"This auspicious thriller romance hero!"

THE RA... REQUEST

"You had a nightmare. See if you can get back to sleep," Patrick said, his voice ragged. He turned away. "I can't trust myself to stay longer."

"Why not?"

"Because nothing can come of it."

"Well, something can come of it—if you should feel the same way." Amanda was astonished at her boldness. She was all but throwing herself at him, asking him for marriage.

"All right. I want you. I suppose only a fool would turn you down. When you go to London, I'd like you to become my mistress."

"I cannot be your mistress. You don't know me if you think I could. It hurts that you would even suggest such a thing!"

"A beautiful love story, sizzling sexual tension, and a page-turning mystery that will keep you guessing until the very end."
—Barbara Dawson Smith

"Elizabeth Parker is a refreshing new talent."
—Cynthia Wright

GILDED SPLENDOR

ELIZABETH PARKER

LOVE SPELL ◆ NEW YORK CITY

LOVE SPELL®

November 1993

Published by

Dorchester Publishing Co., Inc.
276 Fifth Avenue
New York, NY 10001

If you purchased this book without a cover you should be aware that this book is stolen property. It was reported as "unsold and destroyed" to the publisher and neither the author nor the publisher has received any payment for this "stripped book."

Copyright © 1993 by Elizabeth Parker

All rights reserved. No part of this book may be reproduced or transmitted in any form or by any electronic or mechanical means, including photocopying, recording or by any information storage and retrieval system, without the written permission of the Publisher, except where permitted by law.

The name "Love Spell" and its logo are trademarks of Dorchester Publishing Co., Inc.

Printed in the United States of America.

*To Robert and Jaime, with love.
And
to Rose Seeman and the women of Romance Authors of the
Heartland. Thank you for your friendship and support.*

GILDED SPLENDOR

Prologue

England, 1847

A young girl parted filmy lace curtains and gazed out at the lawn gently sloping from the terrace. The February evening, unseasonably soft and warm, caressed her skin. A fresh scent of pine trees wafted on the breeze. She smiled to herself. What a glorious evening to be alive—the beginning of 1847 with the whole world ahead! Surely things would work out somehow—they must!

Turning from the window, she gracefully perched at her dressing table, a confection of shirred cream-colored lace. She took up her curling iron and gazed in the mirror. The smoking oil was heated, and with a slender finger, she gingerly tested the wand. Satisfied it was hot, she began taming the curls in her waist-length hair. Working with each strand of honey-colored cornsilk, she hummed a familiar child's singsong from her nursery days.

Footsteps sounded in the hall. The girl jerked toward the door, an expectant smile lighting her features. Her arm bumped the oil warming lamp and knocked it off the dresser. In moments her gossamer dressing gown and long golden hair were splattered with burning oil. Flames rose quickly, licked at her, engulfed her. With a scream, she ran toward the door, grasping blindly for the knob.

It wouldn't turn. *It wouldn't turn!*

On the other side, a hand held the door shut. An ear listened against the smooth wood for long moments. Finally, the anguished screams of "I'm burning! I'm burning!" died away, and a shadowy figure stealthily retreated down the hall.

Agonizingly Sylvie Emerson died and all that remained from the fire were miniatures of the beautiful girl of eighteen, the memory of the tragic accident of her death, and a charred jeweled box.

Chapter One

England, 1895

She wished him dead. Oh, dear God! She wished him dead!

Amanda Prescott gazed into the beloved face of her father, wasted and gaunt on the sweat-soaked pillow. How handsome and full of life he had once been. Sunken blue eyes, which had once sparkled at his "Mandy," were now closed in pain. She thought of his lively laughter and tall, erect body as he used to toss her up in the air, her skirts and red hair flying, before gently setting her down and taking her tiny hand in his. Now the body, a frail skeleton racked with fever, little resembled the man he had been.

Tears stinging her eyes, Amanda clutched his

frail, cold hand and rubbed it, trying to chafe some warmth into the bony fingers. Part of her fervently wished she could impart life from her body into his, but—she suppressed a shudder—she could not. His death would leave an immense chasm of emptiness in her life. She would miss him deeply, dearly, but he'd suffered for so long. She could only pray for his release. Soon. Sweet Heaven, let it be soon.

"I love you, Papa," she breathed. "I wish you could find peace and join Mama."

As if hearing her voice in his delirium sparked a memory, John groaned, "Clarice?"

A lightning bolt of pain jabbed Amanda's heart. Mama, buried in the little churchyard just three weeks ago . . .

"No, Papa, Mama isn't here. It's Amanda. You rest now. Hush." She placed a hand on his brow, smoothing back the damp hair from his pallid forehead.

Her father struggled to open his eyes. As they fell on his daughter, they cleared and filled with love. "Amanda," he whispered.

"Yes, Papa?"

"Get Mama's jewel box."

"Yes, Papa." Amanda gently placed his hand back on the sheet, crossed to the bureau, and picked up a fabric-covered box. "Here it is, Papa," she said, placing it on the counterpane in front of him.

Feebly, John opened the box, and Amanda watched his trembling fingers fumble with the contents. At last, he withdrew a cream-colored envelope closed with a large seal of red wax. With a shaking hand, he held it up to her.

"I hid this here . . . when Mama died. Take it to Helene Winter . . . my childhood friend . . . Pinewood House." He struggled for a ghostly, gasping breath against the rattling in his chest. "Show her . . . this."

John's thin fingers pulled out a small, jeweled box. Amanda gasped. Despite its slightly charred edges, it was a beautiful creation with alternating diamond shapes of yellow gold and strawberry-colored enamel, rose diamonds encrusting its hinged lid. Amanda gazed in puzzlement. She had never seen it before, nor could she imagine her parents possessing anything so valuable.

"Papa," she asked, her eyes wide, "where did you get this?"

"Take it to Pinewood House. It's your turn—for your life." Her father's voice came out a hoarse croak.

Amanda shook her head in bewilderment. He struggled to raise himself on one elbow. "Make me happy this one last time . . . so I can rest easy."

Dry, heaving hacks wrenched John's bony frame, overcoming him with a fit of coughing. Amanda cried out in despair at his suffering. "All right, Papa," she soothed. "I'll do as you ask. Please lie back, and be still now."

"You'll go tomorrow?"

"I will go—soon. Now don't worry."

"... must go into the hands of Helene Winter, the Marchioness of Swinton. No one else."

John collapsed onto the pillows and closed his eyes. Amanda drew a chair beside the bed, took his hand in hers, and anxiously studied him. The exhaustion etched on his face showed his energy was drained, but he might rest now. She sighed and sat back, massaging her aching neck with trembling fingers.

It had been a long year—an interminable time of caring for her dying parents. She'd poured all of Papa's meager savings from his schoolteacher's salary into medical bills, but the ministrations of the village doctor had proved of little use.

Images of broken sleep, innumerable long nights of heartache, and bloodstained pillowcases filled Amanda's mind. She was so weary of illness.

During the past twelve months, Amanda's youth had died, drained from her by the heavy demands placed on the shoulders of an eighteen-year-old girl. Never again would she be a carefree child. While her friends had been attending parties and meeting young men, she'd missed out on everything. They'd paraded gaily by her window, on their way to sledding parties and dances, the boys chasing the girls, screams and giggles piercing the air. Their muffled laughter had risen up to her through the isolating panes of the sickroom window.

Though she longed to be with the young people, she would have done anything for her parents, and in that year of caring she had not only grown up, but found a quiet strength. She had faced the suffering which she learned came with love.

Yet an aching longing lingered deep inside her which couldn't be denied. Papa and Mama had insisted that a beautiful world existed beyond their little village and the stifling sickroom. Clarice had been a fledgling actress on the London stage before John Prescott had swept her off her feet. With little money, they'd set up housekeeping in his small village. Their home had been filled with light, laughter, and a joyous lasting love. Then illness ravaged their lives. Desperately wanting their daughter to discover all the *joie de vivre* they'd known, they made her promise that after they were gone, she would grasp with both hands all the beautiful experiences and bright sensations life had to offer.

She supposed that, in the future, the proper thing to do would be to look for a beau and settle down with her own house and family. She shook her head in rebellion. With no dowry, no family name or connections, the husband she was likely to acquire would be a poor worker. Though Amanda wanted children someday, she hesitated to face a life of hard work and drudgery.

She wanted more! She'd learned too well that life was short and fragile. She intended to make the most of it, to drink deep of all the varied pleasures the world had to offer. When her end came, she would be able to think back over beautiful memories rather than regrets.

Amanda's lips curved upward into a small smile. An idea she and her parents had lovingly polished bright over the years nibbled at the back of her mind. Why couldn't she go on the stage as her mother had? She'd read aloud to entertain her parents, and they'd always listened raptly, complimenting her ability. They'd sworn she'd inherited her mother's elocutionary talent.

But respectable women did not go on the stage, and the ones who did were not received into proper society. Amanda shrugged. With no name and no fortune, she couldn't hope to be received into society anyway. She itched to get out and do things! Treading the boards of the theater might be the ticket to an adventurous and exciting life! As an actress, she could travel to exotic places, meet people, and have exciting adventures.

Life beckoned to Amanda like a siren. Somewhere out there, beyond the sickness, grief, and suffering, there must be happiness, brightness, and gaiety. But where? She was determined to find it, vowing to herself and her parents that she would someday venture to London and live a marvelous life. Now, only to please her father, she would make a brief stopover at Pinewood House on the way.

Gilded Splendor

One thing Amanda knew with certainty—she would remember her parents as they had been before the illness. She must put the sad memories of their suffering behind her. Once it was over, she would never enter a sickroom again—not for anyone. Not as long as she lived!

"I promise, Papa," she whispered.

She sat back in her chair with resignation to begin the long night's vigil.

"Jonathan, I'll bet you anything you like, Patrick can get that girl into bed tonight," challenged Lord Algernon Douglas.

Three friends assessed Patrick Winter, eleventh Marquess of Swinton, relaxing at the table with them. If ever a man could get any girl he liked into bed, it was Patrick. His tall, muscular body filled out a well-cut evening suit. He carried his powerful physique with an air of elegance and calm confidence, his carriage and bearing erect. Black hair shone above well-chiseled features and intelligent green eyes. His lips curved up at the corners as if he were always relishing some delicious, sensuous joke. But now he merely looked at Algernon with an air of amused detachment.

Algy leaned his chin on his hand and grinned across the white linen tablecloth of the Cafe Royal. Algy's eyes, behind wire-rimmed glasses, took on what might have been an amused gleam if he hadn't been so obviously drunk. As it was, he was having trouble merely keeping his eyes focused on his friend or anything else.

Patrick snorted a short chuckle. "I'm sure I can get her into bed, Algy. But I don't know as I want to."

Viscount Jonathan Mellon sized up his two friends across the table. As in most of their escapades, the outcome was all a matter of whim—was Patrick in the mood for a conquest tonight? Lately, he'd been in such a state of lethargic boredom that everyone had noticed. Evaluating him, Jonathan doubted Patrick would half try with the young lady in question. Savoring a quick victory, he smiled and relaxed back into his seat.

"I believe I'll take your bet, Algy. I don't believe Patrick has the, shall we say, inclination to succeed tonight."

"I beg to differ," Algy slurred. "Patrick is a dashing man-about-town. Nothing can stop him, especially with the ladies. We all know that, now, don't we?" Algy ended in a drawl, his chin slipping off his hand. Catching himself, he jerked upright from a forward fall and jabbed at his glasses, teetering precariously on the end of his nose.

"The bet is for a sum of one hundred pounds," he said loudly.

"A hundred pounds, Algy?" questioned Jonathan.

"A bit steep." The usually silent Lord Freddy Lawrence blinked his eyes owlishly.

"That's the bet," declared Algy. "She's an

actress, so he has a head start. We all know what kind of woman an actress is, don't we? She's bound to be loose of morals and tight of—"

"Algy," warned Patrick, "there are ladies present in this restaurant."

"Besides," Algy continued, unfazed, "it's not as if he hasn't bedded dozens of actresses before. Why, just last month, there was Mrs. Kepplewhite, and before her—now let me remember—wasn't it Lily Hammond?"

Patrick suppressed a yawn behind his hand. "You keep better track than I do."

"But this girl, now . . ." Algy stared in admiration at the woman across the room. "Wasn't she wonderful tonight as Juliet? What fun!"

Patrick pulled a long swallow from his wineglass and cast a glance across the crowded room of the London restaurant. The lady in question was damned fine, that was obvious—excessively pretty, but her expression was empty. At any rate, she was the best thing Patrick had seen in the Cafe Royal lately, and he'd been going there for after-theater suppers for more years than he cared to admit. He studied the luscious young woman and waited for the familiar rush of heat and tightening in his groin. He felt nothing.

He glanced around the restaurant. The Cafe Royal was alive, throbbing with life. Tables teemed with the cream of society, enjoying a late-night supper after the play. Wineglasses clinked, and silverware tinkled gaily above the animated chatter. Candles gleamed brightly. Loud laughter erupted here and there around the room, making the air dance. In the background, an orchestra played the latest rage—a new Strauss waltz. An exciting, shining night. It was all so very lovely. Patrick grimaced. Why did it seem so empty and superficial?

As though sensing Patrick's lack of enthusiasm, Algy baited him. "Coward!" His voice rose. "You can't let me down tonight! Show your stuff and win my bet like a gentleman!"

The young men around the table laughed, assessing Patrick, awaiting his answer. Algy had clearly stepped beyond his bounds. It was not the first time, though, and probably wouldn't be the last. They waited for Patrick to put Algy in his place.

He didn't.

Lately, Patrick had been exceedingly distracted. The plays, the luncheons and suppers in town, the Saturday-to-Monday weekends at the country houses, the ingenues and their mothers who pursued him, other men's easily conquered wives—nothing satisfied him anymore. Perhaps it was turning thirty that made him think he wanted more from life. He wasn't a boy any longer. He wanted—no, needed—something substantial to grab hold of, something with heart and soul and meaning. Unaccountably, the thought made him pensive and sad.

"Patrick, do pay attention." Algy's insistent

voice brought Patrick sharply back to his surroundings. "Are you going to win my bet for me or not?"

"Oh, yes, Algy," said Patrick, realizing his friends were waiting. "You are more than a little drunk, I believe. So I won't let Jonathan take advantage and relieve you of your father's money. You'd only have to go crawling back to him for more, and you've been doing that too much of late. I suppose I'd better win the bet for you." Besides, maybe the proposition would spark some interest into the evening.

"Ho, Jonathan!" gloated Algy, rubbing his hands together in gleeful delight.

With a sinking feeling, Jonathan realized the bet was lost, but he endeavored to hide his disappointment. "Well, he might try, but that doesn't mean he'll succeed."

"You just watch!" said Algy with smug enthusiasm. "And get your money ready. Now to the terms. Patrick must take that delectable young lady to a hotel—any hotel you choose, Patrick. There you must stay with her all night, making mad passionate love, and to prove that you have done so, we'll be waiting in the hotel lobby in the morning at eight o'clock. You must come down with her and turn over to us some article of her underclothing as, shall we say, a souvenir."

"Algy, you are impossible," Patrick said with a laugh. "You must promise me one thing, however—that you won't embarrass the young lady when we come down in the morning."

"Of course not. What do you take me for? Besides, maybe she relishes applause in the bedroom as much as she does on the stage. Now, hand your money to Freddy, Jonathan."

The two young men put down their money. After all the pounds had been collected and placed into the hands of Freddy for safekeeping, three pairs of eyes turned on Patrick expectantly.

"Well, I'm off," he said, rising. The three friends clapped, at first loudly and then quietly as Algy hushed them with a giddy giggle. Patrick looked askance at them over his shoulder and began threading his way through the dining room tables.

Several sets of admiring female eyes followed Swinton as he made his way across the room. He was a study in contrasts—his broad shoulders and rippling muscles looked as though he could win at any skilled sport or rough work he took on, yet his aristocratic carriage and fine clothes were clearly those of a peer who needn't do anything at all in life if he chose not to. The understanding depths of his green eyes shone with compassion and warmth, yet the curves of his full lips hinted at strong sensual appetites and a passionate nature. He carried himself with a commanding air of self-confidence. Women gazed at him with unconcealed admiration; men's eyes followed him with envy—Lord Swinton's reputation preceded him.

Gilded Splendor

Patrick reached the actress's table and swept a glance over her. Enormous brown eyes turned up to meet his. Her gaze ran down his form, registering approval of the magnificent man before her. Her mouth curved into a sweet smile. Patrick swallowed. Where was the urge to bend down and lick with his tongue just where the corners turned up?

"Yes?" she purred coyly. "Did you want my autograph?"

Her autograph? She was clearly used to admirers coming up to her after theater performances, and she thought him a common fan. The idea irritated him immensely. Suddenly the bet took on new interest. It would be his pleasure to take more than an autograph from this young lady tonight. He hid his annoyance with an elegant bow.

"Madam, I greatly enjoyed your performance at the theater. If you will allow me, I would like to stand for a bottle of champagne for you and your guests," he said, turning graciously to the others at the table.

"Why, thank you." The lady flushed with obvious pleasure. "I'm glad you enjoyed the play. Won't you sit down and join us for a moment?"

Smiling, Patrick took a chair beside her. She turned to face him, and he was struck by her ethereal beauty. She had been lovely and graceful on the stage, viewed from a distance, but at close range, he could smell the musky fragrance of her body. Her full breasts rose and fell, their lush roundness seeming ready to burst her décolletage at any second. Patrick imagined reaching out to cup their creamy whiteness in his hands, massaging into the lace of her dress with his thumbs to find hardened nipples . . .

She was speaking again. He raised slow, dreamy eyes to hers. "I'm sorry, madam. What did you say?"

"I was asking if you are a fan of Shakespeare? Do you attend many of his plays?"

"Oh, yes. I find The Bard illuminating and inspiring. Especially when Juliet is played by so lovely and talented an actress as yourself."

Her finely chiseled cheeks blushed a delicate shade of pink. If she was actually embarrassed by his compliment, she couldn't have been acting for so very long, thought Patrick, filing away this information for future use. She was not quite so sophisticated as she thought she was. He would have to be careful to let her down easily after he was through with her. He hated to hurt a lady's feelings when he had to drop her.

But that would all come later. He ruthlessly shoved the thought from him, pasted on his most charming smile, and leaned toward the lovely young girl. It was all so damnably easy.

"Can't thank you enough for winning me that hundred pounds, old man."

Algy lazily twirled a lace-trimmed garter around his finger. The two men were breakfasting at a coffee house, squinting painfully against the bright morning light. Freddy and Jonathan had long since gone home to bed, and Patrick fervently wished to do the same.

The attention of an elderly lady at the next table was drawn to the object Algy was slowly waving through the air. She raised her eyebrows in stern disapproval as she realized what it was.

"Well, I never!" She turned with a huff back to her companion. The two dowagers put their heads together and whispered furiously.

"Would you put that damned thing away?" said Patrick irritably.

Algy hastily stuffed the frilly garter into his pocket. "I'll just keep it, if you don't mind," he said.

"Be my guest. Though what you'll do with it boggles the mind."

"Oh, I don't know. Maybe put it in a scrapbook I'm keeping on you. Now for the juicy details. Tell me—how was it—last night I mean?"

"Oh, Algy."

"Was she a deliciously bad girl, hmm?"

At his imploring look, Patrick relented. "She was rather bad, and you know I prefer bad girls. But she was a sweet thing, not altogether innocent and yet not jaded. I plan to see more of her for a while. Are you satisfied?"

"If you are. If you are. Actresses!" Algy sat back and sighed. He thought for a long moment, then leaned toward his friend. "Seriously though, the hundred pounds will come in handy. I was running a little short."

"You're always running a little short, Algy."

"Don't I know it? It's deucedly hard being the second son. 'The heir and the spare' is fine, except I'm the spare," he said wryly. "My brother gets everything, and I'm reduced to living on a pitiful allowance." Once again, Algy chafed at the unfairness of English hereditary laws, a common theme of his. "You're just lucky you're an only son."

"Oh, I got everything, as you say. Including some things I could have done without." A trace of bitterness laced his voice.

Algy turned to his friend, concern written plainly on his features.

"What's the matter with you, Patrick? You've been downright morose lately. You running short too? I can't imagine that, though." Algy drummed his fingers on the tablecloth. "I know! Why don't you settle down with a good girl for a change? Instead of always picking up bad ones!"

A jab of sudden pain stabbed Patrick's heart, but he kept his expression relaxed, betraying nothing of his underlying emotions. "I'll probably never settle down, Algy."

"Why ever not?"

"We've had this conversation a million times, old man. Let's just drop it."

Patrick longed to confide in Algy. Sometimes

Gilded Splendor

the wall of secrecy and deception he lived behind stifled him. What a relief it would be to just talk freely and sort through his troubles with an understanding friend. And he knew Algy was a good friend. But Patrick had suffered alone in silence for so long, he doubted if he could be forthright now or in the future. Besides, why burden Algy with something neither could do anything about?

Algy was clearly waiting for some kind of answer, and Patrick decided to distract him.

"I am running short, old friend. This damned agricultural depression has reduced the income from our estates to a dangerous level."

"Really? I'd no idea. You're always so lucky—I mean skillful. Why don't you just sell off a painting or two? That should cover it. Or, I know! We'll go to America and find you a rich heiress to marry. All the boys are doing it. Why, just last month, the Duke of Lancashire married that Littleton girl from New York. He'll be set for life. He told me he's going to refurbish the family manor in Ireland—morbid old pile needs it. Not to mention the money he'll have to spend on his mistress! The new wife isn't half bad-looking, either. . . ."

Algy prattled on, and Patrick stared through him, not seeing him. Get married to an heiress. Yes, that would solve his money problems, as it had for so many of his friends—peers who barely managed to maintain their lifestyle, existing on credit, but in reality poverty-stricken.

Marriage might have been an answer to his problem, but Patrick knew he could never bring himself to marry. His grandmother had drilled into him that he must never form a lasting attachment to any decent woman. The onus of his family's disease was too much for an outsider to face. A frightening number of his forebears, his grandfather included, had succumbed to it, and his father would have if he had not died young.

Patrick knew he would also get sick. Long ago, unwilling to accept the dire prediction, the black cloud hanging over his head, Patrick had gone to the family physician, Dr. Sterling, who had diagnosed his grandfather. The doctor had verified that the Winters were cursed with a disease passed down through the men of the family. He had spoken with chilling frankness about the ramifications of the illness.

Patrick had been forced to accept the prospect of spending his future ailing in a sickroom. His initial heartbreak and fury had, over the years, deadened into bleak resignation, casting a pall over his life. He'd accepted it, but could he in good conscience pass the disease on to children, or saddle a wife with the grief of it?

No! He had decided to put an end to the Swinton line and the Swinton tragedy. Promising his grandmother and himself he would never marry, he contented himself with dallying with prostitutes and women of nobility with questionable virtue. They knew how to protect themselves against an unwanted pregnancy. He never saw any one woman for very long.

The idea of marriage and children was forever closed to him.

Patrick lifted his cup to his lips, but the coffee had grown stone-cold. Tucking his sorrow back into a hidden corner of his heart, he tiredly rose.

"Algy, I'm going home. I advise you to do the same."

"But what about the heiress? Haven't you been listening to a word I've said? How about dining with me tonight?"

"No, I'm going out to Pinewood House today. I'll see you when I get back to town."

Amanda trudged up the long, winding road to Pinewood House. Aching with fatigue, she gripped her heavy satchel and concentrated on placing one foot ahead of the other with careful precision. The plodding pace blotted out the weariness from her mind and helped her make progress up the stone driveway. She'd been traveling for three days in omnibuses, coaches, and finally walking the remainder of the way to the estate. Trying to conserve the small amount of money she had, she'd eaten little along the way. It was a draw as to which ached more—her travel-weary bones or her empty stomach.

The road turned and twisted through the estate. Huge nameless trees clasped and entwined their branches like bony fingers over the road, their dark limbs sinisterly black, glistening in the drizzle.

Deep thunder rumbled, and a cold rain filtered from gray clouds roiling overhead. Amanda shivered, clutching her cloak close about her throat. She pushed aside the hair plastered wetly against her cheeks and peered up the drive as it broadened into a wider sweep. Rows of mammoth green pines took shape in the mist, looming on either side of the drive like silent sentinels. Amanda realized with a start why the estate was called Pinewood House.

At the end of the drive, the manor, like a fairy-tale castle young girls dream of, rose into view through the mist and gloom. Tall and stately, its facade extended on and on with rooms, windows, and turrets. Gray stones rose in four peaks across the top of the building. Below, mullioned windows rose up three stories tall. At one end of the building stood an attached conservatory, its glass windows now darkened in the deepening twilight.

In awe at the grandeur and richness of the place, Amanda approached closer through the valley of towering pines. She finally arrived at a fountain, now unused and still. Twin flights of stone steps curved around it to the right and left. She chose the right set, turning a corner at the top, to find they had joined again in front of a heavy, ornate wooden door. Summoning her strength, Amanda extended a cold hand to lift the heavy brass knocker.

Gilded Splendor

At length the door opened to reveal a servant in blood-red livery. He cast a scathing glance down his nose at her, suspicion clearly written across his features. She swallowed nervously. She must look a wet, bedraggled sight!

"What do you want, girl, at this time of the evening? The servant's entrance is at the back of the house. Go back there. Cook will give you something to eat. Then be on your way." The massive door began to swing closed on its hinges.

"Please, sir." Amanda put out her hand to detain him. "I've come to see the Marchioness of Swinton."

The footman stared at her, his sharp features registering full surprise. Painfully aware that her dripping hair and bedraggled clothes made her look anything but presentable, Amanda stood her ground. The servant sniffed disdainfully, and once again began to close the door.

"At least give her this letter," Amanda cried out. "Please!" She thrust a crumpled envelope into his unwilling hand. He held it gingerly between thumb and forefinger as if it were soiled, but he deigned to glance at the handwriting.

"This is addressed to the Marchioness of Swinton, girl. Where did you get this?"

Amanda wiped her wet cheeks with the back of her hand and drew herself erect. She said with all the dignity she could muster, "My father, John Prescott, gave it to me for Her Ladyship. Would you inform her that I am here, please?"

"Well," the servant registered a wary glance. "I will see if she has any knowledge of you. You can wait in the foyer."

He opened the door a trifle wider, and Amanda gratefully slipped inside. In the foyer, comforting warmth enveloped her. In a daze, she watched the footman's stiff retreating back. The encounter had drained her last reserve of energy. She marshaled her waning forces for the upcoming audience with the marchioness. A little rest and sustenance first would have been much welcomed.

Wearily, she glanced around the opulent foyer. Its contents blurred in an image of marble tiles, dadoes, an enormous glass chandelier, and shining oak balustrades rising up twin stairs to the left and right. She was only slightly aware of a profusion of decorative objects. From a distance floated the tinkling sounds of a piano and the light lilt of a woman's laughter.

Her eyes came to rest on a mahogany table in the center of the hall. A tall vase of white roses rested on the shiny surface. They must have been brought in from the conservatory, she thought, fighting to remain upright.

"Her Ladyship will see you now," the servant announced. "Please follow me."

Pulling her attention back to the task at hand, Amanda trailed the man into a large library. Soft gaslight flickered on a profusion of ornate furniture, busy wallpaper, patterned carpet, and innumerable bric-a-brac. Every inch of space

Gilded Splendor

was filled with dark furniture, heavy drapery, or elaborate adornment—marble-topped tables crowded with family photographs in sterling silver frames, ostrich feathers pluming out of vases, fans attached to the walls, and reproductions of Pre-Raphaelite paintings. Amanda had never seen a room so cluttered with an overabundance of rich and expensive decoration.

A voice floated out, cool and silky. "Miss Prescott."

Amanda turned to face a tall, solidly built lady who appeared to be in her midsixties. Silver hair was meticulously arranged high on her head. Her once-beautiful face was delicately etched with a tracery of fine lines. An elaborate puff-sleeved dress of silvery blue exactly matched her eyes. It swept to the floor, as ornately decorated as the room. She held John Prescott's envelope in her hand.

"I am the Marchioness of Swinton. You wished to see me?"

Bedraggled and unkempt, Amanda faced the elegant woman. Unconsciously, she raised a trembling hand to her hair, then forced herself to bring it down and straighten her posture.

"Your Ladyship, I am pleased to make your acquaintance. I'm Amanda Prescott. My father was John Prescott. He asked me to come and see you."

"John Prescott? I don't quite... Oh yes, I remember him. It's been many years. Where is your father now?"

"He died two weeks ago." Amanda's voice broke, but she coughed and continued. "My mother died three weeks before that."

"I see." The marchioness turned slowly, letting the envelope drop to a nearby table. "Won't you sit down? You look as though you've had a long journey."

"Thank you," Amanda said, almost falling into the horsehair sofa the woman had pointed out. Her muscles quivered, whether with cold or fatigue Amanda didn't know. She would have welcomed a civilized offer of tea, but it was not forthcoming.

"I knew your father quite a long while ago. But I haven't seen him or heard from him in years. This is quite a surprise that John would send you here to me now."

"Yes, I was also surprised—my parents had never mentioned you or Pinewood House before."

"And what do you want here?" the marchioness asked, suddenly pivoting to stare into Amanda's face. A trace of coldness lurked beneath the surface charm.

"Madam, I don't want to impose on you. My father's dying wish was that I should come to see you. Why, I don't know." Amanda's words trailed into silence.

For several awkward moments, neither woman spoke. Then Amanda remembered the jeweled box in her satchel. She bent over her bag, drew forth the beautiful object, and held it out

Gilded Splendor

to the older woman. Its rich jewels sparkled in the gaslight.

"My father gave me this just before he died," she said.

Eyes wide, the marchioness stared at the box, her face blanching a deathly white. Slowly, she rose, and like one walking in her sleep, took the box from Amanda's hand.

"Sylvie's box," she said softly, turning it over and opening the lid to peer inside. "Oh, Sylvie," she whispered, closing her eyes. After a moment, she shuddered and turned to face Amanda again, setting the jeweled box on a table.

"I will read your father's letter now, if you don't mind," she said.

"Of course."

The older woman turned her back to Amanda and opened the envelope, splitting the sealing wax with a long silver letter opener. Long moments passed while she read silently. Amanda could not see her face, but she detected a slight tremble come over the older woman's statuesque body.

At last the marchioness spoke as if from a long distance. "Of course, it's a dreadful nuisance right now, what with guests this weekend, and my grandson, Patrick, home."

Amanda had had enough. Tired, exhausted beyond belief, she took her cue from the other woman. She rose, retrieved the box from the side table, and returned it to her satchel. "Well," she said, "I've done what my father wished by coming to see you. I wouldn't want to inconvenience you any further. I'll take myself on to London now. Good day."

"What will you do in London?" Surprise registered in the woman's voice.

"Find employment, of course. I'm sure I can find a suitable living there." Amanda's weariness increased with each breath. If she didn't get out of the stifling room immediately, she would faint. "With your permission," her voice quavered, "I'll go around to the back. Your servant said I might get something to eat before I leave."

"Miss Prescott!" The steely and imperious voice stopped Amanda before she reached the door. "I have no intention of turning you out. You will stay the night. In the morning, we'll sort all this out."

Amanda wavered uncertainly at the abrupt change. The marchioness's voice softened, charming and silky once again. "Won't you please me by staying tonight? I wouldn't want to think I had turned out John Prescott's daughter."

Hearing her father's name again, Amanda wearily gave in. "All right, Your Ladyship. Thank you."

The marchioness pulled a bell rope, and a slight girl in a crisply starched maid's uniform of black and white came to the door.

"Maude, show Miss Prescott to the blue guest room. She will want some supper sent up, and prepare her a hot bath."

Gilded Splendor

"Yes, ma'am." Maude curtsied and waited to show Amanda out.

"Thank you, Your Ladyship," said Amanda. The older woman had already turned back to her desk, rereading the letter, but Amanda sensed cold eyes on her back as she followed Maude from the room.

"Just this way, miss," said the little maid. Amanda struggled with her heavy satchel, and Maude sprang to take it from her hand.

"Here, I'll do that, miss."

Amanda was only too glad to let the girl have the heavy burden, and she followed her up the long winding stairway. At the top landing, Amanda paused to catch her flagging breath. Glancing over the railing at the set of thickly carpeted steps she had just ascended, she was overwhelmed with a wave of dizziness, coupled with weakness and hunger.

A door burst open, and laughter spilled from a room. A shaft of yellow light flooded the hall until a large shape blocked its gleam. A tall man barreled out, looking back over his shoulder. Before Amanda could utter a word of warning, he hurtled forcefully into her. His powerfully muscled body jarred the breath from her, almost knocking her down. Quickly turning around and grabbing her shoulders, the man straightened her and held her upright in a strong, tight grip.

"Hullo! What have we here?"

"Your Lordship!" Maude cried in a startled voice.

Amanda's hazy gaze traveled tremulously up a broad chest to an amazingly handsome, arresting face, all craggy strength and beautifully even features. Dark hair flowed straight and thick, and a comma of its rich blackness fell casually over his forehead. Amusement and interest gleamed down from deep, hazel-green eyes.

His gaze caught and melded with Amanda's, and she felt a gentleness come into his hands. He repeated his words, more softly this time. "What have we here?"

Amanda's last bit of strength seeped from her. Unable to stand a moment longer, her traitorous legs wobbled and gave way. Her eyelids fluttered shut. Strong arms wrapped around her, lifted her up, cradled her.

A sensation of warmth and comfort enveloped her as she was cuddled snugly against the man's solid chest. His uneven breathing fanned her cheek as he held her close. Before the blackness moved in, she could have sobbed with gratitude and relief. Instead she sank gratefully into a still and silent void.

Chapter Two

"Oh, but Mr. Patrick—this ain't at all proper, sir."

"Nonsense, Maude. The girl is soaked to the skin and freezing. Somebody's got to lift her into the tub and get her warmed up—and quickly—or she'll catch a fever."

She had appeared so suddenly and surprisingly in the hall, then fainted dead away. Patrick had scooped up her unconscious form and carried her into the bedroom. Setting her on the edge of the bed, he propped her limp body against his chest and drew a slim, white arm out of a soggy sleeve.

The girl's head lolled against his shoulder, drawing his glance to her face. He heartily approved of her even, beautiful features—

a finely molded forehead, straight, sculptured nose turned up slightly at the tip, delicately curving full lips that innocently tempted him. Her damp hair was the titian red-gold that never failed to weaken his knees. His mouth curved into a bemused grin. He'd always had a weakness for that particular shade of red hair.

Alarmed at the ghastly paleness of her translucent skin and the way her eyes remained tightly closed as if in pain, he quickly sobered. Hurriedly, he pulled the other arm from its sleeve, peeled the cold, clammy blouse away from her wet skin, and tossed it aside. He turned his attention to the skirt, petticoats, and wet chemise beneath, silently thankful he didn't have to wrestle with a heavily boned corset—she wasn't wearing one, and didn't need one.

"The lady will be mortified when she finds out, sir."

He yanked off the last of the wet clothing.

"How do you know, Maude? Who is the lady? Anyway, I believe I've seen the female form before, and I doubt this one has anyth—"

Struck speechless, Patrick's lips parted and he remained suspended, inanimate, stunned by the vision of loveliness in his arms. He had viewed beautiful women before, quite often if truth be known, but this was surely one of the most exquisite females he had ever laid eyes on. Her full, uptilted breasts and rosy nipples curved down into a small waist, then widened again into rounded, womanly hips.

Gilded Splendor

She indeed had no need of a corset to cinch her in, he thought approvingly. He could have spanned her waist with his hands. His gaze continued its slow path down her flat belly, wandering to the soft velvety triangle of hair below. As his eyes traveled the girl's lush, seductive body, his own reacted involuntarily, tingling and stiffening.

The girl's eyes fluttered open, but he couldn't refuse his senses such a banquet. He continued to stare at her. Boldly. Frankly. Her eyes grew wide, and she brought up a hand in an attempt to hide her breasts.

"What do you think you're doing?" she asked icily, pushing at him with her other hand.

"Here—stay put! You'll get sick!"

The girl grimaced. "I don't get sick!" she spat out from between clenched teeth.

She struggled against his detaining hands, until Patrick lost his patience and unceremoniously plunked her into the steaming tub. Water splashed up to soak his immaculately pleated shirtfront as he leaned over the tub. In the next instant, the girl slapped him smartly across his face.

Patrick reared back from the stunning smack, his muscles tensed with an instinctive reaction of icy, lethal anger. Slowly, menacingly, he raised a hand to rub his smarting cheek. A pair of stormy blue eyes stared up at him, defied him, dared him to try something! He was taken aback by the show of courage from a waif so cold, so wet, so tired, and so alone. His icy anger melted as suddenly as it had appeared, and his hard mouth softened.

"Right," he said.

The girl frowned up at him from the tub. Warm liquid sloshed over her breasts, wetting her creamy skin. His fingers itched to rub the wetness slowly into her warm flesh. Perspiration beaded on his upper lip. He longed to throw off his own clothes, climb into the bath with her, and make the water slosh over the rim of the tub in waves of sensuous motion.

He couldn't remember the last time he'd been so aroused by the sight of a woman. Why? Was it her overwhelming beauty that made his body ache for her? Was it her feisty show of spirit? Or was it her vulnerability, her need for his protection as he'd undressed her and handled her naked body? He longed to find out what he'd stumbled on—a lioness or a lamb.

A discreet cough behind him brought Patrick abruptly to his senses. Made sharply aware of another presence in the room, he straightened. Turning around, he faced the maid whom he now realized had left the room and had gone to the kitchen.

"Spoon that hot soup and brandy into her, Maude. I think she'll be revived enough to get herself out of the tub with your help later, so I'll retire."

"Yes, m'lord," said Maude, sitting down beside the tub, a spoon and bowl of steaming soup in her hands.

"Get her right into bed, then."

"Yes, sir." Maude glanced over her shoulder at him. "I can handle it from here, m'lord." Her wide brown eyes twinkled, but he couldn't detect any impertinence in her voice.

"Yes, well, then . . . Thank you, Maude."

He couldn't resist a parting glance at the redheaded vision in her bath before he reluctantly went out the door, closing it softly behind him.

"Heart of gold, has Mr. Patrick," said the maid, her voice unsteady. Amanda noticed Maude's lips twitch into a giggle, which the little maid discreetly covered with a cough.

"Here's your soup now, miss."

Amanda tasted a sip of the wonderful hot liquid Maude spooned into her. Then a swallow of warm brandy burned in a slow trickle down her throat. She waited a few moments, her muscles tensed, but the impertinent man who'd been ogling her failed to return, so she lay back with her eyes closed and sighed. The hot bath thawed her out, relaxing her aching muscles. Soon she was warmed to the bone.

The maid moved about the room, folding clothes and turning down the bedsheets. What a wonderful change to lie back and have someone else take care of her! "Thank you so much," she murmured dreamily.

"Not at all," returned the maid.

A blazing fire crackled cheerfully in the hearth, while the sputtering candles cast a golden glow. Cold wind and rain spattered outside against the window, but the snug bedroom was cozy and warm. Amanda blissfully relaxed to the point of drowsiness.

"Let's get you into bed now, miss, before you drown," Maude said eventually, helping Amanda up and out of the tub. Dutifully, Amanda raised her arms and allowed Maude to slip a long, soft nightgown over her head and down her body, now rosy with warmth.

"Who is Mr. Patrick?" asked Amanda as she gratefully slipped between clean sheets in a massive four-poster bed.

"Master of Pinewood House, miss. The Marquess of Swinton, grandson of the Marchioness."

Amanda sleepily cataloged his attributes as she burrowed down under the covers. A marquess, and a handsome one to boot! He'd given off a fresh scent which seemed to be a mixture of the outdoors, old brandy, and lime aftershave—quite a heady blend. He was the most attractive man Amanda had ever seen. But he was too bold by half!

"I think he's an angel," she said drowsily, cuddling into a soft pillow, "but an imperfect one."

"Yes, miss," replied Maude. "Heart of gold."

"But he needs to be taught some manners. Maybe I'll just teach His Lordship a thing or two!"

Gilded Splendor

Maude laughed softly. "Nobody teaches His Lordship!"

But Maude's words were lost to Amanda. She was already fast asleep.

Brilliant rays of sunshine filtered through sheer gauze curtains. Birds chirped and twittered in the whispering pine trees outside the window. From the height of the sun, Amanda judged it was late morning. She lay in bed, admiring the lovely room, trying to piece together the tattered happenings of the previous day. The bright cheerfulness of her surroundings contrasted with the mystifying questions swirling through her mind.

Why had Papa sent her to Pinewood House to meet the Marchioness of Swinton? Such an elegant, wealthy woman. Amanda was at a loss to understand what her simple, unworldly father could have had in common with Helene Winter. What in the world had they meant to each other? What had occurred between the two of them in the past? What had their relationship been?

And what was the significance of the charred, jeweled box? How strongly the marchioness had reacted to the sight of it! How had Papa come by the box, wondered Amanda, and why had he never shown it to her? How desperately they'd needed money during his and her mother's illnesses! They could have sold the box, and used the money for doctors' fees. It might have prolonged both her parents' lives! But Papa had kept the box hidden, never revealing its existence.

Perplexed, Amanda shook her head. She wanted answers, and she would have them. She hoped the opportunity would soon present itself so she could question Helene.

And on top of everything else, fumed Amanda, why had she given in to her coldness and fatigue last night? Fainting, for heaven's sake! That wasn't like her. Remembering her hideous weakness of the night before, a momentary fear clutched her heart.

She tossed her head against the pillow, resolutely pushing away her anxiety. She'd never been sickly; she wasn't about to start now! *Papa said I should get out and live among cheerful, healthy people, and that's what I'm going to do!*

Cheerful, healthy people... Her thoughts leapt to the tall, handsome man of the night before. The Marquess of Swinton. She went over each detail of his appearance—the lock of black hair falling over his forehead, his marvelous green eyes, the way his lips curved ever so beautifully. Strong arms and muscular physique. Now, he was the very picture of health!

Amanda burrowed down into the covers and drew them up to her chin. Tremulous shivers ran down her spine, and a smile turned up the corners of her mouth as she contemplated the

Gilded Splendor

master of Pinewood House.

But what an arrogant, impudent man! Amanda's grin changed to an irritated frown. Aristocrats forever wore the same expression—insolent, smug, cocksure of themselves.

And him staring so freely at her nakedness! A hot flush of embarrassment swept over her. She wished she'd slapped him harder! If he ever dared insult her again, she would! And yet she had to giggle, picturing his rapt expression. She had certainly caught and held his full attention!

A knock sounded softly at the door, and Amanda quickly sat up in bed. "Come in!" she called.

The door opened and the pert little maid in the black and white uniform entered, her arms laden with towels.

"Good morning, Maude," said Amanda.

"Good morning," returned the maid, placing her burden on the dresser. "How are you feeling today?"

"Much better, thank you. I wasn't really sick at all, just tired from my journey. I want to thank you for your kind attention last night."

"You're welcome, miss. I'm here to help you dress. Lady Swinton has assigned me to be your lady's maid, if it pleases you."

"I don't need a maid. I've never had one."

"Oh, you'll need a maid at Pinewood House to help you dress and arrange your hair and all that."

Elizabeth Parker

"Well, if I do, I'd like it to be you. Won't you tell me a little about yourself?"

Maude's eyes widened in surprise. She wasn't used to being on intimate terms with her employers or their guests. She'd found that servants could live out their entire lives serving the family members in an English country house without ever being known as real people to their employers. Why, the servants at Langly Manor had to turn their faces toward the wall if they were caught in the hallway when a family member passed! But this lady radiated such warm sincerity that Maude swallowed and hastened to answer her.

"I was born here at Pinewood House. M'dad is Reggie White, the gardener, and me mum, Hilda, was cook's helper until she died last year."

"Your mother passed away? My parents died recently."

"Oh, I'm sorry, miss. I still have m'dad, though. He's a great gardener, if I say so meself. He's made the estate grounds beautiful as ever."

"Have you always been a lady's maid?"

"I started out in the laundry. I used to spend my entire days from sunup to sundown ironing Her Ladyship's flounced petticoats. But since then, I've moved up. Now I'm as good a lady's maid as you could want."

Maude came to an abrupt halt, sensing she'd been running on. She dropped a curtsy in apology.

Gilded Splendor

"And do you plan always to be in service, Maude?"

"Oh yes, like my family. 'Course, someday I might marry." Maude's face flushed a bright crimson, and she lowered her embarrassed gaze to the carpet.

"Do you have a young man?"

Maude couldn't help herself. She warmed to her subject.

"Well, Harry—he's the groom's helper—we've been keeping company." Maude sighed. "But we can't see each other, even to talk, except on the one day a week we have off. It's very hard. I can't wait until we can get married."

"And then you'll continue to live at Pinewood House?"

"Oh, yes. Pinewood House is a grand estate. I wouldn't want to go nowhere else."

"Well, I wish all the best for you and your beau."

"Thank you, miss."

Pretending to straighten the curtains, the little maid glanced surreptitiously at Amanda. Surely this wasn't one of the aristocratic ladies of the nobility. They were too snooty, scarcely giving a body the time of day, ordering her about all the time, looking down their noses if they noticed her at all. But this miss was warm and friendly. Maude couldn't understand it, but she decided in that moment that she liked Amanda and vowed to be a good lady's maid for her, even a friend, if a friend were ever needed.

"Her Ladyship has invited you to join her in the morning room when you're ready to go down. May I help you dress?"

"Oh, of course," said Amanda, rising in an instant.

After bathing at the nightstand, Amanda donned the best dress she possessed, a black muslin day dress. Seated at the dressing table, she allowed Maude to brush and pile her hair into a high chignon. Maude was quite good with her coiffure, delighting Amanda with the result.

"Well, Maude," she said finally, appraising herself in the mirror, "I think we're going to get along famously." She regarded her dress. "It's plain, but it will have to do."

"You look lovely!"

Maude peered over Amanda's shoulder, and their eyes met in the mirror. Maude's shining admiration reassured Amanda that she looked presentable, if not in the height of fashion. They winked conspiratorially, and Amanda nodded that she was ready.

Maude led her down the broad sweep of stairs and pointed out the morning room. Amanda, feeling more up to facing the marchioness after a good night's rest, and hoping to get answers to her questions, straightened her shoulders and knocked at the door.

"Come in." Lady Swinton's elegant voice floated out from behind the door.

Gilded Splendor

Amanda entered and was completely enchanted by the most lovely room she had ever seen. The morning room was as elaborately decorated as the library had been, every available inch filled to overflowing with ornamentation, but it was a completely feminine room, decorated with cabbage roses and velvets in shades of rose and mauve. The furniture was light and airy, and statuettes had been placed artfully on delicate tables. Gilding picked out the white wordwork in muted gold. From behind a curved writing desk, Lady Swinton rose gracefully and glided toward her.

"I hope you have recovered from your journey, Miss Prescott."

"Yes, thank you," said Amanda, dipping into a slight curtsy.

Lady Swinton motioned toward a flowered sofa, and they both sat down.

"Let's dispense with formalities." Lady Swinton smiled. "I shall call you Amanda, and you may call me Helene, yes?"

Amanda nodded, and the marchioness continued.

"I'm happy to say I knew your father a very long time ago. He was a sweet little boy in service to our family. Over the years, we lost touch, as so often happens, but now here you are—his daughter, like a memento from the past."

Ah! thought Amanda. One of my questions answered. She smiled, imagining Papa as a little boy in short pants, running around the estate.

"I think it would be delightful to ask you sometime about my father when he was young, if I might."

"Yes, of course. Your father was about eight years older than my baby boy, Austin. They played together around the grounds when they were little. Then your father's family moved away. Austin grew up and got married and had Patrick—my grandson."

Amanda resisted the urge to blurt out with enthusiasm that she had met Patrick last night. She held her tongue, embarrassed that she might have to relate the details of their meeting. Better to let His Lordship explain the bath situation to his grandmother, if an explanation were required.

"Patrick is out today—who knows where?" continued Helene. "He lives rather a wild life, I'm afraid. Oh, nothing dangerous or harmful—he's just a high-spirited boy who loves a good time more than anything else on earth."

Amanda couldn't help thinking the virile-looking man she had met the previous night was much more than a high-spirited boy. Much more!

"Of course, Patrick owes it to himself to have fun while he can."

The expression sounded odd to Amanda. "While he can?"

An edge came into the older woman's voice, and her eyes turned sharp, scanning Amanda's face, assessing her.

Gilded Splendor

"Do you know what was in your father's letter?"

The abrupt change of subject and the directness of the question startled Amanda. She suddenly felt she was in the presence of an adversary. "No, the letter was sealed, so I didn't open it."

"You have no knowledge of its contents?"

"No, Lady Swinton."

"Are you quite sure you never discussed the letter with your father? Did you ever discuss me or my family?"

"No, never," Amanda answered uneasily. That was something that bothered her, too. If the Winters took Papa in and treated him like another son, they must have played a big part in his life. Why had he never mentioned them, never reminisced about his childhood growing up on the estate and playing with Austin?

"Have you ever met a man named Thomas Gray?" The marchioness's eyes glittered as they probed Amanda's expression.

"Thomas Gray? No, I don't think so. Who is he? Was he mentioned in my father's letter?"

Helene failed to answer. Instead, she seemed to look inward, her face masked with an inscrutable expression.

Unbidden anger rose in Amanda. She hated being interrogated in such a fashion when she had so many unanswered questions of her own. But somehow, she sensed this was not the time

Elizabeth Parker

to confront Helene. She studied the marchioness's impenetrable facade, and got the distinct impression that while Helene was very willing to interrogate, the woman would not be so willing to provide answers.

If Helene would not be forthcoming, Amanda decided, it would be best to play a waiting game, to sit back and take in all the information she could glean. Then she could mull it over, before deciding how best to confront Helene.

Her distress must have shown on her face, because Helene suddenly smiled, her voice once again silky and charming.

"Please forgive me for questioning you, Amanda. I hope you'll consider staying on here at Pinewood House for a while. In his letter, your father asks that we get to know each other, and I would be very happy to do so. Besides, you're in mourning and you really have no place else to go for the present, have you?"

The gracious words made perfect sense, but somehow, Amanda didn't quite trust the marchioness. Helene's mercurial moods seemed to change so suddenly and so alarmingly. Amanda sensed the woman wasn't being completely honest, that she had another reason for inviting her to stay. They had been sparring, point and counterpoint, ever since Amanda had entered the room.

"I was on my way to London," Amanda said uneasily. "I should really continue on. I merely thought to carry out my father's wish by stopping to see you first, although I did wonder why he sent me."

"Well, perhaps he knew you'd be safe and well cared for here at Pinewood House. I think your father would have wished it so."

But Helene's answer wasn't good enough, thought Amanda. Why would Papa maneuver to have her be cared for at Pinewood House, when all along, he and Mama had encouraged her to live in London and be an actress? The more Amanda learned, the more frustrating the questions that bothered her.

"You are too kind," she demurred, not quite sure what to say.

"Then it's all settled, isn't it?" Helene rose. Once again, she was all charming warmth, smiling at Amanda, extending her hand in a friendly gesture.

Amanda admitted to herself that a short period of rest in the lovely mansion might be appealing. But more importantly, she wanted the rest of her questions answered, now more than ever. She made up her mind, and nodded her assent.

"I am just finished with my letter-writing," smiled Helene. "Would you like me to show you something of my home?"

"That would be lovely."

Amanda rose and followed Helene on a leisurely stroll through the beautiful building. She found Pinewood House a great old English country home, filled with antiques and treasures that could only have been acquired through generations of a family living in the house and loving it, each successive generation building on, collecting, adding to, and treasuring its contents. Well maintained, it had obviously had money and love lavishly poured into it over the years. Amanda could not help but admire the fine mansion.

The two women passed through room after room—rich, well-appointed rooms—the gold room, the sitting rooms, the conservatory, the music room, the sun room. Helene displayed each setting and object with pride. The mood of each room seemed to play fleetingly across her face, her features expressing her love and possessiveness.

"A home is something always to be treasured and preserved, don't you agree, my dear?" she asked.

"Yes, I do."

"Did John Prescott leave you well provided for?"

The abruptness of the question left Amanda disconcerted. "We lived in a small cottage and didn't have much money, but we loved our home, and were always happy in it."

"I see."

They came to a large open room, its expansive wood parquet floor gleaming and shining with wax. "This is the grand reception hall. Here, we Winters have entertained for many generations."

Gilded Splendor

The large room was surrounded with woodwork of carved mahogany and diamond-shaped leaded windows. Heavy wall hangings and tapestries were lavishly patterned with grape vines and leaves intertwining lush flowers. Around the edge of the room, family portraits displayed Winter ancestors in old-fashioned garb and graceful poses.

Amanda strolled down the row, admiring the collection of portraits. She halted abruptly, spellbound by a painting of two beautiful young girls. They reclined in artless, aloof refinement upon a sofa, like graceful felines. Their identical cornflower blue eyes gazed down at her, seemingly alive. Both were dressed in flowing gowns of white muslin, and each had wound pink ribbons among the flowing strands of her hair. One of the girls closely resembled Lady Swinton, eerily revealing how fresh and beautiful she must have appeared in her youth.

The marchioness gazed up at the portrait over Amanda's shoulder.

"Who are they?" breathed Amanda.

"That is a portrait of me and my sister Sylvie. Everyone called us 'the beautiful Emerson girls.' She was one year older than I. She was lovely, wasn't she? But she had many faults. She died when she was just a young girl. It was a great tragedy for our family, as you can imagine. Let's go on, shall we?"

Reluctantly, Amanda followed Helene from the room, but couldn't help glancing back once more over her shoulder at the haunting, lovely sisters in the portrait. They embodied every resplendent fantasy Amanda had ever had about aristocratic life.

They halted at last before large double doors in an upstairs hallway. Helene swung the doors open wide to reveal a large room which served as a linen closet. She threw open door after door of the huge built-in armoires. Amanda gasped at the linen's meticulous organization. Each size towel, sheet, and pillowcase had its own special place on the shelves, which were lined with a deep vermilion paper and edged with white lace. Piles of snowy tablecloths and stacks of towels all showed the embroidered Swinton monogram.

Helene took out a snowy sheet and lovingly fingered the raised stitchery of its monogram. Her face mirrored her ecstasy.

"I keep stockpiles of extra linens, food, and paper goods in my home," she said. "One never knows when one will have unexpected guests or an emergency of some kind. Why, we've been known to host 400 people, including guests and their servants, at our Saturday-to-Monday house parties. I like to acquire what's needed and always keep it in top condition. I like for things to be nice."

"Everything is lovely," said Amanda softly. Helene didn't respond. She seemed lost in a world of her own.

Gilded Splendor

"Once I own something," the woman continued, "whether it's a sheet or the man who lies under it, I keep them. Always."

A shiver skittered up Amanda's spine. For a moment, she wavered, unsure whether an answer was expected. But Helene sighed deeply and replaced the sheet on its shelf. She closed the closet doors and smiled heartily at the young woman by her side.

"Well, Amanda," she said briskly, "it looks as if you will be needing some clothes. I happen to have extra clothing around here, too. Let's go and see what we can fit you up with." Her eyes twinkled so merrily that Amanda was reassured all was well, and couldn't take offense at the generous offer.

They climbed another set of stairs to a third-floor guest room. A closet there contained a number of beautiful dresses, and they picked out five of the prettiest gowns.

"I'll send Maude to help you try them on," said Helene. "And now I'm feeling a trifle tired. I think I shall go to my room and lie down for a while. I will see you at dinner tonight, yes?"

"Yes, thank you, Lady Swinton."

Amanda smiled at the older woman's back retreating gracefully down the hall. But as she returned to her own room, she pondered the Winter household. Lovely as it was, the house harbored an underlying, distressing sense of unrest and strain. The marchioness loved her beautiful home, of course. That was obvious, and only natural. But why was she so intent on keeping it? Was there some question that she might lose it?

Amanda frowned in puzzlement. Helene had murmured "Sylvie's box" that first night. The Sylvie who had once owned the jeweled box must be the Sylvie of the portrait, Helene's sister. Again, the question of how the box had come into her father's possession haunted Amanda.

And what did the marchioness mean when she said Patrick should have fun while he could?

The brooding questions, added to the ones she already had, assailed Amanda as she walked slowly down the hall, her arms piled high with the colorful dresses. But when Maude met her at the door, and activity engulfed them, she was distracted—for the moment.

Boring. When had his life gotten so damnably boring?

Patrick paced the well-waxed floor. It wasn't quite time to go out. Algy and his friends hadn't arrived yet, and he had absolutely nothing to do. To stave off his increasing ennui, he decided to find something to read in the well-stocked library.

He sauntered toward the room, but halted at the open door, arrested by a titian-haired vision in a fetching dress of light blue stripes. She stood on tiptoe on the top step of the tall library ladder. Her back to him, she was absorbed in examining the volumes.

Gilded Splendor

A very shapely back she had, too. Her slim hourglass waist flowed into the lushness of womanly hips, and he could detect trim ankles beneath a flounce of deep lace edging the bottom of her skirt. He'd seen that figure before, but with not so many clothes on.

Patrick smiled in devilish delight. He might have some fun. Treading with quiet stealth, he halted directly beneath the ladder, and spoke up loudly at her. "May I help?"

"Oh, no, thank you, I—"

The woman glanced down from her precarious perch on the ladder. She halted in midsentence, her voice faltering. Her eyes widened in recognition. He looked up, molding his face into a picture of wide-eyed innocence.

"What are you looking for? Perhaps I might direct you to a certain book."

He grabbed hold of the ladder which was leaning against the bookshelved wall, and set it to shaking ever so slightly. She grabbed on for dear life. "No, thank you."

"I'd really like to be of help, if I can." He shook the ladder harder in his eagerness to assist.

"No, please!" she cried out in alarm.

"Now there's a splendid tome!"

Patrick leaned across with an abrupt long-armed reach which sent the ladder careening away from him. The young woman pitched down into his outstretched arms, screeching as she fell. He caught her nicely in a flurry of petticoats and lace.

"Now look what you've done!" she said belligerently.

He smiled down at her and clicked his tongue against his teeth.

"My, my. How clumsy of me!"

She kicked her foot impatiently. "Thank you for catching me. You may put me down now."

He held her closer, tighter. "Say, this reminds me of last night! Seems you're always falling into my arms. Can this be a plan on your part, or is it purely unpremeditated?"

The woman wriggled in embarrassment, but he still didn't set her down. He merely drew her closer against his chest. Telltale crimson stained her cheeks.

"I assure you, sir, I didn't plan to fall off the ladder. What a ridiculous notion! Do ladies always fall for you?"

"Actually, yes," he admitted with open honesty. "Sometimes with clever ruses like falling off ladders, or fainting, or having some kind of weak fit."

"Of all the—! I assure you, I have no designs on you. In fact, you made me fall! Now put me down!"

"Or what? Will you slap me again like you did last night?"

She kicked out in frustrated impotence. "Oh, how could you bring that up? You might know it would embarrass me. A gentleman wouldn't have mentioned it." Her voice rose in agitation. "Besides, you know you deserved that slap!"

Gilded Splendor

"Lady, when a beautiful woman is presented to me in a state of revealing undress, my eyes are bound to take in the view."

"I was not presented to you. You put me in that state of undress, if you'll remember." She redoubled her efforts to get free, pushing her fists against his chest, as if the conversation had turned loathsome.

Patrick chuckled. "Right. Or you would have caught a fever and died, most probably. Maybe I should have left you to lie shivering on the floor all night."

The woman stopped kicking and peeked up guiltily into his face. "Well, I don't mean to seem ungrateful. You were very kind to take an interest and help me."

Her blue-eyed gaze melded with his, her voice turning sweetly contrite. Patrick's senses jolted. Her pulse beat and swelled against his chest. She was so soft, so warm, so alive in his arms. The womanly scent of her nearness overwhelmed him. A strong, heady pull of sexual attraction tugged at him. His instinctive response to her was so powerful, he cleared his throat, pretending not to be affected.

"All right, I've apologized for not being properly grateful. Now please let me down." She spoke softly, her eyes still locked with his.

"I will, milady, but first . . ."

Without warning, he bent his head and took possession of her lips. She struggled in outrage and surprise, but he kept his lips firmly planted on hers. The kiss lengthened, and he slowly tasted her delicious sweetness. She stopped struggling, relaxing in his arms. His lips moved over hers, explored their crevices and secrets, parted them with his tongue in a slow, sensual movement. Quivering and sighing softly into his open mouth, she seemed to melt. His body stiffened into an erect hardness. He longed to have her naked again, so he could . . .

What the hell was he doing?

Abruptly, Patrick ended the kiss and set her back on her feet. The suddenness of the action seemed to disorient her for a moment, but she shook her head and found her presence of mind.

"Well—that's better," she said. He caught a quick glimpse of the confusion in her eyes before she bent to straighten the folds of her gown.

"Not as far as I'm concerned, but I thought I'd better . . ." Patrick stared down at her through hazy eyes. "Who are you?" he asked softly.

"I could very well ask the same of you. Is your name Patrick?"

"Patrick Winter, Marquess of Swinton. And you?"

"Amanda Prescott."

"A lovely name, but I'm surprised it isn't Lillie or Aphrodite or Helen. You're so charming, you've quite bewitched me."

Amanda arched a smile. "I'm afraid I'm no charmer, come to bewitch you. I'm simply a houseguest of your grandmother."

Gilded Splendor

"Oh, you are indeed a charmer, and a very decorative one. I think you could distract and amuse me very well, if you set your mind to it."

"I'm sure you're able to keep yourself well entertained. And I hope I have more to do than be a charmer or a decoration."

"Oh, there's nothing wrong with being a decoration. Look around." Patrick gestured around the room with an outstretched arm. "The house is full of them. Decorations keep our minds off more weighty and pressing matters."

"Sometimes that must get a little dull, though."

"Dull?"

"I mean," she searched his face, her eyes radiating intelligence, aliveness, "looking only at the surface of everything. The deep dark secrets beneath the surface decorations might prove more fascinating."

A brief stab of pain pierced Patrick's heart. "No, I don't think so," he said.

When he looked back at her a second later, he had allowed a mask of calm reserve and control to come down over his features. She would discover nothing in his expression. He smiled slightly. "Haven't you learned that all women are decorations? Or they should be. Pretty decorations meant to shine and be worn on the arms of gentlemen."

"On the contrary, I've known few decorative women and even fewer gentlemen."

Elizabeth Parker

"You were very decorative the other night."

The telltale blush again crept up her cheeks. "I wish you would not speak so to me."

"Or what? Will you leave in a huff?"

"No, I'm staying—for a while, at least. My father asked me to come to Pinewood House, and your grandmother has asked me to stay on."

"Do you think that's wise?"

"What do you mean?"

"I mean that you've aroused the beast in me, Miss Amanda Prescott. And the beast is lord of this manor, accustomed to getting what he wants, when he wants it."

"Does that include me?"

"Would you like it to?"

In a precise, unperturbed manner, she carefully gathered up her skirts and headed for the door. "Sir, I'm not accustomed to that sort of flirtation, so I'll take my leave now, if you don't mind."

Before she left the room, she turned back with one last parting shot. "I suggest you find yourself another decoration," she said with regal dignity.

Patrick ran his tongue over his lips, savoring the lingering taste of her. "No, you'll do quite nicely," he murmured softly to her retreating form. "Quite nicely indeed!"

He laughed, shaking his head. Turning back to the library, he was surprised to discover his boredom had completely disappeared.

Chapter Three

The next day, a Friday, Amanda descended the stairs to find servants rushing madly to and fro over the mansion, polishing, cleaning, opening windows to air out bedrooms, cutting flowers, and laying in food. To Amanda's dismay, Maude informed her that guests—about twenty-one in all—were coming for a weekend Saturday-to-Monday visit.

Amanda planned to avoid the company. What could she possibly have in common with a crowd of wealthy, sophisticated peers? She didn't relish being embarrassed by her lack of background, money, and social grace. She hoped her presence wouldn't be required at what would most likely be an elegant gathering.

Elizabeth Parker

At four o'clock that afternoon, Lady Swinton summoned Amanda to join her in the library for tea. As Amanda had feared, Lady Swinton wanted her to be on hand to meet the weekend's guests.

"You can be a great help to me," said the marchioness, handing the girl a cup of tea.

"I would be happy to help, but what can I do?"

"You can agree to play bezique with Mrs. Charteris on Saturday afternoon. She doesn't play bridge, and is much too deaf for reading aloud. I'm afraid everyone else will be out riding at that time, and all my guests must be seen to."

Amanda drew in a deep breath, and Helene continued.

"These people are landed aristocracy, to be sure, but they're also my friends, going back many years. You will find they're not so formidable."

"But, Helene," said Amanda, "I'm afraid I don't play bezique. I've never had the occasion to learn the game."

"Oh, how vexing! Well, what can you do, my dear? Maybe a practice round of charades?"

Seeing the look on Amanda's face, Helene hurried on. "No, perhaps that won't do. But could you help me by just chatting pleasantly with the dear lady for an hour or two? By that time, we'll all be back for tea, and can relieve you of your duties."

"Certainly. I'll do my best," said Amanda, not at all certain of how she would entertain for an

Gilded Splendor

hour or two an elderly deaf woman she'd never met.

The guests began arriving the next day. Amanda, concealed behind the lace curtains of an upstairs window, watched their carriages pull up under the portico. As each fine lady emerged gracefully from her carriage, a debonair gentleman at her side, Amanda's dismay grew. Their clothes, high-born expressions, and bearing were elegant and proud, their laughter haughty and gay.

It seemed that protocol was very strict and sleeping arrangements were of the utmost importance to the success of the weekend. Each guest had his or her name on a card fitted into a brass frame on the bedroom door. As the guests were shown to their rooms, Amanda remembered hearing the painstaking instructions given by Lady Swinton to her housekeeper as to their placement in the various guest rooms. Certain ladies had to be placed near the rooms of certain gentlemen, and Lady Swinton had been very knowing about who was having an "understanding" with which wife, and which couples had broken off since the last weekend party.

Listening to the detailed instructions, Amanda had mused that the nobility would never tolerate that kind of behavior in the lower classes. The thought also crossed her mind that perhaps a certain lady might be placed near Patrick's room, but she promptly tossed her head and declared it didn't matter to her anyway.

That evening, a gala dinner had been planned, and Amanda was instructed that all would be dressing for the occasion. She swept down the staircase at seven o'clock, wearing the finest of her borrowed dresses. Tightly cinched into a creation of cream satin tinted with a floral pattern, its crimson velvet sleeves puffed full, Amanda knew it was the most becoming dress she'd ever worn. Maude had piled her hair high and added a spray of flowers. She was girded to meet the aristocrats face-to-face, determined not to show how unsophisticated and shy she really felt.

Amanda advanced slowly down the stairs, carefully minding the train of her dress. From the bottom step, a low whistle of appreciation greeted her.

A slim young man in a cutaway coat leaned against the balustrade, gazing up at her quizzically from behind wire-rimmed glasses. "Hullo! I don't think I've had the pleasure?"

"Good evening," said Amanda.

"Good evening! I'm Algernon, Patrick's friend. And who might you be? I thought I knew everyone who was coming this weekend."

"My name is Amanda Prescott. I'm staying with the Winters for a short while."

The man's clear eyes gleamed with pleasure behind his glasses as he took in Amanda's face and figure. "Now why the deuce hasn't Patrick mentioned you before? Unsporting to keep such a lovely lady a secret from his best friend."

"I only met Patrick when I came here two days ago."

"Oh, I see. So you two are not old friends—not just yet, at least."

"No, not yet."

Algernon's face curved into a smug smile as if he had made an important discovery that might prove extremely interesting. "I'm sure that will be remedied in the near future."

He bowed to her, extending a bouquet of hothouse orchids. "Please let me present you with these. I just came from the conservatory. I'm sure Patrick would want you to have them."

Amanda admired the exotic blooms. "Thank you. They're lovely!"

"Smashing!" The man gallantly held out his arm. "May I?"

Taking his arm, Amanda wondered why he smiled so craftily to himself. They went into the drawing room where the guests were assembling.

"Amanda!" Lady Swinton greeted her with a flourish, took her arm from Algernon, and introduced her around the room. Amanda had a fleeting, quick glimpse of the faces she passed. She tried to place in her mind each name which was mentioned—Lord Delamere and his vague but charming wife Lettie, their son Ian just up from Oxford, a handsome man named Mr. Guy Cust who scanned her figure with an appraising glint in his eye, Mr. Willie Monmouth and his beautiful wife Cynthia, Lord Alfred Perry, a delicate young man who hovered by an older, taller man introduced as a playwright, Miss Julia Stoddard, just five feet tall but radiating vitality and intelligence. After that, the other guests became a blur. There were too many to remember.

As the introductions drew to a close, Amanda was led to a sofa by the fire. She happily dropped into it, content to sit and observe the group. Hands folded demurely in her lap, she watched the people around the room. They were a charming and varied circle, and it was evident they were of the peerage—so different from the ordinary people Amanda had known all her life. These people stood taller, more confidently; they seemed healthier, possessing a certain smug air of assurance bred into them. And all because of an accident of birth.

But Amanda had not been introduced to the person she was most interested in seeing. Her eyes roved restlessly about the room, scanning for a tall man with black hair and fine green eyes.

Talk swirled around her. Discussions about the current plays running in London, how good the local hunting was this season, the Prince of Wales and his latest paramour. Amanda picked up a train of conversation between two exquisite women standing nearby.

"My dear, Bertie is wonderful, of course. But he gets easily and fatally bored."

Gilded Splendor

"I heard the Duchess of Landower kept him very entertained at Hawthorne last week by introducing him to a young Mrs. Hamilton."

"Yes, but he'll be looking for new entertainment in a week or two. He gets so restless! And what is one to do? When you run out of diversions and professional beauties, the only way to keep him happy is to provide ever finer food and accommodations. Why, the Dunlops have spent themselves almost into ruin, just trying to keep the prince entertained."

"Yes, so easily bored. He's almost as bad as Swinton. Impossible to pin either of them down to one woman."

"I'd like to be pinned down by Patrick, I can tell you—directly beneath him."

"Why, you have been, haven't you, dear?"

"It was luscious! But you know Patrick—what a flirt! I think he might be incapable of a lasting affection."

"Well, it's all worth it though, isn't it? There's nothing quite so thrilling as being able to say that one has entertained the Prince of Wales and the Marquess of Swinton—on separate occasions, of course."

The two ladies twittered and passed by Amanda. Her face flushed in consternation at their conversation, especially the part about Patrick.

She turned her attention to a couple sitting near her. They seemed to be very much in love, with soulful looks and much whispering. The young man brought the woman's hand to his lips and held it there, gazing deeply, romantically, into her eyes. Moments later, an elderly, mustachioed man came up behind the couch, and good-naturedly addressed the woman as his wife. Shock at the brazen behavior rocked Amanda.

The group used a private language all their own, especially the younger members, who spoke practically in code. They played at clever verbal games, words not meaning what they should have. Everyone had a sentimental nickname, like "King Arthur" and "my adored gazelle." Amanda followed with interest the punning, flirting, improvising, and double entendres that made the room fairly dance with life.

Helene flitted about the room. Each woman she swept by kept asking, "Where is Patrick this evening?"

Everything else was forgotten the moment Amanda saw Swinton enter the room, a lovely dark-haired woman on his arm. Stunning in black evening dress, his crisp white shirt set against the tan of his rugged face, he smiled down at his companion and whispered something that made her smile up at him fetchingly. Amanda wanted to tear her gaze away from the couple, but couldn't. Patrick's sinuous grace mesmerized her.

"My dear Miss Prescott, you are quite lovely," a voice said behind her shoulder. "May I have

Gilded Splendor

the privilege of sketching you?"

Amanda turned with surprise and noted an impish-looking man with a monocle and drawing pad. She recognized him as an artist who'd been introduced as Granville.

"Why, of course, if you like," she said. He came around and dropped to her feet in front of the sofa.

"Just carry on as you were," he said, and muttered again, "Lovely, quite lovely," before beginning to sketch.

A young man came up behind the artist and watched over his shoulder. Algy joined them, and soon a small group had gathered, all exclaiming about the clever sketch and its beautiful model.

The center of attention, Amanda was beginning to feel quite flattered and charmed by the group. How nice they all were to make her feel so at home and one of them! She smiled and relaxed in the comfortable atmosphere.

Across the room, a pair of smoldering green eyes watched her with interest. Patrick stood quietly in an alcove, alone now, a shoulder propped against the wall. He lifted a cigarette to his lips, and through a swirl of smoke, observed Amanda across the crowded room.

Bewitching woman, he thought. Intriguing woman. Lovely woman. She fairly lit up the room. He was quite used to a varied assortment of people coming and going at Pinewood House. People of all descriptions, from houseguests, to friends of the family, to servants, all lived under his roof off and on. But he couldn't remember any as lovely as this waif he'd picked up in the hallway and placed in her bath.

Her red hair shone, highlighted with the rich gold of old coins. Her blue eyes could flash and sparkle with spirit, and yet, in the library, she'd melted so exquisitely when he held her in his arms and kissed her.

Her appealing body filled out her dress to perfection. He savored the memory of creamy high breasts and milk-white skin. He could have spanned her slender waist with his fingers, and he longed to go over now and do just that. His body stiffened in what was becoming an immediate reaction in her presence.

Who was this Amanda Prescott? Where had she come from? He'd meant to ask his grandmother the previous day, but they'd been discussing finances and had gotten so caught up in the distressing dilemma, Pinewood's financial crisis had consumed the conversation. He hadn't had a chance to question Gram about their beautiful young houseguest.

One thing he was sure of—Amanda Prescott wasn't an aristocrat. She hadn't fainted to be seen in a state of undress by a strange man. Any of the titled ladies he knew would have screamed or swooned in a fit—or pretended to, at any rate, merely for propriety's sake. He grinned and gingerly touched his face where she'd slapped him.

Gilded Splendor

And what about the most important point? Was she a good girl? Or, more to his liking, a bad one? The answer to that question would determine if he would get to sample the pleasures of that lush body. If she were a shy virgin out husband-hunting, he would have nothing more to do with her, but if she had acquired experience at love or was even married... He fervently hoped she was as bad as bad could be! Determined to find out, he pushed away from the wall.

Extraordinarily flattered by the attention she was receiving, Amanda ran her gaze around the room to see if Patrick had noticed. He had disappeared, and that fact made her heart sink.

"She makes a lovely decoration, doesn't she?" A deep masculine voice, smooth and silky as soft velvet, came from behind her. A shiver went up her spine as she recognized Patrick's resonant voice, but she didn't turn around.

"Yes, lovely," said the artist. "There—I'm finished."

He turned the pad around to show Amanda his creation.

"It flatters me," said Amanda. "It's too—"

"Not at all. Here, you may have it, if you promise to sit for me again tomorrow." He signed his name at the bottom of the sheet and tore it off the pad with a flourish, handing it toward her.

"If I may," said Patrick, reaching over Amanda's shoulder to take the sheet of paper before she could reach for it.

"Here!" protested the artist. "I gave that to Amanda."

"Granville, you can draw others," returned Patrick. "I would like to have this one, if the lady agrees."

Granville glanced up testily at Patrick for a moment before falling into good humor. "Of course, old chap. If it's all right with Amanda."

She smiled and nodded to the artist as he got up to leave. The guests drifted away, and Patrick came around the sofa to sit down beside her. From the corner of her eye, she glanced at his long legs stretched out in front of him. The muscles of his thighs seemed ready to burst the seams of his tight trousers.

She looked up earnestly into his searching eyes. They were intelligent eyes under prominent brows, piercing her with hypnotic intensity, seeking to penetrate her very soul. A woman could easily get lost in their green depths.

"Why did you want that picture of me?" she stammered.

"Oh, I don't know. I need a pretty decoration for my room here at Pinewood, and this will do nicely."

There now, he's ruined everything again! Amanda scowled at him in vexation.

"Why do you persist in calling me a decoration, Lord Swinton? It's becoming tedious. Besides, what about your companion I saw you come in with? Isn't she a much prettier decoration than I?"

Patrick grinned maddeningly. "Jealous?"

"Of course not! Why would I be?"

"I don't really know. You're easily the prettiest girl here tonight. And you've made a conquest of most of the men."

"Thank you, but I didn't set out to make any conquests."

"Why not? Wouldn't a tryst or two make your visit here more interesting?"

Amanda raised her eyebrows, but before she could answer, Patrick's earlier companion advanced toward the sofa, her red lips protruding in a pretty pout. Frowning, Patrick rose.

"Patrick, you're taking me in to dinner, aren't you?" the woman simpered at him, ignoring Amanda. "I think it's about time."

"Diane Warfield, Countess of Craven, may I present Miss Amanda Prescott?"

The woman, forced to acknowledge Amanda's presence, glared down her nose with barely concealed impatience. "A pleasure," she said coldly.

"Good evening," returned Amanda.

Diane pulled on Patrick's arm possessively and tried to turn him around, but Patrick remained solid and immovable. With his free arm, he motioned for Algy to come over.

"I'm sorry, Diane, but there's been a change of plans. I must take Miss Prescott in to dinner. Algy has been longing to accompany you, haven't you, Algy?"

Algy threw Patrick a startled look, but quickly recovered. He bowed and gallantly held out his arm to Diane. "Would you do me the honor, Countess?"

Frustrated rage flickered in Diane's eyes. "Well, I'll see you later, Patrick, and that's a promise." Without glancing at Amanda, she took Algy's arm, and he hastily led her away.

Patrick turned back to Amanda with a wide smile and held out his arm to her. She silently took it, her heart in her throat. No man had ever championed her in such a way before. It may have been rude to Diane, but Amanda couldn't help the rush of pleasure thrilling through her. The gong sounded, summoning the group in to dinner.

Amanda toyed with her food during the meal, acutely aware of the marquess's tall presence in the chair close beside her. He exuded potent masculinity. His handsome good looks made her stomach flutter, and she could barely swallow. He calmly chatted throughout the meal, completely at ease, wanting to know all about her. His slow smiles and interested questions drew her out and put her at ease. She found herself warming to him and opening up. She told him of pleasant things, of happy memories, preferring not to spoil the evening by dwelling on the sad times. Instead, she described her childhood and the simple country life she'd known.

He nodded his head. "There's no place on earth like the English countryside. God, how I love

Gilded Splendor

it! The streaming hedges, the gorse bushes, the fresh moist air. Sometimes I go out riding, and my horse takes me to another world, far away from man."

"Yes, I agree. When something is wrong, nothing soothes me like getting away from everyone and wandering about in nature," she revealed.

They smiled at each other, and she imagined taking his hand and walking in shady glens with him.

He leaned back in his chair and studied her.

"And what will you do now?" he asked. "What are your plans for the future?"

Amanda hesitated. She didn't want to appear foolish, revealing her presumptuous ideas about becoming an actress. No one, except her parents, had ever told her if she had any talent or not. Besides, she knew the gentry didn't approve of going on the stage. It was considered bad form, if not downright immoral. He might look down his nose at her and sneer. Or worse, laugh. But his sincere green eyes registered warmth and interest, encouraging her to confide in him.

"Well, since I had such a quiet childhood, I've always craved life, activity, and excitement. I've toyed with the idea of being a London stage actress."

She waited for his derisive laughter, but none came. Instead he said quietly, "An actress. Well, you've got the looks for it, I daresay. And you seem to have a depth of feeling you could draw from to enhance your roles. You might do very well."

She could have thrown her arms around him. With a rush of glad gratitude, she reveled in his kindness. He was like no man she had ever met. His physical presence aroused feelings that titillated and teased her. And he seemed to understand her as no one ever had before. They might have been friends forever. She lowered her gaze to her plate, lest he discover the strong current of affection overflowing in her heart.

"How soon will you storm London?"

"Well, I'll stay here, for a while, at least. Your grandmother asked me to stay with Mrs. Charteris tomorrow afternoon while everyone else is out. I'm to keep her entertained. That's why I'm here tonight. Your grandmother asked me to come and meet her."

Patrick grinned. "Dear old lady she is, too. But she's quite deaf. How are you going to entertain her?"

"I don't know."

Patrick threw back his head in lighthearted laughter, and Amanda had to ruefully join in.

"I can't remember when I've had a more relaxing and entertaining dinner, Amanda. Thank you for that. I'll tell you what I'll do. I'll help you entertain Mrs. Charteris. I rather like the old lady, and she's always seemed to like me."

"How will you entertain her?"

"Oh, I'll find a way. Be in the library at two o'clock tomorrow afternoon and you'll see."

He raised his wineglass to her in a silent salute.

Patrick raised his whiskey glass in another toast, this one imaginary, to Amanda Prescott. Tilting back his head, he drained the glass. The fire had nearly gone out in the empty library, and the clock in the hall had just struck two. All the guests had long been in bed. He sprawled in a leather chair, his thoughts returning again and again to Amanda.

What a delightful dinner companion she'd been! He genuinely liked the girl. Once he'd broken through her shyness, he'd discovered that besides her splendid body and exquisite face, she possessed a lively intelligence. A delightful conversationalist, she shared his love of the countryside, sweetly interested and responding to him as if he'd been the only man in the room and the most brilliant talker in the world.

But what really drew him was her air of quiet strength. Opposite of the silly, jabbering, scatterbrained society women he knew, Amanda seemed to be a woman capable of dealing with anything life could throw at her. What had produced such calm character in one so young? How far could a man go with a woman like that standing solidly behind him, helping him, cheering him on?

He shook his head to clear it. All that was beside the point. She was obviously a good girl,

Elizabeth Parker

damn it! Why the hell did she have to turn out to be virtuous? All he'd wanted was a lusty roll in the hay with her superb body, but she was most probably a virgin. Unsophisticated. Hadn't even been to London. A simple country girl.

He had to take that back. Amanda was a country girl, but she wasn't simple. She'd said she wanted a life of excitement, to see places and do things. She wasn't looking for love, wouldn't settle down in a staid, comfortable marriage to a farmer until she absolutely had to. Well, more power to her!

He'd lived what she would probably call an exciting life, sampling all the world's pleasures, and in the final analysis it had all failed to satisfy him. He hoped she would find more lasting enjoyment than he had. If anyone could find meaning and fulfillment in a life on the stage, she could.

Patrick refilled his glass with whiskey. Still, if she wanted excitement, he could provide it for her! It would be pleasurable to seduce her, and that was what she really meant by excitement, wasn't it?

Deep down, he knew it wasn't. The thought of deflowering, jading, possibly impregnating, and then discarding her was distasteful to him. She deserved better than that. After she had had her little taste of freedom, he had no doubt she would settle down. She deserved a man who could love her forever, marry her, provide her with healthy children and a home of her own.

Gilded Splendor

Not a man who would someday be diseased, dead.

Patrick shuddered.

No, he'd meet Amanda and Mrs. Charteris the next afternoon, then return to London with Algy. It was the decent thing to do. He didn't trust himself to keep his hands off the girl, and why put temptation in his way? To remain in close proximity to her would only be frustrating in the extreme. Better to stay away from Pinewood House until she was gone.

Amanda Prescott was a good girl, and that was that.

The next day promptly at two o'clock, Amanda ventured to the library. Patrick was already there, chatting conspiratorially with Mrs. Charteris. The plump dowager, who had at first seemed dreadfully overpowering and formidable to Amanda, was now talking animatedly. She looked ten years younger and seemed to hang raptly on his every word. Her lined face actually beamed as she bent toward Patrick and giggled like a schoolgirl.

Amanda entered the room, and the two became aware of her presence. Patrick rose to greet her.

"Mrs. Charteris, I believe you have met Miss Amanda Prescott. Miss Prescott, Mrs. Charteris." He bowed elegantly and gave Amanda a meaningful look which Mrs. Charteris couldn't see. Amanda tried to ignore the look. She stifled a smile, somberly taking the woman's proffered hand.

"My dear Miss Ascot," intoned Mrs. Charteris. "Patrick here has just been telling me the most scandalous things—very naughty of him, but very amusing. Won't you sit down?"

"No, Mrs. Charteris," said Patrick. "This is Miss Prescott, and I'm going to entertain both of you ladies, if you will allow me. Please come along."

"Oh?" Mrs. Charteris tried to rise from the plump sofa cushions, not an easy task, but finally accomplished with much huffing and puffing and Patrick's steady arm. Her beady eyes glittered with excited interest. "I do love a mystery. Where are you taking us, you mischievous boy?"

Amanda looked at Patrick questioningly, but he merely shrugged. "That is for me to know, and for you ladies to find out. This way, please."

The trio left the house and crossed a wide expanse of lawn down to a small pond, shining blue, dotted with water lilies and fern fronds, nearly hidden away among the tall trees and lush greenery surrounding it.

"How lovely!" exclaimed Amanda. Both she and Mrs. Charteris held lace parasols over their heads to shield their complexions from the sun.

"This is Spirit Lake. Would you like to go out for a row?" asked Patrick, pointing to a white boat bobbing at the end of a small dock.

Gilded Splendor

"What's that?" asked Mrs. Charteris loudly.

"Let's go out on the lake!" Patrick boomed into her ear.

"Oh, yes, please!" she exclaimed, clapping her plump hands together.

"Good. Here, I'll help you both in. Mrs. Charteris, if you'll allow me..." He held out his hand and the good lady stepped gingerly off the dock and into the swaying boat.

"Dear, oh, dear!" she cried out in alarm. But Patrick had tight hold of her and saw her safely seated in the bow of the boat.

"Come, Amanda," he said then, turning back to where she still stood on the dock's edge. He grinned up at her wickedly. With a smile, she reached to take his proffered hand.

A sharp crack split the air. Amanda froze, her hand suspended, inanimate. The noise reverberated through the trees, rent the silence around the lake.

Patrick grabbed her hand and pulled sharply. She fell face-forward onto the dock, rapping her head sharply against the wooden planks.

Patrick's narrowed eyes looked off tensely into the distance, scanning the trees along the opposite shore, before he bent down to Amanda. "Are you all right?" he asked, taking her face in his hands.

"What was it?" she asked in confusion.

"Gunfire," he said tersely and turned toward Mrs. Charteris. "Oh, my God!"

Amanda followed his gaze and gasped. Mrs. Charteris was sprawled in the back of the boat, her legs askew, blood dripping down her ashen, unconscious face.

She'd been shot!

Chapter Four

Time stretched to a standstill. The sunny day took on an unreal, unnatural brightness. Amanda, her limbs immobilized, gaped in wide-eyed horror at a trickle of red blood slowly oozing down Mrs. Charteris's chalk-white forehead. What had happened? Amanda couldn't marshal her confused thoughts into a coherent answer.

Patrick sprang into action, leaping into the boat, lunging toward Mrs. Charteris. He gently settled her head in the crook of his arm, whipped a snowy handkerchief from his pocket, and pressed it to the wound.

"Mrs. Charteris," he whispered.

When the woman failed to respond, his desperate gaze flew to Amanda, disbelief written across her features. His tortured green eyes begged her to make sense out of the ghastly accident. His naked look of anguish, replacing his usual guarded expression, shocked her almost as much as the accident itself. She extended her hands toward him in simple despair.

An old man hobbled from the gardens in a quick limp, hoe still in hand. His head whipped back and forth in dismay between the two figures in the boat, one sprawled with her legs at an odd angle, the other crouched over her. "Heard the shot, Y'r Lordship. Can I help?"

"Reggie!" called Patrick. "Help me get her out of the boat!"

The two men lifted Mrs. Charteris's lax, heavy body from the boat and lugged her up the sloping green lawn toward the house. Several other servants came running, meeting them halfway, grabbing hold of an arm or a leg to help carry the burden. A young housemaid put an arm around Amanda, chafing her shoulders as they followed behind.

The somber group progressed slowly up the lawn. Guests crowded on the patio, nervously jostling, asking questions in shocked tones. Their voices increased in volume until the situation threatened to get out of hand. Rigid control returned to Patrick's face, tightening his features, veiling his distress. His years of breeding rising to his aid, he took charge.

"Harry," he ordered a groom, "go quickly and bring Dr. Sterling here. He's in the next county this weekend at the Becktons'. Hurry, man!" The

Gilded Splendor

slender groom took off at a run for the stables.

On the terrace, guests parted worriedly to allow them to carry Mrs. Charteris through. Patrick gestured with a nod of his head. "This way, Reggie," he said and led him through the French doors into the salon.

They gently laid Mrs. Charteris on a sofa. Her hand, its skin pale and paper-thin, fell limply to the floor. The guests crowded around the narrow doorway. Patrick drew Amanda in and gently but firmly closed the door. With a searching, appraising look, he saw her to a seat.

"I'm all right," she whispered.

Patrick nodded and knelt down by the prostrate Mrs. Charteris. A servant produced a wet cloth, and Patrick quickly grabbed it and smoothed it across the lady's forehead, wiping away the blood to get a glimpse at the severity of the wound. Where he turned the cloth, it bore a bright red stain.

Amanda watched Patrick's calm control as if he were a lifeline of strength, the only sane thing in a frightening world. What happened? she thought in bewilderment. To that dear old lady? She steeled herself against hysteria by training her eyes on Patrick. Keeping him in her line of vision brought a measure of calm to the disordered turmoil inside her.

"Oh, my lord!" Lady Swinton, her face ashen, stood frozen at the doorway, white knuckles grasping the door frame. She swayed slightly as she surveyed the chaotic scene.

"Gram!" Patrick's strong voice carried across the room. "It's all right. We've sent for Dr. Sterling—"

He was interrupted by a low moan from Mrs. Charteris. Her head thrashed from side to side, and the good lady opened her eyes. When she saw Patrick bending over her, she managed a weak smile. "Some entertainment! Humph!"

Patrick slumped, his face relaxing into a relieved grin. "I'm sorry about that. Next time I promise it won't be quite so exciting."

"Eh, what? Next time? Are you mad?" She attempted to sit up. "What happened?"

"Now you just lie back and take orders from me for a while. We think a gun was fired, and it seems to have grazed you. I think you're all right, but we'd better let Dr. Sterling make sure."

"Sterling? That quack? Let me up."

"Quack, is it?" A male voice boomed behind Lady Swinton, and a tall man with snowy white hair hurried into the room. Without breaking stride, Dr. Sterling drew his arm around Helene's waist and led her to a chair. "Sit down, Helene, before you fall down. Luckily, I was on my way over for my usual weekend visit, and met your footman on the road. Don't worry, we'll soon have everything set to rights."

Turning to the sofa, he frowned. "What have you been up to, Mrs. Charteris?"

"Someone tried to murder me. Now they've brought you to finish the job."

"Let me see."

Gilded Splendor

The doctor knelt down, and Patrick rose to make room for the examination. With the immediate responsibility lifted from his shoulders, Patrick expelled his tension in a long breath. He turned to regard his grandmother, still, silent, and white in her chair. He went to her and gently took one of her hands in his. Leaning down, he whispered in her ear. Helene raised her troubled gaze to her grandson, and as she listened to his quiet words, a look of immense relief and hope flooded her upturned face.

Across the room, Amanda, unable to take her eyes off Patrick, watched them. Gone was the teasing playboy, the flirtatious man-about-town. In his place was the solicitous comforter who'd encouraged her to become an actress. Infinitely gentle, kind, and tender, with a warm strength that inspired confidence, he soothed his grandmother, and the woman quietly regained her poise. Both lifted their heads as Dr. Sterling spoke.

"Just a slight graze. Mrs. Charteris will be fine. But as a precaution, I think we should see her home to rest quietly for the remainder of the weekend."

"Humph," muttered Mrs. Charteris, who by this time appeared quite ready to lie down in peace and quiet. She rose shakily, and Reggie jumped to provide a steadying hand under her elbow.

Patrick crossed to her. "I'm so very sorry." His voice spoke a promise. "We'll find out who was careless with his rifle, believe me."

"Naughty boy, was it carelessness? I thought maybe someone was trying to do me in."

"No one could want to harm you. I'll find the reason for this accident."

She patted his hand. "Fine, fine."

"Reggie," Patrick said, turning to the servant, his eyes filled with gratitude, "thank you."

"Y'r Lordship," said Reggie solemnly. He bowed and helped Mrs. Charteris out the door.

Dr. Sterling perched beside Lady Swinton and gently clasped her hand in his. He bent toward her solicitously, his expression registering deep concern.

"Come, Amanda," said Patrick, grasping her hand and leading her from the room. She followed in silence as he led her toward the conservatory.

In the hall, she turned to him. "How could such an awful accident have happened?"

A muscle quivered in his jaw. "I don't know," he said grimly. "But I'm damned well going to find out."

Potted palms edged the glass-enclosed conservatory. Vases of orchids and fragrant roses flowered in abundance. The late afternoon sun caught each pane of the floor-to-ceiling windows, staining the wall of glass bloodred.

Patrick led Amanda to a flower-laden arbor and turned her to face him, taking her soft cheeks between the palms of his hands. She's so beautiful, he thought. What if she'd been shot, along with Mrs. Charteris? If anything had happened to her . . . He pictured her lovely face marred by a wound, her bright hair streaked with blood. Revulsion shuddered through him, and he gritted his teeth.

"It wasn't your fault, Patrick. And there is no real harm done as long as Mrs. Charteris recovers."

Patrick regarded the slender girl before him, and thoughts of Mrs. Charteris fled his mind. "What about you, Amanda? You could have been killed. My God, when I think . . . !"

Passionate intensity laced his voice, unnerved her. A stray black curl had fallen in disarray over his forehead. Gently, she pushed it back into place, allowing her fingers to play through his soft warm hair in a feminine, comforting gesture.

Patrick closed his eyes at her soft touch. "Ah . . ." he breathed.

They both stopped completely still, caught in the moment. Amanda slowly brought her hand down, and he opened his eyes. His green gaze captured her blue one, and her heart flipped over in response. He radiated strength and virility, yet was meltingly tender. Would he kiss her again? She recalled the ecstasy of his warm, strong lips on hers, and an aching warmth pulsed between her legs. Her breasts rose and fell with her breathing, tingling against her chemise.

"The way you make me feel," she whispered, "I'm sure it can't be quite proper."

He fingered a loose tendril of her hair and sighed. "Sometimes I get tired of caring about what's proper. Remember what you said in the library about delving beneath the surface of things? We go on year after year, preserving the amenities and the rules, hiding behind our elaborate decorations. We forget that all our determined efforts can be obliterated in a single second."

Amanda remained silent in the face of this logic.

"You're very special, Amanda. I hate to think of you disappearing at a moment's notice."

"I'm still here," she said softly.

"Yes, you are. And that's the problem."

"Patrick!" A voice interrupted from behind. Dr. Sterling and Helene entered the conservatory. Patrick quickly dropped his hands to his sides. Dr. Sterling smiled, while Helene eyed the couple, an inscrutable expression on her face.

"Patrick, come with me. I need your help in speaking to our guests and relieving their anxieties. You won't think of going back to London now, will you, son? Not with all the confusion here."

"No, I'll stay and help."

Helene's face registered relief and satisfaction. "Dr. Sterling will see Amanda to her room. I'm sure she would like to rest."

"Oh, no, please let me stay."

At a commanding look from Helene, Dr. Sterling stepped forward, took firm hold of Amanda's arm, and resolutely led her from the room. As the older man pulled her out the door, she turned back for one last look at Patrick. He gazed at her for another moment, his eyes radiating regret and longing, before he dutifully turned to his grandmother.

Patrick strode out a back door of the mansion, his boots clipping sharply against the cobblestone path. Amanda—her warm fresh scent, her touch, her womanly gentleness—filled his senses. He longed to find her and take up where they'd left off in the conservatory. But he knew he shouldn't. He had decided to leave her alone, hadn't he?

He steeled himself against his desires, drew back his shoulders, and riveted his attention to the problem at hand. If he hoped to find any answers about the shooting accident, he had to get out and search the grounds now while the clues were still fresh.

Patrick didn't for a moment believe anyone was out to kill Mrs. Charteris. He very much doubted that the old lady had any enemies with a motive strong enough to shoot her.

But had she been hit merely by accident? A careless hunter with a bad aim? Or had she been mistakenly wounded by a shot meant for him? He scoured his mind for any sore loser he might have beat at gambling recently. Or an irate husband who might have discovered he'd been in the wife's bed? Patrick readily admitted he wasn't lily-white or innocent of wrongdoing, but he honestly couldn't come up with anyone who would want to kill him.

That left Amanda Prescott. He hated his next thought. Could the shot have been meant for her? Images of titian hair and endlessly deep blue eyes swam before him. She was enchanting, but was she really as innocent as she appeared? He'd already decided she was a good girl, and thus not to be seduced. Maybe he would have to reevaluate his assessment. Maybe Miss Prescott had a past that was catching up with her. If so, it would have to be dealt with before it further endangered everyone at Pinewood House.

That morning, he'd asked his grandmother what she knew about Amanda Prescott's background, and why she had asked the girl to stay. She had revealed very little, except that Amanda was the daughter of John Prescott, whose parents had been employed on the estate as maid and stable hand. Amanda had come to Pinewood at her dying father's request, and Gram, out of sympathy and kindness, had invited her to stay. Because of her fondness for little Johnny Prescott, she had offered Amanda temporary shelter. Patrick smiled. It was so typical of Gram—taking in a stray kitten out of the kindness of her heart.

And that was all he really knew of Amanda's background. It wasn't enough, not nearly enough.

An unruly thatch of brown hair caught his

eye. A lanky young groom lounged beside the barn.

"You, Harry," Patrick called, not breaking stride. "Come on. Let's see what mischief we can find on the grounds."

Harry scrambled to his feet. "Aye, m'lord."

The two men went the same way down the lawn that Patrick had taken with the women that afternoon. As they strode side by side, Patrick appraised the young groom out of the corner of his eye.

"You're acquainted with most of the servants on the place, aren't you, Harry?"

"Yes, sir. Know 'em all."

"Any of them own a gun?"

"Not that I know of. What'd anybody in service here need a gun for?"

"That's what I want to find out."

Harry stalked on in uneasy silence. Patrick glanced over and caught the wary look on his face.

"I'm not saying I blame any of the servants, or that I think one of them has to be guilty of something. But I want to find out who fired that gun today, Harry. Do you know anything about it? Heard any of the servants talking? Idle gossip? Anything like that?"

Harry thought for a moment. "No, m'lord, I haven't heard no gossip 'bout no gunfire."

The men walked on, and Patrick realized how little he really knew about the private lives of the estate servants. "You're seeing that little maid,

Maude, aren't you? Reggie White's daughter?"

Harry's eyes widened in surprise. "Why, yes, sir. We've been keep'n company 'bout a year. Didn't realize you'd noticed."

"That's fine. Just be sure and observe all the proprieties, eh, Harry? Reggie is by way of being a special friend of mine. I would hate to see anything untoward happen to his daughter."

"I have only the highest respect for Maude, Y'r Lordship. Don't worry on that score."

"Right. Here's Spirit Lake. You take the left shore, and I'll take the right. Give me a shout if you find anything out of the ordinary."

"Yes, m'lord."

They split up and wended their separate ways around the lakeshore. The afternoon sun had passed its zenith, but still-radiant rays dazzled and danced off the water. It would have been a good day for boating, thought Patrick with a twinge of regret. He would have liked to have seen the sun reflected on Amanda's face as he rowed her out on the water.

He passed the dock, caught sight of the unoccupied boat still bobbing on the lake, and guilt swept over him. He intensely regretted that two ladies in his care had been subjected to danger. He prided himself on totally controlling every situation. He had long ago mastered himself and his errant emotions, and he was damned if he wouldn't master everything else in his life, too. He deplored the feeling of helplessness that swept over him. He had vowed to avoid feeling powerless for as long as possible.

Finding out who had fired the shot, and why, would give him something to do, something important to distract him from boredom and doubts, from his dread, and the panic that threatened to engulf him lately.

Maybe it would also distract him from his thoughts of Amanda. He should leave her alone, but somehow she attracted him beyond just the physical. Inexplicably, he was drawn to her quiet strength and warm understanding as though he were a frozen ice statue, and she the sun. He hoped he could find the strength to stay on at Pinewood House and still resist her charms.

Patrick raised his gaze from the path and discovered he'd gone nearly all the way around the lake. Harry plunged toward him through the overgrown bushes ahead.

"What did you find, Harry? Any footprints? Spent shells?"

"Noth'n. Noth'n at all."

Patrick squinted up at the sun. "Well, it's getting late. Let's go in. We can try again tomorrow."

"Yes, sir."

Harry followed Patrick up the lawn, and they parted at the house. Suddenly bone-weary, Patrick went in, drained of all energy and enthusiasm.

His grandmother met him at the door. "Patrick, where in the world have you been? I need you."

"Looking for clues about the shooting, Gram. Afraid I didn't find anything, though."

"Well, I need you now. Diane, the Countess of Craven, is very upset about the accident. She's been crying and carrying on, until I don't know what. She's in the library now. Won't you go in to her, dear, and try to soothe her? I'm afraid if we don't calm her down, her panic will spread to the other guests. Then the whole weekend will be ruined—if it hasn't been already."

"Don't fret, Gram. I'm sure the weekend can be salvaged."

"Walk with her in the garden, why don't you? That will amuse her and take her mind off things."

Damn! thought Patrick savagely. The last thing he needed this afternoon was his petulant mistress foisted on him. He longed to shrug off the request, but noting the worry on his grandmother's face, he set his jaw and turned dutifully toward the library.

Dr. Sterling had ordered Amanda to lie down. She knew she should try to relax, but she couldn't quell the anxiety running through her mind.

Why? Why had Mrs. Charteris been shot? Had it been an accident? Amanda fervently hoped so. Anything else was unthinkable.

Yet a niggling doubt remained. What if Mrs. Charteris hadn't been the intended victim? What if the shot had been meant for someone else—for Patrick? She imagined him lying wounded on the dock, and a sickening sensation thudded her stomach. How would she feel if anything bad happened to him?

Thoughts of Patrick filled her mind and made her body flare to life. The warm potency of his touch in the conservatory still tingled on her cheeks. His masculinity moved her in a way no man ever had before, arousing strong new feelings. She wasn't quite sure how to deal with his palpable effect on her.

She admired his strength in handling the situation with Mrs. Charteris and his grandmother. His wonderful gentleness in the conservatory reminded her of her father's caring concern. Memories of home flooded through her. She slumped down on the edge of the bed. Until this moment, she hadn't realized how much she missed the warm tenderness of her parents.

"Oh, Patrick," she whispered in the silence. "I wish—"

A tentative knock came at the door, and Amanda looked up.

"Come in."

Maude stuck her head around the door. "Is there anything I can do for you, miss? I heard about the ruckus."

"Oh, Maude. Please come in. Is everything all right downstairs?"

Maude deposited a tea tray onto a small table. "Well, Lady Swinton is fit to be tied. She's trying to get things back to normal. Mr. Patrick n' my Harry went out to search the grounds."

"Oh, I hope they'll be careful! The person who fired the gun might still be around."

Amanda's worried look wasn't lost on Maude. "Mr. Patrick knows what he's doing," she hastened to reassure her. "Never you fear."

Maude poured out the tea.

"Was that your father who helped carry Mrs. Charteris?"

"Yes'm, that's m' dad, Reggie White."

"He was a great help," said Amanda, sipping from the delicate cup.

Maude smiled warmly. "Her Ladyship is organizing things downstairs, miss. Shall I help you change for a walk in the gardens before teatime?"

Amanda sighed. The women at a Saturday-to-Monday house party did nothing but change clothes! Each day required at least four changes: an elegant silk costume for breakfast, a tweed suit for lunching with the men who were out shooting, a tea gown, and the most formal brocade or velvet evening dress for dinner. And no woman dared wear the same ensemble twice in a weekend! Amanda had been provided with her borrowed clothes, but the constant changing bored her.

"Thank you, but I think I'll dispense with the afternoon walk. I'll stay here and drink my tea. I won't need anything else."

"All right, miss. I'll come back later and help you get ready for dinner," the maid said, shutting the door.

Gilded Splendor

Amanda went to her window, overlooking the enclosed gardens below. She admired the gracefully symmetrical arrangement of color, thinking the Winters were lucky indeed to have servants like Reggie and Maude to look after them.

Couples strolled two-by-two through the sheltered maze of hedges. Here and there, pairs snuggled on wrought-iron loveseats, whispering in private tête-à-têtes. Amanda had noticed how the women eagerly waited to be invited for afternoon walks with certain gentlemen—the more walks and the more gentlemen, the better.

Amanda viewed the pretty scene, admiring the ladies' dresses and the lovely garden flowers, when a flash of scarlet gown caught her eye. Around the corner of the gazebo meandered a striking woman with jet-black hair. Diane Warfield, Countess of Craven.

Amanda smiled, remembering Diane's rude snub, and how Patrick had chosen her over Diane as a dinner companion. A second later, the smile froze, then faltered to a thin line. Patrick emerged from around the gazebo, attentively hovering at Diane's side. The brunette smiled up at him adoringly, her arm crooked in his.

Patrick's smile was charming as he led the countess to a shady bench. They huddled closely on the small seat, their heads bent conspiratorially together. A lightning flash of jealousy struck painfully through Amanda's heart. She clasped her hands tightly.

So that was the way of it, she thought. How

could he be so careless with his affections? Something dramatic had happened between them a few moments ago. A woman was almost killed! Danger and strong emotions were shared, drawing them together! Everything had happened so quickly, she couldn't go back to her old life as if nothing had happened, could she? But it seemed he could. *Everything has changed for me, but he's not affected at all!*

"Well, of all the—" she fumed. "And only moments ago, he said he'd like to keep me around. He certainly found a replacement quickly enough!"

Amanda struggled to calm her roiling emotions. "What in the world am I doing?" she asked herself. "Making a bloody fool of myself, getting all starry-eyed! I wanted London and the stage. That's what's important. Nothing else!"

Fingers splayed against the glass, she spoke to the man below. "What they've said is true. I only forgot for a moment that you're nothing but a . . . a . . ." She couldn't think of any words bad enough to describe him.

Whirling away from the window, she tossed her head defiantly. "Special indeed!"

Chapter Five

A steady rain drizzled drearily from a troubled gray sky the next morning. After a light breakfast brought by Maude, Amanda chose to stay in her room, reading and resting. Worn out by the accumulated tensions of the past few days, she tried to forget the shooting and the myriad questions that had been driving her to distraction. Mostly, she tried to forget that the Marquess of Swinton existed.

Mercifully, the houseguests departed. Amanda wanted to avoid meeting any of them as they took their leave. She could truthfully say she'd made some new friends among them, but she'd already said good-bye to Mrs. Charteris, and to Granville, the artist who'd been so kind to her. She didn't want to take the chance of running into the Countess of Craven. She knew she would be tempted to act just as rudely as the woman had been to her, and why should she lower herself to that level?

She certainly didn't want to see Patrick, the glib-tongued turncoat. She couldn't trust herself to be civil to him, and she thought she owed him that at least. After all, it was his house in which she resided, even though it had been his grandmother who had invited her to stay. Besides, he might work his magic spell on her, eliciting warm, maddening responses she was unwilling to feel. He had a way of making her good intentions and firm plans all but fly out the window, and she resented the fact that His Lordship could so easily charm her against her better judgment.

Amanda frowned at the book in her lap, willing herself to concentrate, but Patrick invaded her thoughts, no matter how hard she tried to banish him. Her initial admiration for him had faded, replaced by distrust and confusion. Thinking about the scene in the garden, she realized again what a ladies' man he really was, how everything said about him must be true, and how easily he spread his charms about to any available female. She shook her head. It would be best to avoid him until she was ready to travel to London.

The book fell open on her lap, forgotten. London! How could she be mooning over a man when she had London to look forward to! Had anyone ever fallen in love right before a trip to London? She doubted it. The shining city beckoned enticingly. Surely it must be the place of all riches—stimulating people, fine clothes, delightful plays, the smart clip-clop of horses' hooves on cobblestones beneath the glow of gaslights. The men there would probably be every bit as handsome and charming as Patrick Winter!

Amanda sobered as she pondered her future in the great city. How would she live until she succeeded on the stage? Without money, even London could be dreary and dull. Or worse—some women ended up living off fine gentlemen. She shook her head again, this time more vehemently. That was not an option for Amanda. She would never betray her parents' values.

She focused her attention on her book, which had been lying open at the wrong page. She reread the same paragraph three times without grasping the faintest idea of its meaning. In exasperation, she gave up all pretense of reading and restlessly threw down the book.

Why was she sitting here when she had long ago decided to live in London? She had made her detour to Pinewood House and met the Marchioness of Swinton, as she had promised her father. There was no longer any reason to postpone her journey. She would inform Lady Swinton and Patrick that she would be leaving.

She decided to find Maude and tell her the news. Together, they might start preparing her clothes for the journey. She donned a day dress and wandered downstairs to search for Maude.

After half an hour and a peek into every nook and cranny, Amanda admitted defeat. The little maid was nowhere to be found in the house. Amanda knew Maude shouldn't be dallying outdoors when there was work to be done, but perhaps she had ventured out for a breath of fresh air.

Amanda stepped through the French doors into the garden. The rain had ceased. The steamy, moist air hung heavy, the green hedges dripped. The grass underfoot, drenched with moisture, showed the imprint of her footsteps.

A stone walkway led past a fountain fashioned like a smiling cherub. Her fingers trailed through the water as she passed a raised pool. The murky depths of the liquid shimmered a mysterious, cool green—the exact color of Patrick's eyes.

Amanda ruthlessly pushed away the image of his compelling, arrogant gaze and continued down the path. Away from the bustle of the main house, she relished the peace and quiet of the garden.

A low murmur of voices carried through the still air. She rounded a tall hedge and came face-to-face with Patrick and Reggie, sitting together on wooden benches in front of a small, thatch-roofed gardener's cottage.

In spite of herself, Amanda stared at Patrick with frank admiration, finding it impossible to tear her eyes away. His loose white shirt was open at the neck, exposing crisp black hairs at the V of his throat. Tight, fawn-colored riding breeches encased his firm, shapely thighs. He carelessly flicked a riding crop against tall, shiny black boots.

Patrick and Reggie chatted and chuckled together as if they were old friends, not master and servant. Amanda hesitated, unsure whether to stop and speak or continue on her way. Before she could make up her mind, Patrick rose.

"Good day, Amanda. Out for a walk?"

"Yes," she responded stiffly. "The air seemed fresh after the rain."

"Do you ride? Have you tried our stables yet?"

She nodded. "I ride. Perhaps that is a good idea."

"Won't you sit down for a moment?"

Amanda faltered. She didn't want to intrude on their private conversation, but Patrick gestured charmingly to a bench. She took the seat he offered. His eyes remained on her, caressing her, while he continued his discussion with the gardener.

"Could have been a hunter from the shooting party in the next county, lost his bearings. But then why didn't he respond to our shouts?" Patrick turned his gaze back to Reggie. "No, it was something else."

Reggie considered for a moment. "Mebbe the shooter don't want t' own up t' such carelessness."

"If it was carelessness."

The gardener caught Amanda's worried expression. "Patrick," he soothed, "you've always been a worrier—imagining the worst, ever since you were a little boy. I'm the only one t' really see that side of you," he finished proudly.

Amanda was surprised to hear Reggie address Patrick so intimately and informally, but Patrick didn't seem to take it amiss. In fact, he grinned fondly at Reggie. He seemed to enjoy the familiarity, as if his relationship with the gardener was an old and close one he treasured.

"If only the women knew what a serious side there is t' their ladies' man," Reggie chuckled. "What would they do?"

"Run off screaming, I should think," returned Patrick dryly. He assessed Amanda, his eyes twinkling. "Maybe you'll run off screaming, too?"

"There's no need for me to," she replied curtly, "even if you are a ladies' man, as Reggie says. I can resist a ladies' man."

"Can you?"

After a moment, Reggie continued, "My Patrick is what's known as a challenge, and women do seem t' love a challenge."

"I don't," Amanda retorted crisply. "Of course, some women might—like the Countess of Craven."

Patrick snorted. "Don't mention the countess! I had a deuce of a time calming her down in the garden after the shooting incident, but I didn't want her disturbing Gram with her hysterics." He assessed Amanda intently through narrowed eyes. "Is the countess on your mind?"

Amanda could have bitten her tongue for mentioning Diane Warfield. Why should she let Patrick think she was jealous? She wasn't! It was of no consequence to her who he dallied with. She rose and adjusted her skirts in an effort to hide her flushed face. "I think I'll continue my walk and leave you to your conversation," she said.

Patrick and Reggie both stood politely. "Good day," they said, nodding in unison.

Amanda turned back to the house, breathing in deep drafts of the fresh air. For some inexplicable reason, the day, which had seemed sodden and heavy, now glistened with the light of silvery raindrops quivering on each green leaf and blade of grass.

She walked on through the garden, exploring twists and turns in a tall boxwood maze. The leafy greenery rose six feet high, forming an intricate puzzle, and Amanda wasn't tall enough to see over it. She took many a wrong turn before guessing the right way toward the house. It was great fun, and she marveled at the intricate design and the careful planting.

Coming around a corner of the hedge, she halted. Maude stood just ahead, her back pressed against the garden wall. A young man hovered closely over her. His thatch of brown hair was disarrayed as if he'd been in a scuffle. One arm draped intimately and possessively around the young girl's neck.

Amanda ducked back behind the hedge, not wanting to disturb them. She meant to walk on, taking an alternate route, but her steps slowed as Maude's determined voice rang out.

"Stop that, Harry!"

"Aw, come on, minx. Just one teeny kiss."

"Don't! Be a gentleman."

"I ain't no bleed'n gentleman—you know that, Maudie."

"We might be seen from the house. You're too forward."

"That's not what you said t'other night."

"Oh Harry, what if Her Ladyship finds us out? We must be good. We could lose our positions."

"I don't care if we do. We'll go to London. Anyway, she won't find out nothin'. Old dowager can't see beyond the end of her nose."

Fearing Maude might need assistance, Amanda made a move to step out from behind the greenery, but Maude's teary words detained her.

"When my waist starts to get bigger, Her Ladyship'll notice. Then what will I do? She'll never let me stay at Pinewood House. I'll be out on the street—disgraced. You've just got to marry me, Harry, like we planned."

"Now don't cry, luv. We'll get married all right."

"When?"

Gilded Splendor

"Soon as I get back from London with a job. I'll speak to your father, and to His Lordship. We'll have a lovely wedding, go back to London, and have a fine life."

"Oh, Harry. Why do you have to get a job in London? Why can't we live here at Pinewood House?"

"We've been all over 'at before. You know I don't want t' be in service to His high and mighty Lordship all my life. I've got plans, and now they include you."

"They'd better. You know I love you so."

"And I love you. Let's prove it with a kiss here . . . and here . . . and here . . ."

Silence ensued.

Amanda worried over the conversation, but Maude seemed to be in control, at least temporarily. With enough respect for the little maid to forbear startling or embarrassing her, Amanda continued down the path, away from the couple. She made an anxious mental note to keep in touch with Maude when they were both in London, and to be a friend if needed.

Worried and concerned, Amanda headed for her room to change her clothes. Patrick's suggestion that she go out riding appealed to her troubled mind. She needed to get away from the stifling atmosphere of Pinewood House.

After a quick change, she chose a mount from the stables. Soon, Amanda and her horse were flying over the countryside as one sleek body. She'd grown up riding, and the fresh, wet wind against her hair braced her. It seemed like ages since she'd sat a horse, and she reveled in the sensations of freedom and movement.

She finally pulled up on the crest of a hill overlooking Pinewood House. The manor sat poised like a jewel in the midst of a dazzling green setting. She dismounted and sat on the grass beneath a tall oak to survey the glorious view.

Such a beautiful house, she mused. It could have been a happy place, forever solid, comforting—a refuge against all the sadness in the world. But it was not. Instead, Pinewood House seemed like a trap, harboring dark secrets beneath its elaborate decorations. What was her father's link with the Winter family that had brought her here? Why had he sent her to meet the house's evasive mistress, with her mercurial mood swings and her illusive grandson?

Lost in her thoughts, Amanda failed to hear a large black stallion canter up behind her. She continued gazing dreamily at the mansion until a large form threw a shadow, blocking out the sun. Patrick towered above her, hands on hips, booted legs spread wide, his black hair blowing wildly in the wind. He was so handsome, he resembled a Greek god, and Amanda found it hard to breathe. Her heart throbbed inside her breast, beating a fierce staccato rhythm against her ribs.

He sat down on the grass beside her, one forearm propped atop his bent knee. "I see you took my advice about riding, but I would have preferred you'd ridden out with company. Until we find who's been doing the shooting around here, going out alone could be dangerous."

Amanda's throat clutched so tightly she couldn't speak. Their eyes locked. The word spun around inside her head—*dangerous, dangerous*. Oh yes, his lethal charm was more than dangerous. She leaned toward him, impelled by a force she couldn't control. He reached out and pulled her roughly to him. Before she could protest, his mouth came down hard on hers. Not a gentle kiss, like the first one in the library. He took no time softly exploring her mouth, but took it with bruising, crushing force. His lips, urgent, searing, compelling, moved over hers. Her lips parted, and his tongue filled her mouth, sending her senses reeling. The strength of her own response shocked her. Lost in time and place, she felt nothing but the overpowering mastery of his mouth, his maleness.

He lifted his head, and his hooded eyes darkened with emotion. "Leave Pinewood House, Amanda," he commanded roughly.

She blinked in confusion. "Leave?"

"You heard me! I don't want you here, stirring my senses, arousing my desires. I'd like to see you depart the innocent young girl you were when you arrived, with your scruples and your virginity intact."

Amanda gasped in outraged surprise. "How dare you speak to me of such things!"

Elizabeth Parker

But he had already risen to his feet. He strode to his stallion and mounted it. She could feel his sharp eyes boring into her. The horse pranced and turned, its hooves stomping the ground.

"Do as I say, Amanda!" Patrick flung over his shoulder. Spurring his horse, he was gone, plummeting down the hill at breakneck speed.

Amanda stood and brushed the grass from her skirt. She bitterly wiped her bruised, swollen lips with the back of her hand. That was the last time the marquess would insult her! To kiss her like that, then order her to leave, bringing up the subject of her virginity! He was no gentleman!

He wanted her to leave Pinewood House? No more than she! She determined to move forward the date of her departure.

The air in the dining room that evening vibrated with tension. Amanda faced Patrick across the gleaming expanse of polished wood table. In his civilized and proper dinner attire, he looked more deadly handsome than he had in his riding clothes, if that were possible. His shining black hair was combed smoothly back, his well-cut suit impeccable.

He regarded her sore, tender mouth without comment. Self-consciously, Amanda ran her tongue over her lips, moistening them. He smiled slightly, as though amused, his eyes radiating a subtle challenge. Defiantly, she lifted her chin and boldly met his gaze, vowing to get through dinner with as much grace as possible. *And don't think for a moment you can intimidate me!* she fumed.

Helene occupied the place of honor at the end of the long table. Candles in tall golden candlesticks reflected a burnished gleam off the wood-paneled dining room walls. Vases of fresh-cut flowers adorned the heavy white damask tablecloth.

Servants brought in the first course. As always at these meals, the quantity and quality of the food amazed Amanda. Two soups, one hot and one cold, were followed by fish with a choice of sauces, sorbet, and quails as a main course. Sweet puddings and fruits with port followed at the end of the sumptuous meal. Amanda tasted each dish as it was brought to her, but could hardly finish before it was whisked away by a servant and replaced with another.

As if by silent consent, no one brought up the gunfire or the wound to Mrs. Charteris. Conversation centered pleasantly on family friends and upcoming weekend house parties. Helene and Patrick chatted amiably over their food. Amanda ate silently, saying little.

"You're very quiet tonight, Miss Prescott," observed Patrick, cutting into his quail. He raised one eyebrow quizzically.

She lifted her wineglass to her lips and caught the glow of candlelight turning his fathomless green eyes to a deep shade of emerald. A slight question clouded his expression as he regarded her. Refusing to acknowledge his look, she lowered her gaze to her plate. Her blood pulsed in her veins. It was with difficulty that she concentrated on the meal before her. Deciding now was the time, she lifted her lashes and met his gaze. "I am merely thinking about tomorrow."

"And what happens tomorrow?"

"I'm leaving Pinewood House, continuing on my journey to London. Though I hate to decline your gracious hospitality." She let a trace of sarcasm touch her voice.

Patrick's back went rigid, and a slight tension seemed to come over him, but as suddenly as it had appeared, the tension was gone. He merely took a sip from his wineglass and smiled politely. "We'll hate to see you go, but perhaps it would be for the best."

"I think so, too." An odd twinge of disappointment and sadness knifed through Amanda. She would never see him again. Somehow that thought bothered her more than she'd imagined. She dropped her lashes quickly to hide her confused emotions. "I've postponed my plans long enough."

Lady Swinton spoke up from the end of the table. "What's this? Surely you can't think of leaving us!"

Patrick and Amanda pivoted to her in surprise.

"But why not?" asked Amanda.

Patrick frowned in puzzlement at his grandmother's vehemence. "Yes, Gram? Why shouldn't

Gilded Splendor

Miss Prescott go on to London if she wishes? She has nothing to detain her here."

"Why, because... because..." Helene sputtered for a second, then found her voice. "Surely she had better stay until we find out who shot Mrs. Charteris."

Patrick looked skeptical.

"Well," continued Helene, "there may be some danger she should know about. Besides, her father expressly asked her to stay on here awhile. Isn't that so, Amanda? Why, I won't hear of your leaving so abruptly."

Amanda puzzled at Helene's urgent, strident speech—an unmistakable tone of fear had crept into her voice. "But my father only asked me to come and meet you, which I have done."

"Gram, I really think you should respect Miss Prescott's wishes," argued Patrick reasonably.

Helene opened her mouth to reply, but before more could be said, the butler, Eugene, stood at attention before her.

"Pardon me, madam."

"Yes, what is it?" asked Helene irritably.

"Madam, there is a person to see you." The butler's mouth formed the words with obvious distaste.

"Oh, bother. We have not finished our dinner. Who is it?"

"He says his name is Thomas Gray, madam, and he is—" Eugene halted in midsentence, his eyebrows climbing his forehead in surprise. Helene had risen from her chair, her face a mask of deathly pallid white. Patrick and Amanda paused, their forks suspended in midair.

"Wh–what did you say his name was?"

Eugene grew flustered. "I believe he said his name was, uh, Gray, ma'am—Thomas Gray."

Helene darted one quick, reproachful look at Amanda, but the expression disappeared in the next second as Helene visibly wilted. Her shoulders slumped, all her strength vanished.

"Well," she said to herself in a low voice, "I guess it was inevitable." Then she raised her head. "I will see Mr. Gray in the library, Eugene."

Patrick pushed back from the table, his chair scraping the oak floor. "Who is this Mr. Gray? I think I'd better see him with you."

Helene raised her hand. "No. I prefer to see him alone."

"Who is he?"

"He's an old friend of the family. I will tell you about him later. You and Amanda stay and finish your meal."

Helene visibly drew up her strength as she went around the table. Her back was again ramrod straight as she passed slowly and regally from the dining room.

Amanda tossed a questioning look at Patrick. Thomas Gray? There was that name again. During her earlier interrogation, Helene had implied that Amanda might have known this mysterious Thomas Gray. Who was he? Why had Helene

Gilded Splendor

seemed so fearful at his appearance? And what, wondered Amanda, was the meaning of that look of reproach Helene had leveled at her?

Patrick responded to her silent questions. "I'm as much in the dark as you are. But I'll soon get to the bottom of this." He threw his napkin beside his plate. "Are you finished?"

Her appetite gone, she nodded. Patrick came around the table and, taking her arm, led her from the dining room. They paused a moment in the hall and watched a man about Helene's age head for the library. Though tall and slender, there was nothing distinguished about him. His rounded shoulders slumped, and there was a loose, lanky quality about his joints and movements. His light, sandy hair, now touched by gray, was thinning in spots. In his youth, he had obviously been quite handsome, in a careless sort of way. The library door closed behind him, shutting off the stream of yellow light on the hall floor.

"Would you like coffee?" Patrick asked.

"No, thank you, I believe I'll go up to my room."

Amanda gathered her skirts and turned toward the stairs, but Patrick's hand on her arm detained her on the bottom step.

"What have we here? Do I detect a hint of depression? You're not still upset about Mrs. Charteris, are you? Or is your intended journey to London making you apprehensive?"

"Please let me pass."

His hand tightened on her arm, and his voice turned cold. "Why does my grandmother want you to stay so badly?"

"I have no idea. But it doesn't matter, anyway. I intend to leave as I said."

Even though the mysteries go unexplained, she thought to herself in vexation. She had failed to pin down Helene and make her provide answers to her questions. Nothing had been resolved. In fact, Amanda admitted furiously, she was in the dark now more than ever. But she would just have to live with that. She raised her chin. "It's time I left."

"Good."

Amanda jerked away from his hand. "Oh! You're the most infuriating man I've ever met!"

"And you've met so many men."

She ignored his jibe. "When I first came here you teased me. Then you were kind and gentle. I almost thought . . . The next thing I know you're forcing your attentions on me and rudely ordering me to leave! I don't understand you at all."

Retreating once again behind a haughty, aristocratic facade, Patrick stifled a yawn behind his hand. Amanda saw it and clenched her fist, resisting the urge to slap him. He seemed incapable of honesty. She turned away abruptly to hide the hurt tears that threatened to spill over.

"Amanda!" He caught her arm and swung her around to face him. His deep green eyes were filled with regret. "Do you believe in love at first sight?"

Gilded Splendor

She looked at him incredulously.

"I don't," he said. "Not at all. But I believe in attraction at first sight. From the very first, I've been attracted to you—drawn to you, in a way I can't afford to be. I don't want to hurt you. That's why I believe it would be better not to see you anymore. I'm sorry if I've hurt your feelings."

His genuine apology made some of her anger evaporate, leaving only confusion. Why? Why was he so bewildering? His alternating moods baffled her, unsettled her. She gazed into his troubled eyes. She longed to throw herself into his arms and be kissed again and again. She hated the distance between them, and hated the thought that tomorrow she would place more distance, perhaps never see him again. But fierce pride kept her from confiding in him.

"I don't know what to say to you."

"It's a hell of a note, isn't it?"

Torn with conflicting emotions, Amanda couldn't bear to stay in his presence a moment longer. She whirled toward the stairs, but the sudden thought of Maude made her turn back.

"Before I go, there's something I'd like to ask you."

"Yes?"

"If a servant at Pinewood House happened to get into trouble of some kind, she—or he—would receive help. Isn't that right?"

"It would depend what kind of trouble. If it was something small like pilfering sugar, I'm sure something could be worked out. If it were something more serious, it would probably mean the servant would get the sack and be thrown out. I'm afraid Gram would insist."

"But suppose a young servant couple happened to be in love and . . . and . . ." An unwelcome flush heated her cheeks.

Patrick smiled knowingly. "And there happened to be a baby on the way?" he suggested.

Damn the man!

"Yes—supposing that happened?"

"The girl would immediately be sent away without a reference," he said crisply.

At the cool detachment in his voice, Amanda's embarrassment turned to indignation. "But that is so harsh! Many of your weekend guests dallied together. I saw how they formed liaisons, even going so far as to visit each other in their bedrooms at night! You couldn't help but notice it, and nobody said a thing!"

"I'm afraid that's one of the differences between the upper classes and the lower. Guests can do what they please, but if a young girl in service happened to get herself in trouble, I'm sure Gram just wouldn't tolerate it."

Amanda flushed with anger. "I can't believe what I'm hearing! It's the most heartless, cold, calculating thing I've ever heard! Surely you don't approve of such a blatant double standard!"

"That's the way it is. Besides, none of my weekend guests had the misfortune to get caught. They all held up their side. People can do anything they want—as long as they don't get caught. A servant who gets caught is most unlucky—and most careless."

"Ever since I arrived at Pinewood, I've heard how you keep yourself amused. It sounds like you've had an amazing number of different women! And yet you'd begrudge a young couple sincerely in love!"

Patrick's lip curled. "I don't know who's been talking, but surely my bed partners are none of your concern."

His sardonic expression sent Amanda's temper soaring, and she bit her tongue.

"Besides, you're leaving tomorrow, remember? Then you will surely have no interest in what happens to anyone here at Pinewood House."

Amanda lifted her head in defiance. "Perhaps I won't leave tomorrow. Your grandmother wishes me to stay. Perhaps I will."

She started up the stairs. Patrick spoke after her.

"Is there a servant on the place who's in trouble and needs help?"

She pivoted slowly. "No, of course not. There is no one. I was merely wondering, that's all."

Patrick placed one foot on the bottom step. He leaned forward with one hand on his knee and looked up at her.

"If you knew of such a situation, I would be grateful if you would bring it to my attention. I might be able to help."

"You would help?"

"As I said, it would depend on the circumstances."

"And on your damnable, ever-changing mood?"

She didn't trust herself to speak further. The anger raged inside her until she thought she would choke. "Good night, my lord," she said coldly.

He let her advance to the top of the stairs before he spoke again.

"Are you leaving tomorrow, then?"

Amanda had a sharp retort on the tip of her tongue. *Yes, I'm going! What do you care?* she wanted to scream at him, but she forced herself to speak calmly. "Yes. I have no reason to stay here any longer."

With that, she pivoted on her heel and marched away. Patrick's gaze burned into her back until she turned the corner, out of his sight.

Chapter Six

Damn!

Patrick couldn't sleep. He tossed and flopped impatiently back and forth in his bed, bothered by the rain slashing intermittently against the windowpane. Finally throwing off the bedclothes, he jerked out of bed. He strode barefooted to a sidetable and carelessly sloshed brandy into a glass. He took it to the large wingbacked chair beside his window and sat down in the dark to stare out at the storm. Jagged streaks of lightning cracked and flared through the night, followed by booms of fierce thunder. The fury of the tempestuous wind howling through the pines matched his own evil mood.

So she was leaving tomorrow? Good! That was what he'd wanted, wasn't it? Why should she stay? Because of some servant who'd gotten into trouble? He'd silently agreed with Amanda about the unfairness of the moral chasm between master and servant. But he hadn't been about to admit it to her. Why should she stick her nose in? What did she know about running an estate like Pinewood? How dare she dance into their lives and find fault, in her infinite wisdom, with a system that had sustained England for centuries? Even if she was right?

Patrick ran his hand across his whisker-stubbled jaw. Who the hell was in trouble anyway? Which one of the parlor maids had been rolling in the haystack with which groom? He sighed. He'd find out soon enough, whether he wanted to or not. There'd be hell to pay around the place with his grandmother fussing and fuming. It was all such a bloody bore.

Good thing Amanda Prescott was leaving tomorrow. He knew why his grandmother had insisted on her staying. On the way up to bed, he'd cornered Gram and she'd finally admitted she had come to sincerely like the daughter of little Johnny Prescott. Patrick couldn't blame her. He liked Amanda himself. But a niggling doubt remained—was that the only reason for Gram's insistence that she stay?

And who the hell was this Thomas Gray? His grandmother had been upset and evasive when he'd questioned her about the man. She'd pleaded a headache, even threatened tears, so

Gilded Splendor

he'd had to let her proceed to her room without giving him an explanation.

He took a swallow of brandy, his thoughts returning to Amanda. Yes, it was good she was leaving. He had to stay now, what with all the problems, and he didn't relish the thought of having her in close proximity. She was just down the hall, tucked into her sweet little virginal bed. His mouth turned down in sarcasm. Was she asleep? What was she wearing? Was her body naked and white beneath the sheets? He gritted his teeth. Those were just the kind of thoughts he'd been trying to avoid.

He threw back his head and drained his glass. It was good she was leaving. Wasn't it? Damned good.

It was good she was leaving Pinewood House tomorrow, Amanda thought as she prepared for bed. She pulled savagely on the bows as she tied blue ribbons down the front of her white linen nightgown. Nice to leave her brooding questions behind, nice to escape the stifling house with its atmosphere of stress and danger.

There was nothing to keep her here, nothing but Maude's problem. And a pair of icy green eyes.

Amanda sighed, torn with conflicting emotions. Beneath all her sound reasons and logic, she had to admit she wanted to stay. She wanted to be near Patrick. The thought of never seeing him again made her spirits sink.

But why should she want to be near him? He was infuriating. A flirtatious rakehell with plenty of women he could beckon with a crook of his finger. Surely she had nothing in common with the Marquess of Swinton. Surely he didn't fancy her. He hadn't tried for one second to get her to stay. Surely she wasn't in love with him!

Amanda shook off the thought. No! He'd said it—attracted at first sight, that was all. Hardly a basis for a lasting relationship. And her plans for her future didn't include a seduction by Swinton! Tomorrow she would go, and that would be that.

She climbed into bed and pulled the covers up to her throat. The rain poured outside, slashing against her bedroom windows, but she finally drifted off. She turned and tossed on her pillows, only half aware of the storm disturbing her sleep, bringing strange nightmares.

Lightning flashed outside the window, followed by a clap of thunder. In her dream, the thunder became the sharp crack of gunfire near a lake heavily shrouded in hazy mist. Amanda moaned softly and shifted in her bed. Over and over, the shots rang out, sending shafts of fear through her tense body.

The lightning flashed against her closed, quivering eyelids, and in her dream, Maude's tear-stained face gazed down mournfully at a blanket-wrapped object.

Gilded Splendor

Suddenly, Thomas Gray's face appeared, illuminated, grinning for some unknown reason that made her uneasy. He beckoned her into the morning room. She followed him and found it filled to overflowing with bizarre decorations. Instead of displaying quaint, pretty ornaments, the room had been transformed into an ugly, strange potpourri: grotesque masks, distorted drawings on the walls. She lifted a Harlequin's mask and found another lurking beneath it, a frightening gargoyle. Hastily, she threw off decoration after decoration, finding stormy passionate masks hidden beneath each one.

Gray's lank body shook with laughter as he watched her. In her dream, Amanda covered her ears with her hands to shut out the disturbing sounds and fled from him, down a long shadowy hallway. Her legs grew stiff and heavy as she ran. Her strides slowed as though she were plowing through quicksand. She strained as hard as she could, but the harder she tried, the more steadfastly she remained in place. Her muscles cried out in agony, shoulders and legs tense with the excruciating effort. A cold sweat broke out on her body beneath the sheets.

Thunder boomed outside, suddenly releasing her leaden limbs. Set free, she dashed down the dark hall, threw open a door, and ran into Patrick's open arms. In her dream, he was half-dressed in pajama bottoms. Crisp black hair curled on his muscled chest. Warm and safe, she buried her face against him. His strong arms came around her as they had that first night when she'd arrived at Pinewood House in the rain.

"Don't let me go! Don't let me go!" she whispered over and over, clinging to him.

In her dream, Patrick lifted her and placed her on a broad bed, then lay down beside her. His sexual magnetism radiated heat like a raging fire. Taking her chin in his hand, he turned her face up to his and held it in place. At his leisure, he kissed her, slowly, thoughtfully, sending wild spirals of sensation careening through her.

His hands roamed over her curves, molding her breasts and hips. In her dream, Amanda's body betrayed her as she never would have allowed it to in real life, but she wasn't scandalized. She didn't even want to stop him. She moaned softly as his warm lips nuzzled and nipped at the tender places on her throat.

In the next second, he abruptly removed his warm hands and mouth, and disappeared from her side. Icy cold chilled her, and she shivered, bereft and heartsick. He strode away down a long black hall, not turning back once to look at her.

Don't leave! she cried out in her dream. *Come back! Patrick! Patrick!*

"Amanda." His voice. Dream or reality? He sounded so real.

Don't talk now—just kiss me again, she thought hazily.

Someone shook her gently, pulling her from the depths.

"Amanda, you cried out. Wake up. You're safe."

He pulled her into his arms. She came awake and gazed into the dark green heat of Patrick's eyes. He stared down at her with a look of hungry passion, his eyelids hooded and heavy, his mouth drawn down in a grimace. Through the thin fabric of her nightgown, she felt his body stiffen with a pulsing, aching hunger. A current of deep need sprang between them, joining them, binding them.

"Toss you away and forget you?" he whispered. He grasped her more tightly. "I can't let you leave tomorrow. I can't. I'd regret it all my life."

She didn't answer, merely brought her arms up around his neck. He touched her lips gently with his own, hesitating, then tracing them with his tongue, exploring her mouth, savoring her taste. The closeness and intimacy of her body cradled in his arms seemed to drive him over the edge. He groaned and deepened the kiss, passionately, heavily, with open mouth, as if he could draw the life's breath out of her into himself.

They clung together for long moments before he lifted his head. She saw her own desire reflected in his green eyes, desire she had awakened despite all his best intentions, but he carefully reached up behind his neck to draw her hands down.

"You had a nightmare. See if you can get back to sleep," he said, his voice ragged. He turned away. "I can't trust myself to stay longer, or I won't answer for the consequences."

"Maybe I want you to stay. What are the consequences of that?"

Patrick threw her a look of anguish. "Don't say things like that."

"Why not?"

"Because nothing can come of it."

"Well, something can come of it—if you should feel the same way." She was astonished at the bold huskiness that had overcome her shyness. "Or do you care for someone else?"

"Don't be a fool," he said quietly.

"Well, then . . ."

She waited, watching the internal struggle mirrored on his features. She was all but throwing herself at him. They could be married. Why, oh why, didn't he speak?

He squared his shoulders and faced her.

"All right. I want you. I suppose only a fool would turn you down. When you go up to London, I'd like you to become my mistress. I'll set you up in a townhouse where we can have privacy. You can have your own carriage, clothes, a monthly allowance. You won't want for anything. And you don't

Gilded Splendor

have to worry about becoming pregnant—I'll see that you don't."

"Patrick..." Her heart keened with disappointment.

"It's a very good proposition. Made in the best of faith. You won't receive a better one."

"But that's not what I want. I thought..."

Amanda couldn't finish her sentence. What had she thought? She suddenly felt very foolish. What, after all, would a man like Patrick Winter, eleventh Marquess of Swinton, want with her, a poor, obscure nobody? What could she offer him except her body? And that only on weekends for what would be to him a very small cash outlay. She felt cheap and humiliated, and with that came the awful, searing pain. She summoned her pride and drew herself up.

"I cannot be your mistress. You don't know me if you think I could. It hurts that you would even suggest such a thing."

"Amanda—"

"I can't be a pretty decoration worn on your arm. I'm not like your other women, Patrick."

"I know. You're not even remotely like them."

"But you would make me be like them."

It was useless to argue further. It was clear that he regarded her as a cheap trollop, one of many. "Please leave my room," she said quietly.

"Amanda, think it over, please. I would make it good for both of us."

"Please leave—now!"

Patrick assessed her in silence for a moment, then crossed to the door and threw it open. He looked back once, his hand on the knob, an inscrutable expression on his face. Then he walked out and softly drew the door shut behind him.

Numbly, Amanda sat on the edge of her bed. For the first time, she admitted to herself that somewhere along the way, she'd crossed over that fine line between attraction and love. Oh, God, she wished she hadn't!

She stared at the closed door, not really seeing it. Was she blinded by the punishing rain that pounded against her window, or by the hot, heavy tears coursing down her cheeks?

Chapter Seven

Unable to stem the flow of salty tears, Amanda sobbed for what seemed an eternity. Patrick's words left her feeling degraded. The great Marquess of Swinton! Spoiled rotten, he'd always gotten everything he'd wanted. Life and love were cheap to him. What could she expect from a man like that? Nothing but ruination and abandonment! What would her father have thought of Patrick's revolting proposal? Not exactly what he'd had in mind for "his Mandy," she sobbed bitterly.

With the thought of her father, a measure of calm returned. He had thought of her as a lady, had always treated her like one. In her father's eyes, she hadn't been a trollop. Nor had she been one in her own eyes. Her father had loved her. But the nagging question remained—if Papa loved her, why had he sent her to Pinewood to be among the Winters—these people who seemed to degrade love, who had no concept of what love really meant?

Pushing her worries aside, Amanda clung to her anger. She raised her head from her wet pillow and wiped the tears away with the back of her hand. She'd had a decent upbringing, and her training would do her in good stead. She would show the Marquess of Swinton that he was the cheap one, not her. How dare he insult her in such a fashion! She didn't possess a fancy title, but perhaps it was *his* background that was not all it should have been!

Leaving her bed, she paced the room. She realized her nerves must be frayed to cause her to have such a frightening nightmare. Why had she dreamed of Thomas Gray, of all people? He meant nothing to her, despite Helene's implications. It only showed that the longer she stayed at Pinewood, the more troubled she became.

Well, she needn't remain in this mausoleum another minute to be further insulted and distressed! She would leave at daybreak.

Firmly resolved, Amanda grabbed her satchel from the armoire and threw in her few belongings. She would go to London, as she should have done in the first place. She'd had enough of the Winters and their precious Pinewood House! She'd stayed too long.

A fleeting thought of abandoning Maude stabbed her with guilt, but she resolutely pushed it away. Perhaps she could find a way to help Maude once they were both in London, but first she had to help herself!

By the time Amanda finished packing, the first light of a cold, gray dawn was rising over the hills. She drew the curtain aside and peered out. The rain had stopped, and the clouds parted. It promised to be a fine day for travel. But fine or ill, she was determined to be on the road soon.

All thought of sleep had vanished. Energy and resolve bolstered her spirit. She decided to go down to the kitchen before leaving and find some food to take along. She nudged her door open, careful to make no sound. Whether the Winters would begrudge her a little food was immaterial to her, but she didn't want to awaken the slumbering household and invite questions.

Wrapping her shawl closely around her shoulders to ward off the chill, she tiptoed softly down the wide hall. She had almost reached the broad staircase when angry, arguing voices shattered the silence.

Amanda halted dead-still and threw a wary glance toward Helene's door. Oh, dear! Not everyone in the quiet household was asleep. All she needed was to be noticed prowling in the hallway at this hour! Anticipating discovery, she desperately racked her brain for some kind of plausible explanation for her presence, but her thoughts were interrupted.

"How dare you speak to me that way, Patrick?" Helene's voice registered shocked anger.

"Gram, I'm simply trying to gain your attention, to tell you how I feel." From behind the closed door, Patrick's tired voice sounded strained from the effort to be patient and reasonable. Amanda meant to continue down the stairs to the kitchen, but something held her back. She stood outside the door, mesmerized by the sound of anguish in his voice.

"Last night you were begging Amanda to stay on at Pinewood House!"

"That's different! I didn't say you should marry her to get her to stay! For the last time, Patrick, you cannot think of marrying that girl!"

"And I tell you I am going to marry Amanda Prescott, if she'll have me. There's nothing you can do to stop it."

Amanda gasped. Marry? Was that what he'd said? Her heart leapt. With a few words, everything in the world changed!

"But why, for heaven's sake? You hardly know her!"

"Don't you see, I've lived my whole life for you and the family and Pinewood House. Why shouldn't I have a turn for my own

Gilded Splendor

life? Amanda can help me find that life!"

"She's a nobody, a poor girl lacking in the social graces and in all you've been led to expect. She has no family, no dowry, no breeding or background. She has nothing. She is nothing."

Hot shame flooded Amanda, and she lowered her head in humiliation. It was true. She had no background, not the kind the Winters expected.

But Helene had known that all along! The same woman who had been so nice to her initially, who had begged her to stay at Pinewood House, now didn't want her, now criticized her as ill-bred. Why the abrupt change in Helene's attitude? Amanda had noticed Helene's mood swings before, but they'd been slight and infrequent. This new change was much more—disarming, even frightening.

"Please don't speak of Amanda that way," said Patrick. "I don't care if she doesn't have background. She's a strong, beautiful woman with all the qualities I've been looking for. I love her. I need her."

Amanda's gaze flew heavenward. *He loves me! Patrick said he loves and needs me!*

Helene's voice took on a wheedling, cajoling quality.

"Son, I need you. Who will run the estate if you leave?"

"I have no intention of leaving Pinewood House, Gram. This is my home. I've always been glad to have you stay on and run the housekeeping for me, ever since Mother and Father died. And of course, Amanda and I will want you to continue on here after we're married. I'm sure the three of us will be able to get along just fine in a house the size of Pinewood."

"Patrick, you're forgetting one thing!" Steel rang out in Helene's voice. "The Winter curse. The illness that killed your grandfather. The illness your father would have succumbed to had he lived. The illness that will surely strike you. You know all this, Patrick. Dr. Sterling explained it to you. Would you saddle a wife with it?"

Minutes drew out in a long silence. Amanda absorbed the awful, unbelievable words Helene had spoken. *Patrick? Cursed with illness? God, he couldn't be!* Her fingernails cut into her fists clenched at her sides.

"Gram, we're not completely sure I'll ever get sick."

"Can you chance it? Would you have your young wife take care of you in the sickroom? Watch over you, lying there paralyzed with no chance of recovery? Would you ruin her life?"

Stony silence greeted her questions, and Helene's voice pounded on relentlessly.

"Would you have children? Amanda would surely want them. If you pass the disease to her innocent children, she'll never forgive you.

Gilded Splendor

When she sees her little boy grow up to lie paralyzed and in pain, day after day, year after year, slowly dwindling, she'll curse you for selfishly bringing that blight on him."

"Grandmother, for God's sake!"

"Patrick, I'm telling you this for your own good, and for the good of Amanda Prescott. You don't know how it was after your grandfather got sick—the nights of agony, the days of helplessness. How he raged at his fate! How I cried and raged at mine!"

Amanda listened to Helene's recitation, and all the horror and grief of her own experience came rushing back. How well she knew those days and nights of agony! She and her parents had raged against their fates, too, but it had not changed a thing.

"Patrick, you've always agreed that you can't think of burdening someone with that!"

"I know." Patrick's voice was miserable. "But am I not entitled to some kind of life? Where am I to go from here?"

"You will continue as you always have. You don't have a bad life."

An impatient sound erupted from him.

"You know it's for the best. If you truly love this young woman, you'll give her up."

"I love her." A long silence, then Patrick's voice, terrifying in its coldness. "I'll give her up."

"In time you'll see I was right about this, and you'll thank me. You have much to live for—your honor, your responsibilities. Besides, you're young, handsome, and titled. There's a lot of pleasure and life left for you, dear. And I will always be here for you, too."

"Don't worry. I'll continue as I have done, with honor and responsibilities intact. I'll live life to the fullest extent possible from now on. Just don't expect to see much of me around here. The kind of living I intend to do requires the excitement of the city. Maybe some travel abroad. Who knows?" His voice had grown rash, careless.

"Patrick—"

Helene's sentence was cut off. A door opened and slammed shut as he stormed out the other exit. Amanda stood immobile in the hallway, trying to make sense of the tragic words she'd heard.

Patrick's large shadow fell across the hall floor in front of her, and she shrank back into the semidarkness. He strode into the library. Tentatively, she followed and peered around the edge of the open door. She watched him slosh whiskey into a large glass, his handsome face distorted by rage and hatred.

Throwing back his head, he quickly drained the glass, then slammed it down violently on the table and poured himself another. He paused in thought then, his head bent forward. His knuckles strained white around the cut glass goblet until it shattered in his fist, sending shards of glass flying. Blood trickled down his fingers, but he took no notice. He merely picked up a fresh glass from the sideboard and filled it from the bottle.

Amanda wanted to run to him, cradle his bleeding hand in her own, kiss the blood and pain away, but she halted dead in her tracks. She didn't dare enter the room and let Patrick know she'd been watching, listening.

With a groan, he fell heavily to his knees on the thick carpet. The glass dropped unheeded from his hand, spilling amber liquid across the flowered rug. His head fell forward onto his heaving chest.

Amanda bit her knuckle as she watched, his raw, primitive grief overwhelming her. *No more! I can't watch any more!*

Her heart broke as a single, shining tear rolled down the chiseled face of the Marquess of Swinton.

In the chill gray light of dawn, Amanda crept upstairs to her room. Inside, she leaned back against the closed door and expelled her breath in a rush. Trembling, weak-kneed, she sat on the edge of her bed and pondered the incredible conversation she'd just heard. Turning each sentence, each nuance of expression, over and over in her mind, she tried to make sense of it all.

Cursed with illness! So that was why Patrick had lived such a fast and reckless life! Yet, she'd detected the current of sadness beneath his facade of indifference and his devil-may-care attitude. His grandmother had described his bleak future in chilling detail. With prospects like that, what had he to live for besides the pleasure of the moment?

No wonder he grasped every bit of life he could hold on to. No wonder he saw so many different women. Yet, how could he be so irresponsible as to pass along his illness to innocent children? Amanda raised her head. He'd said he would take care that she didn't get pregnant. Was that what he did with all his women? Her heart keened for him. What a sad way to live! Never being able to marry or know the joy of holding his own child.

She understood now why fleeting pleasures failed to satisfy him, why he longed for a deeper meaning in his life. He wanted love and a family—things he could never have.

It was also clear why he'd tried to push her away, even though he hadn't wanted to.

All of this sorrow caused by a dread disease in his background.

She hugged herself, rocking back and forth on the bed, her cold body slumped in despair. *Oh, God! Not more illness! Not Patrick! He's so strong and virile. Reduced to pain and weakness? No!*

And what about her? Hadn't she been through enough? She'd had to face the suffering of loved ones. She never wanted to enter a sickroom again

Gilded Splendor

as long as she lived! Especially not Patrick's.

Amanda's heart pounded with anger and denial. *Why? Why?* she asked herself repeatedly, intoning the words over and over, beating her fists on the bedspread. No answer came. The stillness of the early morning continued, silent, empty, uncomforting.

Amanda paced the floor, the walls of the room closing in. She shuddered, contemplating the illness Helene had described. Paralysis. Pain. Helplessness. Suffering. Death.

No!

She sucked in a ragged breath and shook her head. She couldn't face Patrick's illness. She couldn't stand by helplessly and watch him suffer, watch the one she held most dear taken from her in bits and pieces. Not after her mother and father. Not again. It would be better to lose him quickly, rather than by excruciating inches. To say good-bye and never see him again. To remember him as he had been—vital and strong. To dream of what might have been. Yes, that would be much better.

But how could she leave him now? She had to face the fact that she loved him. And she'd heard him say it—he loved her, too! How could she simply walk away?

Patrick's face swam in her vision until she saw only him, heard only his voice, felt only his hands and mouth. She knew this passion would come only once in her life. She might love again, but it would be a lesser kind of love, not so real, so innocent. Instead of being consumed with unbidden, unbridled passion in her body and soul, she would calculate and compare future men to Patrick Winter. He was her standard now, the guide by which she would measure everyone to come after, and no man would ever be his equal.

There must be some way they could be together, she thought, lying down wearily on the bed, still fully clothed. There had to be a reprieve from this illness. Maybe he wouldn't get sick. And if he did get sick, perhaps it wouldn't be as bad as Helene described.

Patrick, Helene, Maude—everyone she'd met at Pinewood House hid deep secrets behind pretty facades. The house itself seemed to harbor furtive, private mysteries. Staring wide-eyed at the ceiling, her dry eyes burning and itching, Amanda put aside her plans to go to London. She grimly swore she would confront Helene and force her to tell all she knew.

Amanda vowed to rip away the decorations, one by one, as she had in her dream. She would discover the truths, no matter how ugly or passionate, that lurked beneath the elaborate decorations of Pinewood House!

Chapter Eight

Sweat streamed down Patrick's face and chest, dropping in tiny rivulets between Diane's breasts. He grimaced and shut his eyes tight so he wouldn't have to see the face of the Countess of Craven, her white thighs spread open to him on the bed. He thrust in and out of her with savage lunges that made her cry out. He knew he was hurting her, but he didn't care. He drove on, using her pliant body to exorcise his demons. He ignored her cries, pushing harder and faster. She went with him, raking her nails down his back. "Yes, Patrick, yes," she moaned.

Together they bucked and lunged. Their heavy breathing and the rhythmic creaking of the bedsprings obliterated the afternoon traffic noises of London outside the window.

Roughly, Patrick grabbed Diane's legs and raised her ankles high onto his shoulders. When he thrust deeper into her, she flinched in pain. At the same moment, he burst inside her. As he did, a wrenching yell escaped his throat—"Amanda!"

"What did you say?"

The coldness and contempt in Diane's voice brought Patrick crashing back to reality. He recoiled in horror at what he'd done. What in God's name had made him cry out Amanda's name? Struggling to regain his breath, he opened his eyes to find Diane glaring up at him.

"Get off me, you bastard," she snarled.

Patrick pulled out of her, carefully removed his sheath, and lay beside her on the bed. "I'm sorry."

She had already jerked herself upright and was angrily pulling on her wrapper.

"Don't speak to me! How dare you come here and use me in that rough way, like some—some *thing!* And then you have the gall to call out another woman's name!"

He reached for her, but she eluded his grasp. "Diane, come here and let me explain."

"Don't!" She shrugged off his hand and left the bed to sit at her dressing table. "What possible explanation could you have? And who is this Amanda?" Her eyes narrowed. "Not that simpering nobody I met at Pinewood House?

Gilded Splendor

I'll get you for this, Patrick!"

He stood up and drew on his pants. Then he went over to stand behind her, placing his hands on her shoulders. Their stormy eyes met in the mirror. He thought of trying to explain his problems to her, the pain that had driven him to take her as he had. But he failed to find any sympathy or understanding in her steely gaze. He decided it would be useless to try to form an explanation. Besides, he doubted that Diane really cared, despite her protestations.

"Now, Countess. You know you're not the only woman in my life. It's never bothered you before."

"You never acted like this before. You were so rough today, you hurt me. What's the matter with you?"

"I'm sorry. I'll never do it again."

"Damned right you won't!"

"Let me make it up to you. Please."

Diane's eyes brightened in a calculating look. "How?"

"Whatever you say."

She swiveled around to face him, smiles wreathing her pretty face. "Well, there's that beautiful engagement ring we saw in the jeweler's window the other day. Would you like to get it for me, Patrick, my love?" She looked at him pointedly. "Or would you prefer to give it to Amanda?"

Patrick winced, but he smiled carefully at Diane, hoping his next offer would appease her.

"I'm not ready to give a ring like that to anyone just yet. For now, how about that amethyst necklace we saw? It would look lovely with your new Worth gown."

"I don't want the necklace," Diane pouted. "I want marriage and children. I'm tired of being your mistress, and you must be tired of wearing that loathsome thing every time we make love."

"I don't mind it."

"Liar!"

"That's beside the point." Patrick inhaled a deep breath. "When we started out, we agreed neither of us wanted marriage, remember?" She didn't answer. "Remember, Diane?"

"Yes," she admitted grudgingly.

"Now, would you like the necklace or not?"

She studied him a moment, then capitulated. "All right, I'd like it, of course. But this conversation is merely postponed, not forgotten."

"You shall have the necklace. There's my girl." With relief, Patrick turned to find his shirt. "Will I see you next week? Same time?"

"If you have the amethysts with you."

She flung her arms around his neck and smiled knowingly. "Oh, and Patrick, you can be rough again next time—as rough as you like. I rather enjoyed it."

"I know you did."

Patrick let himself out of Diane's townhouse and hailed his waiting carriage.

Gilded Splendor

"The club," he ordered curtly.

Leaning back against the leather seats, he cursed himself. He had sought release in a woman's body, any woman's warm body, but as usual, had failed to find it. He was just as frustrated, just as violently miserable as ever. He should have known better. He vowed to skip the next tryst with Diane, break off with her, and send the necklace by messenger.

What in hell had made him think of Amanda in the throes of his passion? And calling out her name like that? Good God!

He didn't have to think long and hard to find the answer to that one. He was in love with Amanda Prescott. The release he sought could only be found in her arms, and he would never experience it.

He glared out the carriage window. Damn! He would forget her and lose himself in distractions, or die trying! He would redouble his efforts, live fast and furious. It would work eventually. It would have to.

Scenes of London passed by outside his carriage window. The city had a lot to offer in the way of diversions. So did the Countess of Craven. He narrowed his eyes. She was mercenary and shallow, but he thought of her clawing his back in naked enjoyment of the pain he inflicted. Maybe his interest could be piqued and renewed. He might keep that appointment with her next week after all.

He knew he would, and with that sure thought, his stomach jerked violently in a knot of self-loathing. He clenched his fist, welcoming the cold, numbing effect as he allowed his heart to turn to ice.

"Sweat got in my eyes, so I couldn't see a damned thing. The stone wall came at me in a blurred rush."

Patrick's voice rang out in the club, interrupting the snores of napping gentlemen nearby. Patrick noticed, but didn't soften his voice. He was drunk, and he and Algy continued their reminiscences loudly. He was going to have fun if it killed him! He'd gone to his club directly from Diane's, vowing to forget Amanda, Diane, his blasted dreams, Pinewood House, and everything else in his cursed life.

Algy joined in uproariously. "That didn't stop you! You swiped at your eyes with one hand and grabbed the reins with the other! Damn, if you didn't sail over that wall blind!"

Patrick laughed. "You yelled like blazes when you followed me over. Your wail drowned out the huntsman's horn."

"Not to mention the yelping of the hounds!" agreed Algy good-naturedly.

"You yelped louder than the dogs did!"

Algy raised his glass in appreciation, chuckling at the happy memory. The walls of the stately Carlton Club bore huge gilt placards inscribed SILENCE. Most of the club members obeyed the sign, dozing over their newspapers, safely ensconced in the depths of their leather chairs. A servant crept silently over the thick carpet to place drinks on side tables, then disappeared noiselessly.

Loud conversation and guffaws rang out from Patrick's corner of the room, disturbing the peaceful quiet. A special table had been set aside for him and Algy, and no one cared to challenge them into silence. They'd been drinking steadily, and were now ready to launch into the evening's activities.

"Red-coated riders, black-clad ladies on sidesaddles galloping over the downs, flying leaps over fences. We left the others fifty lengths behind," Algy reminisced dreamily.

Patrick picked up the story. "The speed was so intense, we just jumped everything in our path. The hounds raced at our sides. Nobody could gain an inch on us."

"Smashing!" concluded Algy. "Here's to hunting, the second-best pursuit in the world."

Patrick drained his glass and banged it down on the table. "I intend to do more hunting now. Much more."

"That's the Patrick we all know and love!" Algy saluted him with raised glass. "I thought you were too morose lately. But you seem to have come out of it tonight. Maybe it's the influence of Amanda Prescott. Now there's a lovely lady!"

"Get off that, Algernon. I asked you not to mention her."

Algy failed to notice the green ice glittering in Patrick's eyes. "Say, if you really don't want her, would you mind terribly if I tried my hand with Amanda?"

Algy scarcely had time to see Patrick's huge shape lunge toward him. Next thing he knew, a fist twisted his tie painfully tight around his neck. Patrick thrust his face, a menacing grimace, close to Algy's. "If I ever catch you going after her, so help me, I'll—"

Algy struggled and gulped, frightened eyes popping behind his wire rims. Patrick's murderous rage evaporated as suddenly as it had begun, and he abruptly released Algy with a disgusted sigh.

"Calm down, old man. I didn't mean anything by it. I daresay, she wouldn't have me anyway. It's obvious she's in love with you."

"Just drop it."

Patrick regained his seat and passed a trembling hand over his brow. God, what was the matter with him? Hurting Diane, attacking Algy. He was at the end of his rope. It must be all the drinking and binging, the incessant string of parties one after the other. Even when he did stay in, he was haunted by insomnia, pacing the floor, his muscles screaming with tension.

Patrick sighed. Nothing was working. Deep down, he desperately missed Amanda. He longed to see her, hear her voice, wind his fingers through her titian hair, draw her to him and forget himself in her. His self-enforced exile was driving him mad, and just the thought of another man, any man, being close to her was the last straw, calculated to push him over the ragged edge.

He glanced at Algy and, struck with regret, cursed under his breath. Why take it out on his best friend?

Algy looked askance at him and nervously straightened his tie, his fingers fidgeting.

"I'm sorry," Patrick apologized. "I didn't mean it. I've been a cad lately. Please forgive me, friend."

Algy poked his glasses back onto the bridge of his nose and smiled reassuringly. "All forgotten."

"What do you say we move on to Sally's? This club is too quiet. It's getting on my nerves. I want some absinthe tonight. Seems like a good night for it."

"I'm coming. But let's leave that absinthe alone. It's terrible stuff. It'll kill you."

"I hope so."

Patrick rose and stalked from the room. Algy stood and tossed back one last swig from his glass, then hastily followed. He didn't know about this change that had come over Patrick. He still seemed as tense as a tightly strung bow, ready to let fly at a moment's notice. But Algy forgave him. They'd always been the best of friends, intensely loyal to each other, and he wouldn't abandon him now when he seemed to need a friend so badly. Anyway, they were headed in the right direction. Sally's establishment never failed to please. Maybe that would relieve some of Patrick's tension.

Several hostile gazes followed them out, relieved to see the loud, unruly youngsters depart. Then newspapers were lifted again, and the Carlton Club returned to normalcy and silence.

Time weighed heavily on Amanda's hands the next few days. Itching to be active, she had discovered that life for a woman on a country estate was restricted to the point of uselessness and boredom. Outwardly the picture of peaceful grace, she worked on a piece of Berlin needlepoint for a parlor pillow, one of the few projects approved of for a woman. She plied the needle back and forth in the canvas until her fingers ached and her eyes blurred, but she hardly felt the discomfort or saw the colors or pattern she was working on. Her mind seethed with activity.

The more she thought of Patrick, the more she chafed. Her questions boiled down to one overpowering doubt: exactly what was the nature of the Winter illness? Could it really be so terrible? Was Patrick sure to get it? Somehow, she had to discover the truth of those questions and the other matters that had plagued her, no matter how much the answers might hurt.

Then there was Maude's predicament. Amanda had gently, but skillfully, pried out the secret of

Gilded Splendor

her pregnancy, and an address in London where Harry was staying at his brother's. Unable to bear waiting anymore for Patrick's return, on the previous evening she'd taken her courage into her hands and written him a letter, imploring him to return to Pinewood House to help her with an urgent problem. Before she could change her mind, she'd hastily sent a servant to post the letter. There was nothing more to be done for the present.

Amanda pricked her finger and threw down the sewing in disgust. Oh! Sitting quietly was driving her mad!

An idea clicked in her mind, and she looked up with sudden inspiration. There was another person who had been around the estate as long as Helene—Reggie White. The old man was a link to the past. He must know something about the family illness, and he must have been acquainted with Papa, the little boy who had the run of the place and did odd jobs. Perhaps Reggie could tell her what Helene would not.

"I'll go see Reggie!" Amanda left her chair and rushed from the house. She found the gardener hoeing in a crescent-shaped garden of exquisite proportions. An ocean of blooms, all white, from alabaster to ivory, vanilla to moonstone, wafted lightly on the breeze, creating subtle waves of textured pattern. Mingled scents rose on the air in a heady, fragrant aroma.

Intrigued by the splendor of the garden, Amanda gasped, "How extraordinary!"

Elizabeth Parker

Reggie looked up from his hoeing. "I'm glad you like it. Mr. Patrick has always been partial to the White Garden." He scratched the loose dirt with his hoe.

"Did you do all this?" she asked, awed.

"Yes, miss, over the years."

"Maude said you were an excellent gardener. Now I know what she meant." Reggie smiled broadly at the mention of his daughter. Noting his warm expression, Amanda took heart, encouraged to question him.

"Reggie, I'd like to talk to you, if I may."

"Yes, miss?"

"You seem to know the Winter family so well. In fact, you seem to love them, especially Patrick."

Reggie straightened and leaned against his hoe. "Well, I do love Mr. Patrick. He's like a son t' me. I've known 'im since he was born. Took care of 'im in some of 'is scrapes."

"I thought so."

"And you feel somethin' for 'im, too, miss. I can tell by your eyes!"

Amanda felt a hot flush creep up her cheeks. The gardener turned discreetly back to his hoeing, but she gently plucked at his sleeve. "Will Patrick get sick?"

A cloud of pain darkened the gardener's face. He laid down his hoe and slowly wiped his hands before answering.

"He's next in line."

"Is it really that bad?"

Gilded Splendor

"It's bad." The gardener's short, simple answer spoke volumes.

She had to know. "In what way?"

"Well"—the gardener looked off into the distance—"with his grandfather, it came on sudden, a fever and the shakes. Seemed like just a summer cold, but it didn't get better. They sent 'is Lordship t' the sea for a change of air, but he came home weaker'n a kitten. It got so he couldn't hold up 'is head or talk."

A sudden image of Patrick lying weak and helpless pierced Amanda's heart.

"Dr. Sterling and the family did ever'thing they could for 'im, but he was in pain, lingerin' on. I thought 'er Ladyship would go mad, watch'n 'im suffer." Reggie's face closed in hardness, his mouth tightening. "When he died, she said there could be no more marriages in the Winter family. Said she'd never wish that on another wife."

Amanda swallowed, her throat tight. "But Patrick's father married," she said.

"He was headstrong. Wouldn't listen t' 'er Ladyship. He ran off with that pretty young girl. Was 'er Ladyship angry!" Reggie pursed his lips and blew out a long, meaningful whistle.

"I can imagine," said Amanda. "Then what happened?"

"Well, they had my Patrick, and they were happy. But when he was three, their carriage turned over. They were both killed."

Amanda remained silent. What could she say? There seemed to be no words to express her sorrow for the Winter family tragedies.

Reggie, lost in thought, finally roused himself and drew his attention back to the girl before him, studying her for a long moment.

"Reggie," ventured Amanda. "Did you know my father, Johnny Prescott?"

"Yes, I knew 'im. Nice little boy. He played with Austin. Then his family moved away."

"Do you know any reason why he might have sent me here to meet the marchioness?"

"No, miss." Reggie squinted his eyes, pondered the question, then shrugged in defeat. "I don't know."

"Well, thank you for talking to me."

Amanda turned to go. Her talk with Reggie hadn't provided any information about her father, and it hadn't absolutely confirmed that Patrick would get sick, but Reggie's description of the Winter illness had been chilling, underscoring the horror of Patrick's prospects.

She had rounded the edge of the crescent-shaped garden when Reggie called out, "Miss Amanda!" He hobbled up, out of breath, his hands full of white roses. "Patrick's been miserable these last few years—searching for someth'n. Maybe that someth'n was you." He thrust the flowers into her outstretched arms. "I have somethin' else for you. It might help you and Patrick."

"Oh?"

Gilded Splendor

"A diary. Belonged t' Sylvie Emerson."

"Sylvie? How in the world did you come by it?"

"She liked t' sit here in the White Garden and write in her diary. She forgot it one day, and I picked it up. I meant t' give it back t' her the next day, but that night, she died—burned in a fire."

"Yes, I know she died," breathed Amanda, the enormity of the tragedy stunning her into silence.

"I meant t' give the book t' the family, but I—" Reggie bowed his head. "Excuse me, miss— I read some of the diary. Out of loyalty t' Miss Sylvie, I just couldn't 'ave her heartbreak spread around for people t' laugh at."

"Her heartbreak?"

"I almost destroyed the diary, but something held me back." Reggie looked at her shrewdly. "Now I'm glad I kept it. I'll see about finding it. Haven't looked for it in years." He squinted his eyes, trying to remember the diary's whereabouts. "You and Patrick can read it together. It's prob'ly time he saw it, too."

He tipped his hat to her and turned back to the White Garden.

Amanda headed for the house, her nose buried in the roses, deep in thought. Dear Reggie.

But what did he mean by Sylvie's heartbreak? He'd raised more questions than he'd answered. The harder she tried to find the truth, the more it evaded her. She sighed. Perhaps the diary would clear things up.

Elizabeth Parker

A slight movement caught her eye, drawing her gaze up to a second-story window above. A figure stared down at her from its hiding place, shielded behind the curtain. Amanda raised a hand in greeting, but the wave died stillborn in the air.

Who was it? The filmy lace obscured and blurred the features, making detection impossible. She couldn't even make out if it was a man or a woman, but someone had definitely been watching her and Reggie in the White Garden.

A chilling, malevolent evil rained down at her from the watcher above. Amanda's steps faltered and her hair rose, tingling the back of her neck. A moment later, the curtain swung gently back into place, and the figure retreated out of sight.

Icy panic stole up Amanda's spine. Never in her life had she felt such spiteful, malignant hatred directed her way from another human being. She shivered and goose bumps raised on her arms. Unmindful of the prickly thorns, she clutched the roses tightly against her breasts, ducked her head, and hurried on into the house.

At four o'clock that afternoon, still unnerved by her chilling encounter outside the White Garden, Amanda barged down the hall, on her way to confront Helene. She'd had enough subterfuge and mystery. It was time for answers.

Girded for battle, Amanda was taken aback when she reached the library. Startled, she found

Gilded Splendor

Thomas Gray had arrived there ahead of her. He sat calmly taking tea with Helene.

Slouching in a chair, his lanky long legs stretched out beside Helene's elegant, perfect posture, Gray looked strangely out of place. How long had he been at Pinewood House that afternoon? Had he been the one watching her from the window?

"Oh, dear," fussed Helene. She frowned and rubbed at a minuscule dot on the embroidered white tablecloth. "Graves, there's a spot on the linen. Please bring another."

"Yes, Your Ladyship." The footman dutifully removed the snowy linen.

"Amanda, sit down. We've had a bother about the cloth, but it will soon be set to rights. This is Thomas Gray. Thomas, Miss Amanda Prescott."

Gray half rose from his chair, acknowledging the introduction, and Amanda nodded nervously to him. The footman brought another cloth, placed the tea tray, and left the room. As they took their seats, Helene poured out the tea, presiding as hostess over the little ritual. Reaching to a tiered cake stand, she arranged crustless cucumber sandwiches and delicate cakes on Dresden plates, with the effortless grace acquired through years of reigning as queen of Pinewood House.

Amanda regarded her over her teacup. She'd never known anyone quite like Helene—charming, yet regally distant, aloof. Helene resembled Amanda's mother in her devotion to family, but there the resemblance ended. Amanda's mother had been a simple, loving woman, while Helene possessed wealth, position, a veneer of worldly sophistication, and a far more complex personality.

"Now we can sit back and enjoy ourselves," said Helene with a sigh. "I do so love this part of the afternoon, don't you? It's peaceful and relaxing."

Amanda felt anything but relaxed as the three sipped from bone china cups and munched on the sampling of delicacies. Gray remained silent until Amanda, making her voice casual, probed, "Have you had a nice visit today, Mr. Gray?"

"Yes, Helene and I had a long chat," he responded. "She showed me some of the house. It's decorated beautifully, isn't it?"

Which part of the house were they in? wondered Amanda. What role did he play in this family? Did he know her father long ago?

Helene smiled. "Over the years, we've collected things. Mementos from the past which are maybe not useful, but beautiful."

The past. An ache gripped Amanda's heart. "Memories can be beautiful, when they're not painful," she ventured, looking down into the remains of her tea.

"Surely you're too young to have painful memories," Helene said skeptically.

The old familiar sadness jabbed through Amanda like a knife, but she swallowed the last sip of tea, resolutely forming an answer.

Gilded Splendor

"I had a good childhood, but when my parents became ill, that happiness ended. I nursed them until they died. It was very hard to watch them go that way." She drew in a breath. "So I understand why you watch carefully over Patrick. I know he may become ill."

Helene frowned in Gray's direction. "Who told you that? It's something we rarely mention."

"But why not? Why keep it a secret?"

"Why drag our family business before the eyes of others? Winters don't need or desire pity. Besides, the subject is painful. Patrick was deprived of his grandfather and his parents. Now he may be deprived of much more. We naturally prefer not to speak of it."

"More tea?" asked Gray, leaning forward to take possession of Amanda's cup. She glanced at him warily, wondering how much he knew of the family history. He handed the cup to Helene and smiled politely. "Ah, well, Mr. Wilde says in his new play that we live in an age of surfaces."

"But what lies beneath the surface, Mr. Gray?" asked Amanda.

"Perhaps that's best kept private," said Helene sternly.

"I've grown fond of Patrick," ventured Amanda, "and I—"

"Fond?" Helene sighed and patted Amanda's hand. "My dear, what a shame. It won't do. If you know about the illness, then you must know you can have no future with my grandson. None at all."

Amanda winced at Helene's firm, merciless words, but she defiantly shook off the patronizing patting and lifted her chin. "It's not completely certain he'll get sick, is it?"

Helene threw a sharp glance in Gray's direction. "Whatever do you mean?" she snapped. "What have you been told? Of course he'll get sick! All the Winter men have been sick."

Helene's teacup tilted precariously in her saucer, threatening to spill the dark liquid on her silk gown. Gray leaned forward and took it from her before any damage was done. "Now, Helene," he soothed.

"You have a visitor, madam," announced the butler behind them. "A policeman."

"Policeman!" Helene's eyes popped open, but she struggled to regain her composure. "Show him in." She signaled to the footman. "Graves, clear the tea things."

An unprepossessing little man entered the room and stood before the group. "Detective Inspector William Sweeney of Scotland Yard, at your service, ma'am." His stubby fingers fidgeted with a droopy hat, but his darting, intelligent eyes above a long, walrus mustache pierced them, sized them up, and categorized each one in the record book of a razor-sharp mind.

"Thank you for seeing me, ma'am." He coughed delicately.

"What is it, Inspector?"

"I'm down from London to investigate an unfortunate occurrence in the neighborhood.

Too much for the local constable to handle, if you get my meaning."

"Yes, Inspector?" prompted Gray.

"You were acquainted with Lady Brighton?"

"Of course. We're neighbors and very old friends," Helene replied, then drew up, startled. "Inspector, you said *were* acquainted . . . ?"

"I'm afraid, ma'am, I have bad news. Lady Brighton was found murdered yesterday."

All action in the room hung suspended for a heart-stopping moment. The only sound was the clock ticking audibly on the wall. Amanda watched in consternation as Helene paled, her hand fluttering to her bosom. "Murdered? Why, I . . ."

Gray rose to step between Helene and the visitor. "Here, now! You're frightening the ladies!"

Inspector Sweeney shifted a cool, appraising eye to Gray, at the same time withdrawing a pencil and crumpled notebook from his pocket. "Who might I have the pleasure of addressing, sir?"

Helene leaned forward. "This is Mr. Thomas Gray, an old family friend, and Miss Amanda Prescott, a visitor."

The inspector scribbled their names on his notepad. "How long have you been visiting in the neighborhood?"

"I've been here a few weeks," said Gray. "And I believe Miss Prescott arrived shortly before I did."

"Where are you staying, sir?"

"At the Newhaven Inn."

The inspector turned back to Helene. "You have a grandson, I believe. May I speak to him?"

"Patrick is not here. I—I think he's in London," stammered Helene.

Inspector Sweeney held up his hand, palm outward. "Not to worry. I'm simply informing all the residents hereabouts, warning them to take proper precautions. We're asking all who live in the vicinity not to venture outside alone until we can apprehend the murderer."

"We will be careful, of course," Gray said.

"One more question, if I might," said the inspector. "Did Lady Brighton wear makeup? Lip rouge, perhaps?"

"Makeup!" Helene snapped to attention. "A preposterous idea! She was from a fine family, not some trollop!"

"I see." Inspector Sweeney chewed his lower lip thoughtfully.

"Why do you ask such a question?" asked Gray.

"I can't say. Don't like to give away clues before we can finish our investigation. Sorry to have bothered you. With your permission, I'll just question the servants." The inspector backed toward the door. "Please be careful, and contact me if you think of anything that might help." He bowed, hat in hand. "Good day."

Helene glared at his departing back in righteous indignation, then sank into her chair with a shudder. "Lip rouge! What a grotesque idea!"

Amanda watched Gray stare for long moments into Helene's disturbed eyes. The chill in the room grew, becoming a palpable, living thing. The anxiety that had gripped Amanda all afternoon coursed through her and refused to go away.

Chapter Nine

Patrick was home! Amanda flitted around her room, dressing for dinner, almost dancing with excitement. She hadn't seen him since the night he'd asked her to be his mistress. He'd pledged to his grandmother that night to give her up. How would he act toward her now? What would he say? Would he whisper words of tenderness, despite his grandmother's dire warnings? Amanda ran her tongue lightly over her lips. Perhaps he would kiss her again! Butterflies quivered in her stomach. Or would he retreat into cold, icy silence?

She took special pains with her toilette, even giving in to Maude's wheedling and donning a corset, which fashionably drew in her already small waist. Maude arranged her curls in a

Gilded Splendor

becoming upsweep. Amanda never painted her face, having been taught only fallen women used makeup, but she allowed Maude to lightly dust a little powder over her nose.

"With your fresh skin and lovely high color, you don't need makeup," said Maude admiringly. Then she looked over her shoulder and whispered, "They say that poor strangled lady's lips were painted red, like a common tart's."

Maude and Amanda shuddered simultaneously. The murder was the talk of the neighborhood, gossip and rumors running rampant. And it was not the first time a local woman was injured, thought Amanda. She was reminded of the unfortunate incident when gunfire hit Mrs. Charteris. Could the two acts of violence be linked in some way?

"Here," she said, shaking her head uneasily at the distressing thought. "Help me with my dress."

Maude hurried to gather up the full skirt decorated with silk ombré roses and slip it over Amanda's head. The dress swished down over her hips with a rustle.

When she was ready, Amanda tiptoed in white satin slippers to the top of the curved staircase. She leaned over the polished wood banister to search the foyer below. Servants crossed the hall beneath her, white lace caps bobbing, arms loaded with flowers from the conservatory. Lemon oil glistened on the furniture. Crystal prisms in the gas chandelier sparkled and danced, light reflecting off hundreds of cut glass ornaments. Amanda smiled. *Funny how the world glimmers just because Patrick is here . . . he's here . . . he's here . . .* Her anticipation at its peak, she couldn't wait a moment longer.

Below in the library, Patrick turned and sucked in his breath. Good God, an angel in white floated down the stairs. When had she ever looked more radiant? Fervently wishing the sight of her didn't stir him so powerfully, he stared in admiration, completely at her mercy, incapable of wrenching his gaze away.

Billowing skirts, layer upon layer of white gauze, floated down from her cinched waist. Her low décolletage revealed creamy, curving breasts. White baby's breath caught and intermingled with a riot of curls. And her face! Her eyes were twinkling stars of light, her skin glowing with moist, dewy freshness. She reminded him of a soft, luscious éclair, filled with cream, vulnerable, young—just waiting for the right man to bite into her succulence, taste her sweetness.

"Careful," he warned himself under his breath. "Careful."

Despite his best efforts, Patrick couldn't quell his rush of breathless, giddy response. He strode from the library, meeting her at the foot of the stairs. His glance swept from her face down the exquisite curves of her body. She extended a slim hand, and he found himself reaching for it.

Gilded Splendor

Eagerly, their fingers entwined, warmth clasping warmth.

"What have we here?" he murmured, his voice husky.

"Welcome home, Patrick."

Her whispered breath wafted over him softly, seductively. He caught the fragrance of fresh flowers and musky woman. Her eyes eloquently spoke the question—*Do you want me?* The invitation—*Please want me.*

Ah, God, how he wanted her! To fill his hands with her breasts, caress the nipples into thrusting points of desire, bury himself in her. He could bring himself sweet relief, awaken her to exquisite pleasure. Why shouldn't he? She was waiting, breathlessly waiting. He inclined his head and slowly lowered it toward her moist, pouting mouth. His eyelids fluttered shut—

"There you are, my dears!" Helene bustled into the hall.

Tension slammed into Patrick's body. His head jerked up. *Damn!* Jaw clenched in frustration at the interruption, he struggled to control his unruly, demanding body, heavy with the weight of his desire for Amanda.

"Please come to the library before dinner," trilled Helene over her shoulder, moving down the hall.

The heady spell broken, Patrick willed himself to breathe evenly. Amanda's eyes, filled with regret, met his for a second before she demurely lowered her gaze. Cursing under his breath, he took her hand and they followed Helene.

Unwilling to let go of Patrick's hand, Amanda sat beside him on the library sofa. A fire blazed in the hearth, its dancing light reflected in his fathomless green eyes. She gazed down at his long fingers, capable, strong, holding hers. Was he thinking what she was thinking? As he stared moodily into the flames, did he see his masterful hands moving on her body, his mouth devouring hers in a passionate kiss? Scandalous images assailed her senses, flushed her cheeks hot. Her body tingled with alarming, yet exciting, sensations. She wanted to throw her arms around him, be reassured that all was well, hear words of love spoken. She squeezed his hand, but he merely contemplated the fire, giving no sign he had noticed. The undisguised desire of a moment before had disappeared from his eyes.

After a disapproving glance at their joined hands, Helene poured glasses of brandy for all three and passed them around. Amanda withdrew her hand from Patrick's to take the proffered glass and reluctantly forced her attention to Helene. The marchioness did not look quite herself tonight. Her perspiring face was flushed, her normally perfect clothes slightly askew. Her hand shook slightly as she smoothed back a straying lock of gray hair.

"You'll have to forgive me. The visit from the police inspector was so disturbing. And Thomas Gray has just left." Her voice drifted off.

Gilded Splendor

"Will Mr. Gray be staying at Pinewood House?" asked Patrick.

"No, he's staying at the Newhaven Inn. He'll be quite comfortable there, I daresay. He has other business in the area, and prefers to come and go."

"Yes, of course."

Helene's narrow gaze shifted to Amanda and assessed her intently before she said, "Amanda, you've been a welcome guest here at Pinewood House. We're all happy to have you here, dear."

Amanda felt Patrick tense beside her. He shifted on the sofa, crossed his legs, and began tapping his foot in irritated jerks.

"Now I propose to do something for Amanda," continued Helene. "I hope it will be welcome news."

They waited expectantly.

"Mr. Gray has reminded me of my old friendship with Amanda's father. So in Johnny Prescott's memory, I'm giving Amanda a gift—a rather large sum of money. It should provide her with a good start in life when she makes new acquaintances in London."

Amanda gaped in astonishment, struck speechless with the enormity of Lady Swinton's proposal. Patrick was not so hindered. He uncrossed his legs and leaned forward on the sofa. "What put this into your head, Gram? I'm sure you mean well, but—"

Amanda hastily found her voice and interrupted him. "I can't accept the money, Lady

Swinton. I do thank you, however."

"You must accept it! For the sake of your father. He would want you to be provided for."

"I'm sure I can get along quite well on my own."

Patrick shot up from the sofa and shoved his hands into his pockets. "Gram, what's behind this? Does Gray have anything to do with it?" He paced before the fire. "What exactly is Gray to you, anyway? I know you said he's an old family friend, but I think there's something more going on here."

Helene rose. "Let's go in to dinner. We can discuss it all later, but now our food is getting cold."

Before more could be said, she swept from the room. Amanda and Patrick could do nothing but follow.

Patrick barely controlled his curiosity throughout the meal. His grandmother hadn't satisfactorily answered his questions about Gray, and now he had new ones about the gift she was offering Amanda. But he would wait and curb his tongue. He knew from experience that openly challenging his grandmother would only provoke her stubbornness. He would let her take her own sweet time to explain her astonishing proposal.

He became ever more exasperated as dinner wore on, and his grandmother adamantly refused to bring up the topic. After dessert, she excused herself and retired early, pleading a headache.

Gilded Splendor

His nerves on edge, Patrick bid her good night, then took Amanda's arm and swept her into the library. He swung her around to face him, running his hands up her soft, smooth arms to rest on her shoulders. The air between them reverberated with a palpable tension, a flood of unspoken emotion. He'd been painfully aware of her during supper, responding to her close proximity, and now all he wanted was to take her there on the library carpet. He just needed to reach out for her.

Instead, he stepped back and raked his hands distractedly through his hair. He had nearly blown up in fury at his grandmother when she suggested that Amanda make other acquaintances in London. By a miracle, he'd managed to contain himself. Now his emotions again threatened to burn out of control.

Get a grip on yourself, he thought. *Otherwise you'll ruin this girl and everything else.* His first night home, and he was already maddeningly frustrated, tempted beyond endurance. But he'd known it would be this way, hadn't he? He'd known.

Patrick gritted his teeth. Distance. He needed distance and time to think. Searching his mind for a lever to force between himself and Amanda, he ruthlessly ignored his desire and forced himself to look dispassionately at her. He tallied up the events that had occurred since her arrival at Pinewood House. She'd appeared about the same time as the mysterious Thomas Gray. Was there a link between them? Mrs. Charteris had been wounded. A neighbor had been murdered. Amanda had written a letter asking him to come back and help with an urgent problem. Now his grandmother was proposing to give her a large sum of money.

Was Amanda as innocent as she seemed? Nothing had gone right since she had come to Pinewood. But was that somehow her fault?

Patrick studied her wide blue eyes. They gazed up at him adoringly, betraying nothing but youthful innocence and an enormous crush on him. He despised himself for his suspicions, but he welcomed the chilling questions. They allowed him to cool his ardor and bring some perspective to the situation. Who was this girl? Where had she come from? Could she be manipulating them all? What kind of spell was she weaving over Pinewood House? Over him?

He moved to stand away from her across the room. He must voice his suspicions. Either that or he'd take her into his arms, his bed, his life . . .

"What was all that with Grandmother about, do you suppose?" he asked coolly.

Surprise and disappointment replaced the eagerness in her eyes, and he noted it with a mixture of satisfaction and intense regret.

"Don't you know?" she asked.

"Not a damned thing. That's why I'm asking you."

"I think it's a ridiculous idea."

"Do you? Doesn't the idea of receiving a large sum of money appeal to you? It would to me if I were in your place."

"What do you mean?"

"When you appeared here on my doorstep so mysteriously, wet and cold from the storm that night, you were destitute. I'm wondering what made you pick Pinewood House?"

"Patrick!"

"And why you lingered on here, especially when I so pointedly asked you to leave?"

She drew herself up. "I came to Pinewood House for one simple reason—my father asked me to come and meet your grandmother."

"Oh, I heard that story about your father sending you here for old times' sake, but it doesn't wash. Why did he really send you to Pinewood?"

Her throat moved in a convulsive swallow. "I've asked myself that same question a hundred times, but I've yet to find the answer."

"And you never met Thomas Gray before?"

"No." Her voice turned angry. "Why does everyone ask me that? Helene accused me of knowing him, and I've been meaning to ask her why. What are you all implying?"

"I don't know what Gram thinks. But the idea has crossed my mind that maybe there's a connection between your family and Thomas Gray. Maybe you and he are working together to split Gram's money."

"That's absurd!"

Elizabeth Parker

"All I know is that Gram wasn't herself tonight, and she would never give away a great sum of money unless she had a damned good reason—or someone was forcing her hand."

Amanda's eyes blazed with blue fury. He ached to wipe away the hurt and anger with tender murmurs and embraces, but he didn't dare. He couldn't betray his own state. He'd be trying to get her out of her clothes if he took that route. Better to have her angry. He turned aside and dropped into a chair, carelessly sprawling his long legs toward the fire.

"I seem to be accused of something here, Patrick. What's on your mind? If it's the money, be assured I have no intention of accepting it."

"Of course it's not the bloody money. I would just like to know the reason behind the gift, that's all. I don't want my grandmother hurt."

"Your concern for your grandmother is admirable, I'm sure." Her voice dripped with sarcasm. "But what about me?"

He kept his expression deliberately blank. "What about you?"

Amanda gathered up her skirts and said icily, "I'm going to bed before we say things we might regret." She moved toward the door.

"Aren't you forgetting something?"

She halted and turned back to face him.

"The letter you sent," he reminded mockingly, "requesting my help with an urgent problem."

Amanda bit her lip. "The letter was about Maude."

"Maude White? She's well taken care of here at Pinewood. Always will be."

"Not if she's expecting a baby!"

His body stiffened in shock. A baby? So Maude was the one.

"You said she would be turned off the place without a reference. What will become of her? Her beau, Harry, has gone to London. When I sent you the letter, I was going to ask you to find him, before she's thrown out on the street."

Patrick kept his voice casual to hide his discomfiture. "I'll make arrangements for Maude. You needn't be involved. I can handle anything that comes up at Pinewood, thank you."

Amanda tossed her head in rebellion, clenched her small hands into fists, and planted her satin slippers apart. He waited for a sharp retort, but instead, she merely said, "I'd like to stay on here at Pinewood until I'm sure Maude is settled one way or the other. If that's agreeable to you."

He frowned ominously. She gathered up her skirts and quickly left the room.

Patrick gazed after her, restraining himself from calling her back. His accusations, his defenses, the whole world, sickened him.

Amanda stomped down the hall, her white satin slippers thudding on the wood. Sick at heart, she tossed her head. Her hair came undone and tumbled down around her shoulders, but she didn't care. She caught a falling sprig of baby's breath and tossed it to the floor. Who cared what she looked like now?

Her temples pounded. The lover she had hoped to meet tonight had failed to appear. Instead, she'd faced a cold, hard, cynical accuser. She found herself hurrying, almost blindly running, to get away from him and his hateful innuendos.

How dare he? To accuse me of plotting to hurt his grandmother! Of trying to extort money from the family! How could he possibly think . . . ?

Yet deep inside, she knew it was the specter of his illness, the impending doom that constantly haunted him, that cast a shadow over his world, stained it a cynical black. His pain continually drove him to say and do hurtful things, and her heart ached for both of them.

She looked up, flustered, and found herself at the conservatory door. After a hasty glance to the right and left, she slipped inside. The dark room welcomed her with peaceful stillness and the soothing scent of flowers.

Trembling, she pressed her heated forehead against the cool glass wall and gave in to the disappointed tears she'd fought so desperately to hide. They slid unchecked down her cheeks. Her breasts rising and falling, she gasped for breath.

If Helene had purposely thought to drive a wedge between them, she couldn't have done it better, thought Amanda, clenching her fists in frustration.

Gilded Splendor

Voices disturbed her agitated thoughts. Startled, she ducked behind the gazebo and peered across the dark conservatory. A man lurked in the shadows, partially hidden behind the potted palms. Amanda's hand flew to her mouth, stifling her astonished gasp.

Gray!

Fearful apprehension twisted her stomach. What was he doing here so late at night? What mischief could he be up to?

"I've done it! I did what you said . . . you bastard. . . ."

Amanda could barely make out the words, but it was definitely Helene's angry voice speaking to Gray! Incredulous, Amanda peered around the gazebo to witness Helene draw back her hand and slap Gray soundly across his face, so hard she was nearly thrown off balance by the force of her blow. Gray raised his hand to strike her back, but apparently thought better of it. He shook his head and slowly lowered his hand.

"Amanda Prescott . . ." Amanda heard her own name being mentioned. She strained to catch the words, but couldn't hear them clearly. "Lady Brighton . . ." *Oh, God!* " . . . Sylvie's box . . ." *What about the box?* "You said you wouldn't . . ."

Amanda tried to piece together the broken bits and pieces of conversation, but could make neither head nor tail of them. It made no sense. Why was Helene sneaking around to meet Gray this way? What was it she had done at his behest?

And why was she angry enough to slap him? Helene had said Gray reminded her of the past and prompted her to propose the gift of money. Could Patrick have been right? Was there a connection between Papa and Thomas Gray?

Amanda lifted her head to see Gray and Helene walk out from behind the palms. Afraid of being discovered spying, Amanda slipped out the conservatory door and ran for the stairs, just ahead of them. She heard their voices in the hall behind her, but she kept going, breathlessly taking the stairs two at a time.

Had they seen her? She fervently hoped and prayed they had not.

Chapter Ten

The next day, Amanda stood at her window, deep in thought, trying to make sense of Helene's fight with Gray in the dark conservatory. Helene had not mentioned the incident, so Amanda assumed she hadn't been seen in her wild flight up the stairs. But why had they mentioned her? And Sylvie's box? What had made Helene so angry? Totally bewildered, Amanda struggled with the mounting questions that clung like a maze of shadowy, sticky cobwebs.

Her thoughts were broken by a man's hands stealing around her waist, spanning it effortlessly.

"Patrick?" She looked over her shoulder with a tremulous smile. "Algernon!"

"Hello, Amanda. I've been thinking about you

ever since I last saw you." He hovered close and gave her waist a suggestive squeeze.

"What on earth are you doing?"

He grinned wickedly, his eyes mischievous behind his wire-rimmed glasses. "I'm glad to see you! Why, I've thought of nothing else."

Amanda yanked at his hands. For a pale man so slender and slight, his grip was surprisingly strong.

"Does Patrick know you're here?"

"No, and he doesn't really have to know, does he?" He craned his neck to give her a quick peck on the cheek.

"Let me go! You're being ridiculous."

Amanda struggled, but Algy refused to give up his persistent hugging. Losing her patience, she brought her fists down on his clasped hands in a sharp one-two punch and jabbed backward hard with her elbows, sending him flying.

"Ouch!" he yipped, fanning his injured fingers through the air. "What did you want to go and do that for?"

"What did you want to go and hug me for, then?"

Amanda rounded on him, ready to give him a good dressing-down, but she dissolved in laughter at his woebegone expression.

"Oh, Algy," she said when she could catch her breath, "what are you up to?"

"I was sent in here to flirt with you. I was told that—well, that you like me, sort of." Algy's apple cheeks reddened with embarrassment.

Gilded Splendor

"And so I do. But who told you to flirt with me?"

"Lady Swinton. I couldn't very well refuse the old—ahem—our wonderful hostess, now could I?" He coughed behind his hand.

"Well, I do like you, but I'll not welcome any flirtation." Amanda made her voice stern.

Algy wiped his brow. "That's a relief! I really don't know why Lady Swinton put me up to this thing anyway. I never was any good at it."

Amanda turned back to the window. "Maybe she's trying to push us together to keep me out of Patrick's way," she said thoughtfully, and hastened to add, "Of course, you are quite attractive, Algy."

"I am? I mean, yes—I am!"

"Her Ladyship thought you might distract me."

Algy scratched his head. "It's all a muddle to me."

Exasperated, Amanda explained. "She's afraid to have me marry Patrick, if it comes to that. She's afraid he might get the Winter illness."

"Marry? Just what he needs!" Algy blinked owlishly. "But hold on. Did you say illness? Patrick never told me about any Winter illness. Sounds like balderdash to me. Are you sure?"

Amanda nodded.

"Maybe you should ask Dr. Sterling," suggested Algy. "He's been the family doctor for ages. He would know about any illness."

"Dr. Sterling! Of course! When do you think I could see him?"

With a yawn, Algy sprawled on the sofa and examined his manicured nails. "He's at St. Bartholomew's Hospital in London right now, I imagine. He has his practice there."

London! She might learn something from Dr. Sterling, and she could look for Harry, too! She could actually do something, instead of helplessly waiting in the stifling atmosphere of Pinewood House!

Amanda glanced sideways at Algy, her eyes narrowed into speculative slits. "Algernon," she murmured softly, persuasively.

He bolted upright. "Oh, no! I'm not taking you to London! The Winters would have a fit, especially Patrick. I rather value my neck, thank you."

"Lady Swinton would be glad to see us riding out. She would think your flirtation was working. And she can tell Patrick. When he sees how pleased she is, he won't raise any objection."

"But—"

"Algy, I really think since you were so discourteous to me a few moments ago, you should try to make it up, and do as I ask. Then I might forget about that unfortunate hug you gave me." Amanda was not above heaving a large, wounded sigh.

Algy winced and surrendered. "All right, you win. Change your clothes or whatever you have to do. I'll see about having a carriage brought round."

"I'll be right down!"

"That's the Howard place, Faircroft Manor."

Algy pointed to an imposing brick mansion set back in a sweeping, green lawn. The horses trotted smartly past, on the road to London. Bright sunlight dazzled, sparkling and cheerful, from a cloudless sky, reflecting Amanda's happy mood. Now that she had a mission, she felt lighthearted and optimistic, rid of her frustrated helplessness.

"The Duchess of Howard is hopelessly behind the times. Still wears a bustle," Algy informed her. "But not just any bustle—it's a Jubilee bustle! Every time she sits down, it plays 'God Save the Queen.'"

"Oh, Algy!"

"Little twinkling music box notes tripping on the air," Algy said in a falsetto, conducting an imaginary orchestra with his fingers. "Only trouble is, every time she does it, we all have to stand up, no matter what we're doing at the moment. Blasted nuisance, if you ask me."

Amanda giggled and relaxed against the carriage's comfortable leather seats. "Thank you for pointing out the sights, Algy. But your stories are so preposterous, I won't believe a single one!"

"Everything I've told you today has been nothing but the absolute truth," drawled Algy in a droll voice.

Elizabeth Parker

Amanda slipped her hand in the crook of his arm. "I can see why Patrick and you are such good friends. You're fun, as well as kind. I hope that you and I can be good friends, too."

"We already are, love." Algy winked at her conspiratorially.

When they entered the outskirts of London, Algy said, "Now we're coming to the big city. Ever been here before?"

"Never. But I've always wanted to see it."

"I'll just take you directly to St. Bart's and leave the high spots for Patrick to show you."

"Thank you, Algy."

Magnificent buildings and monuments lined London's grand streets. Smart carriages passed on the road, their crests gleaming in the sunlight, their regal inhabitants nodding sedately to one another. Crowds of people jostled along the tree-lined streets.

Amanda glanced down at her gray traveling suit. "Everyone in the city must be ever so sophisticated," she said in a low voice.

"Don't you worry, love. You would do just fine meeting the queen herself. And would the Prince of Wales take a shine to you! I should say!" He licked his lips and twitched his eyebrows, eliciting a giggle from Amanda.

"Oh, Algy!"

The carriage pulled up before a large, dignified building. Its elegant, gray stone facade stood imposing and majestic.

"Here we are! St. Bartholomew's Hospital."

Gilded Splendor

Algy extended an arm to help Amanda from the carriage. "At your service, madam."

They walked under two stone statues reclining over an arched gate, into a courtyard bordered by trees and gaslights. Inside the hospital, they passed through whitewashed halls and climbed a broad stone staircase.

"Dr. Sterling!" Algy called at the top of the stairs, waving his arm.

The tall, white-haired man at the end of the hall turned and strode toward them. "Lord Douglas!" he said, "and Miss Amanda Prescott, I believe."

"Good day, Dr. Sterling." Amanda extended her gloved hand.

"Please join me for tea in my office!"

"That would be lovely."

The doctor's large room was lined with books and a disconcerting assortment of what appeared to be human bones. Stacks of medical journals and papers, weighted down by a collection of paperweights, covered long tables against the walls. Dr. Sterling showed his guests to chairs and poured hot tea, which had been waiting on a small table nearby. When they had refreshed themselves, Algy excused himself to go and find a friend who had just started medical practice.

"Well, Miss Prescott," said the doctor, turning to Amanda. "How is dear Lady Swinton? That shooting incident at Pinewood was a nasty business. I would hate to see her give in to nervousness, although I can't imagine she ever would!"

"She is fine, sir."

"Good. I'm going to see her at Pinewood this weekend. Charming woman—charming!" He rubbed his hands together, his eyes shining. Amanda waited a moment, then coughed discreetly. The doctor started, turning his attention back to the girl seated before him.

"What brings you and Algernon to London? Are you here shopping? Whatever brings the two of you to St. Bartholomew's?"

"I wanted to see you actually, Dr. Sterling. To ask some questions, if I might."

"Ah. What about?"

"About Patrick Winter and the illness that threatens him."

Dr. Sterling's jovial expression faltered. A quick expression flitted over his features, but Amanda couldn't gauge if it was surprise or fright. "Has Helene discussed this with you?"

"No, but I—"

His features hardened. "It would be a very serious breach of trust between doctor and patient if I were to discuss the Winter family with you."

"But I already know quite a bit," protested Amanda. "I merely wanted to find out how I can best help Patrick."

"I would never do anything to displease Helene. If she wishes me to reveal the family's medical history, which is highly unlikely, she'll tell me. She relies on me completely, and

Gilded Splendor

I will not let her down, or betray the trust between us."

Dr. Sterling rose to pace the office and blustered on in stentorian tones. "Helene and I have known each other for years, and she would never expect me to behave in such an unprofessional manner. Why, she depends on me, and the shock of such a betrayal might harm her."

A captive audience to his lecture, Amanda felt her happy mood evaporate. Vexation took its place. She grew uncomfortably warm, prickly heat rising under her collar. Why, to hear him speak, one would think the old man was in love with Lady Swinton!

He finally turned back to his desk, shaking his head. Amanda just caught the words, "What effrontery!" muttered under his breath. She leapt to her feet, her face flushing in anger.

"I'm sorry, Dr. Sterling. I didn't mean to pry."

He glanced up quickly, caught the angry tone in her voice, and bustled around his desk. "Now, my dear, it is my turn to apologize. I'm sure you meant no harm. It's just that your question startled me." He took her arm in a fatherly gesture. "I think you really must confront Patrick with your questions, or ask Lady Swinton. They will tell you everything they feel you need to know. Now, are you off for some shopping?"

"I don't think so." Amanda gathered up her gloves and reticule, and headed for the door. "Thank you for seeing me. Good day."

Heels clicking sharply on the polished floor,

Amanda stepped down the hall in search of Algernon. She bristled with indignation. Of course she hadn't meant to violate doctor-patient confidentiality! She wasn't a child to be lectured to! But Dr. Sterling was hiding the truth, like everyone else! His high-handedness made her more determined than ever to find out about Patrick's state of health.

Amanda discovered Algy chatting in the hallway at the entrance to the hospital. At the grim set of her mouth and the fire in her eyes, he quickly bade his friend good-bye and took her arm. Together they found their carriage and settled into its leather seats.

Amanda gazed out the carriage window, thoroughly disheartened. While they'd been inside, the sky had turned a dirty, ominous gray. She twisted her reticule, fighting the cloud of depression that threatened to settle on her, like the dreary, overcast sky had settled on the afternoon.

"Something wrong, love?" asked Algy warily. "Did you have a nice chat with Dr. Sterling?"

"No, I did not!" she exploded. "He talked down to me, as if I had no business knowing anything about Patrick. Our trip to the hospital was wasted."

"Not wasted! We had a very pleasant day, at least I did. Now don't fret. Patrick will tell you everything you want to know."

"I hate to question him or worry him with my fears."

Gilded Splendor

"Well, let's go back to Pinewood House. Enough of the big city for one day, eh?"

Algy raised his furled umbrella to tap the carriage's ceiling, but Amanda's hand detained him before he could capture the driver's attention. "I have one more stop to make before we leave London."

Algy pivoted toward her, eyebrows raised in surprise. "Oh? Where would that be?"

"I need to look up an address in Whitechapel."

"Whitechapel! A most unsavory place in the East End! Believe me, the slums are not a proper place for you to go." He shook his head, straightening his tie. "No! I'm not taking you to Whitechapel!"

Amanda smoothed her twisted reticule and removed a wrinkled sheet of paper. "This is the address where we might find Harry Tucker. It's the home of Harry's brother."

"Harry? The groom from Pinewood? What do you need him for? Amanda, this is mad. I suggest we go right home."

"I simply must find Harry, for Maude's sake!"

"Maude's sake? The maid's sake?" Algy clearly couldn't believe what he was hearing. He ran his finger nervously around inside his collar, as if it had suddenly tightened. Beads of perspiration broke out on his forehead. He paused, seeming to weigh Amanda's determination against what Patrick would surely do to him.

"Absolutely not!"

Amanda opened the carriage door and extended her foot. "If you don't take me, I'll get out of the carriage this instant and find my own way to Whitechapel."

Algy grabbed her arm. "All right, all right. Now don't get out of the carriage. Give me that bloody piece of paper." He snatched it from her hand. "But I want you to know this is against my better judgment. I think you're being stubborn and obstinate in the extreme."

He called up the address to the driver. Satisfied, Amanda settled back and closed the carriage door. "Thank you, friend. I won't forget this."

"Neither will I, friend." He gritted out the words, his head in his hands. "Neither will I."

The carriage progressed beyond the elegant quarters of Regent Street, past Spitalfields, and into Whitechapel. As they left the quieter, elegant areas of the city behind and entered the slums, a bewildering cacophony of smells and sound assailed Amanda's senses. She crinkled her nose at the distasteful aromas of horse dung, rotten fruit, and open sewers. The loud clatter of carts, carriages, and vendors' cries rang in her ears.

Crowds loitered on corners, watching street entertainers. Amanda tried to follow with her eyes as a small boy darted among long skirts and creased trousers, but the urchin disappeared down a narrow, dirty lane.

"I pity the poor people who live here," she whispered.

"A far cry from Pinewood, isn't it?"

"Yes, and a far cry from the little country village where I grew up. We were poor, but it was clean there, with fresh air. I can't imagine living in such filth."

The unwelcome thought crossed Amanda's mind that young girls who didn't make it as actresses in London might be reduced to life in the slums. She swallowed, wishing she hadn't insisted on venturing to Whitechapel, but she kept her apprehensions to herself. It would be foolish to turn back now, when they were so close.

The carriage pulled to a stop before a cheerless, dilapidated tenement. Algy placed a detaining hand on her arm.

"Please, love, at least let me go in alone. You wait in the carriage. If Harry's inside, I'll bring him out. Do that for me, please?"

Amanda studied Algy's anxious expression. He had really been a dear, and she had caused him such inconvenience. She gave in with a smile. "All right."

"Good. I won't be long."

Algy sprang from the carriage and disappeared into the tenement's dark shadows.

Left to wait, Amanda glared at the filthy street, strewn with garbage. What kind of job could Harry find here? How could he think of bringing Maude and their baby to live in this rat-infested alley? She had to persuade Harry to return to Pinewood House!

"Hullo, miss. 'At's a foine carriage," a low masculine voice drawled. A burly man in dirty rags had stolen up to the carriage window without attracting attention. He reeked with the foul stench of cheap liquor and stale sweat.

"Spare a li'l change for a po' workin' bloke?" He held out a gnarled, filthy hand. He looked more like a hoodlum than any honest working man, but perhaps he had a starving family, thought Amanda. "Of course," she said.

"Everything all right, miss?" called down the anxious voice of the driver.

"Yes, it's all right," she called back, not wanting to get the beggar in trouble. She reached into her reticule and handed a coin out the window. The man's dirty face screwed up with resentment.

"C'mon, luv. Don' you 'ave some'at more'n this?" he whined in a drunken slur.

"I'm sorry. That's all the money I have."

"Aw, have a heart, Y'r Ladyship..."

Despite his pleading words, his voice had turned sly and calculating. He grasped the carriage's door handle and slowly turned it. Amanda shrank back in fearful disbelief. What did he mean to do? The carriage door swung open, and a grimy hand reached toward her.

"Here now! Be off with you!" a strong voice boomed on the other side of the carriage.

Amanda stared out the window in amazement. "Patrick!"

The drunk released the door handle and teetered in a mocking bow. "Why, if it hain't His

Gilded Splendor

Lor'ship 'isself!" he slurred. Advancing slowly, menacingly around the carriage, he stooped to pick up a large stick on his way.

Fearfully, Amanda craned her neck to watch out the back window. Gesturing to the driver to keep his seat, Patrick met the drunkard behind the carriage. They faced each other, crouching warily. The drunk swung his stick in a sudden wide arc aimed at Patrick's head. Patrick ducked, and with a mighty uppercut, connected his fist with the man's jaw. Amanda winced at the sound of flesh cracking bone. The stick flew into the air, and the man landed on his backside in a heap of rubbish. Patrick advanced menacingly toward him, but the drunk had had enough; hastily scrambling to his feet, he ran off down a back alley.

Amanda breathed a sigh of relief to see him go. She stared at Patrick. He seemed to be all right. Panting slightly, he shrugged his broad shoulders to straighten his jacket and watched the man beat a hasty retreat.

Algy emerged from the tenement building and halted in surprise. "I say, Patrick! What are you doing here?"

Patrick whirled, his face a dark storm cloud. "I might ask the same of you!" he snarled. "Why did you bring Amanda to a place like this?" He climbed into the carriage and slammed the door. "I'll see her home," he said curtly.

"If you say so, old man," returned Algy, shamefacedly. "I'll grab a cab."

Amanda leaned across Patrick and spoke urgently out the carriage window. "Algy, where is Harry?"

"He wasn't there. The place was empty to the bare wood floors. An old hag said the family moved away. She didn't know where."

Amanda stamped her foot on the carriage floor. How frustrating and vexing!

"So the whole trip has been wasted. I'm sorry I dragged you to London for nothing."

Patrick unceremoniously pushed Amanda back to her side of the carriage with a force that made her head bump against the seat cushion. "It was a damned fool thing to do, Algernon," he said, then banged on the carriage roof. "Drive on!"

The driver cracked his whip and they lurched forward, leaving Algy standing in the road behind, shaking his head mournfully at the departing carriage.

Moodily, Patrick massaged his reddened knuckles. "Are you all right?"

"I'm fine. But you were awfully hard on Algy."

"No more than he deserves, the scoundrel!"

"Why scoundrel? Just because he accompanied me to London?"

He turned on her. "And look what happened! While he was mooning around inside some old building, you were left alone in the carriage and attacked by a drunk! God knows what might have happened if I'd been a moment later."

"It wasn't Algy's fault! I made him bring me."

Gilded Splendor

Patrick grunted. "Then you're a damned fool, too!" He gritted his teeth. Amanda lapsed into silence, realizing they were both tired and frustrated. Patrick glared out the carriage window, maintaining an ominous silence until they were out of the slums. Finally, Amanda spoke.

"How did you find us today?"

"Maude said you'd ridden out with Algy," he answered grudgingly. "I dragged the address out of her."

"Hmmm. Very clever. I hope you didn't have to beat her."

Patrick threw a scornful glance, but she managed to keep a straight face.

"This is no joking matter," he exploded. "If you want to go somewhere from now on, I'll take you!"

"Why? What do you mean, from now on?"

Patrick drew a ragged breath. "I guess you'll hear about it soon enough anyway."

A flicker of apprehension crept up her spine. "Hear about what?"

"There's been another murder near Pinewood. The duchess of Howard, one of our neighbors."

"Oh!" she said in dismay. The amusing lady with the bustle.

Patrick set his lips in a grim line.

Fear, stark and vivid, clutched Amanda's heart. "Was she strangled like Lady Brighton?"

"Yes," he said tersely.

"W–were her lips painted red?"

"How do you know about that?"

"I heard gossip." Amanda felt as if a hand had gripped her throat like a vise. "No one is safe," she said in a small, frightened voice.

Lines of tension furrowed Patrick's face. "I'm going to see that we're all safe."

"What do you mean?"

Patrick slammed his fist into his hand. "No more sitting around, waiting to get sick. No more hated, detestable frustration. No more living like a depraved dissolute."

"No one thinks of you that way!"

"My life has been a miserable failure. Wine, women, gambling—nothing has had any meaning. Instead, I've found myself constantly absorbed by"—he threw a telltale glance in her direction—"by things I can't have. Enough!"

Amanda had also had enough. Enough skirting around issues, enough secrets, enough speaking at cross-purposes. She clenched her fists in determination. *He must talk to me about his illness. We have to face it.* Perhaps this was the opening she'd been waiting for—the moment to pierce his armor.

She plucked at his sleeve. "Patrick, when I came to Pinewood House, your grandmother told me you should have fun while you can. She has encouraged you to be dissolute. Why?"

Patrick threw her a quick, searching look, then fixed his gaze on the scenery passing outside the window.

"It's something our family never discusses."

"Please talk to me," she begged.

He hesitated, obviously at war with himself. Amanda waited with bated breath. Would he open up to her? Tell her about the family secret that had marred his life? Pensiveness shimmered in his eyes. His brows furrowed, knitted with indecision.

After what seemed an eternity, he nodded slightly. "I guess you deserve an explanation," he admitted grudgingly. "After all the lies and games, I owe you that, at least."

He focused his attention on a tassel at the carriage window and became absorbed in carelessly flicking it back and forth. "Gram believes I'm going to be ill someday," he said smoothly.

"And are you, Patrick? Going to be ill someday?"

Dropping all pretense, he let go of the tassel and swung around to face her. "Yes. I am."

He stared into her eyes, probing for her reaction. She swallowed, making an effort to remain calm and keep her roiling emotions from showing. "Tell me," she said quietly.

Now that the subject was in the open, his words tumbled out, and she listened raptly.

"My grandfather succumbed to an inherited disease, passed down through the men of our family. My father died of an accident too young to get it, but I'm next in line. It took me a long time to face it. Growing up, I burned with rage and bitterness. I was filled with self-pity, begged the gods to spare me. I denied it, refused to believe I would ever become ill. But over time, I learned to accept my fate. I ran Pinewood House and pursued pleasure with a vengeance, but I decided never to marry or father children." He steadied himself with a deep breath, then continued. "Now you see why there can be nothing between us."

Pain gripping her heart, Amanda lifted her chin. "Surely there's something you can do," she said.

"Don't hold your breath. I've been through that with Dr. Sterling. There's nothing to be done." He gave a resigned shrug. "But I have found something to take my mind off things. One last mission I can perform."

Mission? Sick with dread, Amanda asked, "What is it?"

"I'm going to discover and expose the neighborhood murderer. I'm going to end the rampage of dirty tricks and killing, and make my neighborhood safe for the families who live there."

"But that could be dangerous for you!"

"What have I got to lose?"

Amanda watched his resolute expression, fear for him uppermost in her mind. This wasn't quite the solution to his problem she'd anticipated. When she'd said to do something, she'd meant to override his grandmother's objections and love her. Instead he was proposing a far more dangerous course of action.

Amanda swallowed in fear. "How will you find this person?"

"Examine the crime scenes, the clues, the suspects, taking care all the while to avoid attracting the attention of the police. They would probably try to stop me."

"I wish they would stop you! I wish you wouldn't do this. I'm afraid for you!"

"I've got to do something. Maybe for once in my life, I can be of some use to somebody."

Amanda saw it was fruitless to argue with him. He'd let down his guard for a brief moment, long enough to tell her about the illness, but his admission had not brought them closer. He'd immediately rebuilt the defensive walls between them, strong as ever. She rode the rest of the way in fearful silence, imagining the worst.

When they finally turned up the curved drive of the estate, the cloudy day had turned cold. They were surprised to see a group of people gathered in front of the house.

"What's going on?" Amanda asked. "You don't suppose they've been looking for us?"

Patrick half rose in his seat and instructed the driver to hurry on a little faster. "Hardly likely. No one knew we were going out today." A worried frown creased his brow. "What the blazes?"

The carriage pulled up, and they quickly disembarked. A small group of servants huddling in a circle on the front steps of the mansion silently parted to let them pass.

A body, familiar and beloved, sprawled on the steps. Amanda clutched Patrick's arm. Reggie lay on the flagstones in an unnatural position, his neck bent at an odd angle. Kneeling beside him, Maude clutched his hand, weeping convulsively.

Memories flooded Amanda's mind, vivid pictures of herself bent over her own father, clutching his lifeless hand, weeping over him. The pain came rushing back, all the trauma she had fought so hard to put behind her.

"No!" she cried out.

At the sound of her voice, Maude raised eyes swimming with tears. "M'dad fell off the p–parapet."

The group looked up as one, their gazes climbing the steep stone wall. The gray parapets loomed forbiddingly, stabbing into the dreary, colorless sky.

"What the hell was he doing up there?" Patrick asked, his voice a rasp of anguish.

"I don't know," Maude wept. "No one knows."

Chapter Eleven

The sad day of the funeral dwindled into gloomy darkness. The sun dropped behind the foothills, glowing bloodred on the horizon. Amanda sat alone in her room, pensively gazing into the deepening twilight, her hands wrapped around a soothing cup of tea. A perfect end to a completely imperfect day, and another unexplained mystery for Pinewood House.

The burial service that afternoon had been traumatic. Reggie had been deeply loved. Everyone on the estate and more friends from the county convened to mourn the gentle man who had spent his life lovingly tending the gardens of Pinewood House.

In the quiet tree-lined cemetery on Pinewood's grounds, Reggie's body was slowly lowered into the grave. Mourners stared at each other in silence over the coffin, tentative questions clouding their troubled eyes. What had the old man been doing up on the parapet? What had caused him to fall? The unvoiced questions loomed large.

Remembering how heartbrokenly Maude had cried at the funeral, Amanda bit her lip. Dr. Sterling had finally given Maude a sedative and put her to bed. Without Harry or her father, what would happen to the poor little maid?

Helene had wept gently at the funeral. Surely she would miss her old gardener.

And Patrick? He had suffered with the rest of the mourners, perhaps more deeply than any of them. His eyes had searched her out before the service, darting her way for a brief moment, registering a haunting pain. Amanda had longed to go to him, to comfort him in some way, but there had been no time, and he'd disappeared into the crowd of mourners.

What a tragic, senseless death. Amanda brushed away a tear. A brooding restlessness seized her, and she found it impossible to sit still. The air in the room grew stale and stifling. Her cup clinked against the saucer, as she remembered the last time she'd seen Reggie alive.

The White Garden. Something unknown, inexplicable, beckoned from that green world of living plants Reggie had loved so well. She left

Gilded Splendor

the house, her footsteps taking her down the path toward the White Garden. Moving quickly through the twilight, not knowing why, she was irresistibly drawn to Reggie's gardener's cottage.

Deserted and forlorn, the ivy-covered building stood silent. All around lay scattered reminders of Reggie, as if he would be back any moment to pick up his life where he'd left off. With an aching heart, Amanda touched his hoe leaning against the window, ran her hands over his red sweater where he'd dropped it on a bench, fingered his clay pots holding tender white buds. Reggie wouldn't be here to plant and tend the new flowers. Not ever. Desolation settled over her like a gray, heavy cloud.

Swallowing a lump in her throat, she placed her palm against the cottage's wood door. It creaked open, and she peered into the shadows of the unlit room. Against the far wall, a figure sat, silhouetted in the gloom.

"Hello," he said simply.

Patrick's presence in the cottage didn't surprise her. It seemed inevitable he should be there, sitting in Reggie's chair. He leaned forward into a single shaft of light. Gray circles rimmed his bloodshot eyes. His ebony hair was tousled as if he'd been raking his hands through it. He'd taken off his jacket and tossed it on a bench nearby, rolling up his shirtsleeves to expose the soft, dark hair of his arms. In his hand, he held one of Reggie's white roses.

Amanda crossed to him. He raised troubled eyes to hers and solemnly handed her the rose. "I'm glad you've come," he said. "Stay with me awhile."

She took the precious flower and smoothed its velvet petals. Patrick had never given her a gift before. She would press it, and treasure it always as a reminder of him.

"I'll stay as long as you want."

She sank to her knees beside his chair, and they sat in silent communion, sharing their common grief. The evening shadows lengthened. Finally, Patrick broke the silence, his low voice intense. "I did love that man."

"I know. I know."

"He's always been here for me, ever since I was a little boy. His spirit seems to be here still. Can you feel it?"

Amanda gazed around the room filled with Reggie's things. Her glance fell on a basket of cut flowers waiting to be carried to the house. "Yes," she said, "I feel his love all around us."

A glazed look of despair spread over Patrick's face. "What was he doing on that parapet? He had no reason to go up there."

"Can't anyone say?"

"No." He shrugged his broad shoulders. "What does it matter anyway? He's dead."

Tears slipped down Amanda's cheeks. Patrick cradled her cheek in his palm, and she nestled into his hand, drawing comfort from his touch. He gently wiped a teardrop away, then brought

Gilded Splendor

his wet finger to his mouth. "Salty," he said absently, then shook his head in bewilderment. "I've tried so hard to make Pinewood House a safe, protected world. Now it seems to be falling apart." His shoulders hunched forward in despair. Raw, wretched grief etched his face. He rested his elbows on his thighs and dropped his head into his hands. "God, what am I going to do?"

Amanda's heart squeezed in anguish. She must comfort him somehow, break through his lonely wall of pain. But how? What solace could she offer? With a sharp intake of breath, she realized the only thing she had to give was herself. She closed her eyes for a moment. *Please forgive me, Papa. I know you understand.*

She tugged gently on Patrick's hand. "Sit here beside me."

Patrick blinked down at her, startled at the suggestion. Warning bells sounded inside him. What was she doing? He hesitated, but she nodded reassuringly. The gentle pressure of her hand pulled at him persuasively. Against his better judgment, he found himself saying, "Maybe just for a minute."

He eased himself down onto the stone floor beside her, and she leaned close against him. Just touching her eased his pain a little. Her youthful beauty radiated vitality and life, like a shield between him and the death and suffering all around.

"You help me, Amanda," he said. "Sometimes I think you're the only thing in this bloody world that can save me."

"I want to help," she replied softly.

"But you torture me, too. Other times I think I'll die of wanting you." He heaved a shuddering sigh as his arms went around her shoulders. He would hold her close for only a moment, just a brief moment.

"This is wrong," he whispered. Yet even as he said it, he pressed his lips against her silky hair and inhaled her fresh, young scent. Instinctively, his body responded, his groin stiffening with tingling desire, and the familiar, inevitable struggle raged within him again, as always. He shouldn't be this near. It was insane, infinitely dangerous. His fingers hungrily stroked the folds of her sleeve, rubbing the soft fabric between his fingers in a silky caress.

Her eyes! Deep, dark seas of blue gazed into him with heartrending tenderness. He screwed his own eyes tightly shut to escape what he saw there, and leaned his head back against the cottage wall.

"We need to get back to the house," he rasped.

Amanda looked at his face, shut and guarded. The gloom threw odd shadows on his cheeks, bringing out the chiseled planes. He was fighting her, himself, the whole world. Her nervousness left her when she saw how his mouth had hardened into a taut line. She was determined

Gilded Splendor

to make him relax, to see his lips soften into sensual fullness. Forgetting herself, thinking only of him, she grew bold.

"In a little while," she whispered.

Gently, she took his face in her hands and drew it down to hers. Her lips touched his, lightly, softly, no more than a gossamer flicker of butterfly wings.

At the touch of her kiss, a fierce longing welled up from the base of his spine, filling him, consuming him. His need was unbearable, and he sensed himself losing control.

His eyes flew open, and he reared his head back, breaking the seductive contact of her lips. "Do you know what you do to me?" he choked out, his voice a growl of anguish.

She reached around to grasp the back of his neck. Slowly, inexorably, she pulled his face back down to hers. Her lips pressed firmly against his in another kiss, silencing his objections. Her kiss held nothing back, all trusting, giving eagerness, and his willpower shattered. He couldn't fight anymore—not himself and her, too. With a deep groan, he kissed her back, traced the curved bow of her lips, tasted her sweetness. He pummeled her mouth with an intrusive, insistent probing of his tongue. She responded with the heady, sweet ardor of surrender, matching his own painful capitulation.

The hungry kiss lengthened, and the ancient passion stirred to life. He'd waited so long. He raised his head, and with a look of despair, drew her to lie down on the warm stone floor. He clung to her fiercely, cradling the warmth of her body against his, raining kisses on her cheeks, her eyelids, her throat.

Amanda lay back and closed her eyes. Unbelievable new feelings swept over her, but she wasn't frightened. Her inexperience loomed before her, but never had she felt so wanted, so needed. He was eager, virile, male—demanding and passionate, and she thrilled that it was she he wanted.

He worshiped her with his mouth, and slowly fanned her desire, awakening it to a flame. Lying in his arms, she framed the hard angles of his face with her palms. He stared down at her, his eyes filled with the age-old question. Nothing mattered anymore, she realized. Not the past or the future, not illness or death. Nothing mattered except this moment and his love. She brushed the white rose softly against his cheek and nodded her assent.

Greedily, he ran his hands down her body and up again to cup her firm, round breasts in his palms. He felt a tremor shimmer through her, but she lay perfectly still, as if afraid to move, lest he stop and draw back. He struggled to breathe, the heady scent of the rose filling his senses. Didn't she know? He couldn't stop now, not to save his life.

He pulled up her skirts, trying to be as gentle as possible, and skimmed his hand up her stockinged thigh. She quivered in his arms.

Heat engulfing him, he moved his lips over hers. As if unable to bear her enforced stillness any longer, she let out a long sigh. Her breath whispered into his mouth in invitation, like the wind through the pines outside the cottage.

It had to be. The dam broke, and there was no turning back. Suddenly, nothing existed for either of them except a wild frenzy of fingers on buttons, undoing laces and ribbons, arms and legs hurriedly drawn out of sleeves, clothing tossed carelessly aside, for the sole purpose of feeling flesh against flesh.

Pausing, Patrick's eyes hungrily drank in the sight of her lush body. He took the white rose from her hand and drew it softly around her breasts before caressing each nipple with the smooth, cool petals. At the touch of the velvet flower, they rose to hardened points of desire.

"So beautiful..." he whispered, filled with admiration.

He drew her fiercely against him, craving her soft curves. His hand drew her thighs apart, caressed her. Supporting himself on outstretched arms on either side of her, he rose to loom above her. Her eyes widened in surprised wonder. He bent his elbows and lowered himself into her, finally, into the inevitable, cataclysmic joining of their bodies.

When she stiffened, his mouth devoured hers, rained hot, moist, open-mouthed kisses in the most delicious places, in the most delectable way, allowing her no time to dwell on the pain. Sipping and swirling, he continued to withdraw and thrust, gently and slowly, until she began to move with him.

The undulating movements of her hips excited him, drove him faster. He closed his eyes then and plunged in and out of her with a driving intensity, an aching hardness. The cottage, Pinewood House, the past and the future—all faded away. He lost himself, frantically, wildly, maddeningly. Love obliterated death in urgent life-affirming movement.

God! She would drive him into sweet oblivion if he'd allow it. In a frantic movement, he straightened and pulled himself out of her.

Patrick lay silent, enveloped in a dreamy haze, overcome with wonder. Amanda had given herself completely, unselfishly. His pain and unrest had been quieted, his deep longing assuaged. But, God help him, he would need to have her again. Soon. He would never get enough of her.

He looked at the woman in his arms, and his remorse was immediate and complete, spoiling the contentment of a second before. Where would he find the strength to push her away? To go back to the old life of loneliness and denial? And yet he had to. He couldn't infect Amanda's future with his illness. He must match her unselfishness with his own.

Sighing, he stared up at the ceiling of the cottage. Details of the everyday world burst relentlessly back into his consciousness. Cobwebs spun an intricate fretwork pattern against the old boards. The wind in the pine trees wailed mournfully outside the cottage walls.

"What have I done?"

"What I wanted you to do. That's all."

"Did I hurt you?"

"No. No."

"I'm a cad. To use Reggie's death as an excuse to—"

"Hush." Amanda placed a soft, gentle finger on his lips. "Reggie would have approved. I love you. It seems so simple."

"It's not simple at all, Mandy."

She raised herself on one elbow to look at him. "What did you call me?"

"Mandy. Is that all right? I think of you as Mandy sometimes."

"Yes. It's just that—nobody has ever called me Mandy except my father, whom I loved very much. And now you."

Patrick looked into her eyes. They glowed with the dewy radiance of a woman in love. Though he tried to deny what he saw there, he was struck with a thrill of elation that made his remorse and regret all the keener.

He was silent for a moment, then sat up in the gloom and groped the floor for his clothes. The stones had turned cold to his touch.

"I never meant for this to happen. I thought about it, of course, but I never meant to carry it this far. Now I've spoiled you irretrievably."

"Spoiled me?"

"For other men."

He heard her sharp intake of breath. She sat up and fumbled for her chemise. "You mean for marriage to another man. But I must marry you now, in case I have a baby!"

"You won't have a baby. I pulled out in time. I damned well better have."

Silently, she mulled over this information, her face revealing her disappointment.

"Amanda, I can't marry you. I won't. Not now or ever. So let this conversation be at an end. You'll hate me for listening if I let you continue."

She paused in drawing on her clothing and leaned closer, her voice intense. "I'll never hate you, Patrick."

"Yes, you will."

"Only if you send me away. That would be the greatest wrong."

In exasperation, Patrick threw down the boot he'd picked up. "Then what do you want from me?"

She drew on her blouse and calmly worked the buttons. "I've come to a decision. You asked me to become your mistress."

"I was way out of line that night. I never should have spoken to you as I did. It was ungentlemanly. I apologize, and I hope we can just forget it."

"I don't want to forget it."

"Amanda, you're not that kind of woman."

"It seems I am that kind of woman—now."

Gilded Splendor

He flinched as if she'd struck him. God, why had he destroyed her innocence? For what? Just so he could forget his own pain in a moment of selfish pleasure? He lowered his head in shame and picked up a boot, keeping his expression deliberately blank. He concentrated on wiping the smudged toe with his sleeve.

"You asked me to become your mistress," she persisted, "and I'm holding you to that."

His head went up at the feisty determination in her voice. Her blue eyes sparked fire, her white breasts heaved with anger. God, she was beautiful!

He grasped her chin and gently raised her face to his. "I'm still going to become ill," he reminded her softly. "Doesn't that idea bother you?"

She lowered her gaze, as though afraid of what he might see there. A slight tremor swept through her.

There it is, he thought bitterly, the hesitation, the disgust. She can't hide it. Of course the idea of his pathetic figure ailing in a sickroom would strike her with revulsion. She must feel the same contempt he felt toward himself.

She must pity him.

God! His muscles stiffened with mortification and anger. He'd be damned if he'd accept pity from anyone, especially her. He hid his painful regret, his awful disgrace, beneath an icy facade.

He released her abruptly and stood up. With a show of casual nonchalance, he withdrew a cigarette from his pocket, lit it, and flicked the match away.

"You needn't worry. I assure you, the disease isn't catching. I haven't come down with anything at all yet, and if I do, it's not contagious. So you see," he said, his voice cold, "our lovemaking was quite safe in that regard."

She lifted her chin. "I'm not afraid of catching anything. I was just thinking of my parents—" She stopped, her eyes clouding over.

"I see," Patrick snapped. "They wouldn't have approved of a family, even an aristocratic one, with illness in its background." He exhaled a puff of smoke.

"No! I—"

Patrick abruptly threw down his cigarette and savagely ground it out under his boot. Why hadn't he kept his damned mouth shut? It pained him that he'd ever told her about his illness in the first place, revealing himself so recklessly, inviting her scorn. He'd spilled his guts to the woman when he should have been taking his pleasure with her! Despising himself for his weakness, he retreated behind a well-practiced formality, assuming the cold, haughty superiority of a peer.

"I'll see you later. I'm sure you can find your way back to the house."

"Patrick, don't go like this! Let me explain." She grabbed his arm, pulling him down beside her. "It's my turn to tell you something about myself."

Gilded Splendor

Her words tumbled out in a rush. "My parents were ill. I nursed them for a long time—it seems like all the time I was growing up. When they died, I swore I would never enter a sickroom again. But I want to be with you, for as long as I can."

"What are you saying?"

"I don't think I could stay on after you become ill, to watch you slowly die. I won't lose you like that. Don't ask me to."

Patrick squeezed his eyes shut, unwilling to look anymore at his world of pain.

"But you might not become ill, you know. Who can say for sure?" Miraculously, the words he'd been thirsting to hear, dying to hear, tumbled from her lips. "And even if you do, we could be together until then."

She wrapped her arms around him. The look of love on her beautiful face insinuated itself into his heart, softened his emotions. Her eyes warmed him, saw right through him.

"Mandy, don't pity me!"

"I don't pity you. I love you! I wanted us to marry, it's true. But if that isn't to be, then I'll be your mistress—anything to be with you."

"You don't know what you'd be letting yourself in for. We'd be together for a short while. Then it would turn ugly."

"Can't I stay with you until that happens?"

"Be my pretty little decoration? And then what?"

"I'll leave if you become ill."

Patrick gazed in wonder at the woman. Her voice rang with sincerity. Her eyes shone with a clear, pure light. From where in her slight frame did that fierce strength come?

"Are you willing to accept so little?" Massaging through her tumbled hair, his fingers gripped her warm skull. She stared into his eyes, filling his senses with painful, urgent intensity. Despite everything, she was his woman, the irresistible object of his desire—sensuous, alive, making him pulse with life in the midst of all his deadness and decay. If he could keep her—even for a short while . . . He was struck with the wild, uncontrollable urge to let the world be damned, to possess her, whatever the cost. "You're so beautiful. And I want you so badly. Don't tempt me this way."

He slowly took her in his arms, angled his head, and drowned in her kiss, a kiss filled with wonder and promise. Her warm lips, yielding, sweet, trembled beneath his own.

Something inside him snapped. No! He could not, would not, ever draw her into the agony he faced. He had vowed never to cross the fine line he'd drawn in his life. He must never again yield to her temptation.

"Amanda, don't do this to me! Don't!"

With a curse, he strode out of the gardener's cottage without a backward glance.

Chapter Twelve

Amanda stood in the flickering gaslight, clad only in her chemise, examining her reflection in the mirror. How odd. She didn't look any different, yet she was irrevocably changed. Surprisingly, no one would be able to detect her loss of innocence from her outward appearance.

Her heart was heavy with a guilty conscience. Her body ached, tender and sore. Yet she had to smile, deeply glad that she and Patrick had made love. We're one, she thought. Nothing can ever change that. Whatever happens, I'll always have that much of him.

Perhaps somehow they could be together a while longer. And if he didn't become ill, they might remain together. Who could say for certain that would not happen? Surely Patrick would come to feel, as she did, that there was hope for the future.

Her fingers lovingly caressed Patrick's white rose. Its fragrance was heady and mysterious, its smooth petals soft as a baby's skin. She smiled as the image of what he'd done with the flower focused in her memory. Her whole body tingled, thrilling again to the touch of cool velvet petals caressing warm flesh. She knew that for the rest of her life, the scent of rose petals would flood her with remembered desire for Patrick Winter.

She placed the flower carefully in Sylvie's jeweled box. "Keep this safe for me, Sylvie," she whispered. "Patrick gave it to me."

A knock on the door startled Amanda from her reverie. Hastily, she tucked the box beneath her folded underthings in the top dresser drawer. Throwing on a wrapper, she padded barefoot to the door and drew it open. Diane Warfield! Amanda's warm emotions froze, her heart congealing to ice.

Diane leaned gracefully against the door frame, her arms folded nonchalantly across her chest. Her lustrous black hair swung down about gleaming, white shoulders. She wore a red silk evening gown, low-cut and revealing.

"May I come in?" she murmured in a low, silky drawl.

No, go away! fumed Amanda. *I don't want to see you, especially not now!*

But she fought to school her emotions. It wouldn't do to reveal herself to Diane. Amanda

Gilded Splendor

instinctively sensed the countess was the kind of woman who would take innocently divulged information and turn it, twist it, use it against the giver to her own advantage.

"Of course," Amanda said carefully, forcing a smile. "Please come in." She opened the door wider and stood back, motioning with her hand.

"How lovely you're still here at Pinewood," said Diane, pushing off the wall. "I must admit, though, I had really expected to find you gone by now."

"I'm still here."

"So I see."

Diane crossed casually to the dresser, picked up Amanda's hairbrush, and began carelessly twirling it through the air. Amanda looked at her plain, well-worn tortoiseshell brush and imagined the expensive set of silver brushes Diane no doubt owned. Unwilling to see her possession in Diane's irreverent hands a moment longer, she walked over and took back the brush.

"That was my mother's," she said, replacing it carefully on the dresser.

"How sweet." Diane sniffed disdainfully and perched on the bed.

"Did you want something?" asked Amanda, anxious to be rid of the woman.

"Helene wrote, telling me how terribly Patrick missed me. He can't be without me for any length of time, you see, so naturally I rushed down to spend the weekend with him and put the poor man's heart at ease." Diane flashed a brilliant, insincere smile. "And when I found you were here, I just had to come and say hello!"

Amanda turned toward the dresser so Diane wouldn't read the uncertainty on her face.

"I must say, Patrick was so glad to see me! That man! Sometimes his attentions can be almost overpowering. He's so—so virile!"

Amanda couldn't believe her ears. Was Diane actually discussing Patrick's lovemaking? Sudden panic gripped her. Why was Diane bragging? She couldn't possibly know about the scene in Reggie's cottage, could she? Patrick would never have told her. That was unthinkable! Wasn't it?

Diane came back to the dresser and sidled up close. Amanda felt the woman's breath, warm and sinuous, against her ear. She steeled herself not to instinctively pull away.

"A sweet innocent like you couldn't possibly understand the passions and special needs of a man like Patrick."

Amanda didn't want to hear Diane discuss Patrick in that disgusting way. She wanted to stop Diane with a few well-chosen words, but like a rabbit staring at a snake, she listened on, mesmerized.

"Special needs?"

"His lovemaking tastes run to the, shall we say, exotic and sophisticated. Only a real woman, an experienced woman who savors the same kinds of pleasures, can really satisfy him. He knows it, too."

Gilded Splendor

Amanda clutched the edge of the dresser, a flood of nausea sweeping over her. Had Patrick been dissatisfied with their lovemaking? Bored with her inexperience? Could he have gone directly from her arms to Diane's? No, Diane was lying—she had to be lying. But the seed of doubt had been planted. Amanda's troubled eyes met Diane's in the mirror.

"There now! I've shocked you," Diane purred solicitously.

"Not at all."

"Surely you knew about us?" Diane feigned surprise. "Patrick and I go way back. We've been friends and lovers for so long, it's practically an accepted fact among everyone we know."

Amanda's heart fell. Of course they knew all the same people, moved in the same aristocratic circles. What had gone on between them over the years?

Diane's eyes raked Amanda's figure, clad in her favorite wrapper, shabby and threadbare. Amanda pulled the robe tighter, trying to protect herself from Diane's critical stare.

"Tell me, dear, where are you from? A little country village, I believe Helene said. And your father worked as a servant on Helene's estate, didn't he? I feel I don't know you half well enough, but I'm discovering the most delicious little tidbits about you all the time."

Amanda turned to face Diane. "If there's anything about my past you wish to know, you have merely to ask. I have nothing to hide."

Diane sighed dramatically. "Your life has obviously been so different from the life Patrick and I are used to. Well, no matter! Perhaps we can still be friends." She shrugged and turned toward the door. "I really must be going. Patrick and I are riding tomorrow, so I'll need my rest, and I promised Helene to drop in and bid her good night."

"Good night," said Amanda, trying to control the shakiness in her voice. She wouldn't give Diane the satisfaction of knowing she had struck a nerve.

"Good night, dear." With a smile, Diane left the room, leaving a trail of heavy scent behind.

Queasiness churned Amanda's stomach. Afraid she might be sick, she ran to the window, threw it open, and gulped in breaths of fresh, bracing air. She knew Diane was playing tricks, most probably exaggerating her relationship with Patrick. And Amanda could only imagine the "special needs" Diane had hinted at. Distressed at the dirty innuendos, she gripped the windowsill, her knuckles going white.

One thing Diane had said couldn't be denied—Diane and Patrick's aristocratic, worldly milieu was quite different from the simple world of Amanda Prescott. They had things in common, shared interests, that Amanda could only guess at.

Amanda fought hard to conquer her spoiled mood, to regain the warm, loving tenderness she'd basked in before Diane's unwelcome visit, but her lovemaking with Patrick now seemed degraded. *I won't let her spoil it for me!* she vowed. *I won't let the countess bother me!*

But the warm glow in her heart had turned to ash.

"I'd like to ask you some questions, if I might, Miss Prescott. It should only take a few moments of your time."

Amanda perched on the library sofa the next day, facing Inspector Sweeney. She'd been surprised when he'd asked to see her. The policeman's manner was all it should have been, professional and polite, but his probing eyes scrutinized her, made her feel oddly uneasy, as if she were on trial.

"I'm speaking to everyone who was in the vicinity, trying to determine motives for the murders that have occurred recently. I hope you don't mind."

"Of course not."

The inspector took out his pencil and notebook. "Were you acquainted with either of the two murder victims, Lady Brighton or the Duchess of Howard?"

"No, I never met either of the unfortunate ladies."

"I see. But you are acquainted with Mrs. Charteris, the lady who was shot here a while back?"

"Yes, I know Mrs. Charteris."

"I believe you were in London with the Marquess of Swinton the day Reggie White fell to his death from the parapet?"

Amanda looked down at her hands folded tightly in her lap and swallowed, her throat constricted. "Yes, we returned that day to find Reggie had fallen."

"Or been pushed," muttered the inspector under his breath.

Startled, Amanda stared at him, but he calmly continued his questioning.

"Do you know His Lordship well enough that you would recognize if he were acting strangely?"

Amanda frowned, perplexed. "Strangely?"

"For instance, has he been coming and going at odd hours? Has he seemed agitated or moody recently?"

Moody? A vision of Patrick's face swam before her, tender, boyish laughter alternating with anguish, dark and forbidding as a storm cloud. "Well, Patrick has his moods, surely, but . . ."

The inspector made a quick jotting in his notebook. "Have you ever heard him mention the two murdered ladies?"

"No."

Inspector Sweeney again wrote himself a note, then tapped his pencil meditatively against his teeth.

Amanda raised her gaze to him. "Why do you ask me about Patrick? I feel disloyal speaking

Gilded Splendor

about my host behind his back."

"He may be your host, Miss Prescott, but I'll tell you, he's been showing up in places he shouldn't!"

"For instance?"

Inspector Sweeney's face flushed. No doubt he felt she was impertinent to turn the tables and ask him a question. "He's been prowling around the scenes of both murders, raising a lot of questions. In fact, he seems to know more about the murders than is warranted."

Amanda tensed her fingers, the nails cutting into her palms. So Patrick had begun looking for clues, as he'd said he would! And the inspector was trying to stop him, just as he'd predicted. She'd said she wanted the police to stop him from pursuing his dangerous course of action, but now she couldn't bring herself to inform on him. She raised her chin defiantly.

The inspector searched her troubled eyes. "Miss Prescott, do you feel warmly about His Lordship?"

Amanda avoided his probing eyes.

"Maybe you know more than you're telling," he continued. "In the police trade, there's a phenomenon known as returning to the scene of the crime."

Amanda bolted from the sofa. "What are you implying? Surely you're not accusing the Marquess of Swinton—"

"I'm not accusing him of anything! Just trying to ascertain the facts."

"Well, I'll not discuss His Lordship any further. And you can be sure I'll let him know of your insulting insinuations!"

"You do that! I've had a talk with the marquess and I'll be questioning him further myself." He replaced the notebook in his pocket and headed for the door. "Miss Prescott, Lady Swinton says you plan to live in London soon. Please remain at Pinewood House until my investigation is concluded."

Amanda watched the inspector leave the room. As soon as the door closed behind him, her shoulders sagged and she wilted onto the sofa, her hand covering her mouth.

Oh, Patrick! What have you done?

Chapter Thirteen

"At home, Mama taught me to iron our clothes. Once I left a huge singed mark on one of Papa's shirts."

Amanda sighed at her feeble attempts to make conversation. Maude obviously hadn't heard a word she'd said. The maid fidgeted with a handkerchief, absent-mindedly smoothing its folds, but her mind seemed a million miles away. The handkerchief fluttered to the floor, and with an audible sniff, Maude stooped to retrieve it.

"Are you all right?" asked Amanda, deeply concerned. "I've been thinking of you, hoping you're feeling better."

"Much better, thank you, now that the funeral's over."

"I'm so sorry. We all loved Reggie."

The rims of Maude's eyes reddened, and tears threatened to spill over. "Without m'dad . . . I'm terrible worried, miss."

Amanda placed a reassuring hand on her arm. "Maude, we'll find Harry."

"But you couldn't find him when you went looking in London, miss."

"No, I'm afraid there was no one at the address you gave me. No relatives, and no Harry."

Maude's countenance fell once again, but Amanda hastened on. "We're not finished yet. I talked to Patrick, and he said he would help."

The maid sighed with relief. "Thank you ever so much."

"Everything will turn out fine, you'll see. You just take care of yourself so you'll have a healthy baby."

"Yes, miss. I'll never forget what you've done for me." Maude smiled her gratitude. "Oh! I have something for you!" She drew a small package from her pocket. "When we went through m'dad's things, we found this with your name on it. I think he was meaning to give it to you, so here it is."

Maude thrust forward a parcel wrapped in brown paper. Reggie had awkwardly scrawled Amanda's name on it.

"Thank you, Maude."

After the maid had gone, Amanda settled herself on her bed and undid the wrapping. In her hands lay a small book bound in red leather. She tentatively opened it. Inside the flap, a fine, sloping hand had written "Sylvie Emerson." Dates were placed at the top of each page, followed by entries in that same neat hand.

Sylvie's diary! What with everything going on, Amanda had completely forgotten about Reggie's promise to give it to her.

"Dear Reggie!" she whispered. "You were as good as your word."

Filled with curiosity, Amanda carefully turned over the book's brittle, musty pages. She halted at a passage that caught her eye. An exuberant Sylvie had drawn hearts and playful cupids in the margins around the entry.

February 5, 1846.
Something wonderful happened today! I was tending the conservatory—I do so love the indoor greenery, the ferns, miniature lemon trees, and jasmine! I was fashioning the loveliest wreath with interlacing sprays and tendrils, when who should walk in, but Thomas Gray! He handed me the prettiest little nosegay he'd picked on the way over, and believe me, I thought his wildflowers more beautiful than all our hothouse roses!

Without a word, he kissed me on the lips. Never have I felt such rapture! Oh, of course, he has kissed me on the hand and taken my arm, as you well know, diary. But he has never kissed me so tenderly and fully before. Then he proposed! On bended knee. I am giddy! Of course, I said yes at once.

Mama, Papa, and Helene are so happy, even relieved, I think. Now their minds are at rest that I won't throw myself at a nobody. They've been in mortal fear I would fall in love with someone I "shouldn't know."

I pressed the flowers of Thomas's nosegay. I'm going to save them in my jeweled box and treasure them always.

Amanda's head jerked up. Incredible! Sylvie and Thomas Gray had been engaged! That somewhat explained his presence at Pinewood House. It wasn't so odd for him to come back and visit the family now. But why did the mere mention of his name always send Helene into a dither? And how had he known of Helene's relationship with Amanda's father? Eagerly, Amanda read on.

February 15, 1846

Our engagement is to last a year—too long!—but my parents insist on all the proprieties. Now all they talk of is my settlement. I dream of the life to come. Now Thomas and I will be able to get away from our chaperones and stroll alone!

Helene and I have been planning my trousseau. I'll be needing day dresses—at least two dozen—evening gowns, blouses.

Gilded Splendor

Mama said I might have all new undergarments hand-made by the nuns at the convent!

We found a picture of the loveliest traveling suit of mauve silk with a matching coat lined in the same fabric! I simply must have one like it.

Helene did the funniest thing. We were poring over the pictures, and she burst into tears. I asked her why, and she said she was so happy for me, and she wished me and Thomas all the joy possible in life! Silly girl! Of course we'll be happy!

I couldn't help but love Helene, seeing her foolish tears. I assured her that soon she too would find a wonderful man to love, at which she cried all the more!

A small smile turned up the corners of Amanda's mouth. So Helene had harbored a soft spot in her heart for the young lovers! She hadn't always been so formidable and aloof! Amanda chuckled. Charmed and fascinated by Sylvie, she found herself caught up in the young girl's sweet, innocent life of fifty years before. The revealing picture of the two sisters, close and loving, warmed her. She was seized with a sudden, overpowering urge to look at their portrait. She hadn't seen it since that first day she had toured the house with Lady Swinton. Slipping the diary into her pocket, she hurried down to the great hall.

Standing before the portrait, Amanda was lost in admiration as she studied the large oil painting of "the beautiful Emerson girls." The girls' delicate faces gazed out serenely, their eyes almost alive. Sylvie's hair floated cloudlike past her shoulders. Amanda felt an odd kinship with the dead girl from the past. People at Pinewood House rarely mentioned Sylvie, but the diary had revealed a young girl in love, spirited and sparkling. What a shame she'd been all but forgotten.

Amanda turned to regard Helene's image, as youthful and radiant as her sister. Now she was an old woman, inflexible and adamant that Patrick must never marry. Amanda tried to picture her as a young girl in love. Surely when they were courting, she and the marquess must have experienced the same pangs of new love, the same fierce desire all young couples feel. Had Helene forgotten? Maybe that was the key—to gently remind Helene of her first love. If she could be made to recall her overpowering emotions from long ago, maybe she would soften, sympathize, and help Patrick be with his love now.

Amanda fervently hoped so. She didn't want to face another alternative—the disquieting suspicion that perhaps Helene's opposition had nothing to do with her forgetfulness about the nature of love, but rather with some sinister purpose. Why had she attempted to buy Amanda off with a gift of money—to get her away from Patrick? Amanda studied Helene in the portrait, fresh-faced, young, and innocent. What kind of woman had she become?

Amanda left the gallery, determined to form a convincing and pretty speech to win Helene over to her side. At the entrance to her room, she halted in surprise. The door hung slightly ajar. Gingerly, she pushed it open and gasped. She could only stand and stare at what moments before had been her orderly room. Now it was in shambles.

While she had been downstairs, someone had gone through, ransacking and overturning every bit of furniture. Her bed was stripped of blankets and sheets. Her clothes lay in a colorful tumble on the floor, disheveled and ripped. All the drawers had been turned out. Nothing had been spared.

A quick, disturbing thought made her stomach quiver. Half in anticipation, half in dread, she tiptoed through the debris to peer into her top dresser drawer where it lay on the floor. It was empty. Sylvie's jeweled box was gone.

With a sharp cry, Amanda flew down the hall like a whirlwind, seeking Patrick, Helene, anyone. She tore through the empty house. The walls of the mansion rang with silence.

The butler glided silently from the pantry, and she yanked at his sleeve. "Where is everyone?"

He gaped at the panic in her voice. "I believe Lady Swinton has gone out, miss. She said she would be meeting Mr. Gray for tea at the Newhaven Inn today."

"How long ago did she leave?"

"About two hours, miss. She should be returning soon, I imagine."

"And Mr. Patrick?"

"Out riding with the Countess of Craven."

"Well, if either Patrick or his grandmother come in, please tell them I wish to see them in the morning room."

"Yes, miss."

Amanda perched nervously on a chair, her shaking hands clasped tightly in her lap. She felt violated, unclean, as though her body had been physically attacked. An unseen presence had invaded her room, disturbed her privacy, gone through her things. But what could she do? As long as her assailant hid, an unknown shadow, obscure, indistinct, she remained powerless. She shuddered at her sense of naked helplessness, loathing her vulnerability.

The moments ticked by, and slowly she calmed, her shock yielding to cold fury. It was abominable! How dare someone enter her room and paw through her private possessions? They had stolen Sylvie's box and the white rose Patrick had given her! She seethed with righteous indignation. They wouldn't get away with it!

After what seemed like hours, Helene finally entered the library, preoccupied and flustered, her eyes red-rimmed as though she'd been crying. Amanda sprang from her chair.

"Lady Swinton!"

Gilded Splendor

"Why, whatever is the matter, child?"

"Someone has destroyed my room! They've stolen Sylvie's box!"

"What do you mean?" Helene made a visible effort to train her thoughts on the agitated girl before her.

"Come see for yourself."

The two women hurried up the stairs and stood at the threshold of Amanda's room, staring in dismay at the mess.

"Gracious!" exclaimed Helene. "Who could have done this?"

"I don't know. I was down in the hall looking at the portraits. When I came back up, I found my room had been turned inside out."

"This is very serious. Patrick will know what to do. Don't go back into the room until he sees it."

"What the hell—?"

Inspecting the chaos, Patrick ran his hands through his hair in disbelief. His gaze fell on a soft, pale nightgown, ripped into jagged shreds and carelessly tossed on the floor. Amanda! Hot fury rose in his chest, almost choking him. He swore under his breath. "Was she hurt?"

"No, Amanda's fine. But she says a quite valuable box is missing. What shall we do, Patrick?"

"Who was in the house at the time?"

"Why, all the servants, of course. I was out myself. I had gone to the inn to have tea with Mr. Gray."

"Why the inn? Why not have him here?"

"We just wanted peace and quiet, and privacy, to talk over old times. Surely there can be nothing wrong with that!"

"How long were you with him?"

"For the entire time! Of course, when I left the inn, he remained there. Patrick, surely you don't think—"

"He's a stranger here, Gram. I'd be inclined to blame him before one of our own servants."

"Oh, it isn't possible, is it?"

"With a fast horse, he could have ridden ahead and beat you home, with plenty of time to get into the house."

"Why would he do it?"

"Maybe he was looking for something, and Amanda's room was the first one he came upon."

Agitated fear clouded his grandmother's face. Patrick swallowed, clamping down on his anger. He had to remain cool. It wouldn't do to further frighten her. He hugged Helene to his chest and planted a light kiss on her forehead.

"Oh, Patrick, what's happening? So many deaths, and now this! I don't think I can take much more! And if you think Thomas Gray might be responsible—"

"Now calm down. I'll take care of everything. It'll be all right." He gave her a reassuring grin. "We seem to be having a run of bad luck lately, don't we?" He rubbed her arm soothingly until he sensed her calming down. "I'm going to find

Gilded Splendor

Amanda and ask her some questions about what happened here today."

"Oh, dear!"

"Let's get you some tea." Patrick saw his grandmother to her room and called a servant. Finally tearing himself away, he barged impatiently through the house. *Where the hell is Amanda? If she's been harmed in any way...*

He barreled into the library and drew up abruptly. Amanda sat, small and vulnerable as a child, dwarfed by the size of her large wing-backed chair. But when she looked up at him, her blue eyes blazed with anger. His heart lurched. She had courage, he'd give her that. He strode quickly across the room and enfolded her in his arms.

"Are you all right? God, if anyone had harmed you..."

"I'm all right. I went up to my room and the damage had been done. I saw no one."

He held her back at arm's length, anxiously scanning her figure, reassuring himself she was safe. She smiled tremulously.

"I'm all right, I tell you. But, Patrick, whoever went through my room took a jeweled box my father gave me. It was the only thing of value I possessed. I feel terrible about its loss!" Her voice quavered with outrage.

"We'll find your box, dear. Don't worry." He released her and went over to pour them each a brandy. "Would you like one? You've had quite a shock."

"Yes, please, maybe a small brandy."

He brought the glasses over and pulled her down close beside him on the sofa. "You say your box was valuable?"

"Yes. It was jeweled and very old. It can't be replaced." She became reflective. "Patrick, do you know, it's the strangest thing—I had never seen the box before my father gave it to me. I had no idea he had it. It was obviously of value, and there were many times he could have sold it when we badly needed the money. But the strangest part is that when I came here, your grandmother said the box had once belonged to Sylvie."

"Sylvie? You mean Grandmother's sister Sylvie? Of the portrait?" Patrick frowned in puzzlement. "Strange."

"Yes. I can't understand how my father came to have the box, or why anyone would want to steal it. Who even knew of its existence, for heaven's sake? Or that I kept it in my room?"

Amanda's face clouded over as if something clicked in her mind. She glanced uneasily at him. "No one knew, except—"

"Yes?"

"Well, your grandmother knew. But, of course, I'm not suggesting—"

Warnings whispered inside his head. Who did steal Sylvie's box? Was the house safe? Had someone evil intruded to menace its inhabitants? Or did the evil spring from someone already inside?

Seeming to sense his worries, Amanda's face reflected her fear. God, she was beautiful, sitting beside him, mere inches away—so vulnerable. His thoughts leapt to the image of her lying naked beneath him on the floor of Reggie's cottage. Her innocent temptation, his abject surrender to lust. Christ.

And after their frantic coupling, he'd thought to just walk away from her. That was a laugh. His senses reeled at the nearness of her body, the soft dewy skin of her cheek. He wanted to possess her again—desired her more than he had before taking her, if that were possible.

And other dangers made her vulnerable. Unseen, lurking dangers. Who had been in her room? He was struck with a fierce possessiveness. He would let no one harm her. No one!

"Please don't worry," he said, making his voice compelling. "You're safe here. I'll take care of you."

Her blue eyes met his gaze. Her cheeks colored, and he knew she also remembered their lovemaking in the cottage. The same hot passion coursing through him also burned in her loins. The familiar rush of heated attraction flared between them like a palpable, living thing. Why was it that despite all the sorrow, the danger—whatever they might be facing—the flame of desire always burned between them, always threatened to leap out of control?

"Will you be all right?" he asked, his voice husky. "I need to question the servants."

She cleared her throat and lowered her gaze. "Yes, go on. I'll help Maude straighten my room."

A red-gold tendril of her hair curled softly by her ear. In a proprietary fashion, he reached out, intending to finger its shiny softness. *Don't touch her.* Abruptly, he pulled his hand away. Willing himself to leave her side, he rose and quit the room.

During the night, harsh wind blew up a thunderstorm. Rain battered a merciless, steady tattoo against the windows. Patrick turned restlessly in his bed, sleep eluding him. His churning thoughts matched the raging squall outside. He'd done all he could for the moment, hadn't he? But it wasn't enough. He'd questioned everyone at Pinewood, and had turned up nothing.

He punched his pillow in frustration. Someone was killing people in the neighborhood, and now evil had crept into his own house, had touched Amanda personally. He was haunted by the sight of her nightgown ripped to shreds. What if she'd returned to her room a moment earlier and caught the intruder? He imagined her lying unconscious alongside her nightgown, bloody and injured among the remnants of her possessions. The danger was getting too close!

He kicked away the blankets and left his bed to pace the carpet. Who stole the box? Someone who merely stumbled across it in a haphazard search for valuables? Or someone who knew of its existence and specifically planned to steal it?

He racked his brain, but kept returning to the same idea. No one knew Amanda had the box except Gram! It was only a short leap of logic to imagine Gram discussing old times with her family friend, Thomas Gray. In reminiscing, Sylvie's name might be brought up, and Gram might mention Sylvie's expensive, jeweled box. Gray probably needed money and returned to the house to steal the box. Patrick made a mental note to ask Gram if she had indeed mentioned the box to Gray.

It all seemed to make sense, but Patrick couldn't help feeling that a piece of the puzzle was missing.

Pensively, he stared out the window into the dark. Amanda. She might be uneasy alone tonight, in the room a stranger had violated. She might be frightened by the storm, knowing that someone unfamiliar had been in her bedroom, touching her things.

Patrick shook his head. He shouldn't go to her. He knew what would happen if he went to her bedroom tonight. He mustn't let it happen. It was up to him, as a gentleman, to control his obsession, to protect her. *Stay away!* he intoned over and over to himself. But in his next breath, he rationalized, *She's alone. She might need me.*

His chest heaved as he fought his conflicting emotions. *Does she really need me, or is it just my own weakness, my insane, overpowering need for her?*

He found himself moving down the unlighted hallway, drawn toward the woman alone in the dark. It was late, the blackness illuminated briefly by intermittent flashes of lightning, but he made his way to her room quickly and unerringly. Pausing outside her door, his hand shook on the knob. Go away and leave her alone, he thought. Don't go near her. Not like this.

Yet he turned the handle and went in. One candle burned as a night-light on a side table. His eyes eagerly scanned the shadowy room, seeking her, then riveted on the bed. Her form was outlined beguilingly beneath white sheets. In the sudden flash from a jagged streak of lightning, she bolted upright and stared at him, her eyes wide, questioning, haunted.

He strode silently across the room and pulled her up into his arms. The sheets slid away and she clung to him, kneeling on the bed, folding his shoulders into a loving embrace. He filled his hands with her tumbled hair, a riot of loose curls. Her familiar, heady scent bewitched his senses. Her body, in its thin nightgown, trembled against him.

"I'll keep you safe, love," he whispered fiercely. But even as he said it, in the back of his mind he realized she was anything but safe with him. "I can't stand to be without you, to have anyone else near you...."

Amanda gloried in his urgent voice, murmuring tender words against her temples, her eyelids, her cheeks. He trailed a hot path across her skin, imprinting a burning sensation with every touch. Her pulse hammered as he pressed his lips to the hollow at the base of her throat. She lowered her head slowly, wanting to feel that warm mouth against hers.

Slowly, seductively, he raised his head. The room lit up for a brief second as a jagged bolt of lightning zigzagged across the sky. A liquid shiver of desire ran through her, pooling in her lower body.

"You're not afraid of me, are you?" he asked.

"No," she whispered. "Never of you. I'm glad you're here."

"I couldn't stay away."

He'd come to her room, her arms, preferring her to the Countess of Craven. Perhaps he hadn't been put off by her inexperience, her lack of lovemaking skill. He didn't seem bored with her—quite the contrary. His eyes and mouth and hands throbbed with a passionate message meant only for her. Amanda's heart leapt with joy.

He inclined his head so slowly she thought she would die before his mouth met hers. After a moment, his kiss deepened, intimately demanding all her secrets, until she moaned softly. The insistent probing of his tongue aroused a hot, sweet ache in her. She remembered the heat of their first lovemaking. It had not been assuaged, merely banked, and now burst into flame again. Sweet heaven, she wanted to repeat the unutterable delight of being joined with him.

Patrick drew her nightgown over her head and tossed it aside. Her white body glowed in the dim candlelight, a sculpture of erotic womanhood kneeling on the bed before him. Greedily, he took in her lush breasts, the dark triangle of hair between her thighs, but she didn't flinch or withdraw from his scrutiny. She held still, poised and open, breasts jutting, completely female, offering again the gift of her woman's body for his pleasure. All for his pleasure. He marveled at the miracle of the giving.

He swallowed, forcing himself to move slowly. He could give, too, as well as take. This time, he would slow everything down, take his time, concentrate on her pleasure, teach her what loving fully could mean. He would anticipate her every desire, do everything she'd ever have dreamed, without knowing she'd dreamed of it.

He cupped his hands around her breasts, lifted their heavy fullness, and brought his thumbs around to massage the nipples. He knew they would be exquisitely sensitive. She gasped, and they both looked down at his moving hands. His thumbs worked lovingly until her nipples rose to hard peaks under his ministrations. She closed her eyes and swayed slightly, a soft moan escaping her parted lips.

Eliciting her response was a powerful aphrodisiac. *Slowly, slowly,* he commanded himself, his muscles quivering from self-imposed restraint.

Gilded Splendor

He laid her back on the bed and hovered over her. Her tumbled hair spread across the sheet, riotous curls framing the pale oval of her face. Moving down, he captured one taut nipple in his mouth and teased it, laving it with his tongue, wetting it, moving it from side to side.

He couldn't resist rubbing his aroused body rhythmically against her leg. Unknowingly, she imitated him, undulating her hips, and he skimmed his hand gently down her body. He fingered her soft triangle of hair with light, gentle touches. Her thighs opened, and he gently slid his fingers into her moist warmth.

Convulsively, she clutched his hair, pulling his head back, but he took no notice. Closing his eyes, he pulled her nipple into his mouth and sucked.

"Patrick..." Her head thrashed back and forth, her hands clutched the sheets. He removed his hand, and her hips rose off the bed, following his hand, trying to regain his touch.

He knew her intense need, her urgent longing. How well he knew it! Incoherent sounds escaped her lips. Knowing he could assuage her longing, he couldn't stand the binding constriction of his trousers a moment longer. He tore them open then. He rose and quickly peeled out of his clothes. He returned to her open arms.

"Patrick," she whispered, "I want—" She dug her fingers into his muscled shoulders. "I don't know what I want."

He rose above her and pressed himself between her legs.

"This. You want this," he hissed.

"Yes . . . yes . . ."

He drove himself into her instant heat. She clasped him tightly, so sweetly, he thought he would die. He gasped with the intensity of his pleasure.

She wrapped her legs around him and held on, moving her hips against him, meeting every thrust. The delicious, wet, pulling and tugging sensations along the length of his shaft were exquisite.

She cried out his name. Knowing she was near fulfillment, he never let up for an instant, suckling her breast, thrusting, pulling, until the nipple pointed unbelievably fuller, stiffened rock-hard in his mouth. His body felt the change in her as she shuddered in spasms of relief.

He lost himself then, his resolve, his mind, his heart. He exploded inside her, his head down, dying in ecstasy, drawing out the unbelievable pleasure for as long as he could.

Finally, he dropped down exhausted against her. Their breathing gradually slowed, and the cool night air chilled them. Gently, he pulled out of her body and drew the covers over them.

He caressed her shoulder. It was bad enough that he'd come to her room and taken her again, but he also knew he should have pulled out in time. He'd gone on, recklessly, carelessly, as if it somehow hadn't mattered.

Gilded Splendor

He sighed. He couldn't think right now. His emotions and his body lay shattered by love, and God, the shattering had been good. He could only bask in the deep satisfaction, the relieving cessation of hunger, the blessed love he felt for Amanda, held tightly in his arms.

He kissed the top of her head, and she placed her hand trustingly on his chest, winding her fingers through his hair. The wind outside clicked tree branches against the window like tapping fingers. He turned his head lazily toward the sound and narrowed his eyes.

"What the—?"

Tension slammed into his muscles. Through the dark, he detected the faint outline of a person's head, peering into the window from outside. A flash of lightning zigzagged wildly. Patrick jerked upright in bed.

"What is it?" asked Amanda.

"Someone is watching us."

Chapter Fourteen

Cold. The room was abysmally cold. Amanda shivered in Patrick's absence. He'd quickly sprung from the bed and hurriedly jerked on his clothes. With a quick "Stay here!" he'd hurtled into the night. There had been no time to protest.

Fearfully, she peered at the window, black with dark and storm. The night air cooled her passion-damp skin, and she could have wept at his abrupt leave-taking. Empty and bereft, she ached. In Patrick's arms, she'd found a natural, warm haven. Now without him, she became aware of her nakedness, the chill of the night air. She pulled the covers to her chin, listening to the steady batter of the rainfall on the window, desperately wishing for his return.

She twisted a strand of hair nervously around her finger, her brain swirling. She had let him make love to her again. The first time, in Reggie's cottage after the funeral, in the heat of the moment, shared pain had drawn them together, cataclysmically, inevitably. That had been bad enough, but perhaps understandable.

What was not understandable was wantonly welcoming him into her room and her bed tonight. She'd allowed him to take lustful liberties again—wanted him to—shamelessly abandoning her virtue for the simple pleasure of loving him. And she wanted him again. Now. In her bed, turning to her, taking her...

She closed her eyes, relishing the memory of their shared delight. The thought of him, his masculine body, and what he'd done to pleasure her started an enjoyable sensation tingling between her legs.

What had made her such a wanton creature? She'd gone from being an innocent, inexperienced virgin to a sensual woman who had offered to become Patrick's mistress. What had caused the change in her?

Looking into her heart, she realized it was her love for Patrick. He'd been her undoing. He had tapped a wellspring of emotion within her, elicited responses that shocked her with their depth and passion. He'd unlocked a surprisingly sensual nature in her by touching her heart as well as her body. She knew what it meant to love and be well-loved, and she was grateful to him for that.

Oh, why didn't he come back? She drew on her nightgown and crept to the window. Her anxious gaze scanned the night's blackness for some sign of her lover, but pouring rain enveloped the grounds, distorted and hid indistinct shapes in the murky gloom. Standing at the window, she shivered and stared into the darkness.

It was some time before he returned, soaked to the skin and shivering with cold from his foray into the storm.

"Oh, Patrick!" she cried, alarmed at his condition.

"C–couldn't find anyone," he said, shuddering. "Know I s–saw a f–face in the window."

"You're chilled to the bone. Get back in bed before you catch your death."

His trembling fingers fumbled with buttons. Amanda pushed his icy hands aside and pulled off his wet clothes. Then she turned back the covers. Not needing much encouragement, he sank into bed. His body was racked with shivers under the blankets. Amanda climbed in and lay beside him, nestling close, warming his chilled body with her own. He wrapped his arms around her and snuggled against her, one leg draped over hers.

"You're all nice and cozy," he whispered. She hugged him closer. Gradually he warmed, and his quivering muscles relaxed. He fell into an exhausted sleep.

Gilded Splendor

Amanda held him through the night, occasionally caressing his cheek, silently watching over him. Half-awake, on the verge of sleep herself, shadowy pictures swam unbidden through her mind. Images of long, silent vigils, watching over her sick parents through the night. *But this is different*, she thought hazily. *Patrick's not sick . . . he's not sick. . . .*

Patrick's arms, still wound around her, shook violently, startling Amanda awake. Gray early morning light faintly illuminated the bedroom. The rain had ceased, but a foggy mist blurred the view outside the window.

She studied him, sleeping fitfully beside her, and a worried frown drew her brows together. During the night hours, worrisome changes had crept over him. His face was bathed in a deathly gray pallor. A light sheen of sweat glistened on his handsome features. His forehead and cheeks were hot beneath her fingers.

At her light touch, he stirred restlessly. "Mandy?" he murmured without opening his eyes.

Alarmed, she disengaged herself from his arms and sat up to get a better look at him. She jostled him, and he opened his eyes. They stared dark and hollow from his pale face.

"Are you feeling all right?" she asked softly.

"Just cold, that's all." His shaky hand cupped her breast. "Warm me up, like you did last night." He exerted an effort to put his arms around her and pull her down beside him, but Amanda resisted.

"It's morning now, and I'm worried about you. I'm going to get your grandmother."

"No, don't do that!" He jerked upright in bed and raked his hands through his tousled hair. "I'm all right. I'd better get back to my own room before people are about. Just one kiss?" He managed a lopsided grin.

"You don't look at all well. You're burning up. I don't think it could have been good for you to go out in the rain last night."

"Out in the rain?" He frowned and rubbed the dark stubble of beard on his jaw. "Oh, yes. Prowler. Couldn't find him though. I'll go out again today. Might find footprints below the window."

"That can come later. First we're going to get you back into your own bed."

She helped him stand on wobbly legs, and together they maneuvered his clothes onto his body. He shivered at the touch of the cool, still-damp garments on his hot skin. Draping one arm over her shoulder, he leaned his weight heavily against her.

"Guess I am a bit shaky. Glad you're here, darling."

Together they made their way down the empty hall. Silence enveloped the mansion. Once in Patrick's room, he removed his pants and shirt with trembling fingers. Amanda turned down the covers on his enormous four-poster bed, and he sank into it with a grateful sigh.

"I think I will sleep just a bit more." He tiredly closed his eyes.

When she was assured he was going to stay put, Amanda expelled a long breath and gazed around his bedroom. Masculine and well-ordered in rich hues of burgundy and hunter green, it was a beautiful room.

She went to his leather-topped desk and ran her fingers over the expensive brass appointments. An ornate silver frame propped on the desk caught her eye. Her own likeness gazed at her from the frame. The drawing Granville had done when she'd first come to Pinewood House. So Patrick had used it as a decoration for his room, as he'd said he would. She smiled over her shoulder at his sleeping figure, touched that he'd given her picture such a prominent place on his desk.

She returned to the bed. An unnatural flush mottled his cheeks beneath the gray pallor. She touched his forehead. He was burning with fever. Misgivings turned to fear as she gazed down at him. A nameless dread lodged in the pit of her stomach. What was wrong with him? He needed help.

Quickly leaving his room, she stepped back toward her own. The servants were stirring below, and she saw a maid enter Helene's door with a tea tray. Amanda hurriedly dressed, then went to Helene's room and knocked softly. "Lady Swinton."

"Yes? Come in." Helene, propped against her bed pillows, sipped a cup of tea. "Why, good morning!" Helene looked surprised. "What brings you here so early?"

"I've just come from Patrick's room. I—I wanted to check on him."

Helene's right eyebrow lifted. "Check on him?"

"I'm worried. He went out in the rain last night. He thought he saw a prowler. Now he's burning with fever."

"Oh, dear. Not more trouble. What could he have been thinking of to go out in the storm?" Helene got out of bed and drew on her wrapper. "Well, let's go and have a look at him. Dear, dear."

The two women hurried down the hall to Patrick's room and bent anxiously over his sleeping form. Restlessly kicking at the blankets, he threw one long, narrow foot out into the cool air, but he didn't wake up. After a few moments, Helene silently motioned for Amanda to follow her out. In the hall, Helene turned. "I think this looks serious enough to call in Dr. Sterling. Thank you for alerting me, Amanda."

Helene pressed her hand to her lips and went down the hall to send a messenger for the doctor.

Amanda spent the morning nearly sick herself with apprehension and worry, beside herself with fright and remorse. "I should have sent him away from my room at once," she told herself over and over. "Then he wouldn't have been

Gilded Splendor

there to see that cursed face in the window— if there even was a face! He wouldn't have gone out in the rain. It's my fault!"

She took up a silent station in the foyer and watched apprehensively as servants bustled to and fro, carrying towels and warm water. Dr. Sterling arrived at the house and remained in Patrick's room for nearly an hour before hurrying downstairs, a grim look on his face.

Behind closed library doors, he conferred with Lady Swinton. They left Amanda alone outside, twisting a handkerchief into knots, her lips pressed nervously together. At length, the doctor left the library and, looking neither right nor left, strode across the hall. He took no notice of Amanda as he rushed purposefully from the house.

When Helene failed to appear after a few moments, Amanda crept to the library door and knocked softly before going in. Helene slumped dejectedly in her chair, her head drooping listlessly into her hand, like a fragile flower at the end of the long stem of her neck.

"Helene, can you tell me how Patrick is? I've been very worried."

"Of course." Helene beckoned Amanda to sit beside her and took her hand. "My boy seems to have taken a turn for the worse as the morning has worn on. He's delirious. I'm sorry to say, Dr. Sterling is very worried."

"Why? Dr. Sterling doesn't think this is the Winter illness, does he?"

"Now, now, he's not certain. It could be something minor." Helene patted her hand soothingly. "But I tell you, Amanda, Patrick's grandfather took cold like this long ago. It turned out to be the first signs of the disease. He was never the same after that. I'm very frightened for Patrick."

Icy fear, stark and vivid, gripped Amanda's heart. She tried to quell her rising panic. "Surely this is different, just a simple chill. He'll get over it, and go on as before."

"He's strong," Helene said in a weary voice. "He has that going for him. But that's what is so frightening about this disease. It attacks Winter men in their prime."

"No." Amanda shook her head in denial. "No."

"If only he hadn't gone out in that storm last night," Helene mused softly. "I don't know what possessed him."

Guilt clawed at Amanda, a suffocating sensation tightening her throat. *It's my fault! My fault!* she wanted to scream. *Let me take the blame! Let him be all right!*

But she remained silent, not wanting to further worry Helene with revelations about her indiscretion. She remained silent, throat aching, eyes wide.

The two women sat side by side, hands clasped, each staring straight ahead into her own nightmare.

* * *

Gilded Splendor

The Marquess of Swinton was ill. The house existed under a quiet hush the next two days, all possible noises subdued. Servants trod softly. Doors were shut quietly. Voices whispered.

Amanda waited in agony for news of Patrick, but there was no change. Guilt weighted her heavy heart. She couldn't eat or read or sleep. She prowled through the house, restless, not knowing what to do with herself, or where to lay her hands.

On the second morning, her progress stopped outside Patrick's door. She hadn't been in to see him. She stood outside in the silent hall, her hand frozen on the knob, desperately wanting to go in. But she wanted him as he'd been two days ago, not as he was now. She wanted him well and strong, laughing, making love to her, fighting her—anything but lying helpless in a darkened sickroom.

Panic swirled through her, threatened to overwhelm her. Tiny beads of sweat broke out on her upper lip. Her hand trembled on the knob. The dread of finding him suffering . . . the rumpled sheets . . . the pain . . . She couldn't face it. She had promised herself she would never go into another sickroom.

I can't. Not even for Patrick.

Her shaking hand fell from the knob, and Amanda backed away from the door, shaking her head in silent denial. She turned and bolted, her frenzied footsteps speeding on faster and faster, until she was nearly running down the hall. Away from Patrick's sickroom.

She fled to Sylvie's portrait. Surely the sweet girl of the diary would understand her dilemma.

As she passed beneath the paintings, Winter ancestors seemed to follow her with moving eyes, silently accusing her. *You did it,* they charged. *You welcomed Patrick into your room and your bed. You let him make love to you. It's your fault, and now you won't even go in to comfort him.*

Amanda reached the portrait of the Emerson sisters and caught her breath in a ragged sob. She gazed up hungrily, seeking forgiveness or solace in Sylvie's sweet face gazing placidly down at her. "You understand, don't you, Sylvie?" she whispered. "I let him make love to me because I love him, and I can't go in to see him because I love him."

The portrait said nothing. Sylvie gazed, enigmatic and silent, out through the lost years.

The late afternoon sun threw long shadows across the parquet floor, creating an eerie red glow. A long ray of light struck the portrait, illuminating the sisters' faces with a gentle radiance.

"They were beautiful, weren't they?" A male voice spoke in her ear.

Amanda jumped and whirled around. Thomas Gray, hands in his pockets, stood behind her, gazing lazily up at the portrait. Uneasily, Amanda wondered how long he'd been there.

Gilded Splendor

"Sorry if I startled you."

Wariness crept over Amanda. A tension about the man distressed her, puzzled her. She wanted to get away from him and return to the privacy of her room, but his dark, mysterious aura compelled her to stay. His hungry gaze lingered on the picture as if it entranced him.

"What was Sylvie like?" she asked hesitantly.

"Well, she was..." He stopped as though searching for the right word. "She was one of the sweetest, most innocent young women I've ever known. She had a pure heart."

"A pure heart?"

"She always saw the good in everybody, hardly realized the bad existed."

Amanda's eyes returned to the portrait as she mulled over his words. After a long silence, Gray turned to her. "I was engaged to Sylvie, you know."

"I know. It must have been very painful to lose her."

"Regrets are eternal, I'm afraid. Thoughts of what might have been sometimes overwhelm me."

"Regrets, yes. I understand regrets."

He looked down at her. "Do you have regrets?"

"Well, I wish... I'm sorry, I'm just very worried about Patrick."

"There was no change when I went in to see him a while ago."

"You went in to see him?"

"Yes, Lady Swinton allowed me to see him for

a moment. Haven't you been in?"

"No."

"Strange. Why haven't you? He's delirious, but all the time he raves about you, calling your name over and over."

"He calls for me?"

"He did when I was in the room. Why don't you go upstairs and see him now?"

Amanda's heart surged with fear, constricting her throat. Her hand rose involuntarily to her high collar, which had suddenly grown tight and binding. "No, I'd better not."

"Why not? He would want you to. Even if he doesn't recognize you, I think on some level he would know you're there."

"No, I—I just can't. Now if you'll excuse me . . ."

She turned her back to Gray and headed for the door. She sensed him following her and quickened her pace. Unbelievably, he pursued her, caught up with her at the door, and rudely grabbed her elbow. His voice, low and insinuating, whispered in her ear with an unwelcome tone of intimacy.

"If you don't see Patrick, and he doesn't recover, think of the regrets you'll have then. I can never recapture the moment when I should have gone to Sylvie long ago and told her things that should have been said. Then she was gone."

Amanda glanced into his lined face. Why was he prodding her? He was a stranger. He couldn't understand her dread of the sickroom.

Gilded Splendor

He couldn't know of the promise she'd made to herself. She turned away, shrugging off his hand. "No. Perhaps I'll see him later."

But Gray wouldn't leave her alone.

"Face what you must. Otherwise you'll be sorry the rest of your life! Are you a coward?"

Surging, frenzied anger swept over her. Heat flushed her face, and her denial came quick and hot. "How dare you! I hardly think you're in a position to judge me. You don't know me. I have very good reasons for not wanting to go to Patrick."

"What's the matter? Won't Lady Swinton let you in? She let the Countess of Craven see him." He persisted, goading her now.

Damn the man! He was like a tenacious little bulldog pulling and gnawing on a bone. She seethed with resentment. Why did he have to torment her? Why couldn't he just let her alone? What business was it of his?

But underneath, she knew he was right, and the realization made her even more furious. She had to face her fears and go to Patrick. Otherwise how would she live with herself? Her anger gave her the strength to respond to Gray's challenge.

"Of course Lady Swinton will let me in! Why shouldn't she? I'll go up and see him now."

Marshaling all the dignity she could muster, she spun on her heel and stalked from the room. Back ramrod straight, she rigidly took the stairs one by one. But when she arrived at Patrick's door, her courage failed and she paused, her hand hovering above the knob.

She closed her eyes and prayed for the strength to go in. When she opened them, she spotted Gray leaning casually against the wall at the end of the hallway, arms crossed lightly over his chest. He, in turn, observed her, a knowing smirk on his face. Drawing herself up, Amanda steadied herself and turned away from him, her face toward the door.

She couldn't go in.

Fear and anger knotted inside her. She was trapped, pulled in two, tormented by her own confusion. *Oh, God,* she thought, trembling, *I don't want to go in, don't want to see him ill, don't want to face this. Hasn't there been enough heartache? It isn't fair!*

Hot tears stung behind her eyelids. At the same time, blurred images of Patrick, gentle and loving, warm and laughing, swam through her tears. Her love for him tore her apart. *I want you, Patrick, I want you.*

Slowly, love conquered her fear. *He's the important one now,* she thought, lifting her chin. *He needs me!*

She pushed on the door. It opened a crack, and she brought her face close to peer into the gloom. She released the pent-up breath she'd been holding and forced herself to draw air into her painfully constricted chest. A rank, medicinal sickroom odor escaped the room, carried on the stifling, overheated air. The

Gilded Splendor

strange smell, recognizable, unforgettable, and frightening, assaulted her senses. She jerked her head back violently. Bile bubbled in her throat. Her stomach knotted with nausea. She bent forward at the waist, fighting her queasiness, willing herself not to be sick to her stomach there in the hall.

I can't go in! She shuddered. *I won't!*

She began to pull the door shut again, when she heard a low moan from the bedroom.

"Mandy . . ." came the agonized whisper.

She froze. It was his voice. Patrick of the laughing-sad green eyes, the virile body, the gentle touch, the loving heart. He needed her.

Almost against her will, she pushed the door open and walked in.

Chapter Fifteen

Amanda forced herself to breathe deeply, ignoring the acrid, medicinal smells that assailed her nostrils. The sound of her name on Patrick's lips, calling her, had melded all her courage and determination like a solid rock inside her. Her thoughts raced ahead, and she faced herself with courageous realization. *Nothing after this will ever seem so hard.*

The drapes had been drawn, and a gloomy atmosphere of semidarkness pervaded the room. The shadowy shape of the big four-poster bed loomed against the wall like a huge monster waving its arms. She realized with despair that the monster had Patrick tightly enclosed in its grasp.

Determined to see the thing through, she

pressed her lips together to stifle any escaping sound, imposing an iron control on herself. *Go toward the bed. Closer.* Reluctantly, she made her feet move across the carpet. *Where is he? Where is my dear?*

She inched closer until she reached the side of the bed. Patrick lay motionless, eyes closed, the sheets drawn up around his neck. His black hair lay plastered damply against his forehead, his mouth drawn down in an unconscious grimace of pain. He was changed, but still recognizable as the man she loved. She swayed slightly in the darkened room, and her heart cried out in agony.

Gingerly, she placed her hand on his head. He started at the slight touch. "Amanda?"

"Yes, I'm here."

"Is that you? I love you, Mandy. Where is she? Is that you?" He mumbled incoherently for a while, then lapsed back into troubled slumber.

Amanda pulled a chair to the head of the bed, clasped his hand in hers, and took up a silent vigil. He was so like her father on his sickbed. The old familiar scene from her memories came to life again. *Here I am,* she thought in desperation, *hovering by, watching helplessly, waiting for some change that never comes. There's no end to the suffering, is there?*

Deep within her, rage rose, desperate and terrible in its intensity. She couldn't bear it.

"No!" she spat out the word. "I will not have this again!"

She gripped Patrick's hand with all her strength, determined to break through to him, determined he should hear.

"Listen to me, Patrick Winter, Marquess of Swinton! You will not die, do you hear me? You will not be sick. You'll get well, damn you. Get well!"

He didn't respond. He simply lay there, not stirring, his eyes closed, his mind in another world far away.

She slumped over him. It was all futile. Everyone was right—it was too late. Too late for him, for her, for a future together. His fate had overcome him, defeated him, and they were finished before they had begun. Amanda's tears, hot and turbulent, spilled over and splashed down on him. Burying her face against his side, she drowned in raw, primitive grief.

"Patrick," she moaned, "not you, too. Please not you, too."

A hand stroked her bowed head, caressed her hair with a gentle touch.

"What have we here?"

Patrick's familiar voice was gentle and soothing. She jerked up, riveting her gaze to his face, her wildly beating heart choking her. He smiled weakly.

"Don't cry, Mandy."

"Patrick," was all she could utter. "Patrick."

His fever broke that night. Helene joyfully declared it a miracle. Dr. Sterling examined him

Gilded Splendor

the next day and declared him out of immediate danger, but warned that he would need to be closely watched. The household drew a collective sigh of relief, and things slowly returned to normal.

On the next evening, Amanda dined with Helene and Diane in the familiar dining room, reassuringly observing the old routines. Now life could go on.

Lost in her thoughts, Amanda ate without speaking. She was deeply glad she'd entered Patrick's sickroom. He had woken up to see her face. Now he would always know she'd cared. It had been one of the hardest things she'd ever done, but she'd conquered her dread and gotten through it.

And Patrick had come through, too, thank God.

But when she thought about why she'd gone into the sickroom, Amanda harbored a lingering resentment toward Thomas Gray and his unwelcome goading. Let him try to intrude unbidden into her life again, prodding and pushing! She'd put him in his place! And she'd ask him about her father, while she was at it.

Across the table, Helene put a fork into her dessert and spoke. "What a relief that Patrick is rallying. My boy seems to be out of danger for the time being."

Bright candlelight flickered joyfully above the gleaming candlesticks, reflecting Amanda's mood. Tonight there were no shadows to conceal or frighten. "Yes, it's a great relief," she answered, blissfully happy.

"And yet," mused Diane with a frown, "Dr. Sterling says this could still be the first sign of something worse. He says . . . well, that Patrick might be an invalid from now on."

A prick of misgiving threatened to burst Amanda's bubble of happiness, but she tossed her head defiantly. She wasn't about to let Diane deflate her good spirits with gloomy predictions! "I don't believe that! We've seen that Patrick is strong enough to conquer illness. He'll never be an invalid."

"Time will tell," said Helene. "Whatever happens, Patrick will get the best of care. He'll want for nothing, and we'll see that he's made as comfortable as possible." She touched a linen napkin to the corner of her mouth, then continued. "However, he'll need help from his family now to fight this. He mustn't be disturbed or agitated by distractions of any kind. He must have complete rest and quiet to recover his strength. In fact, I'm thinking of taking him to Bournemouth for a while. A change of sea air and sunshine might do him good."

A pang of dismay clutched Amanda's heart. "Oh!"

"That is why I think, Amanda, it would be best for you to avail yourself of my gift and venture on to London now," Helene suggested. "We have enjoyed having you here, but now our full attention must be concentrated on Patrick.

I'm sure you understand. And there's really no reason for you to stay. Surely you want to proceed with your own life."

Helene didn't say it, but Amanda sensed the unspoken words. *We don't need you. Patrick doesn't need you. You would only be in the way.*

How eager Helene is for me to go, thought Amanda bitterly, *when at first she had been so insistent that I stay!* The topic of marriage had certainly changed Helene's attitude. But why?

"Are you sure I couldn't be of some help to Patrick? I would do whatever I could."

"No. He needs a doctor's care and complete rest, without distractions. No, it's better that you leave." In the older woman's face, Amanda read utter inflexibility. Helene had made up her mind.

"And the Countess of Craven?" asked Amanda.

"I've asked Diane to stay on," returned Helene. "She's practically family and a great comfort to me."

Diane's eyes gleamed malevolently, and she threw Amanda a smug, triumphant smile. Amanda lowered her gaze to her plate, her appetite vanishing. She concentrated on putting down her fork, carefully arranging it next to her plate on the tablecloth, desperately trying to order her thoughts.

"And what of Inspector Sweeney's request that I not leave Pinewood?" Amanda wondered how conveniently Helene would've handled the inspector.

"No need to worry, my dear. I'm sure I will be able to satisfy any questions the inspector intended for you."

Helene watched Amanda closely then said, "I'm sure you'll want to do whatever is best for Patrick, won't you?"

"Yes, of course."

"Well, then!" Helene rushed on as if the matter had been settled, and, of course, in her mind it had. "I'm quite satisfied that, with my monetary gift, you'll be able to build a good future for yourself. I will, of course, assist you in any way I can. If you should decide to seek a position, I'll help you find a place. You could become a suitable female companion in one of the best families. I'm sure you'll soon make friends. London is such a large, busy place. So much to do. And, if I remember, you said you might try going on the stage. . . ."

Helene chatted on, but Amanda, lost in her own thoughts, had ceased to listen. Yes, it might be best for Patrick if she left. She could see that. Her remaining at Pinewood House would be of no benefit to him now. Hadn't he told her to leave, for the express purpose of avoiding exactly the kind of encounter they'd shared the other night? She, too, had wanted to leave, but she'd stayed, and, against all her best inclinations, had made love with him again. It was her fault he lay sick.

She couldn't blame Helene for thinking only of him.

Gilded Splendor

In one ear, she heard Diane prattle about the low morals of London stage actresses. Her heart slowly broke. She swallowed and rose from the table. "If you'll excuse me, I think I'll go up now and begin gathering my things. I can leave in the morning."

"Fine, my dear," agreed Helene heartily. "A wise decision! I'll have the driver take you to the station where you can catch the morning train, and I'll arrange for the transfer of the money."

"Lady Swinton, thank you for all you've done. You've been so kind, letting me stay here at Pinewood House. But I cannot accept your gift. It's a wonderful gesture, and I'm grateful, but really—I'll be fine on my own."

"Amanda, you must take my gift! I insist. You will displease me immensely if you don't let me do this for you!" A note of desperation had crept into Helene's voice, and a trace of fear flickered in her eyes. "Think about it, Amanda. I'm sure you'll reconsider. This can make a huge difference to the rest of your life!"

Feeling pressured beyond endurance, Amanda said, "I must go up now. Good night." To avoid any more coercion from Helene, she hurried from the room.

At daybreak, Amanda wrapped Sylvie's diary in paper, wrote Patrick's name on it, and left it in a drawer for Maude to find. She'd read the entire diary and she felt its secrets belonged to Helene and the Winter family. She had no right to keep it. She was leaving, and the mysteries in the diary would no longer concern her.

Amanda tucked her few possessions into her satchel and left Pinewood House. She said goodbye to no one, taking the same path she had once walked up, not looking back.

Chapter Sixteen

Crisp autumn air heralded an end to summer. Amanda knelt in the garden and sniffed the damp earth's rich, fertile smell. She dug her hands into the black soil and smiled, remembering how Reggie had extolled the pleasures of working in the garden.

It is good, isn't it, Reggie?

Leaning forward on hands and knees, she turned over the dirt with a small trowel, in preparation for seeds to be planted the following spring. Someone else's hands would drop the small harbingers of life into the soil. She would be gone then, involved in a new life.

Finishing her task, she sat back on her heels and gazed solemnly at her parents' small cottage.

And it's good to be home, she thought.

After a few moments, she rose and went inside. She hung her cloak on a peg and turned her attention to her father's books, occupying a place of honor on the mantelpiece. Beside them stood the room's one decoration, her mother's inexpensive china vase. Amanda lightly ran her fingers over the cracked ornament and remembered how her small, childish hands had accidentaly dropped it. A loving smile touched her lips. Her mother hadn't scolded; instead she'd insisted people were more important than things.

Amanda returned the vase to the mantel and sat down in the rocking chair. The turbulent events of the past several months tumbled through her head as she rocked back and forth. She hadn't traveled directly to London from Pinewood House. Her abrupt departure from Patrick had left her heartsick. She hadn't wanted to face new adventures in a strange city. Not for a while, anyway. So she'd returned home to catch her breath in familiar surroundings, to find the peace that had eluded her. She'd hoped a return to a simpler, quieter life would help her find herself again, eradicate thoughts of Patrick—and the pain of leaving him—from her heart. She had to put it all into perspective and place him firmly behind her before she could take up a new life in the city.

Arriving on foot at the little cottage on a dusky evening, she'd retrieved the cottage key from its familiar place under an odd-shaped rock.

Gilded Splendor

The moment she'd stepped inside the dwelling, Amanda's gaze had flown up the stairs to her parents' loft bedroom. Strange, but it hadn't bothered her as much as she'd anticipated. Facing Patrick's sickroom had dispelled her old sense of despair. She'd faced her dread, and there were no more ghosts. *Thank you for that, Patrick,* she thought gratefully.

The house had stood empty except for a few dust-covered pieces of furniture—beds, a chest of drawers, a bench before the open hearth, wooden steps leading to the loft above. After Pinewood House, the bare wood furnishings had seemed simple, plain, and unadorned, but strangely comforting. There was no elaborate bric-a-brac in this house, no pretty decorations hiding strange secrets.

The welcoming homestead had brought Amanda a measure of peace the moment she'd entered it. The family's landlord had been unable to acquire new tenants during her absence and was only too happy to let her stay on at the cottage in return for keeping it up. She'd begun sewing for the village women, who could have done their own mending and sewing, but they remembered her kindness to her parents, and were glad to help her earn a little money to make ends meet.

Working in the garden, she'd stored up the last of the season's vegetables and fruits, and prepared the soil for winter. Light meals and early bedtimes brought the bloom back into her cheeks, and she had quickly settled into a comforting, predictable routine.

On long walks, relishing the peace of the countryside, she pondered Patrick and his effect on her life. She knew she would never return completely to the girl she'd been before she met him. She didn't want to. That girl had vanished forever. In her place had grown a woman who knew love and the pain of its hopelessness, but who had faced her fears and conquered them.

In the lengthening winter evenings, dreaming by the flickering firelight in the hearth, she sometimes missed the activity and society of Pinewood House, the gay weekend parties, the cozy, chatty teatimes, the stimulating conversation at elegant dinners.

Alone in the silence, she would find herself ruminating on Sylvie's diary and the sad secrets it held. She pondered who had stolen Sylvie's beautiful jeweled box, and the treasure inside—Patrick's white rose. She fondly recalled Maude and wondered if Harry had returned to take care of her and the baby.

She ruminated on what had led her to Pinewood House in the first place. What secrets had been written in her father's letter to Helene? Why had he never mentioned the Winters to his own family? He and her mother may have discussed them, but never in Amanda's presence.

Most of all, gazing into the dancing flames, her mind burned with memories of Patrick Winter. The assessing look in his green eyes probing her very soul, the tender caress of his voice, the touch of his hands on her body—the Marquess of Swinton haunted her. She hungered with the memory of his mouth on hers. Had he forgotten her yet? Gotten on with his own life? Was he well and happy, carousing with Algy, or weak and ill, with his grandmother hovering over him? Amanda fervently hoped the former. She would willingly have seen him in the arms of Diane Warfield, Countess of Craven, if it meant he was well and living his life with gusto.

But that was all in the past, she reminded herself with a firm shake of her head. Those people and that great house were never really meant to be part of her life. She'd been an interloper always, never fitting into their aristocratic milieu.

To relieve her thoughts in the interminable nights, she would take down one of her father's books and practice reading aloud, trying to instill dramatic intonations into her voice.

Slowly, over the months, memories of Pinewood House began to fade. She would forget about the graceful old mansion for hours at a time, only to dream of it at night. Always in her dreams, Patrick's face and form, handsome and virile, loomed before her. She sometimes dreamed she heard his voice, sensed his nearness, but she would always wake alone to find her pillow wet with tears.

* * *

Patrick and Algy shivered together, leaning against the pillars outside the Lyceum Theater in London. Sarah Bernhardt's latest play had ended, and now the two men watched the other theatergoers hurry on to late-night supper engagements. Patrick coughed hackingly into his fist and drew his evening cloak tighter against the cold night air.

"You all right?" asked Algy, his brow furrowed with concern.

"I'm fine." Patrick shrugged dismissively.

"This is the tenth play we've seen in as many nights. We'd better find Amanda soon, or I swear I'll never enter a theater again in my life. Culture is one thing, but this is too much!"

"Thanks for being here," said Patrick. "You're a true friend."

He anxiously trained his eyes on the richly dressed women who filed one by one through the theater doorway, scanning each for a pair of melting blue eyes. But none was the titian-haired beauty he sought.

"What else could I do?" asked Algy, his exasperation apparent. "When you got over your fever—which I'm still not convinced you're totally over, by the way, and don't frown at me like that!—we racked our brains trying to think where Amanda might be. Then you get this idea she wanted to be an actress. Against my protests, you're on the next train to London. What else could I do? I had to tag along and keep you from overdoing."

"Well, I appreciate your company."

Gilded Splendor

"I want to find Amanda as much as anyone, but we've spent all our days and nights haunting the stage doors of every theater in London. We've been everywhere, asked everyone, with no trace of her. Don't you think we'd better give up the search and go home? You're still not in the best of health, you know."

"I'm not giving up, Algy. I can't."

"Why the deuce not? You never had it so bad for any other woman. Why this one?"

"Because I love her."

"Love?" Algy guffawed. "Now that's something I never thought to hear you say. How the mighty are fallen! It's very gratifying to hear you're flesh and blood like the rest of us."

"The rest of us? When have you been genuinely in love, old sport?" challenged Patrick.

"Oh, I've had my moments, believe me!" Algy gleefully rubbed his hands together, then sobered. "But I'm still ready to go home. We've been away long enough. What's that old saying? East or west, home is best, don't y'know?"

Home? Patrick paused. Home! What had Amanda said about home? He racked his brain. What had she said? He searched hazy recollections, trying to remember their first conversation. Amanda had spoken of going on the stage, it was true, but in the same breath, she'd talked lovingly of her childhood home in the country. She'd said that whenever something was wrong, she rambled out in long walks in nature. Her home in nearby . . .

Patrick pushed away from the cold pillar he'd been leaning against. He gripped Algy's arm tightly through his overcoat. "Let's go!"

"Where?"

Patrick flashed a triumphant grin. "I know where she is."

The winter's first snowfall arrived silently during a cold night. Amanda woke to a world blanketed with white, a winter fairyland, each black twig and arched tree trunk traced with a dazzling snowy frosting. Sunlight sparkled brightly, gaily beckoning her to come out, luring her irresistibly from her warm bed. Without stopping to even prepare tea, she wrapped up in her mother's warm wool cloak and ventured out for a walk.

Tramping through the trees, she blew on her chafed hands to warm them. Was it snowing at Pinewood House? Was Patrick allowed outside to drink in the bracing air, or did he sit huddled in a blanket in an overheated room?

Despite the beautiful day, the thought burdened Amanda's already heavy heart. She squelched regrets about Patrick. There were other things to occupy her mind now. She'd discovered her pregnancy soon after returning home.

Here she was—expecting a child and unmarried. Just like Maude. Except she didn't even have the security of a home and job at a place like Pinewood House to sustain her and the baby.

Gilded Splendor

She was completely on her own.

She couldn't—wouldn't—tell Patrick of his impending fatherhood. The worry would only undermine his health. Besides, he might not want the child or her. Many aristocrats had illegitimate children running around, but it didn't mean they married the mothers. Besides, if the child was a boy, he might inherit the cursed family illness, and the last thing the Winters needed was another generation to carry on the horrible legacy.

There you had it. Nothing to be done. She had to go it alone.

She knew what that would mean. She and her illegitimate child would be poverty-stricken outcasts, but she would gladly take on the burden and love her child. She just prayed it would be a girl. She hated the thought of growing to be like Helene—protecting her own son from his impending illness, warning him off marriage and happiness.

Amanda tramped through the still morning, leaving footprints in the previously unmarred whiteness. The fresh, stringent air stung her nostrils and lungs, bracing her, wiping away the night's cobwebs from her brain. Sunlight dappled through the tree branches overhead. It was such a beautiful world! And her baby would be a girl!

She looked up at the clear blue sky and couldn't help but be buoyed. It was a glorious day! she thought. It would be sacrilege not to enjoy the beauty God bestowed on the world.

She couldn't postpone her life any longer, pining for what could never be. What had happened to all her plans for action, to discover the zest of living? Maybe she couldn't have Patrick, but there were things she could do and have! For instance, his child to love and cherish!

Amanda smiled. It seemed like ages since she'd felt the stirrings of happiness. For the first time since she'd discovered the fact of her pregnancy, her heart lightened. She could make her baby and herself as happy as possible. From now on, she'd think how best she could live the one life she'd ever have, how best she could help her child. The Winters be damned! She would begin her new life today. High time, too!

Full of purpose, she quickened her step and turned back toward the cottage. A friendly curl of smoke wound from the chimney, beckoning her.

At the picket fence, she noticed a smart black brougham parked up the street. Who was visiting in the village? She squinted, trying to make out the aristocratic crest on its door, but it was too far away.

She shrugged and kicked the snow off her boots at the threshold. A cloud of warmth enveloped her as she entered the door. Removing her bonnet and cloak with a shake, she scattered a swirl of wet snow through the air.

Gilded Splendor

She hesitated only a second, then turned purposefully toward the loft stairs, taking them two at a time, up to her parents' dark, musty sickroom.

"Amanda."

She imagined for a brief second she heard someone calling her name, but she shrugged off the eerie thought and ran to the window. Parting the curtains, she threw open the sash, letting strong drafts of fresh, cold air and sunlight pour into the room. Her laughter erupted in giddy exhilaration. Turning to the bed against the wall, she jerked off the quilted spread, sending dust particles flying to the ceiling. Plopping on the bed to catch her breath, she clutched the quilt to her.

"Mama, Papa . . ." She spoke the words aloud, wishing she could tell her parents she was going to be all right. She and her baby would be all right!

"Amanda." A deep voice sounded behind her, quiet, yet unmistakable.

Her heart lurched madly. "Patrick?" she whispered.

She spun around, the quilt dropping from her hands to the floor. The Marquess of Swinton stood at the head of the stairs, his tall, muscular body filling the entrance to the room. One booted leg rested casually on the top step, and in his hand he held a single white rose.

"I called at your door, but no one answered." His voice trailed off.

Their eyes met, and a shock of thrilled fear ran through her. It couldn't be! Why had he come here? Why now, when she'd just begun to get over him?

He stood like the lord of a castle, devilishly handsome, his powerful physique encased in a sweeping cloak of fine, expensive wool, his boldly handsome face smiling warmly across the room at her.

What was she to do? Love him again recklessly, without heed for herself, and she would be hopelessly lost for all time. The loneliness and confusion of the past months melded together painfully in her chest. Half in anticipation, half in dread, she clenched her fists at her sides and gathered her strength. *Please make him go away and leave me alone!*

She stared wordlessly at him across the room, her heart pounding in her chest. His green eyes, glowing with love, clung to her. He held out his hand, offering her the rose, but she remained silent, rooted to the bed.

Hesitancy registered in his eyes, replacing the hope, and his square jaw tensed visibly. She couldn't bear the look of faltering, tortured doubt that clouded those green eyes.

"Oh, Patrick," she whispered. In the engulfing silence, she didn't know whether to run into his arms or burst into tears. He made the decision for her. Striding across the small room, he raised her from the bed and clasped her in his arms, enfolding her tightly against him, crushing her against the scratchy wool of his cloak. She grasped handfuls of the rich, warm material in her fingers as he rained eager kisses on her eyelids, her cheeks, her chin.

Their lips met, and in a thirsty passion, she greedily drew in his breath, his lime scent, dear and familiar. The hot firmness of his mouth moving urgently on hers broke the spell of her loneliness. A moan welled up from deep within her.

Oh God, he's back! Patrick came to see me!

Happiness bloomed in her like a bouquet of spring flowers, like the sun thawing the icy shell she'd drawn around herself.

It was so good to be held in his arms again. So good to close her eyes while he took her lips and her soul, awakening delicious sexual aliveness in every fiber of her being. It was so easy to give in, she couldn't help but surrender. She had missed him so, been so alone without him.

A chill spiked through her heart. *You're not alone! It's not just you that you're giving, but another human being, too. Think of the baby. Hold back! You must!*

She stiffened slightly, and Patrick, seeming to sense the barely perceptible movement, loosened his embrace. He held her away at arm's length, but kept his hands on her elbows, as if reluctant to let her out of his grasp.

"I looked all over London for you, haunted all the theaters—the Savoy, the Strand, the St.

James. Saw a lot of actresses, but never a sign of my Mandy. Then suddenly, I knew where to find you."

She had to ask the question that was uppermost in her mind. "Are you all right? How is your health?"

His eyes twinkled in amusement. "Don't I look all right?"

She had to admit he looked remarkably fit. His eyes shone with a clear light, his voice carried as strong as ever, and his muscles bulged beneath his greatcoat, weakening her knees. "I'll prove it to you," he growled.

Before she could answer, his strong arms swept her off her feet. He spun round and round in the small room until they were both dizzy and laughing. They finally wound to a stop, and he set her down.

Serious once again, a sensuous light passed over his eyes. "I'll prove I'm fit as ever, if you'll let me, Amanda." He regarded her with a look of compelling desire. His sexual magnetism drew her like a smoldering fire threatening to burst into flame. Her body tingled with a deep, urgent longing that wouldn't be denied. She yearned to be held in his strong arms, to have her body filled with him, to forget everything in his ardent lovemaking.

He slowly brought his head down, and his lips played on hers, gently nibbling, tempting. "I love you, you know," he murmured softly between kisses. "I would have searched the ends of the earth for you. I can't let you go. I just can't."

His hands cupped her breasts, and he gently backed her against the edge of the bed. He put his arms around her and lowered her onto the soft covers, then straightened to gaze down at her.

Her fingers flew to undo the buttons down the front of her dress while she stared up at him. He seemed to need no further invitation, quickly opening his trousers, then covering her body with his own. His eager shaft, rock-hard, pushed against her thigh, insistent, throbbing, convincing her of his excitement, his desire for her.

He pushed aside the fabric of her dress, exposing her. Turgid and tender, her nipples ached. Yearning for his touch, she arched her back, thrusting toward him. He filled his hands with her breasts' tight, full roundness, rubbing his fingers against their throbbing peaks. She gasped. How had she done without him? His touch, his nearness, his love.

Eagerly, he pulled her dress up to her waist, hastily pushing the petticoats aside. He slid into her. Gasping, she tensed her thighs with the overwhelming pleasure.

"Patrick," she whispered. It had been so long. She felt a tear slide from the corner of each eye and trickle into the hair at her temples.

"Love me, Patrick. Love me."

He acquiesced. She clasped her stockinged legs tightly around him, and he thrust in and out of her, stroking her with his full length.

His eyes never leaving hers, his body worshiped her, renewing their love. They moved together in rhythm, in a dance as old as time.

Mindlessly, she gave herself up to the pleasure, climbing to an unbearable peak, until she exploded with a wordless cry. Exquisite sensations rippled through her, causing him to tense and fill her with liquid heat.

In her heart and soul, she succumbed to him. Once again, she surrendered herself without reservation to this man who demanded her totally.

She loved him, that was all. And that was everything!

After they'd recovered themselves, their senses, their clothes, Amanda let her gaze linger in one last, loving glance around her parents' room. Then, taking Patrick's hand, she led him down the stairs to the warm kitchen.

She drew up the bench and watched him sprawl his long legs contentedly toward the fire before she hurried off to prepare tea. He made himself at home in her little cottage. On her way past, he caught her hand, detaining her, grinning triumphantly up into her face.

"I like it here," he said. "I could be quite happy, living here with you."

"Are you really well, Patrick?"

"Yes, I'm really well. They haven't turned me into an invalid yet."

Amanda smiled and went on to the table, but she felt a stirring of misgiving at the word "invalid." Just hearing the hated expression made her uneasy.

As they sipped their tea, Patrick's large presence seemed to fill the small space. Amanda answered his questions one by one, filling him in with what she'd been doing, how she'd been living.

Finally he sucked in a deep breath. She readied herself for the question she'd known would come. His steady eyes bored into her expectantly. "Why?" he asked quietly. "Why did you leave Pinewood House? Why did you leave me?"

She fingered her teacup before raising her gaze to his. "I didn't want to. I told your grandmother I wanted to stay and help you. But she . . . well, you can imagine how worried she was for you. She—that is, we—decided it would be best if you had complete rest and quiet."

Anger flared in Patrick's eyes. He rose abruptly to stand before the fire. "She sent you away, then." It was a statement of fact, not a question, and Amanda couldn't deny it. "She had no right to."

"We all wanted what was best for you."

"You are what is best for me. Grandmother refused to see that. She has never put my wishes first. Never." He pushed his closed fist against the mantel. "All my life, I've done what seemed to be best for my grandmother, for the family. But since I met you, I've come to realize something I never wanted to admit to myself. Maybe

Gram has been wrong. Maybe she hasn't been doing what's best for me."

"What do you mean?"

"I mean that instead of running from my future and trying to elude it, I'd better stand and face it. I've got some hard decisions to make. Somehow I'm going to come to an understanding with Gram, and see if there's a better way to live with my problem." He turned to face her. "Will you help me, Amanda?"

"What can I do?"

"Return to Pinewood House with me. Stand by me while I sort things out."

Amanda studied her teacup, trying to gain time, her thoughts in turmoil. "How can I return to Pinewood House now?" she asked, thinking aloud. "I would only have to go through it all again—only give you up again later." The words filtered through her constricted throat.

Patrick watched her struggle and her hesitation, his eyes trained closely on her. "There's something else, isn't there?" he asked, suspicion lacing his voice.

Frightened, she stammered, "W–what do you mean?"

"There's something going on with you, Mandy. I sensed it the moment I came here. I knew it the moment we made love. Tell me, dear."

"There's nothing—"

In one swoop, he grabbed her arms and dragged her out of her chair to stand before him. His face close to hers, his compelling eyes riveted her to the spot. She couldn't tear her gaze from his intense face. Confound his sensitivity that always knew what she was thinking and feeling!

"Amanda." She tingled as he said her name.

His astute gaze quickly swept down her body, accurately gauging the size of her waist. "You're having my baby."

She waited for him to draw back in revulsion, tensed for his rejection, but to her amazement he threw back his head and laughed heartily. Then, glancing back down at the bewildered woman before him, he hugged her tight. "I'm overcome with joy, darling! Aren't you? Come on, be happy!"

Amanda struggled to hide her confusion, but felt like laughing with him, hysterically, out of control. Impatiently, she shrugged out of his arms.

"How can I be happy? I've no husband, and our baby might inherit your disease." She bit her lip the moment the words were out.

The smile died from Patrick's lips. He sobered, quickly and completely, at her words.

"It might be a girl, you know. But whatever, the child will need its father. And we can soon do something about your not having a husband! You've got to return to Pinewood where I can look after you. You've got to marry me!"

How long had she waited to hear those words from him? She didn't speak immediately, and he pulled out all the stops, shamelessly plying her with another argument. "There's another reason for you to come back with me. Maude needs you."

Maude! How she had missed her friend! "Oh! How is Maude?"

"She's fine. She had a beautiful baby boy. But Harry hasn't returned. I'm still searching for him. Maude could do with some sympathetic company. Wouldn't you like to see her and the baby, especially since we're going to have one of our own?"

"And your grandmother let Maude stay on at Pinewood House?"

"I persuaded her it would be best." Patrick said it simply, but the firm set of his jaw told Amanda of the fight he'd waged with his grandmother to let Maude stay against the dictates of society.

"What will your grandmother say if I return?"

"You let me worry about that."

Amanda buried her face against Patrick's chest, no longer able to control the tears of nervousness and relief that ran freely down her cheeks. He held her in a comforting embrace, until she raised her tear-streaked face to search the eyes of this man who had asked her to marry him.

Yes, she would return to Pinewood House with him and become his wife. Dreams of a career on the London stage vanished like mist. After all, they were going to have a child!

But her heart was heavy. How could she be

joyful? Now the specter of living with a sick husband and a sick child, nursing them, watching them slowly worsen and eventually die, reared its ugly head. Her old life, the one life she'd sworn never to face again, had come back to haunt her. The future hovered before her, shadowy and vague, fraught with terror and trouble.

The baby will be a girl, she decided, resolutely steadying herself. *It has to be! I won't even entertain the thought of a sick baby boy. The child will be a girl. That's the only way I can get through this with my sanity!*

Patrick placed a gentle, reverent hand on her stomach. "If you'll only love me and help me to get free of my family's constraints, I'll try to make you and the baby happy, darling," he pledged fervently.

She placed her hands over his. "You've already made me happier than I've ever been, and somehow sadder, too. I don't know why. It's strange, this power you have over me. You cause me emotions I never knew existed."

"And you make me feel as if I'm going to live forever!"

Helene drew back the curtains to peer anxiously out the window for what seemed the hundredth time that day. Patrick was expected back from London. Now it was nearly dark. What was keeping him?

After regaining his strength, he had adamantly refused to be dragged to Bournemouth for a rest and change of air. Instead, he and Algy had gone straight to London. He hadn't given her any reason for his going. She supposed the boys craved a mad whirl of high living.

Well, she couldn't blame them. Patrick—all of them—had been deeply frightened by his bout with illness. It had probably shaken him so severely that he was trying to obliterate the fear with his old familiar lifestyle of drinking, gambling, and who knew what else. During their unfortunate quarrel, he had told her he was going to do precisely that. But he had always come back before, and he always would, returning to her and Pinewood House for a respite from his hectic life.

So why had she paced anxiously all day, instead of being relieved? She counted off her blessings: Patrick had recovered and was well again, things were working out with Thomas Gray, Amanda had gone from the house. But Helene had to admit she'd been strangely jumpy all day, and even now she couldn't shake the feeling that something was terribly wrong.

She parted the curtains again. A coach! She made out the Pinewood brougham as it rolled up the drive in the twilight and pulled to a stop beneath her window.

She watched with satisfaction as Patrick leapt from the depths of the coach. *Good,* she thought to herself. *It's about time! I'll have supper served. He'll be hungry, no doubt, and—*

Her thoughts ground to an abrupt halt as

Gilded Splendor

Patrick turned back to hand down a female figure emerging from the carriage door. He bent to kiss her, long and tenderly.

"Of all the . . . ! Who is that?" Helene spoke aloud in her exasperation. "Not more visitors! I wanted Patrick all to myself for a while."

She shook her head crossly and peered down on the couple. They raised their faces to look up at the house, and the light from the front door played on their features. Helene's hand clutched the curtain, and she stared down, frozen in shocked dismay.

"Amanda!"

Chapter Seventeen

"A baby! I can't help but express my surprise—well, shock, really, at this distressing news!"

Amanda's heart sank at the look of cold disapproval on Helene's face. The two women lifted teacups to their lips, but there was little comforting coziness about this afternoon's tea party. The room vibrated with tension.

"I really hadn't expected your return to Pinewood House, and when Patrick told me of this...this child, naturally I thought of the future of my grandson and of the baby. It doesn't look good, Amanda."

An icy chill grew between the two women. Amanda's stomach knotted with tension, and she stiffened under Helene's withering glare.

"The child will be a girl, Lady Swinton. We won't worry about any uncertain future for her."

"You know very well you can't be sure the baby will be a girl!"

"I feel it will be. Besides, we'll be all right once Patrick and I are married." Amanda had tried to be consoling, but the moment the words were out, they were like a red flag waved before a charging bull. Helene clattered her cup abruptly into its saucer.

"Married! I told you before that Patrick should never marry! And if he did, it would be to a lady with a distinguished title, like Diane, the Countess of Craven. How could you do this? And after I offered you such a large gift to see you happily settled in London! Is this the way you repay my hospitality? By entrapping my grandson with a child he never wanted?"

Amanda bit her lip, forcing herself not to show the rage that welled up inside her. Upon returning to Pinewood House the previous day, she had hoped to be welcomed and accepted by Helene, but that hope had been quickly dashed. After a short conference with Patrick, the older woman had taken to her room with a sick headache. Amanda had promised herself she would be gracious to Helene, whatever the woman's reaction. But it was hard to stomach the righteous indignation of the marchioness.

She forced herself to speak calmly. "I'm sorry you feel that way, but I hardly entrapped Patrick. I didn't plan for this to happen."

Helene's eyebrows rose in disdain. "Didn't you?"

"Of course not! Did you ask Patrick if he planned it?"

"I know he did not! My boy would never deliberately take such a foolish, reckless course of action. No, he's the innocent dupe of a calculated plan on your part."

Amanda nearly choked. "What an unbelievable thing to say! I won't listen to any more of this." She stood abruptly, sending her chair falling backward. It crashed loudly against the parquet floor. "Excuse me. Otherwise I'll say things we'll both regret."

Before she reached the door, Helene's voice pleaded to her. "Now, Amanda, come back and sit down. I'm sorry about what I said. I'm just so distraught with all the changes and upheaval in our lives. This newest development is going to take a little getting used to."

Amanda turned and regarded Helene. The woman nervously righted the chair and extended her hand in a gesture of supplication. Amanda sighed. What was she to do? Helene's hostility was apparent, but they must try to get along for Patrick and the baby's sake. Slowly, she crossed the room and resumed her seat.

"Don't worry, dear," soothed Helene. "We'll find a way to solve this problem."

Gilded Splendor

Amanda warily eyed the Marchioness of Swinton, who calmly refilled her teacup. Amanda shuddered inwardly, hoping their lives would not deteriorate into a battle filled with bitterness. She set her mouth into a tight line.

If it comes to that, she thought grimly, *I'll lose a few skirmishes, but I won't lose the war!*

"Baby Reggie is the most beautiful big boy," cooed Amanda, hugging Maude's squirming, robust infant. "But he won't sit still!"

Enamored with the baby, she bounced him on her knee. He kicked out his bare feet and gurgled up at her.

"I think he likes you, miss," said Maude.

"Oh, I do hope so."

The two sat side by side on a bench in the White Garden, admiring Maude's chubby son. With his pink cheeks and rounded limbs, he was the picture of perfect, glowing health. But young as he was, he sported an impish, mischievous expression on his baby face. "He's going to be a handful," said Amanda, fervently hoping that Harry would return to help Maude raise his son.

"I'm so glad you've come back," said Maude. "When you left, I worried about you off in the world all alone."

"I thought about you, too, but I didn't worry."

"You didn't?"

"No, I knew Mr. Patrick would keep you safe

here at Pinewood, and I know he'll find Harry, too."

"I'm not sure I want him to anymore," pouted Maude.

"Why not? Whatever do you mean?"

"If Harry doesn't care enough to get in touch with me after all this time, he can go to blue blazes!" After this outburst, Maude convulsively covered her mouth with her hand, as though shocked at her own vehemence. "Excuse me, miss."

"Maude, I'm sure there must be some logical explanation, otherwise Harry would have been in touch. Patrick will find him and all will be explained."

"Do you really think so?" asked Maude grudgingly, kicking the grass with her toe.

"I know so."

"What have we here?" Patrick's tall, graceful form loped easily through the garden gate. Amanda smiled up at him. As always, his presence sent a delicious quiver through her.

"We have here the most beautiful little gentleman in the world," she said, holding up Baby Reggie for his approval.

"He's a good-looking lad indeed," said Patrick, bending to gently rub his finger on the baby's velvety cheek. He gazed at Amanda, a warm glow enveloping him. How beautiful she looked holding the child! What a special, magic moment it would be when he could witness her holding his own baby!

Maude coughed discreetly and reached to take the squirming Reggie from Amanda's arms. "I think I'll take him up to the kitchen now, miss. He must need his nappy changed."

A twig snapped loudly behind a tall hedge nearby. Maude jumped, causing Baby Reggie to look up at her wide-eyed. She glanced apprehensively toward the hedge and whispered, "Lor'!"

"What's the matter, Maude?" asked Patrick.

"The queerest feeling I've had lately, sir. As if someone's always watching me. Just now, I thought I saw a man's head dart back behind the bushes."

"The deuce!" said Patrick. "Another prowler? You two wait here! I'll get him!" He tore around the hedge at a run. A fearful thought brought Amanda to her feet, and she clutched Maude's arm.

"Last time Patrick went running off like that in pursuit of a prowler, he got frightfully sick."

"But it's not storming this time, miss," soothed Maude. "Mr. Patrick will be careful." The maid's worried countenance belied her words, and she hugged her baby close.

The women waited for what seemed an eternity, listening silently for a sound in the quiet afternoon. The only noise was the low drone of bees, buzzing as they circled their way through the flowers.

"Over here, ruffian!" Patrick's angry voice carried through the stillness. Scratches, scuffs, and grunts floated across the hedge.

"I weren't doin' no 'arm," a voice whined.

Two struggling figures appeared around the boxwood.

"Harry!" At Maude's loud exclamation, Baby Reggie bucked back in surprise. Amanda quickly grabbed the child before he fell to the ground.

Patrick dragged the lanky youth by the scruff of his neck. The young man was obviously reluctant to face the two women, but Patrick forcefully pushed him into their presence.

"What are you doing here?" demanded Maude in an injured tone. "Why didn't you tell me you were back? Where have you been all this time?"

Harry kept his eyes trained on the ground and dragged his toe through the loose soil. Patrick shoved him forward. "Answer her, man!"

Reluctantly, Harry raised his gaze to Maude's face. "I'm here to see you, luv."

She crossed her arms over her chest. "Spy on me, you mean."

"Wasn't sure you'd be want'n t' see me."

"After all this time with never a word, I'm not so sure m'self."

"I've sorely missed you, Maudie."

Her expression softened ever so slightly, and watchful Harry, taking note of it, plunged on.

"Besides, I wanted to see the young'un." Harry motioned toward the squirming infant in Amanda's arms. "Is that 'im, then?"

"Yes, that's Baby Reggie," said Maude.

"He's a good 'un, ain't he!" Harry's face

Gilded Splendor

broke into a wreath of smiles. He took a step toward Amanda, his arms outstretched toward the infant, but she backed away.

"It's all right, miss," said Maude. "He can hold Reggie, just for a minute."

Awkwardly, Harry took the baby from Amanda, sat down on the bench, and dandled him on his knee.

"He's the spitt'n image of his granddad, ain't he?" said Maude proudly, sitting down beside them.

"Well," said Harry in an injured tone, "I'd say he looks a little like me."

"Oh, of course! 'Course he does!"

Amanda lightly took Patrick's arm and motioned to him that they should discreetly leave the couple alone. They turned, but Patrick halted and said, "Harry, why skulk around the grounds like a thief? Why didn't you come back to marry Maude and take care of her and the baby as you should have?"

Harry hastily handed the infant to Maude, and stood to face Patrick.

"M'lord," he began, his face red, "I wanted to get a good job in London and then marry Maude. But m'relatives had moved away. I looked for months, but couldn't find no position. Now how could I bring Maudie and the baby to live in slums like that? They deserve better."

"Why didn't you come back to your job here at Pinewood?"

"I didn't like to do that, sir. Wasn't sure m'job

would be waitin', leavin' so quick like I did. Besides, it's hard for a man to admit defeat. I wanted to make good before I came back." Harry gazed longingly down at Maude and the baby. "I just came today to snatch a look at 'em, don't y'know?"

"Have you been here before?"

"Well . . . yes, sir."

"Was that you prowling about the night it stormed so badly?"

"Aye, m'lord. I never thought to make no trouble."

Patrick's eyebrows drew together in a stern frown. "And what will you do now, man?"

"Guess I'll be leav'n for London tonight."

Maude's expression fell.

"Harry, would it be so bad to live at Pinewood House?" Patrick asked. "I could move you up to head groom, if you like. You and your family could live in Reggie's cottage. We could enlarge it, fix it up into a proper home."

"Oh!" sighed Maude hopefully, darting anxious glances from one man to the other. Amanda winked at her.

"You'd do that for us?" asked Harry.

"Of course. I want you to be a happy family, for Baby Reggie's sake, as well as for his grandfather's memory."

Harry thought a moment, then said gratefully, "You've a good heart."

Patrick smiled, then raised one eyebrow and cocked his head toward Maude, sitting on her bench. "Ahem," he cleared his throat meaningfully.

"Aye, m'lord?"

"What about..."

Harry scratched his head, and Patrick rolled his eyes heavenward in exasperation.

"Oh!" Harry finally picked up the cue. He turned to Maude and fell to one knee in the dust before her.

"Would you do me the honor of marryin' me, Maude White?" asked Harry humbly.

"Yes, Harry, I will."

"And I don't have to go to blue blazes?"

"No, Harry, you don't."

Patrick and Amanda tiptoed away, leaving the little family in peace.

Patrick crouched over his desk, deeply engrossed in estate accounts, when a hesitant knock at the study door interrupted his concentration.

"Mr. Patrick, I wonder if I might have a word with you, sir?"

Eyes still trained on a column of figures, he spoke absently. "Yes, Maude? Everything all right with the baby?"

"Oh, he's all right, sir. This is something a little more, uh, private."

Patrick looked up in surprise. "You have my full attention, Maude."

The maid shifted from one foot to the other, her face red with embarrassment. He waited as she withdrew a small book from her pocket.

"Sir, when Miss Amanda left Pinewood, she gave me something for you. Here 'tis."

"When she left Pinewood? Why didn't you give it to me sooner, then?"

Clearly frightened, Maude thrust the book toward him. She looked as if she might burst into tears at any moment. Careful not to startle her, Patrick took the book from her shaking fingers and turned it over.

"What is it, Maude?" he asked gently.

"I don't know. M'dad had it among his things, all wrapped up with Miss Amanda's name on it, so I gave it to her. When she left, she put it in a drawer with your name on it, but I was so hoping she would come back, I sort of, well, kept it for her. I'm sorry, sir." The little maid bobbed in a nervous curtsy.

"Why have you decided to give it to me now?" Patrick kept his voice gentle.

"Oh, Mr. Patrick, please forgive me." Obviously flustered, Maude's words came out in a rush. "I never knew you very well before. I never thought you were so good. But you've been ever so kind to my baby and Harry and me. Now—why, there's probably nothing we wouldn't do for you. I'm sorry I didn't give you the book straightaway." At this, Maude burst into tears.

Patrick's intervention and help in her personal life had clearly won the little maid's lifelong allegiance. He came around his desk. "I want to thank you, Maude," he said courteously. "You're very kind to give this to me. And don't worry about the delay. I'm sure nothing bad will come of it."

"You're not angry with me, then?" she whimpered.

"Of course not. It's quite all right. Now why don't you get back to what you were doing. I'm sure combining your duties in the house with caring for your baby must keep you very busy these days."

Maude's eyes filled with gratitude. She giggled, her smile a tremulous rainbow through the last of her tears. "Baby Reggie is a handful, all right."

She backed out of the room, punctuating every few steps with a curtsy.

Patrick nodded and looked at the book in his hand. After laboring over his accounts all morning, he needed a break. The book might provide a diversion.

He sprawled onto the horsehair sofa and leaned back against its pillows. His lips curved with amusement. Little Maude. The maid had hidden the book all this time, hoping to return it to Amanda.

He flipped open the cover and noticed for the first time that it was a diary.

"Sylvie Emerson?" Instantly alert, the smile left his lips, and his brows drew together. "What the—?"

He leafed through the pages, pausing at passages that caught his eye. His grandmother's name appeared and his interest was piqued.

April 21, 1846

I vow that sisters are a plague on all girls! I wish I had twenty bothersome brothers— I would trade Helene for all of them!

Helene and I were waiting in the drawing room for Thomas to take us out for a carriage ride. I had on my new silk dress and jacket—the one with the feathers at the shoulder. It's such a becoming dress, and I was so looking forward to the ride! But Helene brought over her bottle of lavender scent. I told her I didn't want any, but she would have me wear it! She bent to give me some, and started at the sound of Thomas's carriage outside, spilling lavender all over my new outfit!

I couldn't go out with my clothes ruined. Helene cried—oh, all genuinely sorry now! So of course, I had to insist that she go on the ride with Thomas, leaving me at home! I could have . . . I don't know what!

Oh well, all turned out right, I guess. Helene declared the ride "wonderful." I, in the meantime, made use of the hours to work on a needlepoint bookmark for Thomas. It's ever so cunning, made up with his initials in bright red.

I threw away Helene's odious bottle of lavender scent!

Gilded Splendor

August 3, 1846

Thomas was out of sorts again today. Nothing I could do or say would please him. He was so fretful and impatient, he would find fault with everything! I'm afraid we quarreled again.

Each time, I promise myself it will never happen again—that I will be what Mama calls "a chaste beacon of uplifting grace and love." She says that women must tame men's brutish natures, channel their wandering impulses into peaceful family bonds.

She makes me want to scream. What am I to do when Thomas is so mean and spiteful? I hope I still, even though engaged, have enough spirit in me to resist being treated in such an abominable fashion!

I cried after he left, and Helene tried to comfort me, saying that he is, after all, a man. She says I don't know how to handle Thomas—as if she does!

I can't help fearing for my future sometimes. If Helene is right, and I don't know how to handle Thomas, what will become of me after we're married?

November 7, 1846

I'm so excited! Helene is in love! She acted so strangely today, and it took some doing, but I made her confide in me that she has found the love of her life. She's been acting most peculiar lately, but I put it down to indigestion or pique! Little did I suspect the real reason!

She wouldn't reveal the identity of her beloved, no matter how much I wheedled, cajoled, and threatened! Imagine! She says it's too soon, and Mama and Papa might not approve. I'm going to do a little spying on Helene to see if I can discover who her beau is. What a delicious secret!

December 12, 1846
Something is terribly wrong between Thomas and me. He is so strange and distant lately. I don't know why. What can be wrong? When I ask him, he says he has worries. Why won't he confide in me? We're to be married, after all. I cry myself to sleep every night.

Patrick's forehead creased into a disturbed frown over the diary. So Gray was engaged to Sylvie! What the deuce could have been wrong with the man? He found his answer in the next entry.

"Damn!"

Patrick finished reading and snapped the diary shut with a bang.

It couldn't be! And yet it was! How the deuce could it have happened?

"Sylvie," he said into the silence, as if the dead girl could hear him, "I am sorry. It wasn't fair!"

Gilded Splendor

* * *

"Grandmother, I'll have a word with you—now!"

Helene halted midstride in the foyer, her hands filled with skeins of Berlin wool. Peevishly, she thrust them in Patrick's direction.

"These yarn colors won't do. They don't match the dining room chair covers. Well, that's what happens when you order things. What a muddle."

"Please come into the library, Gram."

"I'm awfully busy."

An impatient sound escaped Patrick's throat, his temper barely concealed. "Now!"

Helene's eyes widened a fraction. "Of course, dear, if it can't wait."

She brushed past him and held the offending yarn up to the light of the library window. She plucked at it, examining it closely. "I just knew that clerk wouldn't get the colors right. Why, he didn't pay the slightest attention when I took such pains to describe the exact shade of blue."

"Put the damned yarn down!"

Helene stared at Patrick, fully noticing him for the first time. "Why, what a sharp tongue! Whatever is the matter?"

He withdrew a book from his pocket. "I've been reading your sister's diary. I came upon something that deeply disturbs me."

"Sylvie's diary?" Helene stared at the book. "You have it? But I thought Amanda . . ."

"She did have it. Maude gave it to her after

Reggie died. He wanted her to have it. But when she went away, she left it for me."

Helene's thoughts churned. She'd known Maude had given it to Amanda. She had listened outside Amanda's bedroom door and had overheard the conversation between the two women. That was why she had ransacked Amanda's room. It had been frustrating not finding the diary that day, and she'd been forced to take the jeweled box instead, so no one would suspect what she'd really been looking for. But it had all been quite useless. The diary was now in Patrick's hands! And only God knew what Sylvie had written in it!

The yarn slipped forgotten from her fingers onto the library table. "Why dredge up the past, son? It was all so long ago, what difference can any of it make now?"

"Nothing in the past can be changed, of course. But I have to ask you about it."

She sighed. "What is in the diary that disturbs you?"

"I think you know. Why didn't you tell me Thomas Gray was engaged to Sylvie?"

"What difference can it make now?"

"In the entries shortly before her death, Sylvie says you stole Gray's affections from her. She says you bewitched him, and he returned your love. The diary shows a heartbroken girl. She'd been about to call off her engagement, but died before she could do so.

Helene despaired at the disappointed, angry

look on Patrick's face. *Sylvie says... Sylvie says... Damn Sylvie and her troublemaking ways! I won't let her alienate Patrick from me!*

"It's a lie. All lies!"

Patrick narrowed his eyes. "Is it?"

Helene straightened her shoulders and frowned sternly, attempting to bluff him. "Patrick, I don't need to tell you that you had no right to read that diary, or to question me in this way. The diary is private, of a most personal nature, and Reggie should have given it to me. After all, Sylvie was *my* sister. Now, whatever she said in that diary doesn't concern you in the least." She extended her hand. "Give it to me. It would be best if we never mentioned it again."

"But if you and Gray were lovers, then I think his presence here now is—"

"Lovers!" Helene blustered in offended disapproval. "Does the diary say we were lovers?"

"No, but—"

"*You* are suggesting it? How could you? Why, I was just a girl, for heaven's sake! Don't you dare accuse me of things you know nothing about! I've never been so insulted, and I won't listen to another word!"

"But the diary—"

"Sylvie lied. About everything. That was her nature. You didn't know her. I did!"

"It's all so sordid. I don't know what to believe."

Elizabeth Parker

The wind went out of Patrick's sails, and Helene hurried to press her point. "Despite her faults, we all loved Sylvie. I would never hurt my own sister in such a way. If you don't believe that, then we have nothing more to say."

Helene made her voice quaver, and her eyes filled with tears. She saw Patrick's anger melt into deep remorse. He held out his arms.

"I'm sorry, Gram. Of course I believe you. How could I doubt my own grandmother?"

"As for Mr. Gray's presence here now, there is nothing whatsoever improper about it," Helene insisted staunchly.

"I didn't say there was. I just want to know why he's here, that's all."

"Isn't it enough that he's an old friend of our family and enjoys my company? I like having him here. I like recalling our youth."

She stood rigidly in his encircling arms, stiffly refusing to relax her taut muscles, but allowing him to place a kiss on her creased forehead. She held out a trembling hand. "May I have the diary? I would like to read it for myself. I think I have a right to."

"Of course."

He handed it over. She made her expression sorrowful, encouraging his guilt, like heavy chunks of burning coal on his head. She noted his contrite look with satisfaction. She'd show him what a cur he'd been to abuse her in such a way! She watched him close his eyes, as if he wanted to obliterate her aggrieved look.

Gilded Splendor

"It's a shock that after all these years, you know me so little," she said. "I think I'll retire now. I'm a little tired."

Patrick leapt to hand her the skeins of wool. "Will you work on your stitchery?" he asked. He seemed to want to thrust the matter quickly behind them.

She sniffled loudly and refused to take the yarn from his hands. "No, I'm too upset. I'll do it later."

Pausing at the door, she threw him a wounded look over her shoulder. "Son, I'll try very hard to forget the hurtful things you said today." Before he could form a reply, she drew the door closed behind her.

In the hallway, Helene staggered with relief. She'd done it! Patrick was back on her side.

Her hands clenched into fists, she fervently wished none of them had ever heard of Sylvie or her damned diary.

He wished he'd never heard of Sylvie's damned diary! Left alone to pace the library, Patrick gritted his teeth. All his life, he'd stood solidly behind his grandmother, and she behind him. He had always considered her wishes, her desires, because he knew she held the well-being of everyone on the estate of supreme importance. But since Amanda had entered his life, he had unbelievably found himself relegating Helene to second place, forced to question her motives and actions, a turn that would have been unthinkable in the past.

Patrick raked his fingers distractedly through his hair. The hurt look on his grandmother's face haunted him. What had possessed him to accuse her? What did the diary matter anyway? As she had said, the past was over.

Yet a trace of doubt lingered. Why would Sylvie lie in her own diary? Why was Thomas Gray back in his grandmother's life?

Patrick frowned. On a more personal level, would he ever manage to bring Helene around to accepting Amanda as his wife? Lately he'd felt himself thrust unwillingly into the position of having to choose between the two women. His alternatives were equally unsatisfactory.

Patrick slammed his fist into his hand. Enough! He would never betray his grandmother, or accuse her of indiscretions again. He would stand solidly behind her as he always had. Damn the diary! He would never mention it again. And damn Thomas Gray! The man could come or go as he liked, as long as Helene welcomed him. Patrick's decision was firm. At the same time, he vowed again he would damned well not give up Amanda! He would marry her as soon as possible, and everyone would find a way to coexist peacefully.

What he needed was a good hard ride. He headed for the stables, where the comforting smell of sweaty horses and hay would brace him up, and nothing more pressing would assail him

Gilded Splendor

than deciding on which sunlit path to guide his galloping horse.

His course for the immediate future as clear as he could make it, he shook his head wearily. His life was like guiding a raft through tricky shoals, dangerous rocks lurking at every side beneath the surface.

Chapter Eighteen

"Damn Amanda Prescott! Double damn her!"

Diane Warfield paced through Pinewood's maze of boxwood hedges, muttering under her breath, savagely tearing off leaves as she went. The countess's agitated mind belied the serenity of the peaceful garden scene.

"Pregnant!" Diane's long, talonlike fingernails shredded a handful of leaves and hurled them viciously to the ground. "Her innocent act was so convincing! Even I was taken in. And all the time the conniving bitch was letting Patrick breed her! Abominable!"

Diane wanted to scream with rage. All her years of careful planning, playing up to Patrick, cultivating Helene—that insufferable bore!—had all come to naught. She didn't know which was worse—the fact that Amanda was pregnant, or the idea that with *her*, Patrick had always taken such careful precautions to avoid pregnancy!

She supposed she might as well pack up and return to London, but surely she wasn't finished yet. There must be some way to salvage this debacle!

"I could just kill her! Before she has the miserable brat!"

Beside herself with jealous fury, Diane flung herself onto a garden bench. Scenes of Patrick and Amanda making love seared her fevered brain. She imagined their naked bodies writhing in the throes of passion. Had he taken Amanda roughly? Or, the agonizing thought that tortured Diane most, had he found it in his heart to show Amanda the tenderness Diane had craved from him?

"Believe me, Patrick Winter, I'll get back at you somehow!" Beside herself, she pounded her fists on the bench seat.

"Hello, countess," came a soft voice behind her.

Diane tensed, her back stiffening. Who the bloody hell—? She quickly swiped a telltale tear from her cheek, then whirled around.

"Oh, it's you," she said, instantly relaxing and pivoting back to face the garden.

"Something wrong, Diane? Something I can fix?"

Gentle hands unexpectedly massaged her shoulders, startling her. She flinched at the inappropriate touch. "No, thank you," she said, fidgeting.

"Let me help," came the soft, insinuating voice. The hands pressed more firmly, moving up her neck.

Her nerves tensed to the breaking point, Diane shrugged impatiently. "I said no, thank you!"

The hands moved away, to her great relief. She opened her mouth to say something further, but before she could, a narrow crescent looped over her head, swept down past her eyes, and closed around her neck.

A painful tightness cut into her skin. Instinctively, her hands flew to her throat and fluttered there ineffectually. There was nothing to grab hold of, no way to get her fingers beneath the tight circle slicing into her throat.

She choked. Unable to draw a breath, her chest tightened. She tried to scream, but the increasing pressure made it impossible. The only sounds in the still garden were her own gagging, gurgling noises.

In some far corner of her mind that remained calm, Diane realized she would die. Today. Here in this peaceful garden. She panicked to her soul and struggled frantically, gasping for air. Her feet left the ground, but failing to find a foothold, kicked at nothing. Her lungs burned, and she felt her eyes bulge. The pressure increased until she could see only spots and stars. With one last choking gurgle of despair, she flailed her fists ineffectually at the person standing behind.

Why? her mind screamed. *Why?*

Then she slumped, lifeless, and was slowly lowered to the grass. All was again silence among the boxwood hedges. Her assailant bent over the body and removed the narrow instrument of death from around her throat.

"Whore!"

Calm, smooth fingers painted the countess's lips red.

Helene bustled into the drawing room, arrayed in a walking suit of fine gray twill. Tall ostrich plumes waved above the hat perched on her head. Drawing on gray gloves, she eyed Amanda, reading in the window seat.

"There you are, dear. I've been looking all over for you. Have you forgotten we're going to tea with Mrs. Charteris? Hurry and put on your coat. You won't have time to change, but I think your dress will do."

Amanda frowned. She had completely forgotten the planned visit. It was so pleasant to sit before the window with her book. Much as she loved Mrs. Charteris, she wasn't in the mood for going out.

"Can Diane accompany you instead?"

"No, she's in the garden. Then she has to pack for her return to London." Helene sniffed sadly. "So hurry and get ready."

"I'm sorry. I don't feel like going. Might I be excused this once?"

Helene gaped, as if she couldn't quite believe her ears. The plumes on her hat jerked as she tossed her head impatiently.

"If a lady doesn't return her calls, she's guilty of the worst sort of rudeness, and attention would be drawn to it. It's one of the many things you must learn if you want to fit into our milieu, Amanda. A lady hides her moods and impulses, and performs her duty."

Amanda bit back the sharp retort on the tip of her tongue. She'd been trying hard to get along with Helene. If paying the call was so important, she might please both Helene and Mrs. Charteris by going. Telling herself a drive in the fresh air might be pleasant, she gave in.

"I'll get ready at once."

"I've called for the carriage to be brought around, so don't dawdle."

Amanda dutifully started up the stairs to fetch her coat, controlling the impulse to stomp her feet on each stair. Hide her moods! Perform her duty! Being a lady could be stifling and bothersome in the extreme!

"Oh, Amanda?" Helene called up from the foot of the stairs. "I've forgotten my reticule on my dressing table. Would you bring it down for me? There's a good girl."

"Yes, I'll get it."

Amanda turned down the hall and entered Helene's room. One glance told her the reticule wasn't on the dressing table. Her gaze swept the bedside stand and window seat, but no reticule sat among the clutter of porcelain jars, books, and silver-framed photographs of long-dead Winters.

"Amanda!" Helene's impatient voice rose from the stairs.

"Coming!"

Hurriedly, she threw open the elaborately carved doors of the armoire. Helene's familiar lavender scent drifted out. She pawed through the colorful profusion of clothes, then raised her gaze to the shelf above, shoving aside a collection of hatboxes and scarves.

Suddenly, blindingly, the sun's rays picked out a brilliant flash of gold, catching her eye. She peered closer and froze, her hand suspended in midair. After a long moment of disbelief, she reached up and drew Sylvie's jeweled box down from the shelf.

She stiffened with the shock of discovery. As its implications hit her, nausea rose in her throat. Slowly, she sank onto a boudoir chair and gazed at Sylvie's box. Hesitantly, she lifted the lid. Inside lay the white rose Patrick had given her. Its unmistakable scent wafted up to her, but now its sickening sweetness seemed cloying, decayed. Her stomach churned with distress.

"Amanda! The carriage!" Helene's voice rose in urgency from the hall below. "For heaven's sake, what can you be doing?" Footsteps sounded on the stairs. "We mustn't keep Mrs. Charteris wait—"

Helene froze in the doorway, her astute eyes flickering over Amanda, the box in her lap, and the faded rose in her hand.

"I'm afraid Mrs. Charteris will have to wait," Amanda said quietly.

"Well, for heaven's sake!" Helene came to life and bustled into the room, drawing off her hat and gloves. "That looks like Sylvie's box! Wherever did you find it?"

"On a shelf in your armoire." Amanda's voice held a faint note of reproach.

Helene didn't reply immediately. Her silence and her look of unease brought to the surface all the doubts and suspicions Amanda had harbored for so long. *It's now or never*, she thought, eyeing Helene. *I want answers!*

"Lady Swinton, how did this box happen to come into your possession?" She couldn't keep the suspicion out of her voice. "It was stolen when my room was ransacked!"

"Why, someone must have placed it there. Of course! The thief planted it."

"Who would do that? And why?"

Helene failed to answer. Horrible suggestions grabbed Amanda's mind. She leapt from one doubt to another, lighting on the question that had been perplexing her for some time. Was Helene a thief? If she had stolen Sylvie's box, was it true she had stolen Sylvie's fiancé so long ago?

"Helene, is Sylvie's diary true? Did you steal Thomas Gray from her?"

Surprise filled Helene's eyes. "Oh, yes," Amanda said quietly, "I read Sylvie's diary before I left Pinewood House."

When Helene failed to respond, Amanda pressed on relentlessly. "Why didn't you marry Thomas, then? Once you had him, you didn't want him, I suppose."

The accusation stung Helene into retort at last. Her cheeks mottled. "How dare you!" she blustered, her eyes snapping. "I never stole Thomas from Sylvie! He was infatuated with me, all right, but I tried to discourage him. Do you think I wanted my own sister's fiancé? I sent him packing!"

"Then why is he back at Pinewood House now?"

Helene slapped her gloves into her hand. "You know very well why, Miss Innocence!" she said, her voice rising. "You're in cahoots with him! And you've been trying to poison Patrick against me, too!" Agitated, Helene paced the room.

"What do you mean?"

Helene paused to stare at Amanda with accusing eyes. "You gave Patrick the diary, didn't you?"

"No, I—"

"And come now, do you really expect me to believe you don't know why Thomas is here?"

"I don't know."

Helene drew a deep breath and searched Amanda's eyes for long moments. She seemed to reach a decision. "All right, I'll tell you. Your father sent Thomas here to Pinewood."

Amanda gaped, incredulous. "My father?"

"Before he died, your father dredged up the past, told Thomas lies about me. When Thomas first arrived, I thought he still loved me, but I soon found out differently. He's here to get money out of me, for you and for himself."

"Get money?"

"Blackmail. He threatened to tell Patrick I seduced him way back then and stole him from my sister."

"But that's exactly what Sylvie's diary says! So it's true, isn't it?"

"It's not true! Not a word of it."

"And even if it were true, surely Gray can't blackmail you for an indiscretion that happened years ago."

Helene drew herself up proudly. "My grandson has always looked up to me. I won't have my reputation besmirched!"

"Then tell Patrick! He'll know how to deal with Gray, and that will be the end of it!"

"No! Don't mention it to Patrick!" Helene hesitated for a fraction of a second. "I'm afraid there's more to it than that! Thomas Gray is dangerous!"

"Dangerous?"

"Remember when Mrs. Charteris was shot? That was Thomas, aiming at Patrick. He didn't want Patrick to interfere with his scheme, and he thought with Patrick gone, there would be more money for him."

Amanda's eyes widened. "That's monstrous!"

"Then he pushed Reggie off the parapet. Thomas had been spying, and knew Reggie had Sylvie's diary. He knew if its contents were known, his blackmail scheme would be over."

Mrs. Charteris! Reggie! Their injuries had been accidents, hadn't they? Or had Thomas really been behind them? And what about the murders in the neighborhood? Good God, Gray was odd, true—but evil? A cold knot of fear formed in Amanda's stomach. A distressed sound escaped her throat, but Helene's words continued to pour out in a rush.

"It seems incredible, doesn't it? Of course, there's no way I can prove any of these things. So I've been paying Thomas, hoping he would leave all of us alone."

"Why didn't you tell all this to Inspector Sweeney?"

"I've been so afraid. You just don't know what I've been going through." Helene subsided, seemingly worn out by her revelations. With trembling fingers, she drew a delicate lace-edged handkerchief from her sleeve and dabbed tiny beads of perspiration from her brow.

Amanda rose and gazed unseeing out the window. Helene's revelations were mind-boggling. No wonder the poor woman had been flustered on so many occasions. How often she had come in from being with Gray, her eyes red-rimmed, her mood agitated. The poor woman must have been out of her mind with fright all this time.

Amanda turned to her, filled with pity. "You thought Thomas Gray and my father and I were all together in a plan to blackmail you? That's why you never trusted me. No wonder we could never be close."

"I've been so afraid, Amanda! Thomas is insane. I think he's been committing the neighborhood murders, too. Poor Lady Brighton and the Duchess of Howard! I didn't want Patrick or anyone at Pinewood House to be his next victim. I thought if I paid him enough, he would eventually go away, and the whole frightful thing would be over. But it just keeps getting worse and worse!"

Amanda shivered with sheer, black fright. It seemed logical that Gray was the murderer. He was physically strong enough to strangle two women and push Reggie. And now Helene had provided him with the motives to perform the heinous deeds—if he were indeed truly insane. He had always seemed strangely odd to Amanda. Besides, who else could it have been? Everything pointed to Gray.

Amanda gazed with wonder at the Marchioness of Swinton. She hadn't realized the depth of the secrets at Pinewood House. It was unfathomable that Helene would be silent about murder in order to cover up indiscretions that had happened so long ago. Amanda drew her shoulders back. Patrick would have to be told, no matter what Helene said. Helene's reputation would just have to be besmirched, and an end put to Gray's evil.

A smirk came over Helene's face. Amanda shivered. How often Helene's expressions were inappropriate and confusing! Of course, the poor woman had been beside herself with fright. That might account for some of her irrational mood swings.

Amanda crossed the room and put her arms around Helene. "It will be all right," she soothed, patting the older woman's arm. "You won't have to face this alone anymore. I'll help you. Perhaps now we can be friends." Amanda filled her voice with determination. "It will be all right. You'll see—it will be all right."

It will be all right, thought Patrick.

They would all find a way to coexist peacefully, though he was at a loss to imagine how this might be accomplished. The residents of Pinewood House continually seemed to be at cross-purposes.

He hoped he would be more successful working things out at home than he had been investigating the neighborhood murders. He'd been to Lady Brighton's and to the Howard place, Faircroft Manor. He'd pried, snooped, questioned servants, and searched the crime scenes, but he'd failed to turn up any clues pointing to the guilty party. In fact, about the only thing his determined sleuthing had accomplished was to make Inspector Sweeney suspicious of him.

But he wasn't done yet. He still had a few cards to play, a few stones left unturned.

He headed for the house, taking the shortcut through the hedges. As a boy, he had long ago divined the pattern of the boxwood maze. Now the labyrinth was as familiar to him as the back of his hand. A turn here, crisscross there, a dash around this corner, and . . .

He stumbled against a large, soft form in his way.

"What the blazes!"

The Countess of Craven lay slumped on the grass.

"Diane? Are you hurt?" He bent over her. "What's the matter?"

He gingerly took hold of one shoulder and turned her over, then rocked back on his heels in shock. Her neck was marked with a telltale slice of pink. Her lips had been smeared with a garish red, the color standing out vividly against the purplish hue of her skin. On her cheek was a faint smudge of black. Sick with horror, Patrick felt her throat for a pulse, but there was no sign of life.

"God—Diane!"

Diane, of the laughing dark eyes—now glassy and unseeing. Diane, with her lust for life—now inert, her life extinguished.

Patrick jerked his eyes around the garden, looking for her assailant, but the peaceful scene was empty except for him and the corpse. He looked back down at her. Wretched guilt filled him. He and Diane had used each other over the years, for their own selfish purposes. Maybe Diane's character had been lacking in some ways, but he hadn't always treated her with the care and respect he should have. And she certainly hadn't deserved this—murder on his own estate where she had thought to be a safe and cosseted guest!

Wanting to do something—anything—for her, Patrick carefully arranged the folds of her dress around her. He held her hand and stroked it tenderly. "I'm sorry, Diane!" he whispered. "Truly sorry for everything!"

Patrick stared at the dead woman, and slowly, anger replaced his remorse, chilling him with icy, lethal fury. In the garden stillness, he bent down and vowed to her lifeless form, "By God, I'll find out who did this—and make them pay!"

Chapter Nineteen

"It was horrible." Patrick slumped forward, his head in his hands. "Horrible!"

Amanda studied him from her position beside him on the settee. If Diane, Countess of Craven, had been found dead in the garden, none of them were safe at Pinewood House. She shuddered with horror. Poor Diane. Amanda couldn't say she had liked the woman, but the countess hadn't deserved to be brutally murdered.

Amanda swallowed, her throat tight with apprehension, as she tried to gauge Patrick's mood. She gazed wide-eyed at his broad back, noting the shudders that racked his body. It was only natural that he was upset. But how much? Had he loved Diane?

Gilded Splendor

"I know how hard it must have been for you to find her that way, loving her and all." Amanda tried not to let jealousy creep into her voice.

Patrick pivoted to face her. "Oh darling, I didn't love Diane. I love you!" He placed his hand reverently on her stomach. "And our baby."

Earnestness radiated from his expression, and Amanda, believing him, expelled a breath of relief.

"But she didn't deserve to die that way!" He frowned ominously. "I'm going to discover who did it and why."

Amanda brought a shaking hand to her lips. What would he do? Plunge headlong into more danger? She gazed into his disturbed eyes, like two churning green pools. In spite of his roiling emotions, she detected a force and strength of character reflected there. He could handle anything that came along and now was the time to tell him all that had been preying on her mind.

"Patrick, I've had a most disturbing conversation with your grandmother. She told me things I haven't been able to get out of my mind. Terrible, unbelievable things. I—I can hardly fathom them."

Patrick leaned forward with a baffled expression. "Go on," he prompted.

"She said things about Thomas Gray, about Sylvie and my father and the diary—"

"That damned diary! Let's just forget it. I gave it to Gram."

Surprised, Amanda raised her eyebrows. "You did?"

"She's maligned in the book, and I thought it only right that she be able to read it and defend herself. Besides, it belonged to her sister. Gram has a better right to it than you or me. I've more important things to occupy my mind right now. And, as far as Thomas Gray is concerned, he's really none of our business. Gram assured me his activities have been quite proper here at Pinewood."

"But she told me that Thomas Gray is the murderer!"

He sucked in his breath and rose from the sofa, fists clenched. "How in the hell would she know?"

"Gray has been blackmailing her with information from the diary! And she thinks he's insane—that he killed those neighborhood women."

"Why the deuce didn't Gram tell me?"

"She's been beside herself with fright! She fears he might hurt us."

Patrick paced a moment, deep in thought, then turned to face her. "All right. I'll handle Gray, but until I do, I'm sending you and Gram up to London, out of harm's way."

"I won't leave you!"

"No arguments!" He bent over her and smoothed a curl from her cheek in a conciliatory gesture. "I want the two of you out of danger. I've work to do, and I don't want

Gilded Splendor

to be constantly worrying about you."

He pulled her up, enfolded her in his arms, and drew her head down against his chest, trying to soothe her, but she was having none of it. She raised her head sharply and pushed her fists against him.

"But you'll need help! I can help, Patrick."

"No, you'll do as I say. Just until the danger is past. Think of our baby. And you can help me by looking after Gram. Won't you do that, dear?"

"But what will I do in London? I'll go crazy sitting around, helplessly waiting to hear."

Patrick smiled fondly. "I'll tell you what you can do. Granville has been pestering me to let him paint your portrait. Go and sit for him." She opened her mouth to object, but he silenced her with a raised hand. "I want you to have your wedding dress made—the most beautiful dress in the world. Gram will help you. And then you can wear it for the portrait. It would please me enormously. And as soon as you return, when all this is over, you'll marry me in that dress!"

Seeing the delight on his face, Amanda's heart lightened. It was wonderful to see a glimpse of happiness replace the worry that had lately etched his features. Reluctantly, she gave in.

"I'll do as you ask," she said, "but you must promise to be careful! From what your grandmother said, Gray is dangerous and insane! Please tell Inspector Sweeney!"

Patrick's jaw hardened. "Don't worry," he said, his voice ominous "I can take care of myself—and Thomas Gray, too."

Amanda gazed excitedly from the window of Helene's carriage as it clip-clopped through London. The high noon sun shone brilliantly, reflecting her happy mood. She had just come from the final fitting for her wedding dress.

She sighed in happiness, grateful for Helene's help and advice through the arduous process of poring over fabrics and designs. The older woman had refused to listen to a word about cost, had eschewed all the ordinary, simple designs and had, with unerring firmness, guided her to choose a confection of shirred cream-colored lace. Helene said the gown reminded her of the past, and an old-fashioned gown would best fit the mood and occasion of a wedding at Pinewood House. Besides, the frilly dress would somewhat camouflage Amanda's pregnancy. Like something out of a fairy tale, it was decidedly the most beautiful garment Amanda had ever seen.

After the final fitting that morning, Helene had pleaded a sick headache. Nearly prostrate, she had reluctantly agreed that Amanda might go on to her next appointment without her. Now, after dropping off the weary woman at their hotel, Amanda was on her way to Granville's studio to make an appointment for her first sitting.

Gilded Splendor

Amanda had never been to an artist's studio before, and she was eager to drink in the aesthetic ambience. Would it be decorated in a romantic, foreign fashion, with a Bohemian flavor? Maybe even slightly decadent? She smiled to herself, a shiver of anticipation tracing up her spine.

This was an adventure of the kind she had been yearning for, for so long! Perhaps now, as soon as Patrick apprehended Gray, they would all be able to relax and get on with their lives. After they were married, Patrick would surely introduce his new wife to the larger world, help her sample some of the pleasures of living she had yearned for. They would go to exciting places and do new things—like having her portrait painted in an artist's studio!

She hadn't seen Granville much since the first house party when he had so kindly drawn her into the group by sketching her. He had been so gentle, so attentive, that she looked forward eagerly to renewing their acquaintance.

The carriage drew up before a row of fashionable brownstones. Sunlight glittered off the curtained windows. After the driver handed her down, Amanda tripped lightly up the steps and tapped the brass knocker. A little woman, stooped with age, opened the heavy door and ran her eyes up and down Amanda's figure.

"You must be Miss Prescott," she said. "This way, please."

"Thank you." Amanda followed the woman's unsteady footsteps down a long hall, and after a discreet tap on the door, heard Granville's voice chime out, "Come!"

The servant opened the door a crack, then retreated down the hall. Amanda entered a room shrouded in darkness. After the bright noon sunlight, the studio was like a forbidding cave, at odds with her happy mood. She peered through the gloom, squinting to adjust her eyes to the change in light. "Mr. Granville?" she called, unable to make him out.

"Over here." A quiet voice came from the shadows.

She reached out her hand, groping through the dark, and it was grasped by cold fingers.

"Oh!" She jumped, startled by the touch of the clammy skin against hers. "You frightened me."

"I'm sorry," Granville said benignly. He led her to a tall stool. "Won't you have a seat?"

Amanda perched unsteadily on the stool, twitching her nose at the heady reek of paint and turpentine.

"I'm so glad you could come to my studio today," said Granville, sitting near her and taking up a pad and charcoal. He began sketching lightly, his eyes never leaving her face. "People so rarely come to me. I usually have to go to their country homes to do my paintings."

"It is delightful to see your studio," bubbled Amanda, regaining some of her earlier enthusiasm. "I am surprised about one thing, though.

Gilded Splendor

Why is it so dark? I thought artists needed plenty of light!"

"Well, we won't start the actual painting today. Just a few preliminary sketches." His voice was quiet, almost sad. "I don't need the light for that, and I prefer darkness, don't you know?"

Amanda remained silent, uneasiness creeping over her. This wasn't the Granville she remembered, so eager to please and fit in. This Granville seemed withdrawn, mysterious.

Her eyes adjusting to the gloom, she scanned the large studio. Her spirits lifted as she realized it was just as she'd imagined. Peacock feathers plumed out of large vases sitting on the floor. Several small nude statuettes adorned side tables. Dark red damask had been tacked on the walls, and in the sketches hung on the fabric, Amanda recognized many of the aristocrats she'd met since coming to Pinewood House. There was a drawing of Algernon, and Mrs. Charteris, even one of Helene.

"Oh!" she exclaimed with a pang of dismay, her gaze halting on one of the drawings. "You've drawn the Countess of Craven. How beautiful she was!"

Granville glanced over at the drawing, a gleam of malice in his eyes. "Yes, her portrait was one of the best I've done, but she was a poor model—flighty and fidgety." He paused in his drawing, and his calm, smooth fingers, holding the charcoal, poised above the paper. "However, I suppose I should feel honored that she chose to let me paint her at all."

"But why not? You're everyone's favorite!"

"Yes, I'm the darling of the carriage trade, am I not?"

Granville's voice sounded cynical, derisive. Amanda gazed at him wide-eyed. He was frightening her badly. She moved off the stool and headed for the door.

"I'm afraid I really must be going," she whispered. "Helene isn't feeling well, and I told her I would not be long."

Granville shook his head, as if trying to rid himself of gloomy thoughts. Then, seeming to remember his guest, he sprang from his chair and rushed to her side. "Have you chosen your wedding gown, dear? Is it ready for you to pose in?" His voice had returned to normal, and now rang with bright cheer. "I'm sure it must be lovely."

"Yes, I had the final fitting just this morning. It's to be delivered at our hotel tomorrow."

"Quite so. Excellent!"

Granville took her arm and walked beside her. "Amanda, I'm sorry I'm not quite myself today. I've been ill. Please come back tomorrow, bring your dress, and we'll begin the portrait. I promise to be more, shall we say, amusing?"

He shook her hand firmly, and his large eyes seemed to beg her forgiveness and urge her friendship and acceptance.

Gilded Splendor

"Yes, of course," she returned. "I'll see you tomorrow. I hope you're feeling better."

With a smile, Granville saw her out the door and down the brownstone stairs, where he handed her into the carriage.

"Until tomorrow, then?" he asked.

"Until tomorrow."

The sun hid behind a bank of gray clouds framing Pinewood House. Chill raindrops pelted down, giving the darkening air a gloomy atmosphere of foreboding.

Patrick prowled his room uneasily, like a caged panther. Where the hell was Thomas Gray? He had told Inspector Sweeney of his suspicions and the inspector and his men had made inquiries about Gray. But he hadn't been seen at the Newhaven Inn for days. In fact, he had disappeared right after Diane's murder. Had he gotten scared off and slipped out of the country?

Patrick shrugged, trying to restore a measure of calm to his soul. At least now he knew who to search for. It was only a matter of time. And despite the police efforts, he would continue the search on his own, and when he found Gray, he would bring the crazy bastard to justice. With Amanda and his grandmother safe in London, he wouldn't hesitate to launch a full-scale attack against the murderer, no matter what the consequences were to himself.

Patrick lit a cigarette. Relief flooded him, knowing that his family was out of danger.

Thank God, Amanda had agreed to go to London. He couldn't wait to see her again when she returned to Pinewood House. And she would bring a portrait of her lovely self with her. Would it show her belly slightly rounded with his child, or would Granville discreetly hide the pregnancy? Patrick smiled. He hoped the picture would show the evidence of their lovemaking.

God, how he missed her! The sound of her voice, the touch of her hand. Eager for even a sight of her, he crossed to his desk to glimpse the charcoal drawing Granville had made of her. Reaching for an ashtray to stub out his cigarette, he knocked the picture to the floor.

"Clumsy!" he muttered, bending to retrieve it from the rug. He turned it over, cutting his finger on a shard of glass. "Damn!" He sucked the blood from his fingertip.

A premonition of fear clogged his heart. What kind of bad luck did this portray?

He expelled a jerky breath. To hell with luck! He would make their luck for them!

Gingerly, he plucked the shards of glass from the frame and placed them in the wastebasket. A drop of red blood mingled on his hand with a smudge of the drawing's charcoal.

Instantly, Diane's image flooded his mind. Bloodred lips. Dark smudges on her cheek. Of what? Dirt? Soot? Slowly, he raised his head. Artist's charcoal?

"My God!" Ice-cold fear struck Patrick's chest. "Granville?"

Gilded Splendor

He imagined Amanda posing, vulnerable and innocent in her wedding dress, before the artist, alone with him in his studio. Would Granville ask her to paint her lips? A little more color?

A ragged cry escaped Patrick's throat. She was there at his own urging! She had only gone to please him. "God, what have I done?"

In anguish, he grabbed a pen to send a message to Amanda, to stop her from going to Granville, but in the next moment, he threw it down impatiently. Hell, he could ride faster than any message boy!

He yanked on his boots and threw a jacket over his shoulder. In a frenzy, he tore through the house. Past Maude, who cried out "Mr. Patrick!" in bewilderment. Out the front door, knocking the surprised butler back on his heels. Down to the stables, yelling for his horse.

Harry led a saddled mount from the stable, and Patrick grabbed the reins, threw his leg over, and kicked savagely into the horse's flanks.

"What's the matter?" Harry yelled after him into the rain, but Patrick didn't look back. He took the fence in a leap, heading the shortest way through the fields toward the main road.

He leaned forward, low over the horse's neck, and rode hard. He would ride his horse into the ground, if he had to. Through the mist, he pounded toward London. The cold rain stung his face, but he rode on, oblivious.

One thought raced through his mind, pounding over and over, in time to the galloping horse's hooves.

God, let me reach her in time!

Chapter Twenty

Frilly and elegant in her wedding dress, Amanda perched on the high stool in Granville's studio and tried not to fidget. She wanted to do everything just right in her first portrait sitting, and she had barely set foot in the studio door before the artist had resumed yesterday's litany of complaints about the Countess of Craven's rudeness. Amanda took her place before the high windows, folded her hands in a pose of tranquility, and endeavored to be the perfect model.

Granville pulled aside heavy maroon drapes, letting sunlight flood the studio. He studied Amanda, squinting through his monocle, then sat down and began to draw in silence.

The sun's heated rays warmed her hair, lulling her into soporific drowsiness. The moments wore on, and she let her imagination wander sleepily to pleasant images of her own little family—Patrick, her, and a healthy baby girl—the three of them picnicking on the wide, sloping green lawn of Pinewood House. Their friends—Algernon, Helene, Maude, and others—were there, too, munching on chicken legs, laughing and teasing. She could almost smell the fresh scent of the grass, hear the soft wind whispering through the pines. It was an image of restful peace and happiness she devoutly hoped would come true someday.

"Here, here! What are you dreaming about?" chirped Granville peevishly. "I must say, your mouth has changed—it's quirking up in an odd little smile—not what I want at all!"

Jolted out of her reverie, Amanda straightened her back and sobered her expression. "I'm sorry."

"There's something different about you." Granville frowned and regarded her thoughtfully, stroking his chin. "You seem to have put on a little weight since I saw you last."

Amanda felt a furious blush creep up her face, the heat suffusing her. She couldn't meet Granville's probing eyes. Her hands unconsciously twisted together.

"My God," he said slowly, as if realization was dawning, "you're not..."

With her eyes lowered, she waited in agony for him to finish his sentence, trying to determine how she would frame an answer, but the

Gilded Splendor

moments drew out in shocked silence, and he said nothing more.

From the corner of her eye, she dared to take a peek at Granville. His eyes radiated a hard, stony anger that puzzled her, as if he were taking the news of her pregnancy as a personal affront to himself.

After what seemed an eternity, he placed his charcoal on a nearby table and picked up a length of thin wire. Slowly, he twisted it in his hands, examining it, fondling it.

"I use this wire to hang my picture frames," he said. "It has other uses."

He left his place at the easel and circled behind her. She wanted to swivel around to see what he was doing, but she didn't want to antagonize him further. *Is this the way artists work?* she wondered uneasily. Perhaps he needed to get a different perspective on his subject.

Granville paused at her back. A trickle of nervous perspiration dampened her high dress collar. Raising one hand, she tugged feverishly at the tight lace. In a lightning-fast motion, a loop of wire swished down past her face. It circled around her throat and cut sharply into her fingers. She jerked spasmodically.

Oh, God, what was he doing?

She tried to work her fingers to loosen the wire, but it sliced into her flesh. Locked in a death-grip, they swayed back and forth in the silent room, like partners in a grotesque, macabre dance. Amanda was dimly aware of Granville's gasps and pants in her ear as they struggled.

He twisted her sideways, lifting her feet off the floor. In another moment, she would lose her seat on the stool and hang in midair, unable to gain a foothold.

In desperation, she grabbed at a nearby table with her free hand. Her fingers closed over an artist's putty knife. She snatched it up and stabbed backward blindly. The pressure on her throat instantly relaxed as Granville dropped the wire and leapt back.

She gasped a breath of healing air and swung around to face him. The sight of the putty knife sticking out of his shoulder made her blood run cold.

Granville yanked it free and hurled it across the room. He faced her in silence, as if gauging her strengths and weaknesses. Then, with the stealth of a panther, he moved toward her, his smooth fingers curved into thin claws. Sheer, black fright swept through her, and she clutched at the baby in her stomach.

No, her mind screamed. *No!*

The door burst open. Granville's eyes twitched for the briefest second toward the sound, and it was all she needed. She crouched, scooped a handful of charcoal dust from the floor, and flung it upward into his face. He bellowed and doubled over, grinding his fists into his eyes.

Gilded Splendor

From the doorway, a blurred form rushed across the room and smashed Granville's face with a cruel uppercut.

Patrick? Thank God!

Granville arched backward and fell heavily to the floor. Patrick leapt on him. He flipped the artist over and held him down with one knee. He drew Granville's hands behind him and tied them together, twisting around them the picture wire Granville had dropped.

Patrick reached out, pulling Amanda up, enfolding her in his arms. "You're all right. Thank God, you're all right," he crooned over and over. She clung to him, exhausted from her efforts.

A nasty laugh from Granville captured their attention. His monocle smashed on the floor beside him, he regarded them with narrowed eyes, his cheek resting on the wooden floorboards. A satanic smile curled his thin lips.

"Funny thing," he whined. "No one ever wore a gown like that for me. I've been allowed into the country houses to paint their grand ladyships, but as to any further intimacy, there they draw the line. I'm not one of them, you see."

Amanda and Patrick drew apart, fascinated by the madman writhing on the floor. "I was the tarts' plaything, their toy. They used me for their own amusement and then threw me aside. But I showed the whole world what they were— nothing more than painted whores with their red, decorated lips." His mouth drew down in an ugly sneer.

"You're sick," Amanda whispered.

The look of malicious evil she recognized from before returned to the artist's eyes as he regarded her.

"I was surprised the Winters allowed you into their exclusive little circle," he directed at her with cold fury. "And landing the Marquess of Swinton! What a coup! Look at you—pregnant by His Lordship, trapping him into marriage. Well, the aristocrats won't accept you any more than they did me."

Amanda gasped in shock. His cruel words pierced her, fed into her insecurities. Hadn't she always known deep-down that she would never fit into Patrick's milieu? Before she could say anything, Patrick broke in. "Don't listen to him, Amanda. He's unbalanced—mad."

A wistfulness stole into Granville's expression as his voice whined on maliciously. "That day I first drew you at Pinewood, I thought you were different. I imagined we could be soul mates on the fringes of society. But I see now you're like all the rest."

"The rest?"

"A decorated whore."

Patrick moved toward him, menacing with clenched fists. "That's enough, Granville!"

Amanda gazed sadly at the artist lying on the floor, twisting futilely against his bonds. His air of isolation, his profound loneliness, moved her to pity. She detained Patrick with a firm hand. "It's all right," she said softly.

He quirked his brow, a question in his eyes, but she smiled up at him. "It doesn't matter what he says. Now we know who shot at Mrs. Charteris and who was behind all the trouble in the neighborhood. He can't hurt us anymore."

Patrick nodded.

She was struck with a sudden, chilling thought. "Do you think Granville could have killed Reggie, too? But why would he?"

Patrick studied him quizzically, but the artist had apparently decided he'd told them everything he was going to. He closed his eyes and turned his face toward the wall.

"Who knows?" Patrick shrugged. "Maybe Reggie was on to him. Or maybe Reggie wasn't pushed, after all. Maybe he just slipped and fell."

"But why do you think your grandmother said all the trouble was caused by Thomas Gray?"

He frowned. "She probably assumed if Gray was crazy enough to try blackmailing her, he was crazy enough to kill. Besides, Thomas Gray was the only stranger to come into the neighborhood. Granville has been visiting us for ages. Gram would have no reason to suspect him."

It seemed to make sense. Amanda gave Patrick a tremulous smile, but she couldn't shake her uneasiness. Had she caught a flicker of doubt in his eyes? Or had it been just her imagination?

"Anyway," he reassured her, "the murderer has been apprehended. The neighborhood will be safe now. Nothing can harm us anymore." He drew her into his warm embrace. "Let's go home."

Chapter Twenty-One

Amanda opened the conservatory door and discovered Patrick bent over a plant, his broad back turned. Engrossed in what he was doing, he obviously didn't hear her come in.

She hesitated for a moment, watching him. His crisp black hair, shining in the sunlight, waved over his collar. His jacket stretched taut across broad back muscles, narrowing into a slender V at the waist. Her eyes wandered farther down to his sturdy thighs encased in tight leggings.

The sight of his powerful body, so gloriously masculine, aroused an itch of desire between her legs which she tried to suppress. It was indecent how much and how often she wanted him. Surely, an unmarried woman, and one expecting a baby besides, shouldn't be forever desiring union with a man, even if they were to be married!

He straightened, and around his back, she glimpsed the tips of a handful of snowy blooms. A tiny smile crept onto her lips. White roses. Their symbol of love. She guessed he was picking them for her. Powerful, hot emotion swept over her, clutching her heart. He was so dear—a man so powerful, yet capable of infinite tenderness. She had grown to crave that tenderness. She might as well admit it—she loved him with all her heart, and she didn't care if it was indecent!

She stole up behind him and wrapped her arms around his waist in a tentative hug. His surprised, indrawn breath heaved against her breasts, but he didn't move, except to lightly caress her forearms crossed in front of his waist.

"What have we here?" he whispered.

"The woman who loves you!" She spoke boldly, surprised at her own forwardness.

Swiftly, before she could unclasp her hands, he pivoted on his heel to face her. A luscious scent rose from the bouquet crushed between them. They laughed and drew apart.

"For you, madam." He bowed with a flourish and held out the white roses.

"Thank you, my lord," she said, smiling, burying her face in their dewy freshness.

"Tomorrow you'll carry a bride's bouquet." His voice rang deep with promise.

"Yes, tomorrow is the day." She couldn't quite

believe it, even yet. Their marriage was finally to happen. All was in readiness. A new bodice had been made for her wedding gown, since the first one had been stained by blood. Granville's wire had cut into her fingers, and they'd dripped red stains onto her dress. Resolutely, she shoved the memory aside. She would marry Patrick tomorrow, and all would be well. It must be!

He lifted his head and closed his eyes, his arms encircling her shoulders, drawing her against his chest. She burrowed close, laid her head against his warm shirtfront, and listened to the comforting, regular beats of his heart.

"We're home," he whispered. "Safe—quite safe." Again the quick indrawn breath. "Our baby will be healthy. You'll see, Amanda. I'll never let anything harm you."

"I know." She stood on tiptoe to reach his mouth with hers. He stood still, letting her run her tongue over the warm planes of his curved lips, until, with a moan, he tightened his grip on her and kissed her back. Warmly, sensually, he deepened the kiss, drawing it out until she was weak with desire. She ran her hand down to caress the hard bulge in his trousers.

Abruptly, he pulled his head back. "The baby . . . I don't want to hurt you," he whispered, his voice a harsh rasp of need.

"You won't," she urged. "You'll never let anything harm me, or our baby."

She increased the pressure of her hand on his aroused flesh, making him groan. Her breasts ached, her heart pounded. "Make love to me," she pleaded.

"Here? Now?"

"Yes!" she said, squeezing her hand around him.

He needed no further urging. He swept her into his arms, strode to a flat bench, and laid her out on it. His greedy eyes never leaving her, he stripped off his coat and vest.

"Will this do, milady?" he asked, opening his trousers.

"Love me," was all she could say.

He tossed up her skirts, hastily undid the laces of her drawers, and placed his hand on her mound, his fingers sliding into her wetness.

"Whatever milady commands—" He never finished his sentence. She reached her arms around his neck and drew him down to her, bringing her legs up around his waist. He replaced his fingers with his turgid flesh.

"Ahhh," she sighed. It felt so good. So wonderful to be joined with him, to be one with the man she loved. She moved with him for long silent moments, lost in the wondrous strokes, the overwhelming, building emotion until, with a wordless cry, she shuddered in waves of ecstasy around every glorious inch of him.

Watching her expression of rapture, he moved inside her silky sheath, loving her with all his might. God, he adored her! He would never be able to prove how much, convince her of his need for her, cherish her with his heart

Gilded Splendor

and soul, but he would die trying. He died a little then, pouring his love into her, a great, overpowering surrendering of himself, forever.

Amanda twirled to and fro before her mirror, delighting in the lovely patterns of the candlelight's glow on her frilly wedding dress.

Tomorrow Patrick would be hers, all hers, forever. She was already his—he must know that. She smiled secretly, thrilling to the memory of their lovemaking in the conservatory that afternoon. They had found true happiness and fulfillment together, leaving an afterglow of peace.

A knock sounded lightly, and the door opened almost immediately. "May I help with that?" Helene asked from the doorway.

Amanda eyed her uncertainly. During their stay in London, Helene had seemed to accept the upcoming marriage, even attending Amanda's fittings for her wedding gown. Though their relationship seemed to have improved, there were still hidden tensions. Helene acted warmly, but Amanda didn't trust her. This was the same woman who had vacillated so disturbingly—wanting her to stay, wanting her to go. What did Helene want now?

"Yards and yards of ecru lace," smiled Helene dreamily. "That dress reminds me of a very long time ago."

"It is beautiful, isn't it?" said Amanda.

"Yes, a confection of shirred cream-colored lace." Helene studied the dress a moment longer, then said, "Come here, dear. Let me brush your hair for you."

Uneasily, Amanda settled on the stool in front of her dressing table. Helene picked up the tortoiseshell brush and gently drew it through the shining red strands.

"Such lovely locks," crooned Helene. "I knew someone once with hair this beautiful."

Helene's eyes glazed over as she gently brushed, running her fingers through the curls. She hummed a strange singsong, a child's rhyme from the past. Mesmerized, haunted, Amanda closed her eyes, drawn into the odd little tune. The tension drained from her shoulders, and after a time, she leaned into the brush strokes.

"You must understand," murmured Helene in a conversational tone, "Sylvie always got everything she wanted—the best clothes, all the men, our parents' attention. She was the favorite, you know, with her hair and personality. But there was one thing I wanted more than anything else, and that was Thomas Gray."

Amanda's eyes flew open.

"I suppose he was flattered to be the object of such intense devotion. He couldn't withstand my ardor—nor I his."

Amanda stared at Helene in the mirror. Something about the woman's expression was out of kilter. Maybe it was the way her eyes shone with an unnaturally bright light. The hairs on Amanda's neck rose, prickling her scalp.

"So you and Thomas loved each other, after all," she asked softly, not wanting to break the spell.

"Of course." Helene shrugged, as if loving her sister's fiancé were the most natural thing in the world.

Amanda held her breath, willing the woman to continue. After a few moments of silent brushing, Helene said, "Your father was our go-between. He carried letters and love-notes between Thomas and me."

"My father?"

Helene's eyes reached dreamily into the past.

"Little Johnny Prescott. A godsend. I could never have had such intimate contact with Thomas if it hadn't been for that boy. Such a good little courier, carrying tokens between us: my handkerchief, the gift of a flower, lovenotes, the times and places of our assignations."

Resentment burned in Amanda's heart at the thought of the couple using her father, an innocent little boy, to make their sordid arrangements. What must he have thought of the situation? He must have been confused at the least. And all for what? What had it accomplished?

"Why didn't you marry Thomas after Sylvie's death?" she asked.

Helene shook her head. "Sylvie's death was horrible, tragic. We both felt guilty, as if we had caused it in some way. I tried to reason with Thomas, but the luster had gone from our relationship. One morning he could stand the guilt no longer, and just disappeared. Eventually I married the marquess of Swinton."

"Why? If you loved Thomas?"

"Right after Thomas ran off, I found out I was . . . expecting his baby. I told Swinton it was his to give my child a name."

Helene calmly brushed Amanda's hair into thick curls around her fingers. A wildness in Helene's dreadful bright eyes belied the methodical logic in her voice. Amanda thought with alarm of the words "method to her madness."

"If I had revealed the real father of my baby, do you suppose Swinton would have married me and raised the child as his own? Oh, no! Not in those days. Not my husband. The family tradition, the great Swinton name and title, meant everything to him. My baby and I would have been without this house and the world I wanted for us."

"Then everything has been a lie . . . all these years."

Helene replaced the brush on the dressing table. "Yes, all these years. It hasn't been easy. Once I started lying, I had to constantly dissemble. But as I've told you, a lady must hide her desires and do what is correct."

"Correct!" Amanda exploded. "Is it correct to lie? Correct to steal your sister's fiancé? Correct to use an innocent little boy in your schemes?"

Helene regarded Amanda with surprise, as if

just now recognizing her. The two women turned away from each other, both unable to face the terrible emotions reflected in the other's eyes. They sat in silence, trying to calm themselves.

"Is it correct to blackmail?" Helene finally spoke up, her voice accusing. "In my last letter, I told Thomas I was going to have his child, but Thomas was gone. Your father must have read the letter on the way, and saved it." She gave a cynical, humorless smile. "After Sylvie died, I gave her jeweled box to little Johnny Prescott to keep him quiet, but what good did that do? All these years later, he used the information against me. His letter you brought to Pinewood said he was sending Thomas here. It warned me to pay you and take care of you, or Thomas would reveal the truth! Of course, Thomas got a little money for himself in the process."

The terrible accusation in Helene's eyes pierced Amanda. So that was how her father had come by the box—Helene had given it to the little boy to shut him up.

"Believe me," swore Amanda, "I had no idea! I've never wanted your money, and I've never been party to any blackmail scheme." Her voice caught in her throat. "I can hardly believe it of my father."

"He loved you," said Helene simply. "Just as I've loved Thomas and Patrick. Your father wanted to protect you and provide for you. That's why he sent you to Pinewood House. Love makes a person do strange things."

Elizabeth Parker

Amanda's thoughts churned. So this was what ultimately lay beneath all the decorations—stormy secrets of passion and the heart. Love had driven them all—her father, Helene, Gray, Patrick, herself. They had all done unspeakable, unbearable things in the name of love.

"You must try to understand and not sit in judgment, Amanda. That would be wrong. You love Patrick, or so you say. Can't you have a little compassion for a young couple who, sinful as it may have been, also loved? At times, the overwhelming pull of love is simply too powerful to resist."

The overwhelming pull of love. Too powerful to resist. Such words from the staid and proper Marchioness of Swinton amazed Amanda. She fully realized for the first time what a maelstrom of emotion lurked beneath the woman's cold, unassailable surface.

Amanda's thoughts flew guiltily to that first time with Patrick on the floor of Reggie's cottage: tangled arms and legs, fevered murmurings, clothes being torn off, surrendering to the irresistible urge to possess a lover. Yes, she knew how desire could push all rational thought aside.

"Love can be powerful," she admitted, remembering how she and Patrick had succumbed to the overwhelming pull of love. They'd tried to resist, knowing there were consequences.

Consequences. Patrick hadn't wanted an illegitimate son who might turn out unhealthy—

Gilded Splendor

Numb horror gripped Amanda. She clutched the edge of the dressing table, her knuckles white. "If Patrick's grandfather is Thomas Gray instead of your husband—then Patrick will never inherit the Winter illness!"

"No. He won't."

All those years! Patrick's grandmother had let him suffer! All those years! Hot outrage welled in Amanda, filling her, consuming her. She whirled on her stool to confront Helene.

"How could you let him live his life under the burden of that lie? You know what it's done to him! He's lived under the shadow of illness and early death, believing he could never marry or have children. It thwarted his entire existence. And you speak of love! It's monstrous!"

Helene lowered her eyes. "From what I've experienced of marriage, I've always thought I saved Patrick from the unhappiness I suffered. He's better off without marriage."

"But that should have been his decision, not yours!"

Helene didn't answer. Instead she gripped Amanda's shoulders, turned her around to face the mirror again, and resumed brushing her hair. Amanda watched in the mirror, glued to her stool, unable to move or tear her horrified gaze from the woman.

"Patrick must never know, never find out who his real grandfather is. What would he think of his Gram if he found out all the lies?"

She hummed her odd little tune again.

"Sylvie makes me do such terrible things."

Amanda smelled the fire before she saw it. A burning, acrid aroma of smoke assailed her senses. With one hand, Helene still plied the brush, but her other hand held a lighted candle to the skirt of Amanda's wedding dress.

Amanda screamed. "What are you doing?"

She jumped up, knocking against the candle in Helene's hand, nearly upsetting the woman. In an instant, the fire spread to Helene's gown, too. Amanda frantically slapped at the fire in her own dress and Helene's at the same time. Greedy flames jumped to the curtains, then onto the bedhangings nearby.

Helene stared in wide-eyed bewilderment at the flames lapping up her skirt. She didn't seem to know what to do about them. She giggled, a chilling sound growing and building in an insane crescendo.

Would it never stop? Amanda's heart raced in panic. *That eerie laughter?*

The crazy, hysterical sound went on and on, unabated. Helene's face twisted into a horrible grinning mask, features distorted, eyes wild.

Amanda shrieked and tried to escape, but Helene, still clutching the candlestick, threw her arms around her, holding her fast. She struggled to break free.

"Now, don't fight," Helene's voice cooed, crazily, eerily. "Stop now! Sylvie says it has to be."

A peculiar crackling sizzled, and Amanda realized with horror that Helene's hair was on fire.

Gilded Splendor

She screamed again and slapped at the flames, oblivious to the pain in her hands.

Helene raised the candlestick high and brought it down sharply on Amanda's head with a resounding crack. Amanda slumped forward, unconscious. The older woman caught her, and they swayed together to and fro.

"Yes, Sylvie," crooned Helene. "Yes, Sylvie."

The door burst open. Clouds of thick, gray, billowing smoke filled the doorway, and in its center loomed Patrick, a tall, formidable figure. Thomas stood behind him, anxiously straining to peer over the younger man's shoulder into the smoke-filled room.

"Amanda! Gram!"

Patrick ran to the two women and wrenched them apart. "Gram, let go. You're on fire! Let go!"

He pried Helene's hands away and propped Amanda up against himself. Wildly, Helene charged them, her arms flailing the smoky air.

There was no time to think, only to react. Patrick's deepest instincts took over, and he made his choice. With a cry of agony, he pushed hard with his free hand, sending his grandmother's burning figure careening across the room.

"Helene!" Thomas's voice cried out from the hallway.

Patrick swept Amanda into his arms and rushed out of the smoke-filled room. The next second he had her down on the hall floor, wrapped her in the rug, and smothered the fire in her clothes. She choked on a breath of the fresh hallway air, coughed, and opened her eyes.

"Thank God," Patrick said on a heavy breath.

Thomas rushed past them into the bedroom. Patrick jerked his head toward the blaze. Amanda clutched his lapels in both hands to prevent him from following Thomas back into the fire.

"Don't!" she gasped.

"I have to." Patrick broke loose and bolted for the door, halted by a volatile wall of heat. The room, a blazing inferno, roiled with sickening smoke.

"Gram!" he yelled into the blaze.

Thomas staggered out, dragging Helene's limp, burning form. He stripped off his coat and wrapped her in it, smothering the flames engulfing her.

Amanda coughed fitfully, and Patrick went back to kneel beside her. He wrapped protective arms around her, and together they watched in silent agony as Thomas gently pulled Helene against his chest.

His eyes swimming with tears, Thomas looked down into Helene's blackened face and fingered a strand of her charred hair.

"Please don't go," he whispered. "The lovers of long ago are reunited now. Nothing can part us ever again."

Helene opened her eyes and gazed up at him,

moving her cracked lips slightly. He bent forward, inclining his ear.

"Sylvie and I forgive you," she whispered.

Helene's eyes stared straight ahead then, open and unblinking, like a doll's eyes.

Thomas's anguished cry rent the air. Tears trickled white lines through the blackened soot on his cheeks. He cradled the dead woman close and rocked slowly back and forth.

Chapter Twenty-Two

His grandmother was dead. Patrick mourned for her during a long, dark night of introspection. At daybreak, the sun shone on a bright new morning. Amanda's room was gutted, but the fire had been extinguished. Now Patrick and Amanda faced Thomas Gray in the library.

"I want answers, Gray," said Patrick. "Do you think you can tell us everything?"

His past bravado gone, Gray's eyes reflected an infinite sadness. His hand shook slightly as it swirled brandy in a cut glass goblet. Patrick leaned over and placed an encouraging hand on his shoulder.

"There's really not that much to tell, I guess. I came to Pinewood House partly to see Helene and partly to blackmail her."

"Cur," snarled Patrick, jerking his hand away.

Gray sighed and went on. "I'm not proud of myself, but there it is. John Prescott wanted his daughter—Amanda, here—to be well taken care of. He made me aware of certain information. I told Helene what I knew, and Amanda, although she didn't know it, brought her father's letter backing me up. Helene was to let Amanda stay here as long as she liked, and also give her a large sum of money."

Amanda raised pleading eyes to Patrick. "I didn't read the letter. I never knew . . ."

"I know," he reassured her. His icy green gaze riveted back to Thomas. "Go on."

"As long as money was being handed around, I thought of myself, too, naturally."

"Naturally." Patrick's voice dripped with sarcasm. "What kind of information were you using for your blackmail? That damned fool diary? I went all through that with Gram. I told her not to worry. I didn't believe she stole you from Sylvie. You were her sister's fiancé, for God's sake! And what if she had? So what? That was all in the past. So what kind of information did you blackmail her with?"

"I'm afraid it's not so simple as that, lad." Gray hesitated.

Patrick clenched his fists, his knuckles going white. He hovered over Gray's chair. "My grandmother is dead," he grated out, his voice low and menacing. "I want to know why, so spill it all now, or I'll—"

Gray half rose from his chair and dropped his glass. Brandy spilled unheeded, spreading a dark stain over the cabbage rose carpet.

Amanda grabbed Patrick's arm. "Please, dear, sit down and let him continue. He'll tell us everything. Won't you, Mr. Gray?"

Amanda's voice was soothing, but Patrick noted a strained, frightened quality to it. He looked distractedly into her tense face. Reminding himself of her condition, he controlled his temper for her sake and allowed her to lead him to the sofa.

Gray nodded nervously. "When I arrived here at Pinewood House, I saw immediately that Helene was very changed from when I knew her. She said things to me I'll never repeat to anybody—things about Sylvie, about her, about me. I knew then she was mad. Must have been for quite some time, what with the secret she'd carried all these years."

Patrick leaned forward, his patience strained to the breaking point. "What secret? What the hell are you talking about?"

"Helene killed Sylvie."

Patrick leapt from his seat. "No!"

He loomed over Gray. Thomas swallowed, his eyes never leaving Patrick's face. "Helene tried to make herself believe I was responsible. But when she saw me again, she had to face the truth, and she snapped." Gray closed his eyes.

"She told me what happened back then. She held the door shut while poor Sylvie burned inside her room."

A shiver crept up Patrick's spine. Was there no end to the horror? Could his grandmother have killed her own sister? If so, she had deluded them all for a very long time. They'd been unknowingly living with a crazed murderess in their midst. He shuddered.

Thomas's voice intruded into Patrick's churning thoughts. "When I saw Helene again, our old feelings for each other revived." Patrick scowled darkly, but Thomas hurried on. "I couldn't help it. She was always an amazing woman. Nothing improper occurred between us, of course. I saw how things were with her. I couldn't carry out my blackmail scheme either. Instead, I tried to reason with her, protect her, see if I couldn't help her regain her footing, mentally speaking."

"If you called off the blackmail, why did Gram try to give money to Amanda?" Patrick demanded.

"I never took the money, and she didn't press the matter," Amanda interjected.

"Helene told me other things that, I suppose, need clearing up," Thomas continued sadly. "She shot at Amanda when she first came here, trying to scare her off, but hit Mrs. Charteris by mistake. Then she killed her gardener. What's his name? Reggie? She saw Reggie talking to Amanda one day in the garden and she had always feared that Reggie knew about her and me and she didn't know what he might have told Amanda. She reasoned that even if Amanda knew about our relationship from Reggie, with him dead, there would be no one to back up her story. So she pushed him off the parapet."

Patrick closed his eyes and held up a hand to silence Gray for a moment. *I was right, after all.* He'd tried to reassure Amanda in Granville's studio, but he had really doubted that Granville was responsible for Reggie's death. He opened his eyes. As it turned out, he'd also been wrong about Gray. He faced the man and nodded for him to continue.

"Helene knew that Maude had given the diary to Amanda, so she ransacked Amanda's room looking for it, and she stole Sylvie's jeweled box to throw everyone off the scent. She was using the neighborhood murders as a cover-up for her own acts." Thomas choked, unable to continue, his eyes filling with tears.

"She came to my room last night to kill me, too," said Amanda with shocked realization.

A dazed silence hung heavy in the room. Patrick's stomach churned with nausea. Everything was falling neatly into place with a fit so perfect, he had to believe Gray's story.

"But can't you see she was desperate?" Gray sprang to Helene's defense. "I knew the truth about you, lad. John Prescott knew. She thought Amanda knew. She was afraid you would find out, and then she would lose you and her home."

"Find out what?" asked Patrick, confused. "If she killed Sylvie, then she was a sick woman. I wouldn't have turned her out. I would have gotten her the care she needed. She always had a home here. My God, you mean there's more?"

"Patrick," Amanda spoke up quietly, "there is something else, another reason for the blackmail. Before the fire last night, Helene told me..." She faltered and threw a helpless glance in Gray's direction.

"Told you what?" asked Patrick, sickened and afraid of what he might hear next.

"I'll tell you, lad." Thomas rose to face Patrick squarely. "Helene and I loved each other all those years ago. I didn't know it then, but she got pregnant. I later found out from John Prescott, who had read a letter from Helene telling me that her baby—your father—was my child."

"What?"

"You're my grandson."

Appalled shock coursed through Patrick's veins.

"And the Marquess of Swinton?"

"Only thought the baby was his. Never knew, but he was no relation to either you or your father."

Like a splash of shocking, freezing water hurled full-force in his face, realization dawned on Patrick. "Then I won't inherit the Winter disease, like Gram always said I would!"

"That's right, lad."

Overcome, Patrick slumped onto the sofa and dropped his head into his hands. Stunned, numb, devoid of feeling, he tried to take it all in. He had grown up in Pinewood House as the future Marquess of Swinton. He had trusted his grandmother, his grandfather, his parents, Pinewood House, his rightful place in the ordered world he knew. But his whole life had been based on a lie! His self-concept was shaken to the core. He wasn't—had never been—the man he'd thought. His whole world had been a fabrication of Helene's disordered mind. Crushed beneath the shattering blow, he could hardly fathom it.

Amanda put her arms around him and hugged him warmly, cradling him against her. "Patrick?" she whispered.

He turned to her in anguish and despair. "Gram shouldn't have done it. Why did she lie to me my whole life? Ever since I was a boy, she let me believe my grandfather was the Marquess of Swinton, and he was never even related to me! She let me believe I would inherit his illness. I don't know which lie is worse! What a goddamned charade!"

"She loved you. Can't you see? If she had revealed that Gray was your grandfather, it would have come out that she'd had an affair with him and borne his child. She'd have been disgraced. Her husband would have thrown her out."

"And later? After my grandfather and my parents died, and it was just the two of us? Why didn't she tell me then?"

Amanda shrugged her shoulders in a helpless gesture. "I don't know."

"I'll tell you," Thomas said. "Her biggest fear all through the years was that she would be connected with Sylvie's death. She thought people would find out she killed Sylvie out of jealousy. There was no way anyone could ever prove it, even if they guessed. But she was too afraid. I guess she'd been lying so long, she couldn't stop."

Patrick shook his head. An overwhelming rage overcame him, and he ground his teeth. "I hate her!" he spat out.

He glared balefully at Gray. "I hate you, too! My grandfather! Why, you're nothing but a lowlife cad and a blackmailer! Why did you ever come back here?"

Overwrought, he clenched his fists, wanting desperately to strike out at someone or something, but he couldn't bring himself to physically attack the sorry-looking old man across the room.

Gray bowed his head. "I came back to tell you the truth."

Patrick leaned forward, muscles taut as a strung bow. He ran his hands savagely through his tousled hair. Ambivalence roiled inside him.

Elizabeth Parker

He still loved his grandmother for all she'd been to him through the years. He couldn't easily shrug off the feelings of a lifetime. At the same time, he hated her passionately for her monstrous deception. He was disgusted to discover he was Gray's grandson, yet an immense relief came with the discovery he wouldn't inherit Swinton's disease. Love, hate, disgust, relief. Conflicting emotions raged and fought within him, until he thought he would burst apart at the seams.

Amanda, beside him, softly smoothed his hair into place. "Do you?" she asked gently. "Do you really hate them?"

They sat together, side by side, in silence for a long time. Gray remained across the room, watching, waiting, his eyes filled with sympathy.

Through his turmoil, Patrick gradually became aware of one thought, one compelling answer—the woman beside him, still there. Warm and loyal. His Mandy. He had a chance with her now, and a life together, if, once and for all, they could get beyond these terrible circumstances. They must try. He turned toward her and drew a ragged breath.

"I mustn't hate them, Amanda. I know that. It would consume me faster and deadlier than any illness I might have inherited. The only way is to forgive and get on with my life."

Amanda smiled through tremulous tears. "And the lie?" she asked gently.

Patrick looked into her eyes. Maybe it could be faced at last.

"Yes, the lie." His chest heaved. In his heart and mind, he shoved off the heavy burden of the past and allowed enormous relief to flood his soul. He was truly free for the first time in his life. A radiant light shone on him, the brightness from Amanda's gloriously happy eyes.

"Now I do not have to live in fear anymore. We can face our marriage with our hearts at ease, have more children and a life together. I'm not a Winter!" A gasping sob tore his throat. "I won't get sick!"

Overcome, he threw his arms around Amanda's waist and buried his face in her lap. For the second time since he'd been a boy, he let the cleansing tears flow. Huge sobs—for all he'd lost, and all he'd found—convulsed him, racking his shoulders.

Amanda wove her fingers through his thick black hair.

"Cry, Patrick. Let it all out. You've earned the right. Then you'll never have to cry about it again."

Epilogue

A baby's thin, high, piercing scream shattered the still air of the White Garden.

Patrick quickly strode to the two babies lying on a blanket in the deep, green grass. "What have we here?" he asked, bending over his small son. Baby Reggie leaned forward, precariously balanced on his pudgy arms. A lock of the infant's hair was trapped under Reggie's plump hand. "I kiss!" Reggie stated emphatically, planting a wet kiss on the baby's head.

"Here, Reggie! Careful! I know you want to play with John, but you're pulling his hair, silly." Patrick good-naturedly patted Reggie's unruly locks, then swooped both boys up into his arms.

"Is everything all right?" called Amanda from

Gilded Splendor

a blanket on the grass, where she sat beside Maude.

"What's Baby Reggie doing now?" called Maude in exasperation.

Patrick strolled over to them, his arms full of sweet-smelling, pink, healthy babies. "Everything's fine. Our sons are just engaging in some rowdy horseplay, that's all."

He deposited Baby Reggie in Maude's lap and sat at Amanda's feet, cradling their tiny son against his chest.

Amanda gazed lovingly at her family. In the year since her marriage to Patrick, she still woke some mornings not believing their good fortune. Life at Pinewood House was everything she'd dreamed, and the blessed miracle of their son radiated health and vitality. She gazed with joy at the wonder before her. Patrick's eyes gleamed into hers over the top of the baby's silken head.

"What's this, a picnic?" Thomas Gray sauntered into the garden, Algy close on his heels.

"What's to eat?" asked Algy.

"Sit down," said Amanda. She plunged her hands into a basket of delectables and handed Algy a chicken leg. He sprawled on the grass as near to the food as he could get.

"Here, I'll do that." Maude quickly set Baby Reggie down and arranged the food on a rug. Reggie took off at a fast trot in the direction of Spirit Lake with Harry, who'd been watching from a respectful distance, chasing after him.

Algy lounged on the grass. The picture of

contentment, he enthusiastically bit into his chicken. "Now this is what I call grand," he said between bites. "I must say you've settled in nicely, Patrick. I always knew you were cut out to be a family man."

"You knew more than I did, then."

"Of course! What do you expect?"

"I expect you to follow suit and get married yourself, Algy," said Patrick. He tried to look stern, but only succeeded in looking amused.

"Think what adventures we could all have then!" Algy gazed over the broad sweep of lawn, his eyes taking on a dreamy quality. "I might just get around to settling down one of these days."

"Oh? Is there someone we don't know about?" asked Amanda innocently, hiding a shrewd smile. "Like that fetching lady you were with at Mrs. Charteris's ball last week?"

"Yes, Mrs. Charteris is fetching, I'll wager—"

"No, Algy, I mean the young lady you danced every dance with—the Duke of Rutherland's daughter."

"Oh, her! Smashing, isn't she? By the way, I was going to ask if I might bring her out to Pinewood next week. I'd like to have you all get to know her."

"I think that can be arranged," said Patrick, his eyes twinkling.

"Might a man hold his great-grandson?" asked Thomas Gray with a smile.

Patrick handed the baby over to him. Meditatively chewing on a blade of grass, he watched

Gilded Splendor

the old man gently coo at the child. In the past year, he had never regretted for a moment letting Gray share their world. From under the doubts and suspicions of the past, Thomas had formed strong bonds with Patrick and Amanda. He had proved a loving grandfather, and it was strange, but somehow he kept alive Helene's memory—not the tragic parts of her life, or her needless death, but he'd often regaled them with stories of a younger, happier Helene. He'd helped Patrick and Amanda see her as a bright beauty who had once embraced life with arms wide open. His presence had been comforting, and he never let them forget his profound gratitude that they'd been willing to forgive and forget.

Everything had turned out for the best, reflected Patrick. He had sold Sylvie's jeweled box, and the money had resolved his financial dilemma. After Helene's funeral, he had also burned Sylvie's diary, and it was only fitting that the diary which had held such awful secrets had been consumed by fire. The flames of deceit had been extinguished and Patrick hoped that the sisters were now resting in peace. As he had watched the pages turn to ashes, he had let the past go and had eagerly looked forward to his future. Selling the jeweled box and destroying the diary had freed all of them of those reminders of Sylvie's and Helene's tragedy.

His gaze met Amanda's. "Shall we go for a walk, love?" she asked.

"Good idea." Patrick rose, took her hand, and they strolled in the direction of Spirit Lake. A light breeze wafted from the water, caressing their skin with the warm scent of summer.

"Happy, milady?" asked Patrick.

Amanda smiled into his eyes. "Yes. Serenely, contentedly, completely happy, Your Lordship."

At the lake's edge, Patrick pulled her around to face him. Gloriously responsive, as ever, she stood on tiptoe to kiss him. Her lips lingered against his, soft, full, and warm. Desire coursed through him, his heart beating with the rhythm of the water lapping against the shore. She moved her hands, stroking his shoulders. Her eyes burned into his with a familiar heat.

He glanced down at the grass and grinned wickedly. A suggestive whisper in her ear brought a blush to her cheeks.

"Here?" she asked, her eyes wide.

He nodded, persuasively caressing her breast and the back of her neck.

"Oh, husband, you do tempt me," she sighed. "But we mustn't provide a decorative little tableau for our company!"

Patrick grinned and pulled her into a bear hug. "When we first met, I called you an amusing decoration, remember? Little did I know what a warm, wonderful woman was beneath the beautiful surface. It didn't seem possible then that you might become my wife and make my life complete."

Overcome with sudden emotion, he heaved

Gilded Splendor

his chest and brought his hand up to cover his eyes. "The sunlight sparkles, doesn't it?" he remarked.

Amanda caressed his cheek. "No more decorations?"

"Nope. And no more secrets hidden beneath. The truth is infinitely more satisfying."

They gazed into each other's eyes, their understanding complete.

She tossed her head and smiled. "When we met, little did I realize what a wonderful man hid himself behind the aristocratic rakehell."

"Rakehell?" Patrick gave in to her teasing and reached out to tickle her ribs. "Why, you little . . . I'll have you know—"

She giggled, pushing him away. "Race you back!"

She took off across the grass, her titian curls flying behind her, riotous in the sunlight. Patrick quickly caught up, laughing as he grabbed her arm.

They ran lightheartedly, then, side by side, up the lawn to Pinewood House, to their family, their friends, and their blessed life together.

LOVE SPELL

THE MAGIC OF ROMANCE PAST, PRESENT, AND FUTURE....

Dorchester Publishing Co., Inc., the leader in romantic fiction, is pleased to unveil its newest line—Love Spell. Every month, beginning in August 1993, Love Spell will publish one book in each of four categories:

1) *Timeswept Romance*—Modern-day heroines travel to the past to find the men who fulfill their hearts' desires.

2) *Futuristic Romance*—Love on distant worlds where passion is the lifeblood of every man and woman.

3) *Historical Romance*—Full of desire, adventure and intrigue, these stories will thrill readers everywhere.

4) *Contemporary Romance*—With novels by Lori Copeland, Heather Graham, and Jayne Ann Krentz, Love Spell's line of contemporary romance is first-rate.

Exploding with soaring passion and fiery sensuality, Love Spell romances are destined to take you to dazzling new heights of ecstasy.

COMING IN NOVEMBER!

TIMESWEPT ROMANCE

A TIME-TRAVEL CHRISTMAS
By Megan Daniel, Vivian Knight-Jenkins, Eugenia Riley, and Flora Speer

In these four passionate time-travel historical romance stories, modern-day heroines journey everywhere from Dickens's London to a medieval castle as they fulfill their deepest desires on Christmases past.
_51912-7 $4.99 US/$5.99 CAN

A FUTURISTIC ROMANCE

MOON OF DESIRE
By Pam Rock

Future leader of his order, Logan has vanquished enemies, so he expects no trouble when a sinister plot brings a mere woman to him. But as the three moons of the planet Thurlow move into alignment, Logan and Calla head for a collision of heavenly bodies that will bring them ecstasy—or utter devastation.
_51913-5 $4.99 US/$5.99 CAN

LEISURE BOOKS
ATTN: Order Department
276 5th Avenue, New York, NY 10001

Please add $1.50 for shipping and handling for the first book and $.35 for each book thereafter. PA., N.Y.S. and N.Y.C. residents, please add appropriate sales tax. No cash, stamps, or C.O.D.s. All orders shipped within 6 weeks via postal service book rate. Canadian orders require $2.00 extra postage and must be paid in U.S. dollars through a U.S. banking facility.

Name _____
Address _____
City _____ State _____ Zip _____
I have enclosed $_____in payment for the checked book(s).
Payment <u>must</u> accompany all orders. ☐ Please send a free catalog.

COMING IN OCTOBER 1993
HISTORICAL ROMANCE
DANGEROUS DESIRES
Louise Clark

Miserable and homesick, Stephanie de la Riviere will sell her family jewels or pose as a highwayman—whatever it takes to see her beloved father again. And her harebrained schemes might succeed if not for her watchful custodian—the only man who can match her fiery spirit with his own burning desire.

_0-505-51910-0 $4.99 US/$5.99 CAN

CONTEMPORARY ROMANCE
ONLY THE BEST
Lori Copeland
Author of More Than 6 Million Books in Print!

Stranded in a tiny Wyoming town after her car fails, Rana Alcott doesn't think her life can get much worse. And though she'd rather die than accept help from arrogant Gunner Montay, she soon realizes she is fighting a losing battle against temptation.

_0-505-51911-9 $3.99 US/$4.99 CAN

LEISURE BOOKS
ATTN: Order Department
276 5th Avenue, New York, NY 10001

Please add $1.50 for shipping and handling for the first book and $.35 for each book thereafter. PA., N.Y.S. and N.Y.C. residents, please add appropriate sales tax. No cash, stamps, or C.O.D.s. All orders shipped within 6 weeks via postal service book rate. Canadian orders require $2.00 extra postage and must be paid in U.S. dollars through a U.S. banking facility.

Name_____
Address_____
City _____ State_____ Zip_____
I have enclosed $_____in payment for the checked book(s).
Payment <u>must</u> accompany all orders.☐ Please send a free catalog.

COMING IN OCTOBER 1993
FUTURISTIC ROMANCE
FIRESTAR
Kathleen Morgan
Bestselling Author of *The Knowing Crystal*

From the moment Meriel lays eyes on the virile slave chosen to breed with her, the heir to the Tenuan throne is loath to perform her imperial duty and produce a child. Yet despite her resolve, Meriel soon succumbs to Gage Bardwin—the one man who can save her planet.

_0-505-51908-9 $4.99 US/$5.99 CAN

TIMESWEPT ROMANCE
ALL THE TIME WE NEED
Megan Daniel

Nearly drowned after trying to save a client, musical agent Charli Stewart wakes up in New Orleans's finest brothel—run by the mother of the city's most virile man—on the eve of the Civil War. Unsure if she'll ever return to her own era, Charli gambles her heart on a love that might end as quickly as it began.

_0-505-51909-7 $4.99 US/$5.99 CAN

LEISURE BOOKS
ATTN: Order Department
276 5th Avenue, New York, NY 10001

Please add $1.50 for shipping and handling for the first book and $.35 for each book thereafter. PA., N.Y.S. and N.Y.C. residents, please add appropriate sales tax. No cash, stamps, or C.O.D.s. All orders shipped within 6 weeks via postal service book rate. Canadian orders require $2.00 extra postage and must be paid in U.S. dollars through a U.S. banking facility.

Name _____
Address _____
City _____ State _____ Zip _____
I have enclosed $_____ in payment for the checked book(s). Payment <u>must</u> accompany all orders. ☐ Please send a free catalog.

COMING IN SEPTEMBER 1993
HISTORICAL ROMANCE
TEMPTATION
Jane Harrison

He broke her heart once before, but Shadoe Sinclair is a temptation that Lilly McFall cannot deny. And when he saunters back into the frontier town he left years earlier, Lilly will do whatever it takes to make the handsome rogue her own.

_0-505-51906-2 $4.99 US/$5.99 CAN

CONTEMPORARY ROMANCE
WHIRLWIND COURTSHIP
Jayne Ann Krentz writing as Jayne Taylor
Bestselling Author of *Family Man*

When Phoebe Hampton arrives by accident on Harlan Garand's doorstep, he's convinced she's another marriage-minded female sent by his matchmaking aunt. But a sudden snowstorm traps them together for a few days and shows Harlan there's a lot more to Phoebe than meets the eye.

_0-505-51907-0 $3.99 US/$4.99 CAN

LEISURE BOOKS
ATTN: Order Department
276 5th Avenue, New York, NY 10001

Please add $1.50 for shipping and handling for the first book and $.35 for each book thereafter. PA., N.Y.S. and N.Y.C. residents, please add appropriate sales tax. No cash, stamps, or C.O.D.s. All orders shipped within 6 weeks via postal service book rate. Canadian orders require $2.00 extra postage and must be paid in U.S. dollars through a U.S. banking facility.

Name_____
Address_____
City _____ State_____ Zip_____
I have enclosed $_____in payment for the checked book(s). Payment <u>must</u> accompany all orders. ☐ Please send a free catalog.

COMING IN SEPTEMBER 1993
TIMESWEPT ROMANCE
TIME REMEMBERED
Elizabeth Crane
Bestselling Author of *Reflections in Time*

A voodoo doll and an ancient spell whisk thoroughly modern Jody Farnell from a decaying antebellum mansion to the Old South and a true Southern gentleman who shows her the magic of love.
_0-505-51904-6 $4.99 US/$5.99 CAN

FUTURISTIC ROMANCE
A DISTANT STAR
Anne Avery

Jerrel is enchanted by the courageous messenger who saves his life. But he cannot permit anyone to turn him from the mission that has brought him to the distant world—not even the proud and passionate woman who offers him a love capable of bridging the stars.
_0-505-51905-4 $4.99 US/$5.99 CAN

LEISURE BOOKS
ATTN: Order Department
276 5th Avenue, New York, NY 10001

Please add $1.50 for shipping and handling for the first book and $.35 for each book thereafter. PA., N.Y.S. and N.Y.C. residents, please add appropriate sales tax. No cash, stamps, or C.O.D.s. All orders shipped within 6 weeks via postal service book rate. Canadian orders require $2.00 extra postage and must be paid in U.S. dollars through a U.S. banking facility.

Name_____
Address_____
City _____ State _____ Zip _____
I have enclosed $_____in payment for the checked book(s).
Payment <u>must</u> accompany all orders.☐ Please send a free catalog.

COMING IN AUGUST 1993
HISTORICAL ROMANCE
WILD SUMMER ROSE
Amy Elizabeth Saunders

Torn from her carefree rustic life to become a proper city lady, Victoria Larkin bristles at the hypocrisy of the arrogant French aristocrat who wants to seduce her. But Phillipe St. Sebastian is determined to have her at any cost—even the loss of his beloved ancestral home. And as the flames of revolution threaten their very lives, Victoria and Phillipe find strength in the healing power of love.

_0-505-51902-X $4.99 US/$5.99 CAN

CONTEMPORARY ROMANCE
TWO OF A KIND
Lori Copeland
Bestselling Author of *Promise Me Today*

When her lively widowed mother starts chasing around town with seventy-year-old motorcycle enthusiast Clyde Merrill, Courtney Spenser is confronted by Clyde's angry son. Sensual and overbearing, Graham Merrill quickly gets under Courtney's skin—and she's not at all displeased.

_0-505-51903-8 $3.99 US/$4.99 CAN

LEISURE BOOKS
ATTN: Order Department
276 5th Avenue, New York, NY 10001

Please add $1.50 for shipping and handling for the first book and $.35 for each book thereafter. PA., N.Y.S. and N.Y.C. residents, please add appropriate sales tax. No cash, stamps, or C.O.D.s. All orders shipped within 6 weeks via postal service book rate. Canadian orders require $2.00 extra postage and must be paid in U.S. dollars through a U.S. banking facility.

Name_____
Address_____
City _____ State_____ Zip_____
I have enclosed $_____in payment for the checked book(s). Payment <u>must</u> accompany all orders.☐ Please send a free catalog.